THE
PRESIDENT'S
DOCTOR

Books by William Woolfolk

THE PRESIDENT'S DOCTOR

THE OVERLORDS

MAGGIE

THE BUILDERS

THE BEAUTIFUL COUPLE

OPINION OF THE COURT

MY NAME IS MORGAN

THE PRESIDENT'S DOCTOR

William Woolfolk

P♥P

A PLAYBOY PRESS BOOK

PUBLISHED SIMULTANEOUSLY IN THE UNITED STATES AND
CANADA BY PLAYBOY PRESS, CHICAGO, ILLINOIS. PRINTED
IN THE UNITED STATES OF AMERICA. LIBRARY OF CONGRESS
CATALOG CARD NUMBER: 73-91652. ISBN 87223-392-8.
FIRST EDITION.

For JOANNA

with all my love

I

In the first-class cabin of the 747 jetliner, Carter Fitzsimmons folded the *New York Times* to place it carefully on the empty seat beside him. It rested on top of the *Chicago Tribune*, the *St. Louis Post-Dispatch*, and the Los Angeles *Times*.

Far below him, the Washington Monument came into view in the cabin window. Then cars raced along the sunlit Memorial Parkway.

To judge from the newspapers, there was nothing to report but wars, rumors of wars, civil insurrection, anarchy, and terror. The Arabs were threatening another holy war with Israel, Malaysia was embroiled in a merciless civil war, the whole continent of Africa was alive with rebellion and hatred. Each newspaper editorialist knew exactly where to place the blame, but each put it in a different place.

NO SMOKING. FASTEN YOUR SEAT BELTS.

We spend so much of our time obeying reflexively the lights that command us. Red light means stop, green light means go, blinking yellow lights advise caution. Lights are the true international language. Even in the remote reaches of the dark troubled African continent from which Carter had recently returned, this language was understood.

Carter could not estimate how accurate the various editorialists were in assessing blame, but there was no doubt they all expected President George Rushton to come up with solutions. *It does seem that my old friend George is going to have his hands full.*

He fastened his seat belt and his long legs nudged into the seat ahead.

The best instruction was to follow the yellow light of caution.

As he was crossing the airport lobby with great loping strides he was intercepted.

"Mr. Fitzsimmons!"

Half a dozen reporters surrounded him with notebooks and pencils at the ready.

"How about Monzania? Are you going to be the new ambassador?"

"We haven't recognized that government," Carter said.

"Do you expect we will?"

"You gentlemen know as much about that as I do. I've been away four years. . . ."

"In Africa."

"In Nigeria."

"Is the President wrong in refusing to recognize?" a diminutive young woman reporter asked.

Carter peered down at her from his extraordinary height. "I can't say he's wrong because I haven't heard his reasons. Since the President knows more about the situation than anyone else, I assume his reasons are good."

She was not deterred. "All African nations recognize Monzania. So do most other countries. Aren't we in danger of being left out?"

"Leaving out the United States would be like leaving out the pianist at the *Emperor* Concerto."

"Does that mean you support nonrecognition?" asked another reporter.

"It means I support Beethoven."

"In other words . . ."

"I have no other words," Carter said firmly. "I'm going directly to the White House now to talk with the President. I'm afraid that's all I have to tell you that even resembles news."

He waved a friendly good-bye. Outside the airport, he stooped into a cab.

At the first glimpse of the historic white mansion rising out of its oasis of green lawn and drooping willow trees, Carter felt a stir of excitement and pride.

The taxi slowed down. On the sidewalk outside the White House, a massed group of blacks was moving in a long ellipse, chanting and carrying placards that called for the recognition of Monzania.

A policeman came out of the sentry booth at the entrance to the White House driveway to open the tall iron gate.

"Identification, sir?"

Carter showed it to him, and the policeman walked to the booth to check the register of expected arrivals. Carter got out of the taxi to wait. Behind him, the shouting of pickets rose in an angry chorus, and there were loud rattling sounds as wooden placards were dragged against the bars of the iron fence.

"A little excitement," Carter said, when the policeman returned.

"Yes, sir." He gestured. "Go right on in, Mr. Fitzsimmons. The party's on the south lawn, right around the turn."

Before he rounded the corner, he heard voices. A slight breeze was blowing and, unseen, he paused a moment. Young ladies with their dresses fluttering and billowing like restless flags were playing some sort of game with hoops. Each time a hoop wobbled crazily or toppled, there were explosions of laughter.

It might have been a scene from an earlier era. The view was expansive and leisurely and green, and Carter was struck again by how much of the Old South was preserved here at the White House.

His gaze was drawn irresistibly toward a woman, the only stationary object in view. She was watching the young people at their game, her chin raised a little, and one hand to her eyes shielding out the sun.

As he approached her, she saw him and jumped up.

"Carter!" She offered both hands and a radiant smile. "You have absolutely no idea how glad I am to see you."

"And now I know why I've been looking forward so much to coming home."

She took his arm. "George is inside working. He'll be here shortly." Holding him captive, Claire Rushton led him toward the game players. "I want you to come and say hello to Marie."

Marie was now a slender, darker, and, in Carter's view, somewhat less lovely version of her mother. She had Claire's erect carriage and willowy walk, and he supposed most men would think her pretty.

He said to her, "We're old friends."

"Of course we are. It hasn't been that long."

"Eight years since you went off to school."

"Have I changed much?"

"You've grown beautiful."

"Oh, my," she said, with a smile almost as charming as her mother's. "I love older men. They do so much for my ego."

As she left to rejoin her friends, he told Claire, "She's lovely."

"Isn't she?" She glanced toward the mansion. "Here comes George."

The stocky figure approaching, wearing a white turtleneck and dark blue blazer, might have been walking across a campus two decades ago. But as George Rushton came closer, Carter saw how he had changed. The rugged manly face had broadened, the hair was thinning in front, and crow's-feet now walked around the clear blue eyes.

"Somehow I thought you were taller," George said.

"You've cut the world down to your size, Mr. President."

The laugh, frank, amiable, unforced, dissolved every other impression.

"I've missed you, Carter. Drop that Mr. President. Nothing's changed except that I won an election."

"I didn't vote for you. My absentee ballot didn't arrive until three days after the election."

George's smile broadened. "If I'd lost by one vote, I'd never have forgiven you. Let's join the festivities, shall we?"

There was no need to, for the party had gathered itself and was moving toward them. Carter had noticed the phenomenon long before his friend became famous. People were always drawn to wherever George Rushton was, as to any source of strength and stability in an uncertain world.

"We'll talk later," George said, before he was engulfed in his admirers and swept off into the gaiety of the birthday party.

Later, in the Oval Office, George Rushton was in a somber mood, listening to the arguments Carter put forward on the subject of Monzania.

"It's perfectly clear," Carter said, "that as long as we withhold recognition from the black government, the former white rulers are going to be encouraged to keep on fighting against the inevitable. And many of our people must be wondering why we, supposedly helping democracies all over the world, are dragging our feet about recognizing a government that represents the overwhelming black majority."

"That's perfectly true," George acknowledged. "But nobody is aware of how far Russia's influence has penetrated there."

"I guess I'm not either."

"That's the real issue. Since the fall of the Brezhnev clique, there's no spirit of détente left. They're pressing us everywhere, in the Middle East, in Malaysia, but most of all in the newly established nations of Africa."

"Like Monzania?"

George nodded. "They seem determined to make that country a satrapy. As long as I'm President, I won't allow it. If that means we don't recognize the government until they establish that they actually are independent to some degree, then that's what it has to mean."

"It won't be a popular decision."

"They didn't elect me to be popular. They elected me to be President." He winced and tugged his neck back against his palm. "I'm sorry, Carter. I intended to make you our first ambassador."

"I'm sorrier than you, in that case. World affairs have a nasty habit of interfering with my career."

"But I have another assignment for you. One that can be much more important. I'm going to Peking soon for a summit meeting, and I'd like you to come with me."

Carter uncrossed his long legs. "I'm flattered. I should point out, though, that I've never even been to China, so I won't be much help. I have only the sketchiest idea about their economic situation."

"I don't want you as an economist. You'll be briefed on what you have to know, so that's no problem. I need someone whose good judgment I can trust."

"Are you sure I won't just be taking up space that might go to someone more useful?"

"I'll be the judge of how useful you can be. How about it?"

From a white marble mantelpiece, the portrait of a severe Dutch lady looked down at Carter admonishingly. When Duty whispers low, thou must. . . .

"Of course, if you think I can be any help."

Rushton flipped the intercom. "Ask Abramson to come to my office as soon as possible." He looked up at Carter. "You know the old fussbudget, don't you?"

It was not a term Carter would have chosen for the distinguished secretary of state, a special assistant on Asian affairs for the celebrated Dr. Kissinger, and a man who had been seriously considered as a vice-presidential choice at the same convention that had nominated George Rushton.

Carter said, "We've never met, but I read his book, *A New Approach to Foreign Policy.* I was so impressed I wrote to him about it."

George made a slight grimace. "He's fine for writing books that profess to see all sides of a problem. But what good is it if the analysis never leads to anything? All he seems able to do is wring his hands and gloom around, wishing the world were better than it is."

That quality would exasperate George Rushton, for in any situation George wanted to know immediately the steps to be taken; then he took them. No matter how difficult a choice, the act of choosing neither rattled nor dismayed him. He understood that power existed only in use, and he had an absolute assurance about his ability to use it. In him, the will and the act were inseparable. For years Carter had watched this man with a mixture of amazement and envy.

With a slight smile, Carter replied, "I gather you and Abramson haven't been getting along."

"He wasn't one my better appointments."

Carter noticed George turning his neck, stretching it against the flat of his hand.

"This damn neck of mine never got back to normal after the accident," George said ruefully.

"Have you seen a doctor?"

"I have a good man now. It's much better than it was."

Adolph Abramson, a small, dark-haired man with shining red cheeks, entered. He shook hands gravely with Carter.

"You wrote me when my book was published."

"I'm surprised you remember," Carter said.

"On their deathbeds authors remember every word of praise, though they may forget everything else."

Rushton broke in, "I've decided to take Carter along on the

trip to Peking. I want you to brief him personally, Dolph. Put everything in context for him."

Abramson turned to Carter. "I'm sure we'll learn from each other. I'll be glad to get a fresh viewpoint."

Rushton said, "I'm not taking you with me, Dolph. I can't afford to leave the foreign policy of this country in limbo. Someone has to mind the store while I'm away."

Abramson did not conceal his surprise. "I've spent a good deal of time preparing for the trip, Mr. President."

"Sorry. I can't leave Elmer Tate here alone. He's going to need you more than I will." George had a quietly firm way of cutting off argument. "I'd like a word with Carter alone, and then you and he can get better acquainted. The sooner you start briefing him the better."

With a nod Abramson accepted the dismissal and left the Oval Office.

"What I'd like you to do," George Rushton said to Carter, "is write out a full report on your impression of what's been going on in Africa the past few years."

"My job was simply to study economic trends and developments within Nigeria."

"I want your viewpoint, that's all. And don't try to write what will please me. Will you do that?"

"Of course."

"Good to have you back. I'm really looking forward to having you along with me on the China trip."

Abramson was waiting for him outside the office, and Carter matched steps with the secretary of state as they walked down a short corridor. It was an awkward moment.

"I'm sorry you're not coming to Peking," Carter said.

"George Rushton is a strong-minded man. Like most Presidents, he really wants to direct the nation's foreign policy himself." Abramson spoke slowly and precisely, and did not waste words. "I don't think he wants me to serve him as Acheson served Tru-

man, or as Kissinger did Nixon and Ford. He doesn't need a secretary of state."

"Every President does," Carter said. "It gives him someone he
can blame if his own policies go wrong."

They passed through a long-windowed conference chamber,
simply furnished with only a massive octagonal table and comfort-
able-looking armchairs along each side. On a far mantel was a
model of a clipper ship.

Abramson said, "Did you know that if you sit in the President's
chair and make a wish, it's supposed to come true?"

"Why doesn't it work when the President sits there?" Carter
asked.

As Carter was leaving by taxi, the pickets had massed closely
just beyond the gates. The street ahead was choked with people.

A policeman came toward the cab, holding up his hands.

The taxi driver shook his head. "I don't know how they get
away with it!" He turned in exasperation back to Carter. "What
the hell do they have to complain about? Down with everything
that's up, that's their motto."

Two police cars arrived and several uniformed men began
working furiously to move the crowd away from the entrance to
the White House.

The driver gunned his engine impatiently. "For two cents I'd
run right through the bastards."

The street was clearing as police struggled with people offering
only passive resistance.

Then a whistle shrilled. A squad of helmeted men galloped
down the street toward the melee.

The driver said, "Ziffren's boys. Now we'll see some action!"

The horses rode right into the massed crowd. Carter heard
cursing and screaming. A bottle flew up in an arc to smash the
shoulder of one helmeted rider. Other riders drove into the mob
with nightsticks swinging. Clattering hooves echoed among

shrieking men and women. A rider was almost pulled off his horse. Gunfire crackled.

The taxi driver watched fascinated. "That's it! Give it to the black bastards!"

Now the crowd was in full flight, and a ceaseless stream of people passed around the stalled taxicab.

A young black, his face bleeding, looked in the front window.

"Beat it, you sonuvabitch," the driver said.

The young black's gaze drifted to Carter in the rear seat. "Look what they did," he said, "Look what they did! You oughta be ashamed, Whitey!"

The driver put his hand full into the young man's face and pushed. "Get the hell out of here, Sambo!"

"That's enough!" Carter said sharply.

"Don't tell *me*, mister!"

An instant later there was the sharp shattering sound of breaking glass and a brick caromed off the steering wheel.

Carter raised his hands to protect himself from flying splinters. The driver's face and hand sprouted thin red rivulets. In one quick movement he was outside, looking for vengeance.

A black woman ran toward him blindly, looking back at helmeted riders in pursuit. The driver's fist came down in a clubbing motion. The woman staggered and fell. In the same instant, a surprised expression came over the driver's face and he crumpled. Near where he fell lay an empty Coke bottle that had struck him down.

Carter opened the door and got out. The woman had fallen near the fender. As Carter tried to help her, she pulled away from him and spat in his face.

"You with *them*, honkey!"

The driver was lying with the wheel of the car almost directly over him. He was bleeding from a gash on the temple, but seemed to be breathing normally.

Carter heard confused shouting and the drumming of hooves, and stood up as a helmeted rider reined in nearby.

"These people need a doctor," Carter said.

"Move along! Clear the street!"

A moment later the street was empty, save for fallen bodies. The galloping of victorious riders was like prolonged bursts of musketry.

2

The six o'clock news broadcast carried graphic reports of the riot. Only one person had been seriously hurt, a young girl who suffered a fractured skull. According to the newscaster, the riot could easily have escalated into something worse except for the prompt intervention of the Security Bureau's special mounted detail.

As the broadcast ended, the telephone rang. When he heard her voice, it was like something that suddenly materialized out of a daydream, a kind of wish fulfillment.

"How'd you get this number, Claire?"

"All things come easy when it's the White House calling. I just told them to get you on the phone."

"Marvelous. Every woman ought to have a husband who's President of the United States."

A hesitance, then, "You haven't seen George in four years. How did he look to you?"

"Just fine. Handsome as ever."

"I'm so glad you think so. He's terribly upset about that riot today. He ought to be getting some rest, but he's waiting for a full report."

"I was in the middle of that riot. It was pretty brutal."

"Mark Ziffren is sure those people wanted violence. He says they'd like nothing better than for someone to get killed just so it would make headlines."

It had appeared to Carter that everything was under control until the mounted troops arrived, but he was not disposed to argue. "It made headlines anyway," he said.

"Oh, let's not talk about it. There are much more pleasant topics. That wasn't a proper visit today, and I didn't get a real chance to be with you. I wish we could make it tomorrow, but my schedule is hopeless. All sorts of conferences. The head usher. The maître d'. The housekeeper. And then a formal dinner."

"Well, I'm free whenever you are. Why don't you call me?"

She ended the conversation cheerfully with, "We need you here in Washington, Carter. Don't you dare go far away again."

Carter called the medical center to confirm his appointment for a physical checkup the next morning. As soon as he hung up, the telephone rang again.

"Mr. Fitzsimmons?"

"Yes."

"This is Jack Elkins. I'm down in the lobby. I'd like to talk to you for a few minutes."

Jack Elkins wrote the most widely read political column in Washington.

Carter said, "I have a reservation for dinner at the Jockey Club and I'm leaving now. Sorry."

He went downstairs. In front of the hotel, a taxi cut quickly to the curb before him, and as he got in he saw that someone was already inside, a man who looked husky enough to be a football tackle.

"Oh, I thought . . ."

"That's okay, Mr. Fitzsimmons."

— 13 —

The large, somewhat coarse face with its slightly prominent nose and deep cheek lines was familiar.

"You're Jack Elkins."

"I've got a couple of things I'd like to check out with you. It won't take long. I'll drop you at the Jockey Club."

The taxi started forward, and the sudden movement pushed Carter down into the seat beside Elkins.

"The rumor is that you're going to Peking with the President."

Carter settled back into the seat. "I have nothing to say to you."

"That's not a very friendly attitude."

"I don't feel very friendly. I read your column this morning. That story about the President and the Soviet party chief."

"It happens to be true. I got it straight from people who were there. They had an argument and George Rushton flipped out. Tried to physically attack him."

Carter said firmly, "He isn't capable of behaving that way. When he's angry, he's more likely to make a joke than anything else."

"You haven't seen him in a while," Elkins said. "He's changed."

"If so, I haven't noticed it." In fact, he had been surprised at how easily he and George had resumed their old friendship, as if resuming a conversation that had been recently interrupted.

"I've even got a theory about what's behind it."

"Behind what?"

"The way George Rushton has been acting. Of course, it could just be that he's sitting in the middle of the world's biggest pressure cooker. But I suspect something else. His marriage."

Carter stared at him.

"It's gone sour," Elkins said.

Carter answered sharply, "George and Claire Rushton are the happiest couple who ever lived in the White House. You don't know anything about them if you don't know that much!"

"Some of my best theories turn up later as hard news."

"This one won't. It's total nonsense."

"I'm certainly not wrong about one thing. George Rushton has been damn uptight lately. And it's showing up in the polls. He's been digging a new hole every month in the popularity ratings."

"Is that the way you measure a President? By how popular he is?"

"I don't carry anybody's flag. I just tell it like it is. Now, about the Peking trip? Would you like to confirm or deny?"

Glancing out the window, Carter saw the taxi about to make a turn. "Your driver isn't taking me to the Jockey Club."

"Okay, okay. He's just driving around."

"I have a seven-thirty reservation."

"You'll get there."

"You're just wasting your time. I'm not going to tell you anything."

Jack Elkins shrugged. He leaned forward and through the glass protective shield gave the driver his instructions.

"And in case you're thinking of trying this again," Carter said, "tomorrow morning I'm renting a car."

In one of the medical center's private rooms on the fifth floor, Carter sat wrapped in a disposable, faintly blue-colored paper robe on the edge of an examination table.

A knock on the door.

"I'm decent," he said.

A nurse entered, a young woman with full lips and an attractive dark complexion. She was carrying a clipboard under her arm and a waxed paper cup in one hand.

She said, "Would you mind giving a small contribution? Use the bathroom in there."

"You aren't the same nurse who gave me the electrocardiogram."

"I've got my own specialty."

"That?"

"This. I also coordinate the various medical reports for summing up." She put the container down and removed the clipboard from beneath her arm. "I'm not supposed to tell, but do you want to know?"

"Yes." He was admiring her figure.

She made a small circle with thumb and forefinger. "You've come through so far A-OK."

"What's ahead?"

"Urinalysis. Rectal. Muscular coordination. You should be getting through in about two hours."

"Two hours?"

"A final report from the lab. Sed rate and X-ray analysis. Then a consultation with our head diagnostician. Dr. Jonathan Vancell. The resident genius."

"I'm hungry."

"Have you had your stomach and digestive tract X-rayed?"

"I must have. I was in the X-ray room almost an hour."

"Barium?"

"The works."

"Well, then, we might risk a glass of milk and a graham cracker. Though you're not supposed to have anything but water."

"Someone should have warned me. I could have brought a box lunch."

"An Irish revolutionary went more than a hundred days without eating."

"I am *not* an Irish revolutionary."

"I know. I know all about you." She tilted the clipboard at him. "In fact, I probably know more about you right this minute than any other living human being."

"Believe it or not, I am more than the sum of my various parts. What's your name?"

"Joyce Hatton."

Her only questionable feature was slightly protuberant eyes, but somehow they only made her seem attentive.

"Have you been on duty all day?" he asked.

"Since eight this morning. It's been a long haul. We had all those people injured in the rioting. Thank goodness only one is in serious condition. And the last I heard she was doing all right."

Carter said sympathetically, "You must be as tired as I am. And probably as hungry."

"I suppose I am."

"Then why don't we have dinner together?"

As usual, putting himself at risk, he had a sudden glimpse through appraising eyes. A loose-jointed, flapping monstrosity who was too tall, too old, too White Anglo-Saxon Protestant.

"Together?"

He laughed. "That was the general idea."

"You're sure you're not making a mistake?"

"I don't understand."

"This isn't a deep tan. It's genetic."

"Does that mean you never have dinner?"

She smiled then. "Eight-thirty okay?"

"Eight-thirty is just fine."

The clipboard she had been carrying was on Dr. Vancell's desk when Carter entered his office, tucking his shirt down into his trousers.

Dr. Vancell was young-looking, lean-featured, and wore a white smock. "It all seems very much in order. Heart sound, lungs sound, all your vital organs performing their proper functions. Uric acid is seven point six, up near the limits of normal. You don't drink a lot, do you?"

"Not any more. Only a little wine."

"Good. On the whole, for a man your age you're holding up pretty well." Dr. Vancell sat back in his comfortable leather chair, took a cigarette and tamped it against the pack. "Smoke?"

"No. Gave that up too."

"Wish to hell I could. Doctors ought to know better." He struck a match and lit the cigarette. "I understand you're a close friend of George Rushton's."

"We've known each other since college."

"I guess you were upset by that stupid column of Jack Elkins's."

Carter said, "It doesn't jibe with the President's character."

"Elkins is a damned fool. Always trying to make smoke where there's no fire. I listen to his weekly show on television, but he never strikes me as sincere. You know, I met Rushton once. If you see him, will you give him a message?"

"Of course."

"You tell the President he's got a good man in Mark Ziffren and not to be afraid to give him his head. He'll do what has to be done to get rid of the goddamn revolutionaries in this country. And tell him not to worry about that girl. She was asking for trouble."

"What girl?"

"I just got word from our operating room. That girl who got her skull fractured during the riot. She died."

That evening at eight-thirty, Carter picked up Joyce Hatton at her apartment house a few blocks from the medical center. She wore a soft shirtwaist dress, russet colored, and in the light of the crystal chandeliers at the Rive Gauche she was almost beautiful.

She was very quiet, almost preoccupied, until finally he asked, over cocktails, "Is something wrong?"

"No. Well, to tell the truth, I'm still thinking about that girl who died today. Only fifteen. A child."

"I know. It was a tragedy."

"Why do those things have to happen?"

"I don't agree that the mounted troops ended the riot. They began it."

"Really?"

He told her how he had been trapped in the middle of the rioting and what he had seen. When he finished, her eyes were shiny with tears.

"That's Mark Ziffren for you," she said. "He's not one of my favorite people."

"From what I've heard, I don't think he'll be one of mine either."

She became more friendly after that. When the waiter came, they both ordered the trout meunière. He asked for a wine list, chose a Puligny Montrachet '53, and noted her slight frowning hesitance.

When the waiter left, he said, "You didn't seem to approve."

"That's the trouble with knowing too much about a man," she said. "Your uric acid. Upper limits of normal. You could tip over into gout. I took another look at your medical chart after you asked me to dinner."

There had been a question on the chart about his marital status; he had checked the box for Divorced.

"What else did you find out?"

"Your social security number. And how old you are."

"Anything more you'd like to know?"

"Nothing I can think of. Well, maybe one thing. Those four years you spent in Nigeria. Does that account for your interest?"

"In what?"

"A member of a minority group."

"Ever since I was twenty years old, I've been six foot seven. That makes me a member of a minority group much smaller than yours."

She laughed, and a further unacknowledged tension was gone. She asked, "Why did you go to Nigeria in the first place?"

"My job."

"I mean your real reasons. You could have worked anywhere if you wanted to."

"Oh, I was probably running away from something." It occurred to him she might assume he had run away to forget his broken marriage, but he did not bother to correct the impression.

"Tell me about yourself," he said.

"My father was black, or mostly. My mother was white—entirely."

"I was more interested in you than your parents."

Her slow smile accepted all the implications. "All right. What would you like to know?"

"Start with the usual. What made you decide to be a nurse?"

"I bought a personalized horoscope. It said I was kind, and

liked to help people in trouble." Her eyes met his; he felt a small shock, as if he had touched an open socket while the electricity was on. "My mistake. I was being flippant, and you really want to know. It was because of my father."

"He wanted you to be a nurse?"

She shook her head, her lips compressing slightly. "He keeled over one evening while we were sitting and talking. By the time the ambulance came, it was too late. I could have saved him if I'd known what to do."

"And you blamed yourself?"

"In a way. I took a job as a nurses' aide in a city hospital."

"And liked it."

"Not at first. That's where I really saw indifference."

"In what way?"

"Patients aren't considered people. Just numbers. The doctors and nurses usually refer to them as 'the census.' Even when the patients line up for treatment they get a number. They're not called by name the way they are in a private clinic. When I went through a ward for the first time, it knocked out all the silly ideas in my head about smiling nurses in nice starched uniforms taking temperatures and pushing sweet old people in wheelchairs."

Something in him responded to her with a warmth that had been extinguished for a long time.

"How did you get to the medical center?"

"I would have stayed on at the city hospital, but I got into a hassle with the supervisor over an asthma patient who was having a seizure. He was turning cyanotic, and she wouldn't give him adrenaline. Nurses aren't supposed to give medication except on a doctor's orders. The man was dying right there in front of us while we were watching, and all she would do was page the doctor in the dining room. Finally I couldn't stand it. I took the keys to the drug closet away from her and gave him what he needed. That was my last day at the city hospital. Now I'm at the medical center taking urine samples and keeping charts. And grateful. When they checked, they were told I was emotionally unstable. I wouldn't have been hired at all if it wasn't for Dr. Thatcher."

"Who?"

"Dr. Marvin Thatcher. The President's doctor. I told him exactly what happened. He spoke up for me. He said if doctors or nurses had to be punished every time they broke the rules, there wouldn't be many doctors or nurses left in the world. A nice man. A good doctor, too, although the dinosaurs at the medical center thought he was too permissive. He left a couple of years ago and started his own clinic."

On the drive back, he found himself wondering how old she was. Twenty-five or -six. No woman as good-looking could have reached her age without having at least one serious affair. Probably several. The thought did not please him.

Throughout the evening they had made progress toward that undefined goal that occupies so much of the energies of a man and woman who find each other attractive. Now he wondered whether to play the least or most aggressive role. *I've had a lovely evening. May I call you again?* Or press the issue and invite himself upstairs for a nightcap? He had so little experience with women that he was utterly unable to gauge what would happen.

Her head was almost touching his shoulder. If he only knew what she was thinking.

Suddenly she asked, "Are you going to be one of those who write your memoirs about the President?"

"Not likely." Their thoughts had hardly been synchronized. "I don't think future historians will need my small contribution."

"How long have you known him?"

"Since college."

"There must be any number of interesting stories you could tell."

The truth was often a good subterfuge. "The most interesting stories can never be told. But that's true of everyone."

At the front entrance to her apartment house, they kissed goodnight. It was then that he had a familiar giddy feeling, as if everything inside him was seesawing.

3

The first time Carter had experienced the sensation was when he walked into a class in college algebra and saw Claire Palmer sitting in the second row. He was placed in the last row so he would not block the sight lines of other students, and from that vantage point he studied her loveliness. By the end of the first week he was in love, although he knew they would never share more than a college classroom. At Webster College a schism divided the sons and daughters of the Yankee establishment, many of whose parents had also attended the college, from the outsiders.

Carter was an outsider. The Fitzsimmonses were an elderly couple who had adopted him and then scrimped to send him to a good school. "After all, school is one of the most important experiences of a young man's life." They expected him to make the kind of friends there that would assure his future success.

But his future had been decided before he arrived at college. Growing up with an older couple, Carter never had the kind of communication with parents that would have prepared him for the modern world. He arrived on campus as if he had been dropped out of the nineteenth century—complete with formal good manners, a stiff correctness of speech, and almost incurably old-fashioned attitudes. Some of this eventually rubbed off, but vestiges remained, and helped to keep him outside the charmed circle.

Claire Palmer belonged in the center of that circle. Her father had gone to the college and so had his father before him. And because she was beautiful, warm, and sympathetic, there was always a cluster of admiring boys.

After midterm examinations, Carter joined a group of nervously keyed-up students who went to a nearby pizza parlor to compare examination results. Claire came in a few minutes later and sat with them. She was afraid she hadn't gotten anything right on the midterms. Everyone comforted her, but as they went on to compare answers it became increasingly apparent that she was telling a near truth. An inspired young man suggested that Carter, "who is such a whiz at math," could tutor her.

"Oh, would you?" she asked Carter.

Never did a knight pick up a lady's gauntlet with more affected nonchalance. "If you'd like me to."

That was the beginning. They met every Tuesday at the school cafeteria to review her algebra, and he prepared her well enough to pass the course with adequate grades. In turn, he learned much from her. She loved poetry, and when she read aloud to him in her small voice, his heart responded. *My vegetable love should grow/Vaster than empires and more slow.*

"What is a vegetable love?" he asked.

"Not of the flesh," she told him.

It was an ideal that Carter accepted. Love did not have to include sex, at least not right away.

By then they had started dating, and it was generally accepted that she was his girl. The impossible had happened, and he was beginning to think about their future. As soon as he graduated and found a job, he intended to speak to her father, a professor of anthropology at Harvard. He would marry Claire, and on their honeymoon they would visit all the romantic places: the Spanish Steps, the Eiffel Tower, St. Mark's Square, the Acropolis.

Then George Rushton appeared on the scene. George was another outsider, but he had begun, even in his freshman year, to move toward the center. He had the unexplainable charisma of a born leader. No one thought it remarkable when George, despite a relentlessly middle-class upbringing, was tapped by the most exclusive fraternity on campus. He was on the school paper, belonged to the chess club, the debating society, the choir. In his junior year, he was elected class secretary. He helped with theatricals as a director and occasionally in a small acting role. He even wrote a one-act play, featuring one Sir Hastepound—an obvious play on *Rushton*—an incorrigible practical joker whose victims turn the tables on him. So far as Carter knew, that was George's only writing effort. At the play's single performance, George Rushton, seated in the first row, began the booing and catcalls, and somehow turned the evening into a personal triumph.

His distinguishing characteristic was tenacity. What he set his mind on getting, he got. In his sophomore year he had turned out for the basketball team. So did Carter, who had a good eight inches on George in height and an advantage in reach, but no will to overcome the slow reactions that let alert players continually steal the ball from him. George Rushton, on the other hand, was always trying to improve. One evening Carter dropped by the gym to get something out of his locker and found George on the court, making run after run at the basket, looping and hooking in shots. When Carter returned two hours later George was still practicing, this time from the foul line.

When the final cut was made, Carter was dropped, and George, despite his lack of height and moderate skills, made the squad.

Carter took Claire to the junior prom. Ichabod Crane and the fairest of them all. Dancing with her, he felt oafish and shuffling beside her dreamlike floating grace.

George Rushton cut in once, and from the sidelines Carter watched. George was a smooth dancer who knew all the steps and other couples stopped dancing to watch him with Claire.

It soon became apparent that George had set his mind on Claire Palmer. Carter saw them walking together toward a classroom and meeting casually around the campus. He waited numbly for the moment to come in which George, in manly straightforward fashion, would ask to talk over the situation, and he despised himself for an inability to act on his own. He felt as if he were a long, soft sofa on which other people sat until he finally took on their shapes and indentations.

The meeting with George took place exactly as he foresaw. George began by saying he considered himself Carter's friend and there should never be any deception between friends. He went on to say he felt a strong attraction to Claire, and he had some hope she shared his feeling. Since she and Carter were not engaged, it was only proper to let her decide between them. Didn't he agree? There was something almost ruthless in his determination to be fair.

Carter understood that he would lose, for Claire's liking him had been some kind of aberration. But he struggled as hard as he could to keep her. Not until she told him she had fallen deeply in love with George and felt he was "so right" for her did he accept defeat. He promised he would always be a good friend— to both of them.

He kept his promise, but began to find solace in solitary drinking. One morning he woke up in a hotel room without any idea of where he had been the previous night. The very next day he accepted an offer from the Institute for Afro-American Relations that compelled him to move to Washington. Although he was pleased to see Claire happy, her happiness was easier to bear from a distance.

George Rushton's political career advanced predictably. He had that rarest of qualities—the ability to help other people defeat their fears. He moved from the party's state committee to the state attorney generalship, then was invited to run for Congress. At that point, along with other reservists, he was called up for duty in Vietnam. He served as an aide-de-camp on the staff of General Mark Ziffren. Carter was sure he would come back trailing clouds of glory—with thousands of Vietcong following captive in chains behind his all-conquering jeep.

One day in November 1966, George Rushton was reported missing and presumed dead in an airplane crash near Tay Ninh.

As soon as Carter heard, he went to the Rushton home on Sparrow Mountain. Claire was holding her fragile emotions together while surrounded with friends, but by late afternoon most of the others had gone. The last to go was the state's leading political power, a gray-haired older man with a crew cut who told Carter sadly that it was a great loss. "That young man had the stuff to go all the way. A natural politician."

Claire told Carter it was silly of him to drive late at night when the guest room was made up and ready. Because he did not want her to be alone, he agreed to stay until morning.

He slept badly. When the grandfather clock in the hall struck four, he got up, put trousers on, and went downstairs to find a book to help him pass the sleepless night. There was a light in the library. He knocked, and Claire opened the door. She was wearing her nightgown and robe, and her hair was in a pigtail. Without any lipstick or cosmetics she looked younger than when he had first met her.

"I didn't know you were awake," he said.

"This was his room. I wanted to be here among his things."

She began to cry, miserably and helplessly. Desperately searching for something to say, Carter told her, "If anyone in the world can pull through this, George can. I wouldn't be surprised to hear at any time that he's turned up alive." He did not believe it.

At last she dried her tears. "You're so good for me, Carter," she said. "It helps just to talk to you."

I love you, he said in his mind.

At five-thirty they went up to their respective bedrooms, and

Carter lay fighting the devil that told him he must help Claire through her time of grief until at last she learned to love him as she had loved George.

A week later George Rushton returned to the American headquarters at Tay Ninh, having spent the intervening days dodging Vietcong patrols while making his way by foot through their territory for almost sixty-five miles. The exploit rated a good deal of newspaper coverage, and earned him the Distinguished Service Cross. Both proved assets when he decided to run for senator. He was elected by the largest majority ever recorded in the state.

That meant he and Claire would soon be moving to Washington, where Carter lived. It seemed as if George was his Jungian shadow, except in this case the shadow always won out. With pained awareness he considered the possibilities: the pleasure of renewing an old friendship, the anxiety of renewing an old temptation. And his oppression was so great it was almost as if his emotions were able to anticipate the terrible consequences that would soon follow.

4

The briefing in Abramson's office the next evening lasted until nearly midnight.

For two and a half hours they covered not only Chinese industrial management but also the mount of rolling stock on its rail lines, and appraisals of China's position vis-à-vis the European Common Market.

When the session turned to the critical problem of Russian-Chinese relations, Carter asked why the Russians were so obsessed with fear of China.

Abramson turned from the window of his seventh-floor office. "Let me put it this way. Suppose Mexico had a population of one billion people. And suppose it was laying claim to large regions of the southwestern United States and was at the same time developing near parity in nuclear weapons. Would we be obsessed about them?"

Carter left with a briefcase bulging with notes and duplicates of documents. He reached his hotel room and inserted the key into the door. In the room a man with his back to him had Carter's attaché case open on the bed and papers strewn out. He was photographing them with a palm-sized camera.

At the sound of the door opening, the man jumped as if struck with a whip. When he turned to confront Carter his hand magically had a gun in it. Carter recognized the graceless two-inch barrel of a Smith and Wesson .38.

A scowl deepened on the man's pyramidally shaped face. "Into the bathroom." His hand and gun indicated the direction. "Move!" He had a midwestern accent.

Though shocked, Carter found he was still thinking. No ordinary sneak thief would be carefully photographing papers from the attaché case.

He said, "You really wouldn't use that gun. The people you work for wouldn't like that."

"You'd better do what I tell you."

"That's the type of gun used by lawmen. I suppose you're a government agent."

The man moved threateningly closer, and the floor creaked as his weight pressed down.

He overlooked how far Carter could reach.

Carter grabbed the hand holding the gun. The startled angry expression on the man's face quickly froze into ferocity as he struggled to free himself.

They wrestled across the room. Carter already foresaw that he would get the gun, and call the hotel desk to have them summon the police. A clear case of breaking and entering, attempted burglary, and . . .

He felt as if he had suddenly broken up inside and everything was flowing down out of him. He began to choke. He collapsed, his hunched shoulders and hands gripping his genitals until his knees touched the floor.

The man bent over him, putting the gun into his pocket. He said accusingly, "You had to make me hurt you."

Carter lay on his side with his legs drawn up, and his shoulders began to shake. He squeezed his eyes shut against excruciating pain. All he could think was that he'd been crippled for life.

Twenty miles away he heard a door close and a tiny vibration reached him through the floor. There was a sweet spoiled smell from the carpet where he had vomited. He moved his head slightly away, and rolled over and flexed one leg with cramped tentative slowness. He could move. He blinked at the horizontally magnified room.

He got into the bathroom to splash water on his face in the basin and gargle. Under fluorescent light his complexion looked soapy. As he turned off the faucet, the telephone was ringing.

"Carter? I was about to give you up."

Claire.

A wrench of pain caught him as he was about to reply, and he gave a small grunting sound that she must have mistaken for hello, for she went on brightly: "I haven't had a chance to send a formal invitation. But George and I would both like you to come to dinner tomorrow night."

The pain was fading.

"Look, Claire, can I call you back? I have to make another call. I'm afraid my room has been burglarized."

At exactly ten minutes before eight o'clock, Carter emerged from a rented Oldsmobile under the archway of the west gate of the White House. He tugged at his tuxedo. Something in his elongated frame offered formidable resistance to the elegance of custom tailoring.

As he entered the dining salon he caught a glimpse of himself in a gold-framed mirror walking with a slight forward stoop, favoring his sore groin. The effect was anthropoidal.

A short, gray-haired man smiled at him. "My name's Thatcher. Dr. Marvin Thatcher. You must be Carter Fitzsimmons. I've heard a good deal about you."

"I've heard about you, too, Doctor."

Dr. Thatcher looked for all the world like a benevolent country doctor. "I hope I draw a better partner than I did last time. One of those glacial beauties who thought conversation would fracture her makeup."

"I know the type," Carter said.

"I don't know how to make small talk at dinner."

"Neither do I. I can never think of a confounded thing to say. Except that the trout is excellent."

"I'll try to remember. The trout is excellent."

"It isn't much good when they're not serving trout."

A butler referred them to a side table on which there was a seating chart of the dining room. They found miniature envelopes bearing their names. Inside was the name of the lady each would escort to dinner, and a diagram of the dining room, showing their places at the table.

Dr. Thatcher winced at his card. "I wish this were my kind of thing," he said.

"I wish I were shorter," Carter said.

They went into the state dining room, a dumpy little man and an elongated scarecrow, both in ill-fitting tuxedoes.

At the table, long minutes blurred into each other while Carter sipped Chablis and remarked to his partner, Marie Loughran, wife of the secretary of the interior, that the Dover sole was excellent. She agreed. Tiny forkfuls disappeared into her rosebud mouth, and she engaged in droning conversation.

She explained what her husband was doing to make the country self-sufficient in energy. "I hope people understand what Tim Loughran is doing for them," she said, referring to her husband for some reason by his full name. "I hope they appreciate it. Do you think they do, Mr. Fitzsimmons? You don't mind my asking your opinion?"

"Not at all," Carter said. "I'm always pleased when people ask for my opinion, because that supposes I have one."

She gave him a fixed smile, and for the rest of the meal she concentrated on the man on the other side.

After dinner, Claire and George led the way into a long rectangular room with arching windows that looked out on the rose garden. Far beyond, in the pale moonlit sidewalk, were the dark silhouettes of the pickets.

Claire came to him. "Did you enjoy talking to Marie Loughran?"

"I'm afraid she found me boring."

"Nonsense. Women don't meet many shy men nowadays. She probably thought you were charming." She looked around smiling, without any particular focus, actually looking to see if anyone was near enough to overhear. "Now, tell me what happened to you last night."

He told her about the nocturnal visitor, the perfunctory visit by detectives that followed. There had been no clue. He had not expected there would be any.

"In my opinion," he said, "he was a government agent. Probably one of those Security Bureau boys."

"Why don't you ask General Ziffren?" She nodded toward a man approaching them. "That's his department."

Mark Ziffren moved with a stiff halting gait but, despite his infirmity, he had the erect military posture that made Carter aware of his own tall man's stoop. He made an effort to straighten himself.

"General, I'd like you to meet Carter Fitzsimmons, a very old friend of the President's and mine."

Ziffren's handshake was quick and strong, but he withdrew his hand an instant before Carter was prepared for it.

Claire murmured, "Excuse me," and drifted away to join another group.

"I understand you're just back from a tour of duty in Nigeria," Ziffren said. His body weight shifted almost imperceptibly toward the right, favoring the crippled side. He had lost his left leg just below the knee when he stepped onto a land mine at Quang Tri.

"Four years."

"Must have been an interesting experience. You had plenty of opportunity to see the Russians throwing their weight around."

"In what way, General?"

"Trying to lure them with grants and loans. What they're really interested in is their oil and gas and commercial markets. I wish somebody could get that through the head of our esteemed secretary of state."

The hum of conversation in the room increased momentarily, and Carter fumbled back through memory for what he knew about this man. Mark Ziffren had served with Patton in Europe, with MacArthur in Korea, and his distinguished military career had ended when he was forced to leave the service, an amputee, during the Vietnam war. Now, at sixty-two, he had a whole new career in government.

"I'm sure he's aware of the problems," Carter said. "I've found Abramson highly knowledgeable."

"I'd advise you take anything he says with a pound of salt. As far as I'm concerned, the sooner people like Abramson are swept out of office, the better off our government will be."

"On the contrary, I think he's been a fine secretary of state," Carter said. Then he added maliciously, "You might have been more impressed with him if your man had succeeded in photographing my briefing notes."

Ziffren lifted a quizzical eyebrow.

Carter said, "I assume it was your man who visited my hotel room last night. . . ."

"Why do you assume that?"

"Since I'm to accompany the President to Peking, that makes me important to security. I think you checked the files on me and decided to supplement them."

"You really shouldn't leap to conclusions." Ziffren glanced sharply up at him. "But suppose you were right. Would you have any reason to fear that kind of surveillance?"

"I assure you, General, there is nothing in anyone's dossier anywhere that would show I'm a security risk."

"Nobody in government can have a private life. You can't expect to be an exception. Don't take these things personally, Mr. Fitzsimmons."

The skin on Carter's cheeks felt hot. "I take it very personally when someone kicks me in the testicles."

Ziffren appeared startled, then amused. "Testicles. A word I don't hear much, outside of hospitals. Don't people like you have balls, Mr. Fitzsimmons?"

They were joined by a group that included Tim Loughran, secretary of the interior, and Senator Halliwell of the foreign relations committee. Frustrated and angry, Carter hovered nearby like a lonely volcanic outcropping. As soon as he could, he excused himself.

Claire returned. "I saw you talking with General Ziffren. Did you get any satisfaction?"

"I'd like to punch him in the nose."

"He arouses strong opinions. I've never met anyone who's neutral about him."

"I don't understand how George could give a man like that so much authority."

"Perhaps you shouldn't try too hard to understand," she answered in a mildly rebuking tone. "As George says, a pedestrian can never think like the one who's driving the car."

In criticizing George, he had ventured into forbidden territory. "Ziffren just raises my hackles, that's all."

George Rushton was in the center of a large admiring group. Apparently he finished telling an amusing story, for everyone laughed.

"Your husband is in good form tonight," Carter said.

She answered unexpectedly. "He always pulls himself together when he has to."

He picked up the faint pulse of a real anxiety.

"Are you worried about him?"

"I don't think he's looking well. And he's lost weight."

"Why don't you speak to Dr. Thatcher?"

"George wouldn't like that. And Dr. Thatcher wouldn't tell me anything, anyhow."

"If you'd like me to, I'll try pumping Dr. Thatcher a little."

Someone was approaching, so she answered quickly, "That would be nice. You're a good friend." Then she added with a bright smile, "By the way, we're having a musicale on Thursday evening. You will come, won't you?"

The other guests descended on them, and Carter looked around until he glimpsed Dr. Thatcher in a corner with a short dark man who was finger-tapping on his chest. The doctor gave him a mildly imploring glance, and Carter went over. After a few moments, the short dark man sensed he no longer had an audience, and left in the hope of finding someone more receptive.

They heard George Rushton's robust baritone laughter.

"He's enjoying himself," Dr. Thatcher said.

"I don't think he's looking well," Carter said. "He's lost weight. And he complained about still having trouble with his neck."

Dr. Thatcher nodded unhappily. "The condition isn't improving as rapidly as I had hoped."

"What is it?"

"Nothing serious. A rupture of an intervertebral disk. Given time, the gelatinous material pushed out from the ruptured disk will shrink and the pressure on the nerve roots will be relieved."

"Isn't there anything that helps in the meanwhile?"

Thatcher shook his head regretfully. "About all I can do is give symptomatic relief. I've tried everything from wet heat to massage to the method Dr. Janet Travell used so successfully with President Kennedy."

"What was that?"

"Trigger-point injections. When a muscle goes into spasm, there's a particular point where an injection of a local anesthetic— usually Novocain—will relieve the spasm and kill the pain. In theory it should only work until the anesthetic wears off, but in practice the relief can last for weeks or even be permanent. Unfortunately, I can't say I've had those results with the President." Thatcher sighed. "His real problem is nervous tension."

"Does tension affect it?"

"Oh, yes, there's a definite physical connection. Tension shortens the long spinal muscles that pull the vertebrae together. That increases the pressure on swollen nerve fibers." Thatcher's hand moved, palm upward, in a helpless gesture. "At one point I I worked up courage to suggest he ought to go for a long holiday to his farm."

"I can imagine the kind of reception that got."

Dr. Thatcher smiled wistfully. "He told me to stick to doctoring and not mess around in politics."

Carter asked, "Do you think it'll be all right for him to make the trip to Peking?"

"I'm sure it will. I'm going along to keep an eye on him." Thatcher made a wry face. "I'd be very disappointed if he had to call off that trip. For me it will be something of a homecoming."

"Oh?"

"I was born and raised in China."

"Were you?"

"My parents were missionaries there, and I didn't leave until I was almost fourteen. It's like my second homeland."

Above the low-key conversations surrounding them, Carter again heard Mark Ziffren's high, thin voice.

"I came up against the Russians in the Second World War," Ziffren was saying. "I saw how they operate. General Patton wanted to drive right through to Moscow. If he had, we wouldn't be having all this trouble with them today."

The universal fairy tale, Carter thought—the wicked Them and the good Us.

He was glad General Ziffren was not coming with them to Peking.

Adolph Abramson arrived at the Vice-President's home shortly after the dinner hour. It was the eighty-five-year-old former home of the chief of naval operations, and was located on the Naval Observatory grounds.

When the Secret Service had wanted to put improvements in the house that would add to its security, Elmer Tate flatly refused. "Nobody's going to accuse me of spending tax dollars to fix up any place I live in. Besides, it's all foolishness. A plot to assassinate me would be the most futile political scheme of this century. What would anybody gain by it? As far as the government's concerned, it'd be two years before they even found out I was dead."

Abramson was met at the front door of the official residence by Gloria Tate, a genial damp woman who looked perfectly at home in an apron.

"Elmer's down in the basement," she said. "What we call the recreation room. Working on his pool game." She always gave the impression of having just come out of a warm bath, but this evening her pink flushed look seemed more pronounced, and the reason became evident when she suddenly lifted up the edges of her apron and sneezed into it. "Bless me," she said. "I must be coming down with something. Elmer doesn't like for me to be sick. It discombobulates him."

"Would he mind if I dropped in on him downstairs?"

"Not a bit. When you're finished, come on up and have a cup of coffee and some of my angel food cake."

"I'd like that."

The basement recreation room was only partially refinished, steam pipes and concrete walls still showing. A full-sized pool table was in the center, a cot against a wall, and two folding chairs faced a small television set.

Elmer Tate was leaning over the pool table to line up a shot and Abramson waited. The cue ball caromed off and rolled slowly down to rest against a far cushion.

Elmer looked up and saw Abramson. "Never could play position. Every time I even think about it, I can't make the goddamned shot."

"That isn't what I hear," Abramson said smiling. "I'm told you're the best pool shark who ever came to this town."

"Now, you must've been talking with Fred Wilson, our esteemed attorney general. Or maybe Senator Halliwell. Those boys learned how to play pool in gentlemen's clubs. Nobody who learns that way ever gets to be any damn good. I learned hanging around the local pool parlor. Worked as a rack boy for a while. That way, you get to learn something about the game." He laid the cue stick parallel with a side cushion. "What's on your mind, Dolph?"

"Have you heard the news about Carter Fitzsimmons?"

"What news?"

"His hotel room was broken into and searched, and he was beaten up."

Elmer Tate shook his head. "This city's crime rate is climbing faster than its unemployment rate. Gloria—she won't go out at night alone."

"This wasn't an ordinary burglary, Elmer. The crook had a miniature camera and was copying papers from Carter's attaché case."

"A spy?"

"Possibly. Carter doesn't think so. He thinks it's the Security Bureau—acting on General Ziffren's orders."

"Wouldn't surprise me any. That gimpy son of a bitch is a little off his rocker when it comes to national security."

Elmer Tate's private conversations were noted for their candor, not to mention his sometimes unprintable language, but for some reason Abramson's strong streak of propriety was not offended by this plain-speaking man.

"Frankly, Elmer, I'm worried about the way things are going. When did you see George Rushton last?"

"Hm. Maybe three, four weeks ago."

"And you're the Vice-President. Most other people in government haven't seen him in months."

"I don't take offense. The Rushtons and the Tates aren't the same kind of folks. Outside politics, we don't have a hell of a lot in common. I like George, admire him in fact, but he doesn't play poker or pool like I do, and his wife gives parties that high-class people go to and talk literature to each other. Me and Gloria wouldn't fit in, and we know it."

"I don't mean socializing, Elmer. I'm talking about the President isolating himself from everyone, including you and his cabinet."

"Nothing unusual about that. Those boys in the cabinet may be bright enough individually, but add them all together and they don't come up to a good case of shingles."

"At least they could help to keep the President in touch with what's really going on. So would congressional leaders, but Rushton has been ignoring them too. He's relying on his inner circle. General Ziffren first and foremost."

Elmer shook his head. "I wish that brass-buttoned bastard had lived in biblical times. Samson could have used him when he needed the jawbone of an ass."

"And Chad Oliver, who guards Rushton's time and appointments and decides who he'll see and who he won't."

"Never could stand that fat-faced pretty boy. Nothing he says is worth a bucket of warm spit. He lies like an ambassador."

"And, of course, Dr. Thatcher. No one knows exactly how much influence he has with the President."

"I kind of like ol' doc. Aren't you leaving out somebody?"

"I can't think who."

"You ought to put his wife in. A man's wife always pulls a pretty strong oar. In fact, you ought to put her at the top of the list."

When the Tates had first come to Washington, it quickly became known Elmer would not respond to social invitations that were not addressed to *Congressman and Mrs.* "I'm not going to have my wife spending her evenings at home without any company but a hound dog and TV set," he explained. As senator, Elmer Tate got into a front-page quarrel with a New York gossip columnist who described Gloria as the dowdiest woman in Washington. His reply, profanely assigning the lady columnist to a permanent booth next to the men's room at Grand Central station where anybody could "drop in a coin and have her," helped to establish him as a personality to be reckoned with and a fiercely protective husband.

"I don't think Claire Rushton has much political influence with George," Abramson said. "She runs their social life—and very well—but she doesn't interfere in other matters. So that leaves him with no close advisers except Ziffren and Chad Oliver."

"I agree it's bad, Dolph. A man in the Oval Office needs somebody around who can look him straight in the eye and say, 'That's bullshit and you know it.' But there isn't anything you and I can do about it."

"I think there's someone who might be on the verge of joining that inner circle. Carter Fitzsimmons is very close to the President, an old friend, and he's already been invited to Peking."

"Is he a good man?"

"I'm impressed with him. I believe he could be a moderating influence."

"Meaning he looks at things pretty much the way you do. Aren't you sore the President is taking him to China instead of you?"

"I was at first," Abramson conceded. "But now I'm glad he'll be there. We need someone to offset the hard line Rushton tends to take with the Russians."

"Whoaa, there. I don't trust those bastards either."

"But you believe our differences can be settled by negotiation. That we can work out some kind of livable compromise."

"I don't think we ought to use the H-bomb just 'cause it's there—if that's what you mean."

"Ziffren does. He's always pointing out that we have three times the megatonnage in nuclear weapons that the Russians have."

"I never met a general who had more sense than Orphan Annie. All that matters is the Russians've got enough to kill every man, woman, and child in this country thirteen times over. How many times do you have to kill people before they're dead?" Elmer looked at Abramson shrewdly. "One thing puzzles me, Dolph."

"What's that?"

"You didn't come here to tell about Ziffren or even how you'd like to get Carter Fitzsimmons over to our side. Jezebel Christ, you don't need my approval for that. You're trying to scare up a different kind of polecat."

"It's your support I want, Elmer."

"Good. Let's cut the fat and get down to the meat. What do you want me to do?"

"You're on the National Security Council along with the President, secretary of defense, and me. And you have one big advantage over either Lester Hawkins or me."

"Yeah. No matter how mad the President gets, he can't fire me. I got my job from the American people, and nobody can take it away from me."

"Exactly."

"What you want me to do is look the President in the eye and tell him when he's full of varnish."

"Especially if you see him tipping over toward Ziffren and his extreme views."

"Pretty scared, aren't you?"

"Yes, I am."

Elmer Tate rubbed his chin thoughtfully. "Hell, George Rushton isn't going to pay any attention to what I say. But I'll do anything I can to stop Mark Ziffren. That humping bastard has got a bomb where his brains ought to be."

5

The car hummed on its way across the state line toward an inn twenty miles below Alexandria.

"I think you're going to like it," Carter said. "It's well recommended."

"I'm never comfortable when I get south of the Mason-Dixon line. Do you think they'll approve of us?"

"I wish you'd get over that particular hang-up. It's out of date."

"Well, I look respectable." She chuckled derisively. "They may think you're taking me across the state line for immoral purposes, but they'll still serve us dinner."

A sign flashed by on the highway: VANCEVILLE, 7 MILES.

"You just had the strangest expression," she said.

"Something reminded me."

"Of what?"

"My wife," he said.

She studied him a moment. "You're divorced, aren't you?"

"Yes."

"I saw it on your form at the medical center. What was she like?"

"Tall and slender. The kind you would call handsome. Her name was Janet McMullen, and she's the daughter of Judge Mc-Mullen."

Toward the end, he thought: *It was probably only because Janet and I loved her father that we kept on believing we loved each other.* To know Judge John McMullen was an experience. A forthright conservative, McMullen had missed a chance to serve on the Supreme Court because he disapproved of Nixon's previous appointments to the Court. When told he was under consideration to fill a new vacancy, he told Nixon, "Why would you choose me, Mr. President? I'm not mediocre."

Carter collected memories of the judge like a miser storing coins. Once, talking about the decline in a President's popularity during his term in office, Judge McMullen remarked that even if Jesus Christ came to reign over the world, it would scarcely be a year before the opinion polls reported that 44 percent thought He was doing a good job, 41 percent didn't think so, 11 percent had no opinion, and the remaining 4 percent never heard of Jesus Christ.

"I'd like to hear more about your wife," Joyce said.

He thought: *Janet might have been a better person if she had a third interest to add to horses and society.* He answered: "She's an expert horsewoman. She's been to the best schools in Switzerland and England, and she knows Princess Anne."

"How did you meet her?"

How? That is always important, isn't it, the actual getting together, drawing together, merging, of two different personalities. It happened because he was the scheduled speaker at one of her Social Affairs with a Purpose. The purpose was organizing aid for Biafra, and the meeting was held at the McMullen farm in Vanceville, which was probably why Janet was chairwoman. At the meeting he made several practical suggestions for sending aid to the Biafrans, and sometime during the long pleasant afternoon he became aware of Janet's interest in him.

Carter was flattered that she found him attractive because by then his inability to make out with women had become a steady painful exasperation. He seethed with unspent emotion, unsatisfied yearnings.

After a short chaste engagement, they were married. He recalled nothing of the intervening time. It was as if he had gone into hibernation and emerged to find himself walking down the church aisle. On his wedding day he was a little drunk.

He did not expect Janet to be good in bed—she didn't seem the type, her moral standards were too high; but she was a revelation. They shared long evenings of pure carnal delight, of a passion so absorbing that he finally came to recognize his previous involvement with Claire as youthful romanticism. That did not make his feeling for Claire less important, but it gave him perspective.

After a while the fierce molten thrill, the exquisite sensations in his nerve endings, began to fade, and he discovered with freshly sharpened anguish that he was thinking again of Claire, her gaiety, her openness. Janet was a closed system. She had immense reserves of silence that, after a time, he no longer bothered to tap. They continued to go through the motions. When she gave a party for an English girl friend visiting New York, George and Claire—vacationing in the city that month—were invited as a matter of course. At the time, George was concluding his first term as a senator and, despite his youth, was being mentioned frequently as a possible candidate for President.

Then he met Anne Demas.

Janet's friend, Anne Demas, had been twice married briefly, first to a famous movie director, and then to a wealthy British publisher. She was a beautiful creature with a voluptuous body, although Janet told Carter (in one of those deliberate moments of jealousy) that Anne was a creation: the synthetic product of a nose job, chin job, teeth capping, hair dyeing, brow shaping, breast firming, and buttock reduction. Apparently somewhere during the fabulous transition to loveliness Anne had lost sight of her identity; the failure of her two marriages had further eroded her sense of belonging in the world.

At thirty, she was making increasingly desperate efforts to accommodate herself to the demands she sensed around her; she had numerous lovers, none of whom stayed long. She got through the long nights with pills, and had made two attempts at suicide. On the evening she came to Janet's party, little remained of nervous stability, but she was still beautiful enough to have almost any man she wanted.

She chose George Rushton.

If Claire had been there, nothing would have come of it, but she had canceled at the last moment because their daughter Marie came down with measles. So George Rushton came alone that evening, met Anne, and that was the beginning.

Several weeks later Carter received a call from George Rushton's secretary, saying he was in New York for a few days and asking if Carter could spare a lunch as soon as possible. They met that very day. In the middle of lunch, George looked up with a pleading expression.

"You've got to help me," George said. "I'm in serious trouble."

"What kind of trouble?"

"Anne Demas wants me to get a divorce and marry her."

Carter was stunned. "You and Anne." Somehow hearing himself speak the words made the incredible more real. "How long has it been going on?"

"Since that party you and Janet gave. She called the next day . . . and, well, there you are. It's something I can't control."

"Why tell me?" Carter asked, his tone stopping just short of: *Keep in mind that I'm Claire's friend also.*

In a low voice choked with inner conflicts, George managed to ask, "What am I going to do?"

George Rushton—confused? Among the unbelievable things that had occurred in the past minute, this had its place.

"I think that's pretty obvious," Carter said. "Unless you want a divorce, you'll have to give up Anne."

"Good God, don't you think I've tried? She's badly disturbed, under the care of a psychiatrist. Threatening to kill herself."

"You have to make a choice. And the sooner you make it, the better for everyone concerned."

George looked at him sadly. "Carter, *please* try to understand. I know you can't see how this could happen, how I could do this to Claire if I really loved her. Well, it has nothing to do with how I feel about her." His head lowered; he looked down as if unable to confront what he was about to reveal. "It's just that, to be frank, she's never been too interested in the physical side of marriage. Anne happened into my life at a bad time. The important thing is that she'll tell everything if I don't marry her. She said she would." George sounded despairing. "I can't see any way out."

"What are you worried about most—your career or your marriage?"

"Claire is all that matters."

"Then it's clear what you have to do. Tell Anne that under no circumstances will you divorce your wife, that you're perfectly willing to confess everything rather than lose her."

"She won't believe me. And she's vindictive enough to go to the newspapers."

"If she does, it may mean the end of your political career. But Claire will stand by you. No matter what Anne decides to do, your marriage will survive."

"God, what a hopeless mess."

"You ought to go away. Somewhere Anne can't reach you."

"Where?"

"I have a cabin that's yours if you want it. No telephone, not even electricity, but all the privacy you need. You can tell Claire you have to get away from work pressures for a while."

"I swear I don't know how I got mixed up in anything like this."

"Neither do I," Carter said, unwilling to forgive more than he had.

The next day George had a showdown with Anne—the details of which he did not reveal to Carter—and left for the hideaway cabin. Several nights later Carter was reading very late in the evening, researching an article for the *Economics Review*. The telephone rang with the alarming shrillness it has at an unexpected hour. He picked it up quickly, hoping it would not waken Janet in the bedroom.

"Carter, are you alone?" There was a hoarse tremble in George Rushton's voice.

"Janet is asleep. I'm in the living room. What is it?"

"I drove thirty miles before I could find a place to telephone you. . . . My God, Carter, can you come?"

"To the cabin?"

"Hurry."

"I'll come in the morning."

"I need you *now*. Please! There's . . . trouble with Anne. I can't think what to do. I'm going out of my mind."

"Is she there?"

"Yes."

"I'll be there as soon as I can."

He went into the bedroom and found Janet sleeping. Before he left the house he wrote a note in the event that she might wake up and find him gone.

Dear: I had to go to the office for research material on the article I'm doing. Back soon. . . .

With any luck he would be back before she wakened, and could destroy the note. He finished dressing, put on his overcoat and a scarf, and went down to the garage. As he backed the car out there was still no sign of movement at the bedroom window.

He drove to the cabin in a little over an hour and parked on a rise in the dirt road. As he started climbing the path between the dense growth of vegetation, he saw a station wagon and a small red Jaguar parked beside it, facing the small tool shed. The station wagon was George Rushton's.

A single light burned in the window of the cabin's bedroom. The porch and the living room were in darkness.

The screen door was closed, but he knocked on the wooden rim. A light went on; the door opened.

George Rushton was wearing an undershirt and beltless trousers with no shoes or socks. He needed a shave.

"Carter, I didn't know how to explain on the telephone." His voice shook. He gestured vaguely toward the bedroom. "I've tried everything I could think of. She was gone before I found her."

A dreadful possibility occurred to Carter. He went to the open doorway of the bedroom and stood looking at a still figure on the bed. Anne Demas wore only a lacy beige slip that had hiked up, revealing the long symmetry of perfect legs.

He did not wish to actually enter the bedroom and discover for himself.

"Is she dead?"

George nodded and his mouth gave a meaningless grimace. He seemed to be holding his nerves together with frayed string.

"How long ago?" Carter asked.

"Around midnight. I thought she was sleeping when I found her."

It was then five o'clock in the morning.

"How did it happen?"

"I found an empty bottle on the floor. Sleeping pills."

Carter went into the bedroom, lifted a limp wrist, and rolled up the eyelids. There was no need, for the body was already cold.

"Have you called a doctor?"

"Not yet. I called you." His wide eyes seemed to be pleading. "I didn't know what to do. I couldn't believe it when I couldn't wake her up."

"What was she doing here?"

George looked accusingly at Anne's body lying on the bed. "I had no idea she was going to try this. On the telephone she was so gay . . . and affectionate. I began to hope she was going to be civilized about it. She told me how much she'd missed me . . .

that it was foolish for us to quarrel. I made the mistake of inviting her. I swear, if she'd even threatened. . . ."

"There will be an autopsy, George. It will show whether she had sexual relations before she died."

"I didn't think it would mean anything."

Carter held the angry words behind clenched teeth. Words would accomplish nothing.

Finally he said, "There's usually a suicide note."

George took Carter into the bathroom. Scrawled in lipstick on the medicine cabinet mirror was: *All you want is fuck, you bastard.*

"Where were you when she wrote this?"

"It was just after. . . . I was in the living room putting out the lights. She seemed all right."

"And then?"

"We went to bed. I woke up at midnight, and something about the way she was lying there . . ." He shook his head dazedly. "I tried artificial respiration but it was too late. I was going for a doctor when I got into the car. Then I got confused, and in the end I called you."

A small pendulum clock struck a single note.

"We'll have to call the police," Carter said.

"I guess there's nothing else to do." With all the power of his will George Rushton had tried to evade this moment, but now its crushing weight was upon him. There would be a front-page scandal, the ruin of his career, a divorce.

Carter sat down, his long thin hands folded in his lap. Most of his awareness centered on the fact of Claire's happiness about to be destroyed. Then another thought struck him, and at first it merely made him angry. He told himself it was ridiculous. But something in its sheer quixoticism attracted him. As he kept playing with it, kneading it like a lump of clay, he became almost pleased with the rude impossible shape.

"Take your car, George, and go."

"What?" George stopped pacing.

"I'll handle everything. Go home."

"What about Anne?" He stared.

"You can't do anything more for her."

"I won't go until I know what you're up to."

"Trust me."

"She's *dead*." His tone suggested the fact was apparently escaping Carter's attention.

"Staying won't bring her back to life. You're not able to think clearly now, George, and you mustn't try to make decisions in your frame of mind."

"The police?"

"You can talk to them later when you've had a chance to collect yourself."

"You're trying to make it easy for me. I can't let you do it. What kind of a heel do you think I am?"

I never called you a heel, Carter thought wearily; but the verdict of self-appraisal is never entirely wrong. He corrected himself; that was unfair. George must have had scores of opportunities, and how many men could go through their whole lives being true to only one woman? Marriage vows did not always take into account the fierce drives of the human animal, against which the most solemn pledges stood like a sand castle against an incoming tide.

He said bleakly, "There's a lot to be done, and it's late. You must leave now, George."

It was a moment before George answered. "All right. If you really think I should."

Watching the station wagon drive away, Carter began to feel ill. It was the backlash of doubt following upon a bold decision. Everything, including the fact that the owner of the red Jaguar lay dead in the bedroom of his cabin, struck him as incredible. Incredulity fathered hope and he hurried back into the cabin, but Anne Demas was lying where he had left her.

A deep shudder went through him, and he hurried to the bathroom. Racking, heaving, he added a fitting touch to the sordid tragedy. Afterward, emptied even of revulsion, he was able to see what had to be done. He went carefully around the cabin, removing traces of George Rushton's presence. An empty tobacco tin, an unfamiliar shaving cream in the bathroom cabinet, a grocery list in the kitchen that George had started to make out. It was fortunate George had not gone to the general store. There was a chance someone there could have identified him. He burned the grocery list, took the shaving cream and tobacco tin into the backyard where he flattened the tin with his heel, then took it and the tube of shaving cream into the tool shed and dug a small hole in the earth beneath a pile of logs and buried them. He scuffed out the tread marks of the station wagon back down to the road, where there were many other concealing tread marks. He searched the red Jaguar but found no papers relating to anyone but its owner. In the living room Anne's brocade purse was on a table. He opened it. About eighty dollars, a scribbled paper with directions on how to get to the cabin, a mirrored compact, a small comb, a mashed lipstick. The paper had been torn off a memo pad and stuffed into her purse. The directions were quite explicit, but there was nothing to indicate from whom she had gotten them. In the bathroom he wiped the lipsticked message off the mirror.

He got into his car, drove it up from the road to the tool shed, and parked next to the red Jaguar. Then he carefully backed down to the road again, leaving his own tire tread marks.

At the train depot in town, from a public telephone, he called the police. By then it was dawn.

When he returned home at nine o'clock in the morning, Janet was at the breakfast table in her dressing gown.

"I got your note. Why did you go off without breakfast?"

Carter was still in the grip of that inexplicable self-destructive force that had carried him through the awful hours of the early morning questions by police.

"I didn't go to the office," he said. "Something terrible has happened, Janet. Before I tell you about it I have to know that I can rely on your absolute discretion. Can I?"

— 51 —

A wary look entered her eyes. "You're acting very mysterious."

She finally gave her word—"I'm a judge's daughter and I'm used to keeping secrets"—and Carter told her everything. He began with her party at which George Rushton met Anne Demas. She did not seem too surprised to hear that George Rushton had begun an affair with Anne. She had never admired George, nor did she quite share Carter's quaint notions of fidelity. Her loyalties were based on her own sense of inner worth, a sense that never allowed her to condescend to casual sexual frolicking. At finishing school she had belonged to the Rara Avis, a group of girls who had pledged to remain virgins until marriage. She was one of the very few who had kept the pledge.

As Carter went on to tell how he had advised George and offered him the Roanoke cabin, Janet's manner underwent a perceptible cooling. As he unfolded the full terrible events of the nightmare evening, her eyelashes seemed to draw lower and lower until her eyes were almost closed.

"Do you realize what you've done?" she asked when he finished.

"For better or worse, I've done it, and there's no turning back. I've given the police a complete statement."

"You'd let everyone think *you* had that rendezvous with Anne Demas?"

"No one can prove differently."

"It'll be our name—yours and mine—that will be dragged through the mud."

"George Rushton's name would mean headlines. My name will hardly rate a mention."

"I won't have it." Her panic was clearly rising—he could almost trace it in the deep flush spreading through her throat up to her cheeks. "I warn you!"

He saw her as if from a distance—strong-willed, handsome. Above all, a McMullen. Daughter of a well-known constitutional lawyer and jurist who once had been considered for the Supreme Court.

"I can't deny what I've said. I told the police I was with Anne at the cabin. And her death was simply an accident."

"That may satisfy the police but it won't stop the scandal. I really think you've taken leave of your senses. What can I tell my father? How would I ever explain it to him?"

"I have no objection to your telling the judge the truth." There was no one whose discretion he trusted more than Jndge McMullen's.

"And have him think me an even worse fool? Imagine my telling him what a stupid thing you've done, and that I was willing to go along with it. Carter, I'm not willing. You have a clear choice of alternatives. Either save your friend George Rushton, or save your marriage."

In that sharp chiaroscuro world of either/or, it was all so clear to her, but there was an element in the situation she was unaware of. Claire mattered far more to him than George. Far more than Janet. As the flames leap higher and all is about to be lost, the martyr scarcely remembers for what cause it is happening. Had he and Claire ever been that close?

"Perhaps it was wrong, but it's done now and I can't undo it." With a considerable part of himself he continued to know its ridiculousness. He would have liked to add, *I'll make it up to you*, but he understood the futility.

"You mean you won't?"

Without hope, he answered, "I can't."

She got up and left the breakfast table. An hour later a taxi departed with her and her luggage.

No one thought of connecting George Rushton with the death of Anne Demas.

At approximately the time Carter was calling the police to tell what happened, George was driving his station wagon north toward the Capitol. Nearing a small town in Virginia, he suddenly veered off the turnpike. It was raining hard at the time and everyone later assumed he lost control on the slick-surfaced highway.

His station wagon traveled about twenty yards before colliding head on with a tree.

On the third day, while the prognosis for George's recovery was still guarded, Carter went to the hospital.

Claire met him in the waiting room, her face drawn tight over a mold of suffering. "The doctors say he should be recovering, but he doesn't seem to be fighting hard enough."

"That doesn't make sense, does it?"

She did not reply directly, but said, "If you tell him it's going to be all right, he'll believe you. He won't listen to the doctors or to me."

"I'd like to talk to him," he told Claire.

When he entered the hospital room, the light was fading. George Rushton was in bed, neck in a brace, with his broken leg splinted and stiffly out before him on the blanket. The part of his face beneath the head bandages was swollen and ugly from contusions.

Carter pantomimed an exit instruction to the nurse. When she left, he went to the side of the bed that George was facing.

"How are you, George?"

He managed a grotesque parody of a smile. "Are the police waiting for me to get out of here?"

"No. I told them that I was alone in the cabin with Anne when she died."

"You? Why did you say that?"

"It was my cabin, and it looked pretty obvious."

"I can't let you take the blame. What about you and Janet?"

"I told her the truth. She gave me her word she would never tell."

"Can we rely on it?"

"Yes."

"And what about Claire?"

"She doesn't know anything more than anybody else."

"She believes that you and Anne? . . ."

"Right now, she's not worried about me. She's worried about

you." Probably, he thought, Claire will never bring herself to mention the scandal. Shocked, sorry for Janet, she would find it hard to believe that Carter, one of the people she cared about, could be unfaithful. In the end, without truly accepting it, she would file it under life's inexplicable mysteries. And she would never reveal her true feelings.

There was a touch of bewilderment in George's next query. "Why are you doing this?"

"I don't know the answer myself."

Carter drove to Vanceville to see Judge McMullen. He admired and loved the frail old gentleman and now had to tell a lie that would be embarrassing to them both.

In the library at Vanceville, Carter learned that Judge McMullen had suspected what was happening to their marriage. In his slow deep voice he began musing about his own wife.

"She was very much like Janet. They say if you want to know what your wife will be like, look at your mother-in-law. Something in that, Carter. We were married for thirty-seven years, and lived together in the happy-unhappy way most married people do. After the honeymoon, a man and woman need something in common." Faded gray eyes probed into his. "Do you want a divorce?"

He was inviting Carter to respond with his own truth.

"No, I don't want a divorce," Carter said, putting down a small tremor of disagreement within himself. "I think Janet is a wonderful woman."

McMullen puffed at his "talking" pipe. "If you mean that, Carter, I'll take up the cudgels for you. I pride myself on having some insight into people, and I know you never had a serious clandestine affair with that woman. You needn't tell me your reasons for making up the story. Only assure me it isn't so."

"All I can tell you is that I'm terribly sorry it happened." He had no doubt that Judge McMullen saw through the transparency of the lie.

The judge's pipe glowed as he took a deep puff. "Janet won't forgive you. She'll start proceedings, if only to dissociate herself from the scandal in the newspapers."

"I'm afraid you're right."

"And you're willing to let her do that?"

"I have no way to stop her."

When Carter left the farm at Vanceville, he was certain it was for the last time.

Three weeks later George Rushton went from the hospital to his home in New Hampshire to continue his recuperation. During this period Carter accepted an offer that would take him to Nigeria to make an economic survey of the country's natural resources.

On his first night in Africa, he lay sleepless under a huge crimson bed canopy in the embassy building with a bottle of Cutty Sark beside him. Mosquitoes buzzed outside the netting while he read over the lawyer's letter informing him that his divorce was final. He found it hard to believe he was reading about the end of that part of his life. The night sounds began to seem peculiar, magnified, menacing, and the murmuring of mosquitoes almost crossed the boundary into indistinct human speech.

Did you really want this to happen? Is this what you were trying to accomplish?

"I think you'd better get out of the exit lane," Joyce warned.

Less than a quarter mile ahead was the exit to Vanceville. In a few seconds he would have been forced to turn.

He moved the wheel slightly, the car swung back into a through lane, and the Vanceville exit fell behind.

"It isn't far now," he said.

The inn was a large red house atop a hill and surrounded by tall old elms. The maître d' led them through a main room where wooden tables were placed with artful simplicity and candle lanterns made a friendly flickering light.

At their table Carter studied the menu.

"Squab?"

She said, "That's one food I never touch. I grew up in a neighborhood that was mostly black, but there were a few Italian families around. They used to raise pigeons on the roofs of their
apartments."

"How about steak *au poivre*?"

"It's the most expensive thing on the menu. And I don't think
it's good for my diet."

"You don't need to worry about your figure."

Her gaze across the lamplit table warmed him. "You're improving. I thought at first you were strictly an 'aw, shucks' character."

"A what?"

"One of those shy types. Very old-fashioned."

"How about veal *cordon bleu*?"

"I made up my mind to take the next thing you suggested. I
think I'm starting to trust you."

"Aw, shucks," he said.

In the past few days she had been in his thoughts with alarming frequency—even in the midst of solemn briefings at the State
Department he would suddenly remember her smile or a frag-
ment of conversation between them. He tried to discount some of
this on the grounds that he had not been to bed with a woman in
months, and that Joyce was very desirable, but he knew it was
more than that. With her, his deep reserve melted and talk flowed
easily. She was the first woman since Claire with whom he could
be himself.

Thinking of Claire reminded him of her concern about George's
health. When the waiter brought dessert and coffee, he said, "By
the way, you were talking about Dr. Thatcher the other night.
How much do you know about him?"

"Personally? He was married to a Korean woman. They had a
young daughter, but after the divorce she took the girl back to
her own country. Now he doesn't really care about anything except his work."

"How good a doctor is he?"

"He's got all kinds of degrees, including one in pharmacology. And if I had anything wrong with me I'd go to him."

"Did you work with him on any cases?"

"Just one. A man who came to the medical center in terrible shape. He had severe stomach ulcers, and no doctor could do anything for him because so much of his problem was mental. He kept working himself into anxiety states that made the ulcers worse. I suppose he could have used a psychiatrist, but he didn't believe in anything like that. Dr. Thatcher undertook his treatment, and before you knew it Mr. Ordiveras was feeling fine."

"Ordiveras?"

"He's an artist. Felix Ordiveras. You know him?"

"I bought a painting from him several years ago."

That had been before Ordiveras got in trouble for including a portrait of Fidel Castro in a mural of great Latin American heroes commissioned for a bank. The bank refused to accept it, Ordiveras sued, and when the verdict went against him he suddenly dropped out of sight.

"He thought Dr. Thatcher walked on water," Joyce said.

Carter signaled for the waiter to bring the check.

"Where would you like to go now?" he asked.

"I have to make this an early evening." She glanced at her watch. "I'm due at the hospital early. If I'm short of sleep, I walk around all day with the inside of my head stuffed with cotton."

He tried not to show too much disappointment. He took her home, and when he returned to his hotel room he sat for an hour at the window and listened to the traffic from the street below. He had not been prepared for the intensity of feeling. When he thought of her, some part of him, for a long time dry and enclosed, filled with a kind of happiness.

She did not replace Claire, who kept a viselike hold on his imagination; but whether or not it was possible to love two women at the same time, it was clearly possible to desire them.

He slept late, and before he was fully dressed he turned on Jack Elkins's morning news program.

While the picture was still blank, he heard the harsh, compelling baritone: ". . . and I can report, exclusively, that one of the men who will accompany President Rushton to Peking is General Mark Ziffren. As a member of the military, Ziffren once advocated dropping nuclear bombs on Moscow. What conclusions are the Russians going to draw from this man's presence at Peking? And isn't it odd that Secretary of State Adolph Abramson, our leading authority on Asian affairs, will not be in the President's entourage?

"Add it up, ladies and gentlemen, and maybe you can guess what kind of questions the Russians will be asking."

Carter turned off the television set.

After breakfast he called Secretary Abramson's office to confirm their appointment for lunch. Abramson asked Carter if he would mind postponing it.

"I expect the Russian ambassador in my office within the hour, and it's going to be a long session. As you imagine, it's in reaction to the Ziffren appointment."

"Are the Russians taking it badly?"

"The ambassador called right after the Elkins news show to ask if it were true. I had to admit it was. He called the appointment a slap in the face and a blatant provocation."

"Did the President consult you?"

"I heard about it last night for the first time. I suppose the President didn't tell me because he knew I'd be against it." Abramson's cultivated quiet voice was worried. "The President doubtless has his reasons, but I wish I knew what they are."

With the afternoon suddenly free of appointments, Carter thought he might go have a look at his old house just outside Georgetown. He could still recall every detail of it. At times, thousands of miles distant, he found it hard to believe that strangers moved among those familiar surroundings, woke in the same bedroom he had shared with his wife. It was curious that he was always able to relate more easily to places than people. He could recall the foster homes he had lived in as a very small child, but none of the foster parents. Even the Fitzsimmonses, the only father and mother he had known, had never really been close to him. Love is not the same as intimacy.

He didn't know who had leased the house from Janet. The present occupants might think he was snooping if he went there unannounced; he decided not to. Nevertheless, sitting in his rented car on the street, he again seemed to enter a familiar foyer, saw the carpeted staircase on the right, looked through the archway into the living room with the painting on the wall, a glorious riot of color at a short distance, a work of tormented intensity as one drew closer. Felix Ordiveras labored for a time, and there it stood.

Janet owned it now, one of the few things he had asked for in their divorce settlement.

On impulse he entered a drugstore and looked up an address in the telephone directory. Then he drove his rented car to an area of antiquated but well-maintained houses inhabited mainly by artists and writers.

The five-story brick apartment house was fairly modern. He could not find Felix Ordiveras listed on any mailbox in the dim foyer. Finally he pushed the bell over MANAGER, and a round-shouldered man wearing a cap answered.

"All rented up. Nothing available," he said as soon as he saw Carter.

"I'm looking for someone who lives here. His name isn't on any of the mailboxes. Felix Ordiveras."

"His name isn't there because he doesn't live here any more."

The manager gave him Ordiveras's new address, and Carter drove to another quarter of the Capitol, a shabby, rundown, haphazard conglomeration of frame houses with flaking paint, dismal stores offering groceries and beer, weed-grown lawns, and littered streets with long-abandoned trolley tracks. This area had no pretense to being Bohemian; it was merely poor.

Two black men were standing on a sidewalk arguing with each

other in a high-pitched dialect Carter could not understand. He found the number he was looking for in lopsided numerals on a rust-scarred mailbox. It was outside a narrow, gray building with a sagging veranda.

After pushing the doorbell twice with no response, he knocked. Someone moved inside the house and the sputtering noise of what must have been a TV set ceased. A curtain at a window moved partly aside.

Carter guessed he was under inspection. At last the door opened and an emaciated man in a shirt and baggy trousers, standing flat-footed in bare feet, stared suspiciously at him.

"What do you want?"

"I'm looking for Felix. . . ." Carter's voice failed as he recognized who stood before him. In five years Felix Ordiveras had aged so much this might be a much older brother, or even his father. "I bought a painting from you a few years ago. One showing the church at San Miguel Allende. I'm Carter Fitzsimmons."

The man studied him more closely, then stepped back. "Come in." He let Carter pass by him into the interior. "I thought you were someone come to bother me. Anna usually deals with them, but she's out shopping. . . ." His shaky voice faded away.

In the living room there was no carpeting, only newspapers spread on a bare floor. At one end of the room was a small portable television on a card table.

"Sit down. That chair is better." Ordiveras guided him to a plain wooden chair. "Why did you want to see me?"

Carter decided not to mention yet what he had come for. "I wanted to look at the work you're doing now."

"Work?" The once deep-black eyebrows, now salted with gray, arched with despair. "I try. Oh, yes, I make hundreds of starts. But I always throw away the little I am able to accomplish. God has taken away from me what He once gave so freely. I spend my time here," he indicated the television set, "trying to put my mind to sleep so it will not bother me with problems of work any more."

"If you're ill, you ought to see a doctor."

"There is only so much that a doctor can do. It is nerves. I can't concentrate. I can't eat or sleep, and sometimes I have stomach pains so bad I think I am about to die." Ordiveras seemed to look inward with shadowed sunken eyes at some private grief.

"If I can help you get medical care. . . ."

"I have the best."

"You're sure?"

"The same doctor I had when I was rich. If not for him I would have been dead months ago. But you aren't interested in that. You are interested in buying something. Isn't that why you came?" The tone and the smile were both wheedling.

"I'd like to look at what you have," Carter answered.

In the adjoining room piled on the floor were a number of sketches. Nothing else was in the room but an easel, a few dried-up paints in a paint box, and a wooden stool. Ordiveras turned over the sketches for Carter. They were fragmentary—a few scribbled lines, a mere suggestion of a pattern.

"You can buy them cheap," Ordiveras said.

"I like that one." Carter was choosing almost at random. "How much?"

"Is fifty dollars too much?"

In Ordiveras's heyday anything from his studio would have cost several thousand dollars; yet fifty dollars was more than this pitiful sketch was worth.

Ordiveras took the money with trembling hands. "You really like it?" he asked.

"A bargain," Carter assured him. At the door, as he was leaving, he asked, "By the way, what's the name of the doctor treating you?"

"Thatcher. Marvin Thatcher. The man is a saint. He worries about me like my own father." His expression became sorrowful, dreaming, as if thinking about that vanished parent. "A great man. I told that to the other person who came here asking about him."

"What other person?"

"Not long ago. A newspaper man. The one who writes that Washington column."

"Jack Elkins?"

"That's the one," Felix Ordiveras said.

6

When the paging device began its intermittent signaling, it went unheard in the pocket of a pair of trousers carelessly thrown across a chair in room 114 of the Wayfarer Motel.

Nearby, in bed, Jack Elkins was concentrating on the charms of one Michele Alpen, an extremely well put together young lady with whom he had arrived at the motel a scant hour before.

On a dresser before the mirror stood a bucket with an empty bottle of champagne. The mirror reflected Jack and Michele on top of the blanket with the bedcovers thrown back. Michele was naked and Jack wore nothing but his blue socks.

About a minute before the buzzer began, Michele was making purring blissful sounds because Jack's tongue was gently laving her pelvic region. He began to move up, leaving behind a canal that still quivered deliciously. He bestowed a love kiss on her navel and with his palm brushed an erect pink nipple lightly. He moved his lips up further, tracing a valley between conically perfect breasts. Everything he did showed the sure control of a man who knew just the kind of sensations he was producing with it. Michele was aroused, welcoming, more than ready when he decided it was time for a short intermission. Nothing made a woman anticipate sex more than to withhold it just when she thought she was about to have it. That added a fine edge of frustration to her desire. . . . He gave her a last kiss under the chin, a final rub of her pubic hair, and rolled away.

"What's the matter?" she asked.

"No rush. We've got all weekend."

That left her without an adequate answer. Since most women objected to the rash impetuosity of their lovers, they had finally achieved an agreed-upon female consensus: A man knows his business if he takes his time. For Michele to protest would be to fly in the face of this pragmatism, so it was easier to hold her peace, bite her underlip, and make him pay when the time came. He would really have to perform.

Jack casually hoisted himself up against the pillow, and reached over to the night table for the pack of cigarettes there.

"Smoke?"

"No, thanks." Her tone said "damn you."

As he tapped out a cigarette, he remembered that his lighter was in his trousers pocket. He got out of bed for it and heard the tiny buzz of the paging system.

"Oh, Christ!" he said. He took out the little device, hardly the size of a lighter. Freed of its pocket prison, the buzzer now became clearly audible. "I'd better call my office."

"Do you have to?"

The lithe perfection of her body made him hesitate. He had invested effort, time, and money in getting her there, and she was at a pitch in which, if nothing happened in the next few minutes, all the preliminary lovemaking would be wasted and he would have an irritable nasty companion.

On the other hand, Adele Moyer knew better than to page him unless it was important.

"I won't be long, honey," he said. Sitting on the edge of the bed, he picked up the telephone and placed a call to the private number. He reached out to pat Michele's thigh but it was no longer there. She had moved to the other side of the bed.

"Hi, Del. What's up?"

"Carter Fitzsimmons is here. He wouldn't tell me what it is, but he says it's important."

"Put him on."

Waiting, he crumbled the cigarette between his fingers and let brown tobacco spray into an ashtray.

"Jack Elkins?"

"Yes."

"I understand you went to see Felix Ordiveras the other day."

"What about it?"

"I have a feeling we should get together."

Carter Fitzsimmons was close to both the President and the First Lady. It might be worthwhile to cultivate him.

"When?"

"The sooner the better."

"I can't now. I'll see what I can do later."

"Tomorrow?"

"Give me a ring."

He put the phone down carefully, not turning toward Michele on the bed. What excuse could he give her for cutting short the weekend? She was not merely another weekend conquest, but an important part of a current investigation.

People might call him unscrupulous, but that was only in his methods; he was scrupulous about not publishing anything he believed to be untrue. When documentation failed him or he couldn't verify a story, he might publish it on the theory that a partial truth was better than none and often helped, merely by being told, to uncover the rest. If this caused him to be labeled "sensationalist" or a "rumor-monger," so be it. That was not how he regarded himself.

As an enterprising young author he had not balked at slightly embellishing the truth. That was what made his first book, about some of the disreputable characters who had sat on the Supreme Court, a scandalous success. The chapter headings about various justices indicated the content: "The Voyeur," "The Public Drunk," "The Anti-Semite," "The Manic-Depressive," "The Legal Lecher," were only a few. The book was published at a time when the country was blanketed with billboards calling for the impeachment of Chief Justice Warren, and irreverence toward the nation's highest court found a ready audience among Court-haters.

As one of the season's talked-about young writers, he was invited to a fashionable marble palace on Washington's most exclusive circle. Here lived Penelope Watson, the powerful wealthy widow of a recently deceased newspaper publisher. In the few brief years since her elderly spouse had passed on to a just punishment, Penelope had amused herself by casual amours with a number of young men. Her interest in Jack was perked by his photograph on the book jacket; it suggested his coarse masculine vigor.

At the time of their first meeting Jack was twenty-seven, and Penelope Watson was no longer pushing fifty—fifty was pushing her. Nevertheless, with dyed hair, slender figure, and surgically restored face she was not unattractive, and she had the indescribable aura of challenge that so often surrounds sexually jaded women. She was a connoisseur of people, and her wealth and social position drew whomever she wished into her presence.

Young Jack Elkins was dazzled by a woman who could comfortably be mistress of a home where even the doorknobs were made of semiprecious stones, terrapin was served on Tiffany silver and Dom Perignon was poured into Waterford crystal goblets. He offered no objection to Penelope Watson's decision to monopolize him.

In the morning he was still abed when Penelope came in giggling because the maid had found hairpins in the sofa and her panties under the cushion. She told him that, by God, he had no idea what a comfort it was to "find a prick that works" after some of the disastrous experiences she'd had. Now that she had herself a good serviceable young stud she had no intention of letting go of him.

It was a mutually rewarding affair. Jack Elkins became the political columnist, three times weekly, for the Watson chain of fourteen newspapers, and Penelope blossomed to a new and serene radiance in the autumn of her life. As her protégé, he met the great and wealthy, and saw them, as it were, in close-up, never to be impressed by them again. One person who did impress him was Penelope's niece, Fanny, who returned from a European finishing school. She was a snobbish young lady of nineteen with a contemptuous mouth and an arrogant air, who dismissed Jack as "auntie's bull moose" and Penelope's friends as "the other ladies of the bordello." In the privacy of the bedroom, Penelope made fun of her niece, called her "Frigid Fanny," and ridiculed her bustless, slender figure.

No one was more surprised than Penelope when Fanny and Jack eloped.

"What must have been going on behind my back," she wailed to her friends. "Heartless miserable bastard. I hope she makes him miserable, and she will. Mark my words."

For a wedding present she sent Jack a box containing a pound of raw hamburger—"your pound of flesh"—shaped into an unmistakable penis and balls.

Everyone tagged Jack as a fortune hunter, expecting Fanny would inherit money not only from her own well-to-do parents but from her multimillionaire aunt. Fanny, to avoid suspicion of this, insisted on living off Jack's income. They moved into a small house on Dumbarton Street. Jack had been summarily dismissed as political columnist for Penelope's newspapers, but his column was so popular that it was snapped up by a syndicate and sold to other papers at a substantial rise in income.

His income was not, however, equal to the demands of his new wife. Fanny had never been given to understand that there were limitations on what she could spend; her bills at fashionable department stores were astronomical; so were the hairdresser and masseur bills. Jack protested the masseur as an unnecessary extravagance. Fanny was hurt: "You *know* how I hate to exercise!" When he tried to economize, she called him cheap and mean, and when he pointed to their rising debts, she said she never would have married a man who could not support her.

Aunt Penelope was right; she made him miserable.

After four years the marriage had deteriorated to a point where Jack was being flagrantly unfaithful and Fanny, who had begun seeing a psychoanalyst, was given to suddenly asking questions like "Who am I?" Late one evening Jack returned to the house on Dumbarton Street and caught her with a lover. Jack beat up her lover so badly he had to be hospitalized, and the next day Fanny left for Reno.

Since then he had played the field, having no difficulty in finding attractive women interested in straight, uncomplicated sex with no afterthoughts or regrets. On many occasions he put his amatory talents to work in his journalistic career. This weekend, one of these occasions, had been progressing delightfully on schedule until the unanticipated paging message.

On the opposite side of the bed, Michele had taken a further step to display displeasure. She had covered herself to the shoulders with the bed sheet.

"Who was that?" she asked.

"Ever hear of Carter Fitzsimmons?"

Her green eyes were unflickering. "He's an economist or something. The President's taking him along to China."

A knowledgeable lass. At twenty, Michele had come to Washington to find an easy government job and a successful man to marry, preferably in reverse order. But she soon discovered that in Washington girls outnumbered eligible men in a ridiculous ratio. That did not in the least mean, however, that men were unavailable. In the first year of her stay in the nation's capital, she had had brief romances with a junior congressman, a member of the Securities and Exchange Commission, an attaché at the Argentine embassy, and a vigorous young lawyer attached to the Department of the Interior. By that time, her phone number was well known and she didn't lack for dates. She was being "passed along."

She didn't mind. There have always been "career pros" in Washington, attractive young ladies willing to sell their favors in return for a good job or a nice apartment and expensive clothes, or simply for the glamour and excitement of being on intimate terms with the semifamous. Michele now worked for an important lobbyist who, when not enjoying her company himself, offered her as an inducement to his clients or to people in government who might assist him in getting certain bills passed or turned down.

"Do you have some sort of filing system in your brain, honey?" Elkins asked with a deep chuckle. "You're too beautiful to be so smart."

"Frankly, I'm pissed off at you right now."

"I figured that from the way you ducked under those sheets. A body like yours, it's a shame to keep it out of sight."

She understood she was being coaxed and liked it. "You're not so bad yourself. But I didn't think we were going to spend all our time talking about it."

"We're not."

"You didn't have to telephone."

"Honey, when that little buzzer goes off it can be anything. A plot to assassinate the Pope or someone tipping me off to a new Watergate. If I don't answer, I might miss out on the biggest news story of the year." He moved toward her on the bed until he was lying prone beside her. He put one hand on the sheet over her abdomen and began to make slow circles with his hand. "I promise if that thingamajig starts buzzing again, I'll throw it out the window."

He gently tugged at the concealing sheet. She held to the edge with her fingertips, without too much determination. When he kissed her, she finally let him pull it all the way down.

He put one hand behind her head and kissed deep into her mouth, exploring with his tongue. Her mood grew passionate. He placed his hand between her warm thighs. Her hips began undulating and when he touched her vagina he could feel it palpitating. Desire surged through his body. He slowed down, waiting. She tensed. "Not this time, baby," he whispered reassuringly.

He drew back and plunged into warm enclosing moisture, drew back and plunged again. Her breath was hot. She began coming, hard. Her teeth bit his arm and held until she had to let go to cry out. Then he felt the shuddering of the little death.

"Enough," she said after a while, tapping him lightly on the shoulder. Like an exhausted fighter he pulled out of her embrace. Their sweaty slippery bodies parted, and he lay on his back breathing deeply.

Michele looked at him. "I didn't expect it to be that much fun."

He grinned. "You can have a rematch any time."

They lit cigarettes and smoked in silent weary triumph. Two satiated gladiators.

"I don't suppose you'd level with me," she said. "What is this all about? I mean, why did Larry give you my number?" Larry Aldoss was the lobbyist she worked for. "Usually he tells me why it's important to make a client happy. This time, no instructions."

"Didn't you ask him?"

"When I heard it was you I didn't give that much of a damn. I've always been curious about you. I used to look at your picture, the one that goes with the column, and wonder—What is he like in bed?"

"You know now."

"That's why I'd like to know more. What are you after?"

"Honey, I'll be honest. It may save me time." She didn't know yet that their long weekend together had been shortened to one night by Carter Fitzsimmons's call. "I've been checking with people who've been Marvin Thatcher's patients to get some clue to the kind of problems he handles and the kind of methods he uses. And I've been having hell's own time getting anybody to cooperate. Most of them think Dr. Thatcher is religion. Lay on hands and heal."

"I never was his patient."

"You saw him in action. I'd like to know what happened that night with Paul William Jayson."

"One more question. Why is Larry doing this? Some favor he wants you to do for him?"

"I've got a few of Larry's secrets hidden away in my files. He'd like them to stay hidden."

"Fair enough. Okay, ask me anything. Jayson's lousy in bed, if that's news."

"Not the kind I'm after. You were cruising with him on his yacht when he had some kind of seizure."

"We never got away from the dock. We were supposed to sail in the morning, but that night about one o'clock he got sick."

"What kind of sick?"

"Peculiar. He got out of bed, saying he was feeling nauseous. He went into the bathroom and when he came out he complained about how fast his pulse was beating. Then he started having numbness in one arm and leg. I thought it was a stroke."

"Did he call the doctor?"

"Not right away. Not until the arm and leg got locked into a kind of clawlike position. I wanted to call an ambulance—I figured he was dying—but he insisted it had to be Dr. Thatcher. He said the doctor was the only one who could deal with it, that hospitals didn't know anything. . . ."

Jayson, too.

"I was plenty scared, believe me. On his next trip to the bathroom he said his head was vibrating. . . ."

"Vibrating?"

"He said he had a feeling he was going to split apart. Then down he went. Unconscious."

"What did you do?"

"What could I do? I went for help, but when I got on deck Dr. Thatcher was coming over the side. So I went down with him to where Jayson was lying like dead."

"What happened then?"

"The doctor gave him an injection. After that I didn't see much.

One of the crew helped put him into bed, and there wasn't anything more for me to do. I went up on deck and just waited around for a while. I went back about half an hour later to see what was going on and didn't believe my eyes. Jayson was sitting up in bed, talking and behaving almost normal. Even his arm and leg had got better. He smiled at me and asked me if Dr. Thatcher wasn't some kind of a miracle healer. He felt well enough to go right ahead with the cruise, but Thatcher wouldn't hear of it. He took Jayson with him to his clinic to keep him under observation. It turned out he'd been treating Jayson for high blood pressure and migraines."

"What kind of injection did he give him?"

"I don't know. But if you'd have asked me, I would have sworn Jayson was a goner."

"Try to think. Didn't Jayson make some explanation to you of what the attack was all about?"

"He brushed it off. Said it was a psychosomatic thing and not as serious as it looked. And he mentioned having had business problems."

"Funny. Jayson always struck me as a tension-giver, not a tension-getter."

Michele gave a studied, sensuous yawn. "Honey, *I'm* feeling relaxed all over. What I'd like now is a nice warm shower."

"Anything you say."

She wrapped a green motel towel around her head before she slipped behind the frosted glass panel. The heavy rush of the bath faucet was followed by the higher spattering sound of the shower. He slid back the stall door and got in the tub. She was standing with her back to him. For a second he held her, then she freed herself of his embrace and handed him a bar of soap. As he started to soap her, he felt the slick warmth of her wet shoulder.

She turned around to rinse off her back, so close that he sensed the writhing begin in his loins. She saw what was happening, and met him more than halfway. With a few tremors and gropings, he found her. She gave a sound between a chortle and a gasp. After a few moments he drew back and out, and she groaned.

She put her mouth close to his ear and whispered, "Oh, Jack, can I?" Her hushed voice stirred him to further excitement.

"Sure. Go ahead."

He blocked the spray with his broad back while her green toweled head slowly descended. Between his thighs a titillating tongue played greedily. He fought the life surging in his limbs until he could no longer bear it, then let go. She sighed deeply, and her hands settled like fluttering soft birds to hold his strong pulsing.

She looked up at him beaming. "You sure are a lot of man."

What the hell, he thought. They were not going to have more than one night, so why not make the most of it. "Let's go back to bed, baby."

He trusted her. She could get him started again.

7

The next morning Carter called Jack Elkins's number and was put through to Adele Moyer.

"Mr. Elkins expects to meet you today. But I never know his whereabouts when he's on the town. You'll have to ask the newsstand operator at the Majestic Hotel."

"The what?"

"The one in the lobby. Mr. Elkins will leave a message telling you where to meet him. Go there in person and identify yourself. Mr. Elkins takes every precaution to protect his confidential informants."

Carter did not think of himself as an informant. "What time shall I be there?"

"The newsstand operator is named Cedric. He comes on after eleven."

It was ten o'clock. Carter picked up the newspaper he had brought back with him from the hotel coffee shop and leafed over pages. Suddenly his attention tightened on a face from his past.

The society page open before him featured a three-column photograph of a London charity ball. There was the distinguished host and hostess, Lord and Lady Ballance, m'lord appearing a bit startled by the camera, but Lady Ballance poised, handsome, and a good deal younger-looking than her husband.

Janet's good looks were the kind that improved with years. Mrs. Carter Fitzsimmons was clearly behind her, and she fit perfectly into her new role.

There are moments in every man's life in which he wonders what there is to show for his effort, and seeing Janet's picture made him reflect that his balance sheet would have to be written in red ink. His marriage had failed, he had no children, few friends, and a career that seemed to be going nowhere. It was not the kind of record he liked to match against his youthful expectations.

Deliberately he forced himself to think about Joyce. He had begun to wonder lately if she was someone with whom he might share a future. His feeling for her was so new he could not be sure it would last—but the fact that he was afraid it would *not* last was significant. It mattered.

At eleven o'clock, in a slightly depressed mood, he took a taxi to the Majestic, a stately hotel that, after decades of neglect, had been refurbished to become a new favorite in an era nostalgic for the leisured grace of an earlier time.

The lobby newsstand had an imitation marble facade around the open area in which newspapers, magazines, and a few best-selling paperbacks were discreetly displayed.

"Are you Cedric?" Carter asked the stooped old man in shirt sleeves behind the counter. "I was told you might have a message."

"You Mr. Fitzsimmons?"

"That's right."

A small sealed envelope was handed over. "He didn't say you were such a tall man."

"I came in disguise," Carter said.

Instructions in the envelope were simple but cryptic. He was to go to Potomac Yacht Rentals and take a sailboat, the *Sooner*

Child, for half a day. There must have been an item in Elkins's files about his having been an expert sailer.

Sooner Child was waiting at the slip and the owner of the rental agency seemed to expect him, so their transaction was completed quickly. Carter removed the cover and straps, unfurled the sail from the boom, and released all the dock lines except the one at the bow. Almost immediately a wind blowing from the stern began to move the *Sooner Child*. He threw off the bowline and, using the mainsail alone, let the boat move out onto glittering silver water.

He had not handled a tiller for some time, but the feel came back quickly, and within a few moments he began to enjoy himself. Listening to the water lapping around the boat, he was reminded of sailing with George and Claire Rushton. One afternoon in particular, while Claire and Janet were making fish chowder in the cabin, he and George had been alone. The quiet wide horizon seemed to unlock George's reticence. He told Carter he had ambitions beyond the Senate, but that he really wondered if he was qualified. "I don't kid myself. The biggest thing I have going for me is singleness of purpose. I set a course and stick to it. But is that enough?"

"That's often the secret of success," Carter said.

George said with attractive self-deprecation: "I don't really do things right. I just don't make as many mistakes as most people."

Encouraged by Carter, always a good listener, George talked about his youth. His father had been a stern parent. "There's nothing like a red raw imprint on the backside to create respect for authority," George said, while Carter silently disagreed, knowing that nothing heals boyhood wounds. "Dad always said I'd never amount to anything. Secretly I've always expected him to be proved right. Perhaps that's what made me struggle so hard to prove he was wrong."

That afternoon Carter came to closer grips with his friend, and no longer felt the resentment of the self-conscious for the self-assured. When the chowder was ready, George ladled it out, assuming the role of a Hungarian waiter (he was a fair mimic), and Carter laughed as readily as anyone.

That was one of their last happy times. A few weeks later George had his meeting with Anne Demas. . . .

Under Carter's expert guidance, the *Sooner Child* moved smoothly toward the middle of the bay. He used his weight on the windward side and clipped along in a steady breeze with the boat heeling at an angle of twenty degrees. Other sails were only distant small fluttering pieces of paper. He moved in a friendly void—without reference points to the past, present, or future. Just as he was beginning to wonder where the rendezvous would take place, he found out.

Jack Elkins emerged from the boat's small cabin to stand blinking in the postnoon sunlight. He wore a white shirt and trousers, and rope-soled sandals.

"We're far enough from shore now," he said.

Carter stared at him. "You must have been pretty cramped."

"Yeah."

"Why the double-o-seven stuff?"

"You can't be too careful with Mark Ziffren."

"What's he got to do with it?"

"Ziffren's boys are always watching me. I'm *numero uno* on his enemies list because I know too much. Including what was on a page mysteriously missing from his service record."

"Missing?"

"It covers the time Ziffren was serving with Patton. They linked up with the Russians and Ziffren met with his opposite number, a Russian colonel, in a border town in Austria. There was some sort of fight and the Russian colonel got zapped."

"Murdered?"

"Nobody knows. Ziffren was quietly shipped home, under something of a cloud. But there's no proof now. That page from his service record is gone. One day, though, I'm going to get my hands on something called *The Suppression of Civil Disorder*."

"What's that?"

"A little book he wrote for the government. A top-secret classification was slapped on it and it was stowed away in the vaults. It's a blueprint for how to take over the country to preserve law and order."

"How can you be sure it exists?"

"I've talked to people who've read it. It's enough to make your hair stand up. He took the first step when he got all the government's investigatory agencies under his damn Security Bureau. Then he built up the riot control force into a paramilitary outfit. They're ready. Officially, their job is to maintain essential services in case of widespread civil disorder. But they practice the same kind of training maneuvers that would be needed for a coup."

"You seem to take it seriously."

"I do. All it needs is one more big step. The President has to declare a national emergency."

"Which he won't."

"Maybe you're right. But I don't like the way things are going." Elkins sat down, watching Carter move the tiller toward the sail in a tacking maneuver. "Why'd you want to see me?"

"Because of Felix Ordiveras. I'd like to know why you're interested in him?"

"Who told you I am?"

"I went to see him. He told me you'd been there."

"My business is getting information, not giving it. But maybe we can make a deal. I got interested in Ordiveras when he was hauled in by a couple of policemen who said he was acting strangely. They were going to send him to the hospital for observation, but he called Dr. Thatcher and was released in the doctor's care. Your turn. Why are you interested?"

"I knew Ordiveras years ago. Bought a painting from him."

"So?"

"I heard he was hard up and dropped in to buy another of his sketches."

"And when you heard I'd been talking to him, you decided to call me?"

"That's right."

"Why?"

Carter hesitated slightly.

"I didn't want you writing a story exploiting him. He's had enough trouble."

"B.S."

"I beg your pardon."

"Bullshit. That isn't why you called."

"Why did I, then?"

"Because you know I've been checking up on Thatcher. And you're worried I might find something embarrassing to your friend Rushton."

"I don't know what you're talking about."

"Something's got to explain George Rushton's behavior."

"*That* again."

"Well, if he isn't nuts, why does he keep acting like he is?"

Carter yanked the tiller. There was a rattle of slides and slugs, and the boat shook violently. The sail slapped back and forth near the mast.

A shower sprayed Elkins, soaking him to the skin.

Elkins began shaking water from his drenched clothes. "You did that deliberately!"

Carter corrected by steering slightly away from the wind until the luffing stopped. "I should have dumped you over the side."

"What the hell for?"

"That was a damned irresponsible thing to say!"

"Don't get mad." Elkins looked uneasily at the distance to shore. "I know you think everything about your friend is on the up and up. But neither one of us knows for sure. If you give me the straight story, I'll print it. How's that? Help me get the facts."

"How?"

"You have an inside track at the White House."

"Are you asking me to spy for you?" The sailboat heeled sharply and began to come about.

Elkins steadied himself. "You might as well have the name as the game."

"That remark doesn't make sense."

"It does as far as Mark Ziffren is concerned. His men saw me come to the boatyard and get aboard the *Sooner Child*. After a little while you came along and got aboard. They've got you tagged."

Watching the approaching shoreline, Carter replied, "I don't believe you."

"I can prove it. Just try not to be too obvious."

At dockside, Carter made the sailboat fast and waved good-bye to the boat rental man, who did not seem surprised to see Jack Elkins. They went to a nearby lot where Elkins had parked his sporty lavender roadster.

They pulled rapidly out onto the river road. Only two cars were behind them; one was a junky station wagon with six or seven people piled into it. The other was a convertible with the top down and a young man at the wheel with a girl snuggling close.

Elkins picked up speed, moved to the left lane, and went up the inclined exit to the highway and sped into oncoming traffic.

"Now, look."

Carter began to turn but Elkins jabbed him with his elbow.

"I told you don't be obvious. Rear vision."

A distance behind, almost obscured by intervening cars, the open convertible with the young man and the girl was now traveling in the same lane.

"It doesn't prove they're following us."

"Watch."

Elkins stepped on the accelerator. The little sports car zoomed ahead, swung out, passed cars on the right, and continued to accelerate while it swung from lane to lane, making a zigzag pattern between cars. Horns yelped angrily.

Elkins took the next exit ramp, clearly marked for twenty-five miles an hour. He went into it at almost sixty. Tires wailed but the little car amazingly kept its balance. He brought it around the winding turn onto a narrow, tree-shaded road. Without slowing down he swung right, jolting over a curb and onto the gradual slope of an embankment that was partially concealed among trees.

A moment later the convertible with the young man and girl whizzed down the exit lane and out onto the road. Then, as if the driver were confused, the convertible slowed until it reached the corner and turned out of sight.

Elkins looked at Carter with a knowing grin. "We're partners."

"Go to hell," Carter told him.

8

That evening the White House musicale was held in the East Room, where part of the spacious white and gold interior was taken up by a removable stage so the guests in the rear could see the performers. Under glittering chandeliers, a crowd of about one hundred fifty had gathered to hear Ray Charles in a specially arranged program of his own music. The usual White House entertainment lasted thirty minutes but this concert went on for almost an hour.

Afterward, guests mingled at drinks and refreshments. Carter found himself paired with Mrs. Mirabelo-Aguas, a talkative Brazilian woman with a special interest in the occult. She was grayishly young, modishly dressed. After Claire Rushton introduced them and quickly moved on, it occurred to Carter that there was more design than accident in the pairing. This seemed to be confirmed when he discovered Mrs. Mirabelo-Aguas was a widow.

"However, I am in constant touch with my husband," she assured him. "There are times when I feel him standing at my shoulder and know that if I turn I will see him. Do you believe in the spirit world, Mr. Fitzsimmons?"

"I haven't any direct experience."

"I sense that you are a man of deep spirituality," Mrs. Mirabelo-Aguas said. "Every intelligent person knows that things exist of which we have no direct experience. At this very moment, there are TV waves passing through the air all around us and yet we cannot see them. We know their presence by the effects they make, pictures on a screen, voices. Can we not also believe the same of spirits?"

"An interesting point," Carter said, managing to meet her eyes while at the same time looking beyond her. Across from them, a space of perhaps six or seven feet, Dr. Marvin Thatcher was talking to a lovely woman whom Carter had been told earlier was chief of the Chinese delegation to the United Nations. Carter picked up small snatches of their conversation. The Chinese woman was telling Thatcher how the Communist regime had built gardens and public ways in what had once been the sacrosanct preserves of the Forbidden City.

Suddenly he noted a silence in his immediate vicinity.

"Would you care for a brandy?" Carter asked his companion.

"Alcohol," Mrs. Mirabelo-Aguas told him firmly, "is a poison in the body."

Conversation languished. He had to make an effort to keep his attention from straying. He was scarcely able to express regrets when a handsome Brazilian friend swooped down upon Mrs. Mirabelo-Aguas to carry her away.

Claire came toward him, disapprovingly. "You let the Brazilian bombshell escape. She's lovely, and has several million dollars."

"And communes with the spirit of her late husband."

Claire smiled. "If it has to be a ménage à trois, why shouldn't the third party be a ghost?"

Sometime later, at the far end of the East Room under the Gilbert Stuart portrait of Washington, Carter found himself in a group with Chad Oliver. Chad, smiling, somewhat unctuous, was making party conversation. He remarked on how few people who live and work in the nation's capital ever consider it their home.

"Ask someone on the street where he is from, and he'll never say, 'I'm from Washington.' He'll say, 'I'm from Los Angeles or Chicago, Atlanta or Pittsburgh.' I've been here ten years, but it isn't home to me and probably never will be. Home is still Charlottesville, where my family. . . ."

"Will you excuse me?" Carter interrupted. "Dr. Thatcher's over there and I have something I must speak to him about."

Dr. Thatcher and the Chinese lady delegate were deep in conversation, and Carter, while too far away to distinguish words, was surprised to hear they were not speaking English.

The Chinese woman saw him first, and turned a bland inquiring smile toward him.

Thatcher said, "Ah, Mr. Fitzsimmons, I'd been hoping to see you again."

"Am I interrupting anything important?"

"Not at all. I was practicing my Chinese with Madame Win. It's gotten pretty rusty, but she insists she can understand me."

"You are fluent, Doctor."

"Well, perhaps what we learn in childhood we never forget. Do you think that's true?" he asked Carter.

"I hope I've forgotten a number of things," Carter replied. "At least I've tried to." He had a stifling sensation in his chest from anticipating what he was about to say. "I was surprised to learn that Felix Ordiveras is a patient of yours."

"Oh, do you know him?"

Carter nodded. "I hadn't seen him in some years. I was shocked at the change in him."

"He's terribly ill." Dr. Thatcher shook his head regretfully. "I'm not sure how much I can do. Miracles in medicine are reserved for a higher power than doctors have." He appeared ready to continue, but George Rushton appeared suddenly.

"I'd like a word alone with you, Carter," George said.

"Of course, Mr. President."

He followed George Rushton across a hall to enter a parlorlike room where the furniture was upholstered in green fabric and the walls were covered with green moiré silk.

Rushton closed the door. As he turned, his attitude underwent a chilling alteration.

"I understand you've been having secret meetings with Jack Elkins."

"I don't know whether I'd call them secret. We've met twice. Once in a taxi outside my hotel, the other in a sailboat on the Potomac."

"At whose instigation?"

"Once at mine. Once at his."

"Can you tell me what he was after?"

"The first time he was checking a rumor that I was to accompany you to Peking. I didn't confirm or deny it."

"And the other meeting?"

"I heard he had visited an acquaintance of mine, a painter named Felix Ordiveras." George Rushton did not appear to recognize the name. "I wanted to find out why."

"You should be careful, Carter. Elkins is not a friend of this administration. Mark Ziffren reported this to me and, fortunately, I was able to assure him you're trustworthy. But you put me into a very difficult position." In the dim light, beaded perspiration was evident along the ridgeline of Rushton's eyebrows. "I want your word that there will be no further communication between you and Jack Elkins."

"If it's important to you."

"When you fraternize with people like Elkins, you get tarred with the same brush. He's a cheap gutter journalist who'd like to destroy me, to tear down everything I'm trying to build." The hand with which George rubbed the side of his neck had a slight tremble. "And he's working with people who are in very high positions. They're trying to get me in every way they can. They're disloyal, unpatriotic, treasonable. . . ."

"Treasonable? That sounds rather extreme, George."

"Don't you think I know what's going on?" The voice sounded as if forced out under great pressure. "Take a look at the pickets outside! That will give you a rough idea of what's happening in this country!"

A chill moved through Carter's body. "Look, George, if you're not feeling well. . . ."

"Damn it, Carter, first you sneak around to secret meetings with my enemies,"—each word now seemed to come off a coil of suppressed rage—"and now you're trying to pretend there's something wrong with me. Whose side are you on?"

"You know better than to ask." Carter felt no indignation; he was far more worried about why George Rushton felt himself surrounded by mysterious sinister enemies.

"I want to work closely with you. But if you're plotting to betray me! . . ." The enormity of the suspicion suddenly overwhelmed George. His face flushed, and his hands clenched.

The door opened, and Claire came in.

"You've been hiding long enough," she announced gaily. Then she became aware of the charged atmosphere in the room.

George Rushton's anger subsided. "I want to trust you, Carter. God knows I need someone I can trust!"

Claire looked levelly at her husband. "If there's one person you know you can trust, it's Carter." She recovered a little of her gaiety. "Time you came back to the party. At least to say good-bye to your guests. They'll excuse you after that. I know you have to make it an early evening."

The diminishing tension was like the fading odor of nitrate from spent ammunition.

"All right. We've finished," George Rushton said.

A few minutes afterward in the East Room, the President with a smile and a wave announced, "Ladies and gentlemen, the evening is still young. Enjoy yourselves." Then he and Claire left for their private living quarters.

Carter found Dr. Thatcher with Madame Win. "I'm concerned about George Rushton, Doctor."

Thatcher nodded. "My impression is that he is quite tired. He's been working too hard in preparation for his trip."

"It's more than tiredness." Carter glanced at Madame Win, then decided to risk it: "I think he was behaving a little erratically."

Thatcher's composure did not waver. "Well, in that case, I'd better check up. By the way, I promised to escort Madame Win on a short tour of the art gallery. Would you take over for me?"

"Delighted," Carter said promptly.

Dr. Thatcher made his apologies and left.

Madame Win looked up at Carter towering over her. "A very great man, your President, is he not?" she asked. "My countrymen are persuaded of it. We are so looking forward to seeing him in Peking."

Her smile was a flash of white in saffron.

Dr. Jonathan Vancell shook Carter's hand cautiously, expressing in the friendly gesture a slight reservation.

"I appreciate your seeing me, Doctor," Carter said. "I know how busy you are."

"Oh, that's all right. Joyce Hatton said you wanted to check with me about a friend of yours. Someone who's now under a doctor's care?" Dr. Vancell's lean, spectacled face took on a concerned expression. "The best advice is for him to do what his doctor tells him."

"Joyce said you are one of the best diagnosticians in the country. I know you can't suggest any treatment without seeing him, but I only want to get your opinion."

"Did she say that?" Vancell was boyishly pleased. "Well, it's rather a large order to diagnose a patient sight unseen, but I might be able to provide a little insight. I'd rather not know the name of the patient or his doctor. That way we can keep it a more or less theoretical discussion."

"I understand, Doctor."

For the next ten minutes Carter told Dr. Vancell all he knew about Ordiveras and the shocking transformation of the past few years. Vancell questioned him closely, and Carter found himself remembering little details that he had not consciously noted at the time. *Did the pupils of his eyes appear dilated? Yes.*

Finally he asked, "From what I've told you, Doctor, do you have any idea what his problem might be?"

"There are a good many possibilities, of course, but a parallel did strike me." He brought a pack of cigarettes from the desk and offered one to Carter, who refused. "The symptoms might be the result of prolonged treatment with a chemical substance."

"I'm not sure I understand."

"Under normal circumstances, the brain is a delicately balanced chemical factory. We're just beginning to understand how easy it is to upset the balance. Drugs interfere with the communication among the brain cells and cause distortions of behavior . . ."

"Drugs?"

"The psychedelics, in particular." The doctor lit a cigarette, enjoying a last drawn-out morsel of superior knowledge before being compelled to share it. "I'd say this man might have been taking something in the amphetamine class."

Carter, taken by surprise, stared down at his hands. "The kind they call wake-ups or eye-openers?"

"Those drugs directly stimulate the central nervous system, exciting the brain cells in somewhat the same way that adrenaline does. They can have the most striking effect on how a person looks, thinks, and acts. The Institute of Psychiatry did very detailed research on amphetamines and their effect on different types of personality. Some of the symptoms you describe are decidedly similar."

"You really believe that?"

"It's a possibility that should be checked. Your friend's symptoms fit the syndrome of a weak-inhibitory type after prolonged use of an amphetamine. Take a look at the Institute's paper sometime."

"I'd like very much to read it."

"Of course, you'll keep in mind that I can't say anything definite about an individual patient unless I can study his symptoms in person. Can you persuade this man to come in and be examined? Informally, you understand. His doctor would still be in charge. I wouldn't want to be accused of poaching on another doctor's territory." Dr. Vancell gave a faint detached smile, as though to dismiss the mere idea.

"There'd be no question of that, Doctor."

Carter left the office and walked down the hall to the little nurse-doctor conference room where Joyce was working over her charts.

"How did you make out?" she asked him.

"The Institute of Psychiatry published a report on amphetamine drug users. Can you get hold of it for me?"

"It would take doing. When do you need it?"

"As soon as possible."

In his own mind he was sure drugs were not the cause of Felix's problem. There was something too simple about that explanation, but he shuddered at what Jack Elkins could do with it. As the President's doctor, Marvin Thatcher's name was news.

Leaving the hospital, he returned to the shabby neighborhood where Felix Ordiveras lived. He hoped to persuade Felix to see Dr. Vancell.

As he approached the sagging veranda, he was struck by a peculiar kind of desolation. His knock on the door was answered by hollow echoes.

"Mr. Ordiveras?"

He walked to a window and tried to peer in, but could see nothing. He returned to the door, and knocked more demandingly.

"Looking for Mr. Ordiveras?"

A young boy about fourteen was standing on the sidewalk watching him.

"You know where he is?"

"I hope you're not a friend."

"Why?"

"I think he died."

"What?" He stared challengingly.

The young man said, "It all happened very sudden. I live around here." He backed off, grimacing nervously, as he saw Carter coming toward him. "I heard his woman say he was very sick. She started carrying on a lot, crying and yelling. Then the doctor came. I heard him say Ordiveras had died. That's all I know." Poised for retreat, he became ashamed of his timidity. "I'm just trying to help. I didn't want to see you banging on that door all night."

"Where is the woman?"

"She hasn't been back since they took him away."

"Who?"

"The doctor. The one who was here and took care of everything."

"What's his name?"

"I dunno."

"Can you describe him?"

"Oh, kind of short, with gray hair. An older man, but kind of friendly looking."

9

Jack Elkins passed a letter over to the attractive brunette secretary in his office.

"File this under Thatcher."

It was a reply from the state department of education, which licenses physicians, to his own letter demanding that the department investigate the qualifications of Dr. Marvin Thatcher. Curtly, the department informed him they found no reason to review Dr. Thatcher's qualifications.

In other words, drop dead, Mr. Elkins.

Well, there were other ways to get an investigation started. He dictated a memo to one of his staff reporters suggesting he locate a patient of Dr. Thatcher's willing to file a malpractice suit. That would open a Pandora's box in which evidence would have to be presented about other patients and the success or failure of Thatcher's treatment.

As Francoise started to type his memo, he wandered into Adele

Moyer's adjoining office. Adele had the mouthpiece of a telephone against her shoulder. She looked up at him.

"It's that bastard at the White House," she said. "I'm holding until he's on."

She meant Chad Oliver, and he needed no further indentification.

Adele said, "Just a second, Mr. Oliver. He'll be right with you." She gestured toward the other telephone in her office, and Elkins picked it up.

"That was really a low blow," Oliver said in his best chiding tone. "I would like to know where you came up with the story that Ziffren is going with the President to Peking."

"Do you deny it?"

"You stirred up everyone from Senator Halliwell to the Russian ambassador. Damn it, Jack, everybody is sticking firecrackers up my ass. The press corps wants to know why the hell I didn't tip them to the story. How'd you get on to it?"

"You know better than to ask, old buddy."

"Someday you'll need help, too."

Elkins said, "When I do, you won't give me the sweat off your balls."

After he hung up, he glanced at the stack of newspapers piled on the floor to the side of his desk. All papers from cities that carried *Elkins's Corner*. Three days between when his copy was submitted and when it appeared. Plenty of time for other people to find out, even to apply pressure to get certain stories edited or dropped. TV was the front burner. Put a story on there, and nobody had time to do anything but sizzle.

TV, however, had never done much for his ego. Not even the most controversial, entertaining news show ever got a decent rating. He ranked consistently in the last ten. He only stayed with it because of the total audience. More people watched him on the boob tube than read him in all the newspapers.

He rolled copy paper into his typewriter, typed out "Corner (Elkins)," and gazed at the sheet with a fixed stare. The column was due on the teletype at noon sharp. Once again, he was ready to acquaint his readers with the failings of the famous, their secret vices, tyrannies, silly antics, personal eccentricities, and pious hypocrisies.

The light on the phone at his elbow blinked on and off irritatingly.

"Adele? I said no calls. The column's due in sixty minutes."

"You might want to speak to this one. Ex-FBI. He's got something buzzing in his bonnet."

The phone call was from a former FBI agent who was convinced he had a front-page item about the bureau's undercover counterintelligence campaign directed against black militant leaders, particularly against Harry Wade, the self-proclaimed messiah of the John Brown Society, who wanted to "unify and electrify" the militant black movement. The ex-agent said he could supply documentation needed to prove what the FBI and its boss agency, the Security Bureau, were up to.

Elkins told him flatly, "That's been going on since J. Edgar Hoover. I'll look at what you've got to offer. But it doesn't seem to be anything I can use."

The man sounded pretty crushed when he hung up.

Adele called immediately. "Anything to it?"

"Zilch," Elkins said. "Twenty years in this business, and I'm supposed to think it's news when a government bureau gets a counterintelligence campaign going."

"Sorry, Jack. I figured you'd like anything on Ziffren."

"I damn well would."

It would be nice to get something on old gimpy-legs, the way Drew Pearson had with that high and mighty General Douglas MacArthur. MacArthur had once filed a million-and-three-quarter-dollar libel suit against Pearson and his *Washington Merry Go Round*. Then Drew learned about a Eurasian chorus girl named Helen Robinson, and how MacArthur had installed her in a suite at the Chastleton Hotel with a car and a chauffeur at her disposal. When Pearson dropped that bombshell, MacArthur suddenly withdrew the suit and paid all the legal fees. He also handed over fifteen thousand dollars in cash to the girl.

No such luck. Elkins had searched Mark Ziffren's life backward and forward, and there was not a penny's worth of scandal. The general, a fire-breathing fundamentalist, had married his childhood sweetheart and remained faithful to her. She had died from cancer a few years ago, and Mark Ziffren still made monthly pilgrimages to her grave.

Jack began typing his column. A few more windbags to puncture. Another phony politician to scalpel. A few titillating paragraphs that didn't have quite enough documentation for more conventional reporters to use.

He finished, not entirely satisfied, and turned it over to Adele to put on the teletype.

"You had a phone call from Carter Fitzsimmons. I told him you were busy and would call back. Okay?"

"Okay. There's no rush. I don't owe that prick anything."

Francoise was holding another call for him.

He picked up the receiver.

"Greg Hazen, Mr. Elkins. I've been thinking about your offer and maybe we can get together."

"I'll make arrangements for where we can meet. Miss Moyer will be in touch."

"Will you bring cash?"

"Don't worry. If you've got anything worthwhile you'll be paid."

Greg Hazen was a former medical attendant at the private clinic operated by Dr. Marvin Thatcher. After their first contact, Elkins had asked Adele Moyer to find out what she could about Hazen. There had been nothing in his computer files, for Hazen was a nobody, but she had hit pay dirt with a source in the Criminal Identification Office of the FBI. Hazen was listed both as Gregory and as "Chick" Hazen. He had served a prison sentence for sodomy, and had several times been arrested (no convictions) for the sale and distribution of pornography.

Adele Moyer arranged for a meeting with Hazen at the "boarding house," a white frame mansion on N Street that had once been a private residence but now offered rooms for overnight guests. On occasion, Elkins used its rooms for confidential meetings. People were always coming and going there, and it would be difficult, if not impossible, to identify an informant. He used a different room for each meeting to be sure no one bugged it in advance.

Half an hour later, Elkins was waiting in a second-story guest room when the door opened and a slight man in a dark suit came in. He had short, graying hair, hard eyes, and the general appearance of a man whose experience in life had made him wary.

Elkins indicated a chair opposite the bed on which he was lying with his jacket strewn carelessly on the white chenille bedcover.

"Quite a runaround," Hazen said, still standing.

"You mean picking up a message at the newsstand?"

"Why couldn't we just meet at your place?"

"You'd have been noticed, probably followed. I go to great lengths to protect the people I work with."

"That's good." Hazen decided now to accept the chair that had been offered. "Look, I've got some hot stuff. I've written it down, as much as I can remember."

"Where is it?"

Hazen took a large envelope out of his inside pocket. "When do I get paid?"

"I never buy a pig in a poke."

"How do I know I can trust you?"

"You've got it the wrong way around. A lot of people do business with me. I've got a reputation to protect. Who the hell are you?"

Hazen shrugged and handed over the envelope. Elkins took out a few scrawled, handwritten sheets.

He glanced over the pages quickly. "I can't make out what's here. You'd better tell it to me. Or read it."

"Okay."

It took half an hour for Hazen to read what he had written.

Basically, what he had to say was that "orgies" had taken place at Dr. Thatcher's private clinic between patients and good-looking male "assistants" and female "nurses" on the premises.

When he finished reading the last page, he added, "Every word is true. It really happened. I'm willing to take an oath."

"You expect me to take your word for any of this?" Elkins indicated the sheets of paper still in Hazen's hand. "I need facts, hard facts, not cheap sexy gossip. What kind of a job did you have at the clinic?"

"Medical attendant."

"What duties?"

"General kind of stuff."

"Mopped up around the place, dumped out the garbage. Did you ever actually *see* Dr. Thatcher treat a patient?"

Hazen's manner turned surly. "Lots of times."

"What was he doing?"

"What any doctor does. It was different with different patients. He gave them medicine—"

"What kind?"

"How do I know? I'm no doctor."

"Did he ever give medicine that wasn't on prescription? You know what I mean?"

"Hard stuff?"

"Anything like that?"

Hard eyes shifted evasively. "Sure."

"You're a liar."

"Now, listen . . ."

"Why did you get fired?"

"We had a disagreement."

"You and Thatcher?"

"Not exactly. But when he heard about it, he said I should be fired. Never gave me a chance to explain."

"Explain what? That you were hipped on pornography and oddball sex. That's why you were fired, wasn't it, Hazen?"

"What kind of a gag are you trying to pull?"

"Your story isn't worth a damn."

"You don't get off the hook that easy."

"I'm not on any hook."

Wary eyes searched his face. "I'm entitled to something. I want one grand."

"I'm not interested in you any more. Beat it." Some bitterness at a lead vanishing in smoke was transferred to the sleazy character before him. What he wanted to find out was the kind of treatment Marvin Thatcher gave his patients, and what he was offered was a souped-up sex yarn!

"Don't try to pull any fancy stuff. We had an agreement." Hazen started toward Elkins's jacket on the bed. "You brought cash. I'll take what you've got."

Elkins rose to intercept him. Hazen made a quick downward lunge at the jacket. Elkins was quicker. A hamlike fist slammed into the side of Hazen's jaw. He went down so suddenly it seemed that he had been going down before the blow struck.

He lay on his side and Elkins rolled him onto his back with the toe of his shoe.

Elkins leaned close to him. "If you try anything, you'll end up in prison for attempted blackmail. I know about you and your record, Hazen, and I'll put you behind bars again so fast it'll make your ears pop."

Elkins took him by the collar of his jacket and dragged him along the floor out of the room. At the head of the stairs, he hauled him erect and gave him a shove. Reeling, grabbing at the banister, Hazen went down the stairs. Elkins watched him plunge out the door.

He returned to the room for his jacket. From the lining of an inside sleeve he removed a small microphone. The recording tape would have a complete account of those so-called orgies at Thatcher's clinic. Francoise would transcribe it into the computer files.

Never know when any kind of information might prove useful.

When he returned to his office, Adele Moyer met him. "You've got a visitor waiting inside," she told him. "Carter Fitzsimmons."

"Anything else happen?"

"They transferred the Washington bureau chief of the *Times*."

"No kidding. Why?"

"You put the last nail in his coffin when you got a beat on the Ziffren appointment."

"What should I have done—tipped him off?"

"He blames you for it."

"I've got so many enemies in this business I hear they're forming a club. Only one membership rule—they never hold meetings. They've even got buttons with FEF on them, for Fuck Elkins Frequently."

Adele laughed. "Does that apply to the women?"

She was the only female office employee to whom he had never made an overture. She was his "good right arm" who presided over the office and accompanied him to Washington's toniest affairs. Having her with him was like having an extra pair of ears, and at any gathering she knew at once which cabinet member would leave when Elkins arrived and why, which senator would keep to the furthest corner of the room, and why. She was far better able than he to detect the nuances of dislike stirred up by his presence.

In his office he checked over messages and calls, noting a bill from the Ma Bell specialist who had been in to check that no new bugs had been placed on the telephone lines. Finally the buzzer sounded.

"Carter Fitzsimmons?"

"Send him in."

Carter entered. "I've got news that may interest you," he said. "Felix Ordiveras is dead."

"How do you know?"

"I was at his house."

"You saw him?"

"Someone there told me."

Amateurs. Take anyone's word for anything.

"What did he die of?"

"I don't know."

It occurred to him that he wouldn't mind slipping a noose further over Carter's neck. If Carter got to where he had nothing more to lose by working with him, he might prove useful.

"Then we'd better find out," he said. "Would you like to come with me?"

"Where?"

"The morgue. That's a likely place to look for a dead person."

At the morgue there were no new admissions under the name of Ordiveras. To be certain, they went down the line to check corpses rolled out of refrigerated shelves for their inspection. Felix Ordiveras was definitely not among them.

"You all right?" Elkins asked as they emerged. He had noted Carter's queasiness.

"I'm fine."

"We'll try Ordiveras's place next."

At the house, Elkins forced the door, which was held only by a slight latch. They went through the rooms carefully. There was no note, no clothing in the closets, no food in the kitchen, no sign of occupancy.

"It's as though no one ever was here," Carter said.

"Somebody cleaned it out. That story about him dying might have been cooked up to fool creditors."

They went up and down the block, interviewing neighbors. They found the boy who first told Carter that Ordiveras was dead, and he repeated the same story.

"Sounds like Doc Thatcher, all right," Elkins said. "We'd better talk to him."

At Thatcher's clinic, the girl receptionist said the doctor was not available and that there was no one else who could give any information. She suggested they call again in the morning.

"We can't wait that long," Elkins said to Carter as they were leaving. "If we want an autopsy, we have to move fast."

"An autopsy?"

"If he's dead, that's the way to find out what killed him."

From his office, Elkins called Thatcher's clinic. "This is the police," he said in a voice changed enough to be unrecognizable. "I'm inquiring about a patient of Dr. Thatcher's who died suddenly. We need a few facts for our records."

"I'm sorry. I'm only at the switchboard. I can't give you that information."

"Then you'd better put me through to someone who can."

After a few minutes he was connected to a woman who said she was the chief nurse at the clinic.

She said, "I'm afraid we can't divulge anything over the telephone."

"Maybe Dr. Thatcher can."

"Dr. Thatcher isn't here at present."

"Listen, if I have to, I'll get nasty. I'll haul the doctor down to headquarters in person to answer questions. I'm just trying to be nice and save him trouble."

After a pause: "How do you know this person you refer to is a patient of Dr. Thatcher's?"

"The doctor was with him when he died."

"If he's a patient, his name would be in the files. Leave your name and telephone number and I'll call you back."

"I'll wait. His name is Ordiveras. Felix Ordiveras."

There was a delay of nearly ten minutes. When she returned to the line, her tone was frosty: "I found his name in the inactive files. He used to be a patient but hasn't been for some years."

"You sure?"

"I'm holding his case record right in front of me. And in very large red letters across it is 'Canceled.' The 'Canceled' refers to his account. There was a considerable sum owing at the time he left. Apparently, the doctor decided it wasn't collectible. He visited Dr. Thatcher for the last time two years ago."

"Isn't it possible the doctor continued to treat him free of charge?"

"I've never seen him as a patient here. You'd have to speak to the doctor about that. He'll be in after ten o'clock in the morning."

The phone clicked off.

"She recommends Dr. Thatcher," Elkins said. "In the morning."

"I don't see any harm in waiting."

"There might be."

"What?"

"I want to know," Elkins replied, with a touch of impatience, "whether Ordiveras died in spite of everything Dr. Thatcher could do for him. Or because of everything he did."

"Now, wait a minute. I don't go along with the idea that Dr. Thatcher is responsible."

Elkins shrugged. "That's your business. I'm going to keep checking."

After Carter left, Elkins called in Adele Moyer and told her to put the staff to work checking funeral homes for an area of seventy-five miles.

"Ordiveras has to be in a funeral home," he said. "Unless Doc Thatcher has him propped up in his closet."

They were still checking out funeral homes when Elkins went to bed at midnight. In the morning, Ordiveras had not been located. Elkins called a friend at city hall, who put him in touch with the chief clerk at the Bureau of Public Records. Elkins hurried down there.

"How long ago did he die?" the chief clerk asked after the files were brought into his office.

"Yesterday."

"Then the death certificate has got to be here in this file." He riffled through quickly and came up with a copy. "Felix Ordiveras —right?"

The certificate listed the basic cause of death as a heart ailment—myocarditis.

It was signed by Dr. Marvin Thatcher.

From the Bureau of Public Records, Elkins went to the district attorney. He asked that an inquiry into the cause of death of Felix Ordiveras be opened immediately.

"I have reason to think that what the death certificate says is wrong."

"You're accusing a highly qualified, reputable physician of incompetence or malpractice."

"An autopsy will prove whether I'm right."

"Thatcher is the President's doctor. I don't want any part of it, Jack."

"But you'll go along."

"Not this time."

"Or I'll have you turning on a slow spit. Seems to me the White Citizens' Caucus contributed to your election campaign. And then their district chief never got prosecuted on a rape charge."

"I simply didn't have a case I could bring into court."

"Even if it's true, who do you think is going to believe it?"

"You are a bastard."

"Didn't anybody ever tell you?" Elkins asked cheerfully.

The district attorney picked up the telephone. "I'll start making arrangements for the autopsy." He called Dr. Thatcher at his clinic. Midway through the call he sat up straighter, listening carefully, replying in monosyllables.

Finally he put the telephone precisely back into its cradle, and turned to Elkins.

"I don't think your inquiry into the cause of death is going to get very far."

"Why not?"

"Felix Ordiveras's body was cremated last night."

IO

As Carter was crossing the lobby of his hotel, the cover of *Time* magazine caught his eye. It showed a photograph of George Rushton staring out the window of the Oval Room. The cover title WAS: HERMIT IN THE WHITE HOUSE?

Carter bought the magazine to leaf through the story. According to *Time*, the President was seeing fewer people than Nixon had, holding no press conferences and refusing requests for meetings with congressional leaders unless approved by Chad Oliver.

Hell, he needs some privacy. It's a man-killing job.

Time went on to say that all important issues were now being decided by Rushton from an "option sheet" prepared for him by Mark Ziffren that gave arguments for and against any course of action. Maximum length: two pages. *Time* thought the method gave too much power to whomever chose the yes or no arguments and that, in any event, Mark Ziffren was a poor choice for the job. *I agree with that*, Carter thought, rolling up the magazine and putting it in his coat pocket.

On his way to the elevator, the desk clerk called to him.

"A note for you, Mr. Fitzsimmons."

The clerk handed over a plain white sealed envelope with an imprint on the back flap: LEADER NEWSPAPER SYNDICATE.

"It was left here about half an hour ago. Delivered by a messenger service."

Carter opened the envelope. Inside was a single sheet of paper with a scrawled handwritten message:

Ordiveras is dead. The death certificate is signed by Thatcher. No autopsy. Body cremated. Convenient way to dispose of proof ... JE.

Elkins's smug assumption started Carter's adrenaline juices flowing. That remark about disposing of proof was totally uncalled for. Why shouldn't Ordiveras have been cremated? Perhaps his wife wanted it that way. Carter was particularly annoyed because he knew Elkins was simply riding a hunch. And, of course, he didn't give a tinker's damn about Ordiveras. It wasn't even Dr. Thatcher he was after. It was the President.

Going up in the elevator, Carter recalled Dr. Vancell's startling theory that Felix Ordiveras might have been suffering from an overdose of amphetamines. A far-out diagnosis. But during his recent confrontation with George Rushton, without admitting it to himself, he had been studying the President at close range. Had there been physical symptoms? The dry mouth and frequent moistening of the lips, the involuntary trembling, the perspiration, the irrational show of temper?

He caught himself up short. He was no better than Elkins if he tried to fit every detail into a pattern, a syndrome.

But wasn't the sudden cremation of Ordiveras's body at least a *little* suspicious?

In his hotel room, Carter telephoned Dr. Thatcher at the clinic. There was a short delay before he heard the familiar voice.

"Mr. Fitzsimmons? What can I do for you?"

"I've heard disturbing news, Doctor. Felix Ordiveras is dead."

"Yes, it happened quite suddenly."

"I was at his house, and there doesn't appear to be anyone around who knows about funeral arrangements."

"That's all been taken care of."

"Where is the funeral being held?"

"It's over. I arranged for his body to be cremated. There wasn't any next of kin."

"The woman who lived with him?"

"Gone. Disappeared. Under the circumstances, I did the best I could."

"Yes. Yes, I understand, Doctor. What did he die of?"

"Officially, a heart condition. But he'd been in very poor health for a long time. A history of bleeding ulcers and anemia. He could have gone almost any time."

"I see. Well, there's nothing more to be done. Thank you very much, Doctor."

He sat by the telephone, his thoughts proceeding with a kind of deliberate aimlessness, until interrupted by another call.

"Carter? Dolph Abramson. Do you think you can stand another evening of socializing?"

"When?"

"The Nigerian embassy is having a reception tomorrow evening. As such things go, this is small—fewer than three hundred guests."

"It doesn't really sound like my kind of thing."

"There's going to be a turnout of the foreign diplomatic corps. It's to celebrate the independence of Monzania. And you can help us get around a sticky situation."

"What is it?"

"President Rushton won't send anyone with an official position. He thinks it might stir up comment and a lot of embarrassing questions. On the other hand, we can't ignore the affair without snubbing some important people. But you're perfect. You're known to the Nigerian embassy."

"They're smart enough to see through that ploy."

"And you're smart enough to make the best of things. Will you go, Carter? I'd appreciate it very much."

"I do have a date."

"By all means, bring her. I'm sure they'll be delighted."

Carter presented the handsomely engraved invitation, with admittance card enclosed, to the carriage man. As he proceeded with Joyce toward the drawing room, he had a presentiment of trouble. This was clearly an important occasion along embassy row. Arriving guests stood cheerfully in the glare of television lights and cameras, photographers maneuvered for position, reporters swarmed. The guests appeared to be from the VIP list of both Capitol society and foreign officialdom.

It certainly was no place, Carter thought, for an unaccredited representative of the United States government. There should have been someone from the State Department or the cabinet.

The buffet table had two suckling pigs in its center, pointing north and south, flanked by great silver trays of sturgeon and caviar, hot and cold hors d'oeuvres, ham, turkey, pheasant, salad, sweets, and a huge rectangular cake decorated with twin flags of Nigeria and Monzania. There were several barmen dispensing drinks, including Russian brandy and vodka, and an orchestra was playing behind the palms on the reception floor.

The trouble Carter had been expecting occurred shortly after he and Joyce finished filling their plates at the buffet table.

"I congratulate you, Mr. Fitzsimmons," a heavy voice said just behind Carter.

He turned to confront a tall, ugly black man with a fringe of curly iron-gray hair, wearing a resplendent uniform with gold braid and striped trousers.

"Colonel Robuto," Carter said.

"I congratulate you for having brought with you such an attractive woman. Such an attractive black woman. Most diplomatic. May I be introduced?"

"Ms. Joyce Hatton, I'd like you to meet Colonel Robuto. Don't be misled by his rank. Colonel Robuto is *the* leading military man of Nigeria."

Colonel Robuto bowed slightly, took Joyce's hand, and brought it to his lips.

"Mr. Fitzsimmons exaggerates. He believes those news stories in which I am described as my country's strong man."

Joyce said, "Aren't the stories true, Colonel?"

"I take my orders, dear lady. We have a President, just as you have. Nigeria is a republic, and the military are of no more importance than in your own country. Or perhaps that has changed here," Robuto said, looking at Carter. "Your President now has a military man to rule beside him."

"If you mean General Mark Ziffren, he certainly doesn't rule beside our President."

A smile twisted Colonel Robuto's thick lips. "Instead of him, perhaps? Many people now believe that he is the most powerful man in the United States government."

"If they do, they're mistaken."

"We know a good deal about him. While at West Point, he wrote a paper high in praise of the German army."

Carter said as amiably as he could, "You can't hold him responsible for something he wrote when a student. He served with General Patton. And you remember what Patton did to the German army."

"We are very disappointed in your President for appointing a man with such warlike views." Robuto paused. "And our friends in the Soviet Union are frankly alarmed. It does not improve the prospects for world peace about which your President speaks at such great length. In fact, comparing your President's words with his actions, we in Nigeria think we see how greatly he has changed —and not for the better. One is tempted to say, as you Americans put it, will the real President Rushton please stand up and make himself heard?" He glanced at the crowded reception room. "For example, here you see gathered the official representatives from many countries. We do not see anyone of importance from your

United States. My country is humiliated by not having an official representative of your government. . . ."

An undercurrent of excitement ran through the crowd. Some of the guests began looking toward the hallway across from the salon.

An aide whispered to Colonel Robuto.

"He's here—now?" Robuto asked.

He hurried toward the entrance of the reception salon, arriving barely in time to meet a familiar figure entering: Elmer Tate, the Vice-President of the United States, looking very uncomfortable in a tuxedo and black tie.

Carter was near enough to hear Robuto's greeting.

"I—I did not know you were coming, Your Excellency. I apologize for our lack of preparation."

Grinning broadly, Tate shook hands. "I couldn't bring the missus. She wanted to come, but she's got a bad head cold."

Suddenly the reception was, in Carter's eyes, a brilliant success. The Vice-President assumed the spotlight, and the Russian contingent was obviously discomfited by his presence.

It was half an hour before Carter had a moment with Elmer Tate alone. "Whoever persuaded you to come made a wise decision," he told him.

"Persuaded, hell! I got an invitation. I don't check my invitations with those boobs at the U.S. protocol office. They play some kind of crazy game where the rules are being changed every minute. Tell you the truth," Elmer Tate added with a grin, "my wife was feeling so poorly she went to bed early. And I was just itching to get out of the house."

The throbbing of tribal drums signaled the chief entertainment for the evening, a special performance of Watusi dancers in raffia-fringed leopard skins, monkey-fur headgear, and anklets of jingling bells. The throbbing beat rose to a fiercely rhythmic staccato, then the frenetic performers entered with their long-limbed vaults, punctuated with earsplitting whoops.

Across the way from Carter, Colonel Robuto stood next to Vice-

President Tate, his ugly face wreathed in smiles. When Elmer Tate whispered something to him, Colonel Robuto responded with a great burst of laughter. Everyone around them seemed delighted.

Joyce said, "The Vice-President seems like a nice man."

"He's soothed some bruised feelings tonight. Robuto is happy, protocol is in its heaven, and all's right with the world."

Elmer Tate departed at eleven, but the party went on. At midnight Carter was dancing with Joyce.

"Doesn't it make you a little uneasy?" she asked.

"What?"

"Being surrounded with all these black faces."

He wondered why she held so tenaciously to a belief that all human problems were somehow based on pigmentation.

"After four years in Nigeria," he said, "I think my color blindness is pretty well established."

"I don't believe people who say it doesn't matter."

"It might be easier if you did."

"It wouldn't be true, though. And that happens to be a topic I know more about than you do."

The music ended on a crashing chord.

"I'd like to go now," she said.

In the car on the way home, he sensed a hostility from which he was not excluded.

Then she said, without preliminaries, "My father was whipped as a young boy because he was too fresh to white folks. His mother whipped him. She did it because she loved him and didn't want anything bad to happen to him."

"Those were ugly times," Carter said gently, "but what has it got to do with us?"

"Everything. My father had the bitterness trained out of him, but I didn't. I found out what was really going on because I had a very good teacher. A black man who really knew the score and never let white people con him."

"Why are you telling me this?"

"I'm scared."

"Of me?"

Her voice was strained. "I know what's going to happen, and I don't have the will to stop it. I'm in love with you."

A strange sort of love, tangled with contrary impulses, hedged by resentment, larded with bitterness, rivalry, prejudice, compromised by a past that could not be changed and by fear of the future. But he welcomed it, nevertheless.

He drove up in front of her apartment house at shortly past one o'clock.

"Too late for a drink?" he said tentatively, feeling a warm betraying flush.

"Why don't you come up? I have that paper you asked for. The one from the Institute of Psychiatry."

He had never entered her apartment, and his first thought was that it clearly did not suit her. The decor was cheerless, with a maroon sofa, black leather chair, and an area rug with a subdued jigsaw pattern. Along a side wall was a tall long cabinet containing a stereo, a television set, and bookshelves.

She interpreted his look. "A sublease."

"Very nice."

"You don't have to be polite. There isn't anything here that belongs to me." She met his eyes. "I never wanted to own anything that it would hurt me to lose." She opened a bar shelf out of the side wall cabinet. "You can have anything to drink, provided it's Scotch."

"Nothing, thanks." He sat down in a chair. He had a sharp anticipation, the familiar mixture of desire and tenderness, a sense of impending disaster, a fluttering of his stomach as if he were approaching a waterfall without being able to gauge the distance of the plunge. Surely she expected something to happen. But unless he made some move, the opportunity would dwindle away and he would find himself on the street, alone, feeling like a fool.

He got up, unfolding his extraordinary length, and went to her.

She looked up, smiling with a certain interest. He had meant to kiss her, but indecision overcame him and he sat down close to her on the sofa instead.

"You know," he said, staring at a painting on the wall, "this place really doesn't suit you." The painting was a large horizontal reproduction of nymphs disporting at a pool while a lustful satyr looked on from behind a clump of bushes.

"You should have seen what it was like when I moved in. He had everything but the mounted head of a girl. Framed nude foldouts, big poster photographs, and lithographs that were just this side of obscene."

His knees rose before him like twin pointed peaks. Now, he told himself. He turned to her, half expecting her to evade him, and with surprise he encountered the full richness of her mouth. His arm about her sensed the slight tremble of her shoulder muscles. When he began to touch other parts of her body, she made no attempt to resist.

At last she stood up to undress. Her body was sculpturally beautiful, a smooth molding of bronze.

Her wide nostrils flared. "Let me look at you."

He undressed quickly. Strongly excited, he moved fully to confront her. Then he buried his face in the dark opulence of her breasts. His cheeks felt fevered against marvelous supple yielding. His breath came sharp and his heart pounded.

He pulled her down onto the couch. "Don't wait," she said. Then her eyes closed tightly, and all became the sweet delirium of consummated love.

He lay with his hands clasped behind his head, slowly regaining control.

Joyce leaned on an elbow, regarding him with a warm appraisal. "You are by far the nicest man I've ever been with."

He kept his tone light. "Have there been many?"

"*That* question."

"You don't have to tell me." It was the foolish curiosity of a middle-aging man, quite aware of being in love and defenseless.

"Yes I do, because you want to know. When I was nineteen, I went to bed with a man I hardly knew."

He had no desire to hear a recital of adolescent promiscuity. Yet he was conscious of the necessity to adopt the right attitude, to appear neither shocked nor indifferent, prurient nor prudish.

"You must have known him well enough," he said.

"It was our first date. He just happened to be at hand when I made up my mind."

He suffered a small spasm, a feeling he had not experienced in a score of years—since he first saw George Rushton look at Claire in a certain way.

She went on, "I'd decided not to let virginity become an obsession with me. With girls, it can. Either you meet some man you like enormously so then it's perfectly natural to go to bed, or you don't meet him, and then you begin to wonder if you'll end up a withered old maid."

"Someone once said that if virginity is a virtue, so is malnutrition." He was pleased to achieve this much nonchalance. "And did he end your obsession?"

"Not exactly. In fact, he gave me a new one."

Obsessively hunting out new lovers to satisfy a discovered appetite. A Good-Time Charlotte.

"Oh?"

"The experience was so dreadful that I didn't look forward to trying it again. All through it he kept asking me, do you like it, baby? I couldn't wait to get out of there. When he called again, I told him I wasn't interested."

"That must have put a dent in his ego."

"I doubt it. He probably decided I just didn't like sex. For a while I thought he was right."

"Then someone got you over it?"

"Yes."

He was intensely aware of her beside him. "Who was that?"

"He was very important to me. In fact, I was much more in love with him than he was with me."

"Maybe you only thought so."

"No, I'm sure. He had very strong convictions, and I didn't measure up to his ideal. I was too light-skinned. He believed only black is beautiful."

"Poor darling."

"The trouble with being my color is you don't know where you really belong."

He thought: *A couple of outsiders. That's what attracted us to each other.*

"How long ago did you break up?"

"Almost two years. If you'd like to know how many men I've slept with since, no one. Not until you."

"Really?"

"I don't make a great to-do about sex, but I do believe in a simple rule. You ought to like the man a great deal. Nothing, but nothing, is more off-putting than having sex with a man you don't really like."

In what he hoped was a suitably commonplace tone, he asked, "Well, what are we going to do? Shall I go home—or stay?"

"Stay. I want to hear about you."

"Me?"

"Women can be curious, too. We have equal rights."

Carter had known very few women intimately. Except for casual opportunities that came swiftly without forethought and ended without consequence, there had been no one until Janet.

"I'm a lot older than you are," he said. "And the most significant love affairs of my life were those that never happened."

"There was your marriage. Why did that break up?"

He decided not to tell her about Anne Demas. "Probably I expected too much. I discovered pretty early that marriage leads only into diminishing expectations."

She said, "Since then?"

"A divorcee who worked at the embassy at Lagos and lived in an apartment next door to the chancery."

"Who else?"

"The sister of a rich plantation owner who fancied herself as an artist."

"I'd rather not hear any more."

"There isn't much more to tell."

"I don't believe you, and I'm jealous."

He was pleased.

II

"There's a surprise waiting for you," Abramson told Carter when
he appeared in his office in the State Building. "The President
asked General Ziffren to sit in on this briefing."

"Well, that should make it interesting."

"If you're ready, we'll begin at once."

They left his office and went to a large terraced room on the
seventh floor where assistants and undersecretaries, aides and ex-
perts, had gathered for a full-dress review of the current situation
in the People's Republic. Seated near the window, General Ziffren
seemed to dominate the room.

Abramson opened the meeting. "I thought we should deal first
with some economic problems. That's an area in which Carter
Fitzsimmons will be particularly interested."

A common misconception, Carter thought, this belief that econ-
omists were, by definition, interested in economics. The truth was
he agreed with its classification as a "dismal science." Usually by
the time he acquired a respectable knowledge of a nation's econ-

omy and its economic geography, he was completely bored with it.

He began taking notes during the discussion about the efficiency of Chinese industrial management, but soon found himself doodling complex cross-hatchings on his pad of yellow foolscap. As he was filling them in, he noticed Mark Ziffren watching him. He tilted up the pad so Ziffren couldn't see what he was doing.

Ziffren smiled. Turning his own pad slightly to one side so it would be away from the others, he showed Carter what he had been doing. He had been making squares, microscopically small.

Another speaker began to explain the situation in agriculture, and the incredible success of the Chinese in feeding their huge population. The famines that once killed so many millions were now in the past. The briefing droned on to a discussion of China's trade relations with the island empire of Japan.

"What I'd like to hear," Ziffren said sharply, as this topic finished, "is what data you've got on their fighter planes and commercial jets."

Abramson called on the State Department expert, who reported the Chinese had only a limited fleet of TU-18 bombers, thirty squadrons of fighter jets based on the French Mirage fighter, and less than fifty commercial jet planes, mostly purchased from the United States.

Ziffren grunted and made notes. Then the session turned to the question of China's steadily worsening relations with the Soviet Union.

"The Russians fear the Chinese," Abramson said. "Almost half of their population consists of ethnic Asians. There are historical reasons also. It was only in the fourteenth and fifteenth centuries that Russia won its freedom from Mongol rule."

Ziffren observed acidly, "Hard to believe they've been thinking about it for over five hundred years."

"They look at time differently than we do," Abramson replied. "Our country is only two hundred years old, but Russian and Chinese history goes back for thousands of years. Their people have grown up thinking of the present generation as only one chapter in a long continuing tale. Any Russian schoolboy will tell you about the treaty of Nerchinsk, signed in 1689, and why they fear some sort of reaction from the Chinese."

"How about the Chinese fear of the Russians?" Ziffren asked.

"Equally real. More so today than ever."

"And with good reason," Ziffren said with high-keyed emphasis. "Now you're in a field I know something about. The Chinese don't have a big armory of missiles and bombers. Their missiles aren't protected by steel- and concrete-lined silos. And their main nuclear research labs and the sites where their nuclear weapons are made and tested, such as the plant near Lanchow and the testing ground at Lop Nor, could be wiped out in a surprise attack."

"What do you think the odds are of an attack taking place?" Carter asked.

"The Russians will move in wherever they think they can get away with it."

"You mean there's a real possibility of war?"

"That's what we've got to expect, and that's what we've got to prepare for."

Abramson listened, his face drawn, his eyes troubled. Carter stared at him across the desk, waiting for him to speak, then saw he was not going to.

Carter said, "It seems a good situation for us to steer clear of."

In the overlapping of voices chiming in, he gathered that was the consensus of the others.

Ziffren listened stonily. "We can't toss in our hand without even playing our cards," he said. "We've got good cards to play."

"The table stakes may be too high," Carter replied.

Abramson stirred out of his silence. "I don't think we want a situation that would put us into a direct confrontation with one side or the other. It's not in our interest to take sides in any struggle between two great hostile Marxist-Leninist powers."

"I leave that decision up to the President," Ziffren answered.

"After all, he's our commander-in-chief. He sees the big picture. The rest of us are just battalion commanders."

This statement evoked a swift flurry of assent. The trouble with the men present was not their knowledgeability (everyone knew a great deal about the subject under discussion), but that they were by convention, tradition, and inclination subordinates. Ziffren's mention of the President had awakened the bureaucrat's fear of being thought "irregular."

Carter slumped lower in his chair. "Even if some agreement did result from the Peking summit, wouldn't it have to be approved by the Senate?"

Ziffren replied, "Only a treaty needs Senate approval."

There was a further rush to confirm this. An undersecretary remarked that an executive agreement, signed only by the President and the Chinese Premier, would be fully binding on the country.

"And the limits of such an agreement?" Carter inquired. "How far can it go?"

The answer appeared to be there were no limits. An executive agreement could cover the same ground as an actual treaty. Each viewpoint was buttressed by the requisite accompaniment of fact and reasons. All opposition to General Ziffren was rapidly vaporizing, and no one present was likely to offer any counsel to conflict with the basic principle he had laid down: The President's authority was supreme.

As the meeting broke up, Abramson thanked everyone for being present. With a nod and a handshake Ziffren departed, moving swiftly despite his stiff gait. Carter admired the way the General dealt with his infirmity. By simply ignoring it, he became more formidable because of it.

Carter was alone with Abramson in the secretary's office, reviewing the briefing, when a buzzer sounded.

Abramson flicked up the intercom. "Yes. What is it?"

"The Soviet ambassador to see you."

"I'll see him right away." He turned to Carter. "He doesn't

have an appointment. A bad sign. It might be useful if you were present to hear this."

A moment later the door opened, and Ambassador Stolypin entered. He was a solid, unpretentious man who had made himself popular in Washington during the era of détente by giving extravagant parties and carefully letting it be known that he had a weakness for vodka and horse races. Since the fall of Brezhnev, he had tried hard to give the impression of a highly independent man who did not have too many strings on him being pulled in Moscow. The impression was, of course, mistaken, but the performance was praiseworthy. A most creditable ambassador.

Stolypin was polite through the necessary introductions, but from the set of his bull neck Carter guessed trouble was not only brewing—it was about to boil over.

"Mr. Secretary," Stolypin said, "my government has been watching your President's recent course with alarm. We find it hard to understand what policy he is pursuing."

"You'll have to be more specific, Mr. Ambassador."

"We feel that President Rushton is trying his best to antagonize the Soviet Union."

"How is he doing that?"

"By his unprincipled, criminal, warlike, and imperialist acts."

"Mr. Ambassador, I can see this is not going to be a pleasant interview. But I really must ask you to skip the invective. Can we get to the specifics?"

Stolypin continued angrily. "We have known for some time that your President is not a friend of the Russian people. But when he tries to shift the balance of world power against us, then we must take whatever measures are necessary to protect our vital interests."

"What makes you think your vital interests are being threatened?"

"We know your President's plan for concerted action with the People's Republic of China. If he follows through with this rash and reckless scheme, there will be dangerous consequences. I warn you in the plainest terms that. . . ."

Abramson's reply, spoken quietly, had a chill, unmistakable emphasis. "Let me tell you, Mr. Ambassador, as plainly as I can, that my country will not accept instruction from you concerning our relations with any other country. We would like to remain friendly with all, including your own. And you have no right to infer that our friendships with other countries are aimed against you."

Stolypin flushed. "I'm talking about an alliance between the United States and the People's Republic of China. In the present world situation only a mentally unbalanced man would. . . ." He stopped, and seemed suddenly at loss for how to continue.

"What leads you to think such an alliance is being considered?" Abramson asked.

"We have our sources of information," Stolypin answered. He sat rigidly, as if to guard himself against any further ill-considered outburst.

"Apparently, your sources are better than mine."

Stolypin asked suspiciously, "You mean you don't know anything about a rapprochement with China?"

"I know nothing of an alliance."

Stolypin paused, shrugged, and his tone became friendlier. "I don't doubt you would lie if it was necessary to protect your country."

"I return the compliment."

A tiny smile touched Stolypin's lips. "I'll give your assurances to my government."

"And I will see to it the President gets your message. Thank you for coming to see me. I hope our next meeting will be under friendlier circumstances."

Stolypin answered so slowly that each syllable seemed to have a separate weight. "Let us really hope that, Mr. Secretary." He stood up and left the room.

"I suppose that's what is known as presenting something in the strongest possible terms," Carter said. "You handled him very well."

"A curious slip of the tongue, don't you think? It might have been deliberate, but somehow I don't think so. I mean when he referred to a mentally unbalanced man. What was your impression?"

"He was referring to the President. And stopped himself when he realized he had gone too far."

"Why would such a thought have been in his mind? If Stolypin suspected such a thing, he would most certainly have reported it to his superiors in Moscow. That's part of his job." Abramson appeared both unhappy and perplexed. "Would that help to account for the Russian aggressiveness of late? They've been pushing us in the Middle East, in Malaysia, Africa, even South America. . . . It might be a way of testing the President's determination and stamina."

"They'd better not push too hard."

"A dangerous game. But few governments can resist playing it if they think they see an advantage. It takes a very delicate balance of force and restraint to let them know when to stop. If there isn't enough force, they will simply push further. On the other hand, if there isn't enough restraint, there's the terrible danger of overreaction. A miscalculation on either side can be fatal."

"Do you think someone has been feeding them rumors about what the President intends to do in Peking?"

Abramson remained seated, staring intently, before he replied with quiet earnestness, "Are you quite sure the rumors would be untrue?"

All the dark leather chairs against the wall in Chad Oliver's office were occupied.

"Do you know what the President's schedule is like?" Chad Oliver asked, his good-looking paunchy face registering dismay. Seated at a long, kneehole desk, he showed Carter a bulging file of papers in a metal holder. "Those are just papers he hasn't been able to sign yet." He held up a thick stack of white five-by-seven cards. "And this is today's backlog. I'm routing problems around to all the other departments." He shook his head, despairing at the impossible task. "Every minute of the President's day is jammed tight against every other."

Carter said, "Squeeze me in somewhere. This is important."

"I've turned down twenty requests from the press this morning. Each one wanted an interview with the President. It can't be done." He ran his fingers distractedly through curly brown hair.

A difficult job at best: The problems of a presidential press secretary had steadily multiplied from the halcyon days when Jim Hagerty served Ike, and Pierre Salinger toiled for JFK, both of whom represented leaders well liked by the public and the media. Bill Moyers's skills had been taxed to the fullest to hold LBJ's critics at bay, and Ron Ziegler's unenviable chore had been to defend an administration at war with the press, the courts, and the Congress. Chad Oliver had begun as spokesman for a very popular President—but in recent months his job had become almost as difficult as Ron Ziegler's had been.

Carter persisted. "I sympathize with your problem, Chad. But I don't need a lot of time, and this is something I must speak to him about. How about this evening?"

"He's scheduled until ten-thirty. That's Senator Halliwell. There's a lot of fence-mending to do and, judging from the way the senator sounds, it could take *forever*."

"How about afterward?"

"It'll be close to midnight. Even a President's entitled to some sleep."

"That's fine," Carter said, ignoring the objection. "I'll be back at eleven. And I don't mind waiting." Turning to go, he flung back, "See you later."

"You won't see *me*," Oliver said pointedly. "I'll be home in bed."

In his hotel room, Carter at last finished the report on Nigeria he had promised George Rushton. He read over the fourteen pages with mild pleasure and surprise. It was coherent, disciplined, convincing. The cloudy anxieties gathering in the back of his mind had compelled him to put other thoughts into a sensible order.

The only puzzle he had been unable to explain was why in Nigeria, where gasoline practically came bubbling out of the sewers and oil revenues were ten billion dollars a year, there was still an energy crisis. But Carter had long ago stopped trying to reconcile economics with common sense. As a science, his profession had a lot to learn from tarot cards.

Now that the chore was finished, other anxieties returned. More and more he was convinced Abramson was right and the President was planning a secret alliance with China. Privately, Carter would have liked nothing better than to let the United States sit back and watch the Chinese and the Russians bully the hell out of each other. It seemed a proper, if Machiavellian end, for diplomacy. But to ally ourselves with one Marxist-Leninist country—against the other? George Rushton must see that it was madness.

It hardly seemed credible that Rushton would consider it. On the other hand, some smart Presidents had committed stupid blunders. Witness the way Truman handled the Red spy scare in the late 1940s—opening the door for Senator Joseph McCarthy. And FDR's attempt to pack the Supreme Court. Woodrow Wilson had kicked away his chance to win Senate approval for the League of Nations. Then there was Kennedy and the Bay of Pigs, LBJ and Vietnam, Nixon and Watergate. A lamentable list.

When Carter returned to the White House that evening, he found his name had been included on the list of the President's appointments. He was directed to the President's study on the second floor.

A woman staff assistant met him in the hall. "I hope you won't have to wait too long, Mr. Fitzsimmons."

It was forty minutes before the door to the study opened and Senator Halliwell departed in a glow of friendly exchanges with

George Rushton. Halliwell, the old mountebank, had obviously been charmed. He beamed as he left, nodding to the staff assistant and to Carter.

George Rushton remained in the open doorway. "Come in," he said to Carter. He turned to the woman staff assistant. "I don't have any more appointments tonight, do I?" A rhetorical question. "Then there's no reason for you to hold the fort. You go along home."

The second-floor study had formerly been known as the Treaty Room. It was a sturdy-looking room wallpapered and curtained in the Victorian manner. A heavy pedestal table occupied its center, with heart-backed chairs around it and a swivel chair at the far end.

George sat in the swivel chair with his feet up on a stool. "Halliwell is a hypocrite of the purest ray serene," he said. "I hated him even when I served with him in the Senate."

"What has he done now?"

"He thinks that taking Mark Ziffren along to the summit is a bad mistake." His voice mimicked a scolding superior tone: " 'If what you'd like to do at Peking is outflank the Soviet Union, you're just tipping your hand by taking General Ziffren as a principal adviser.' "

"A lot of people agree. I was with Abramson today when the Russian ambassador stormed in. His government is worried about what you intend to do in Peking. They haven't forgotten that General Ziffren once advocated dropping nuclear bombs on them."

Rushton's face was drawn in irritable lines. "I hope this isn't what you wanted to talk to me about tonight, Carter."

"Yes, it is. Ziffren is the most violently anti-Russian man in the government. That makes him the worst possible choice to accompany you to Peking. Even a token gesture—not bringing him along—would help to reduce tensions."

"I thought better of you. I didn't think you'd join with spineless characters like Halliwell and Abramson."

"Mr. President," Carter underlined his earnestness by using the formal address, "why bring with you a man who's been known to advocate a preventive war against the Soviet Union? Unless you're deliberately trying to make the Russian leaders think something out of the ordinary is going to happen in Peking."

"I can't let the foreign policy of this country be dictated in Moscow."

"Of course not. But Ziffren's presence will only make the Russians think the whole purpose of the summit is to unite against them."

A shade of uncertainty entered George Rushton's voice. "Did Abramson suggest your coming to me?"

"It's my own idea."

Rushton blinked several times, then appeared to nod. "Perhaps you're right. There's no reason to make them unduly susp—"

There was a distant muffled shout, followed by a series of popping noises. Then a heavy thumping *crunch*.

Carter started up from his chair. Before he got to the window, a man rushed into the room.

He shouted, "Don't move, Mr. President. *You!* Get the hell away from that window!"

Another loud thump.

The man flicked off the light switch and raced past Carter to the window. Darkness outside was faintly illuminated in white and red. He drew back the shade with one hand and, presenting the narrowest of targets, aimed carefully. He fired. Explosive sound reverberated.

More popping noises followed in swift succession. Then a final, isolated, almost silly little one.

Silence. An acrid stinging odor filled the room.

"What the hell's going on?" George Rushton asked. His facial muscles had tightened until his expression was masklike.

The man glanced at him, as his tautness slowly relaxed. "Mr. President, there's been an armed attack on the White House."

Rushton was blankly incredulous. "By whom?"

"About half a dozen of them. The guards outside handled it. But I had to make sure of your personal safety."

"What's your name?"

"William Chalmers, sir. Security Bureau."

"A good job, Chalmers."

"Thank you, sir. I must ask you not to leave this room until we've determined it's safe to do so. When I leave, lock the door behind me."

He checked the chambers of his revolver, inserted fresh cartridges, and moved quickly into the dimness of the hall.

Newspapers the next morning gathered the confusing skein of events into a pattern. At a few minutes past midnight six persons —two white men, three black men, and a black woman—had attempted to storm the White House. They carried pistols and hand grenades. They succeeded in getting through the west gate before being repulsed in a pitched battle with White House security guards. Five of the six attackers were killed, and one man escaped. Two security police were dead.

Last night Carter had sat up talking with Joyce until the small hours. He anticipated her attitude. If there hadn't been four black people involved, would they all have been killed? Or would there have been more of an effort to capture them alive? He pointed out that the attackers had been armed and that two security guards had also lost their lives. It was bad enough without trying to find racial overtones in it.

"Here, would you like to read about it?" he asked now.

Joyce sat up in bed, rubbing a fist in her eye. "No, thanks."

"I have to make a phone call."

Carter lost count of the number of times he dialed 456-1414 before he ceased getting a busy signal and an operator answered with the familiar, "White House."

"I'd like to speak to the President," Carter said.

"May I ask who's calling?"

"Carter Fitzsimmons."

After a short delay, a male voice answered. "Press staff. Can I help you?"

Carter again gave his name and encountered a delay of several minutes before a different male voice said, "Press staff." Once again Carter explained that he wished to speak to President Rushton. The male voice asked for his number and promised to call back.

"I'm afraid it might be several hours, though. Things are pretty upset here this morning."

"May I speak to Claire Rushton, then?"

"I'm not sure she's taking calls at this point."

"Will you find out, please? And call me back as soon as possible."

When the telephone rang, it was Jack Elkins.

"I understand you were at the White House last night when the shooting started," Elkins said gruffly. "I'm trying to put together what really happened."

"All you have to do is read the papers."

"They print what they're told. I'm after the real story. Does it make sense to you?"

"What?"

"Is it possible to find six people that bent on suicide? Lee Oswald, James Earl Ray, Sirhan Sirhan, and Albert Bremer were nuts. You could never get six nuts like that together at one time and send them in to be killed."

"What are you driving at?"

"Just remember what I'm telling you. That guy who got away. You can lay odds that bastard Ziffren isn't going to break his neck to find him."

"I swear to God," Carter said, "I think you're hallucinating."

A minute later the telephone rang again, and a press aide said Carter had been cleared to talk with the President's wife. He asked Carter to call the White House again and inform them of his clearance.

Claire sounded strained, but self-possessed. "You won't believe it, but Marie and I slept through most of it. The ambulance sirens woke us up. By then it was all over."

"How's George?"

"He feels worst about those two security men who were killed. They both had families."

"Have they found out more about the people who attacked the White House?"

"Only that they're members of some revolutionary group."

"Does anyone know why they did it?"

"Mark Ziffren says they were trying to kill the President."

"But *why*?"

"They're fanatics. Like those Puerto Rican nationalists who attacked Blair House and tried to kill President Truman." After a slight pause, her voice tightened with repressed fear. "Oh, Carter, suppose they'd done . . . what they came to do?"

"They couldn't have. How is George reacting?"

"He feels he has to do something to reassure people. He's going on TV tonight."

"What's he going to say?"

"Something to do with national security. George has pooh-poohed all the warnings that General Ziffren gave him. Now he says Ziffren has been right all along."

"I hope he doesn't go overboard."

"How do you mean?"

"What happened was a terrible thing. But a handful of fanatics rushing the White House don't represent anyone but themselves."

That evening as Carter turned on the television set, a commentator was solemnly reviewing the events that had prompted the President to ask for time to speak on the three major networks.

Joyce came out of the bathroom, where she had been taking a shower. She was wearing a plaid bathrobe.

"Has he started?"

"Not quite."

"I'm expecting bad news."

"Why?"

She sat down cross-legged in front of the television set. "Time to rouse the rabble."

"You're being unfair."

"I hope so. I remember some years ago when a bomb was thrown into Martin Luther King's house. It went off and might have killed his wife and nine-week-old baby. When black people heard about it, they got guns and knives, sticks and rocks, and were looking for trouble. Dr. King told them to get rid of their weapons because they had to love their white brothers no matter what they did."

"He was a great man. But don't lose faith in George Rushton. He's no rabble-rouser."

"We'll see," she said.

The TV announcer said, "Now, ladies and gentlemen, speaking from the White House—the President of the United States."

The screen showed George Rushton seated before a small table in the diplomatic reception room.

"My dear fellow Americans . . ." The voice was calm and controlled. "All of you have heard of the senseless assault yesterday upon the White House. All except one of the men who began that assault are dead, so we do not yet know their real motives. But we must not assume that they are any real threat to the security of the nation or the orderly processes of government. . . ."

Carter smiled reassuringly at Joyce. He hoped Jack Elkins was listening.

"However, it is the duty of a democratic government to protect itself against the excesses of those who will not accept the established rules of law and order." Rushton's manner turned somber. "Although their numbers are few, the danger they represent is great. Too many of us are complacent in the face of the danger posed by advocates of force and revolution. Fanatic doctrines are listened to by thousands of credulous people, the kind whose picketing of the White House preceded last night's violence. . . ."

It seemed an unfortunate linking of youthful pickets with the armed attackers. The prestige of a high office carries with it its own form of conviction. Carter wondered uneasily if many millions were at this moment translating the President's words into a new article of faith.

"... I have instructed General Mark Ziffren, head of the Security Bureau, to recommend measures necessary to maintain our full security. As President Andrew Jackson once said, 'we must be prepared to surrender a little of our liberty if we wish to preserve the rest.' To prevent a recurrence of the murderous events of last evening, to guard against violence spreading through the nation, I am preparing stern repressive action...."

Joyce, sitting on the floor in front of the television set, turned to him with a questioning and fearful look.

He did not know what to say.

12

Dinner was late, but Jack Elkins said nothing, for he knew Leo was waiting for him to complain or make any comment that would indicate he was acting "like a big shot." Leo was his older brother, and he and his wife Margaret, a plain-looking blond, lived with their four children in a house in Rockville Gardens that had been bought with the money Jack paid Leo for taking care of his books and making out the payroll. For more serious problems, such as preparing records for examination by the Internal Revenue Service, he used an accounting firm. Leo didn't understand the need for that additional expense when he was perfectly competent to handle all the financial details. That judgment about his competence was strictly his own.

"What'd you think of the President's speech yesterday?" Leo asked. They were in the small, paneled library having drinks before dinner. "You've got to admit he's on the right track. We can't let those fanatics kick us around. The sooner Ziffren clamps down on those people, the better off the country will be."

Jack was sprawling on an easy chair with his drink precariously balanced on his chest. "Ziffren's a goddamn fascist."

"You shouldn't say things like that. You could get into trouble." Leo's earnest round face was concerned.

"Leo, you don't even understand what civil liberties are all about."

"I love my country," Leo said. "I don't like revolutionaries and traitors. If you ask me, they all ought to be in jail."

Jack's glass rose and fell unsteadily, and he kept it from toppling with splayed fingers.

Leo shook his head sadly. "I know how you are. You'll get mixed up in something. Would you like another drink before dinner?"

"No, thanks."

At dinner, Margaret said a grace that included a blessing for the President of the United States.

The dinner was delicious. Margaret's cooking was one reason Jack found visits to his brother's home endurable. Another reason was that he had access to a completely private untapped telephone line. He had been waiting for a particular telephone call for two hours.

When he had first heard of the hopelessly suicidal attack on the White House, he wondered why there had been only two security guards at the west gate. If there'd been more, the attackers might not have tried it. It was hard to figure out what they expected to do if they got inside. There were 132 rooms and 20 baths in the White House. The President could have hidden in any one of them. How could they find him?

Then he began looking at it from the viewpoint that the whole incident had been a setup. Suppose the attackers thought the way had been prepared for them. By whom? By an agent provocateur, someone who infiltrated their organization. Probably the same man who was in the attack party and escaped.

"The kids haven't finished their dinner yet," Margaret said. "And their favorite program is coming on in five minutes."

"Oh, they'll finish in time for that, all right," Leo said with a chuckle.

Jack sat smiling, though not actually *at* anything. He merely made appropriate physical responses while his mind occupied itself elsewhere.

The agent provocateur could not have arranged for only two guards to be at the west gate. That was a crucial point. The attackers would know the kind of firepower that White House security forces had, and they would have to be convinced first that everything had been arranged to make it easy for them. That meant a contact inside the White House, someone who could make sure only two guards were on duty at the west gate.

Elkins had called the captain of the security forces, but had gotten no satisfaction. The captain insisted that the two guards had been there on his orders, and it was his sole responsibility. After all, he pointed out, he couldn't keep maximum strength everywhere. The attackers had simply struck at a weak point in his deployment of security forces.

It could have been that way, but Jack Elkins suspected the captain was covering for someone higher up. Someone who might gain by having such an attack take place because he could use such an incident as part of some larger plan.

Mark Ziffren. This was just what Ziffren needed to put his plan for suppressing "civil disorder" in motion. With more authority from the President, he could move against anyone he considered a security risk. The general had a blacklist that would put Nixon's old enemies list to shame.

The paging signal went off toward the end of dinner. He had asked Adele to signal him as soon as she heard. He said, "That's my office alerting me. A call should come through in a couple of minutes. Do you mind?"

Margaret brushed a falling lock of hair back from her face; at moments like this, when she was in close proximity to the spinning of great mysterious wheels that created the mighty events of the world, she was impressed with the fact that she had a Very Important Person for a brother-in-law.

"You go right ahead," she said. "I'll serve coffee whenever you're ready."

He waited in the small library with a desk, color TV set, and one wall of paperback books. At last the telephone rang.

A soft slurred voice said, "You are going to die."

"We are going to kill you," Jack answered. "We are going to kill your racist ass."

Carter was engrossed in reading when he heard the tapping on his hotel-room door. He hurried to let Joyce in.

She had a long cardboard box under her arm. "I have a surprise for you," she said, as she kissed him. "I bought a new dress. And you'd better be prepared to like it."

She emerged from the bathroom minutes later, swirling around in a loose-flowing long white dress with an embroidered flower design. Her black hair was caught behind with an ornamented barrette. She was making a second circuit when she noted the absent fixity of his stare.

"I don't seem to have bowled you over." She glanced at the paperbound copy of the Institute of Psychiatry Report he had been reading. "Is something wrong?"

"They did a very thorough job. Or at least it reads that way to a layman like me."

He poured a drink for her and she sat down next to him. Consulting the report from time to time to refresh his memory, he told her what he had been reading. There were different categories of human personality, and the psychedelic drugs, particularly amphetamines, had profoundly different effects on each type. Some withdrew into a passivity that was like schizophrenia, others gave no visible emotional signs but their bodies rebelled and developed purely physical symptoms, still others varied helplessly between childish attempts to continue winning favor and sudden equally childish displays of temper.

"Is there another category?" she asked quietly. "One you're particularly interested in?"

He nodded. "In some ways it's the most frightening."

"Frightening?"

"It's the type everyone looks up to, the leaders." He picked up the report to read from it: " 'These are naturally aggressive types who learn to bring their hostile impulses under control and get what they want without a show of belligerence. Their need to dominate is directed into socially useful channels. If exposed to long treatment with amphetamines, their carefully balanced personality starts to disintegrate. Hostile impulses regain control. They begin to believe they are surrounded by enemies trying to destroy them, and they strike back with what often seems to be unmotivated violence.' "

"And that started you worrying about the President?"

"I didn't like that speech he made last night."

"Neither did I. But it doesn't make me think he's on drugs. I've known people who got pretty hostile without any help from amphetamines."

"Jack Elkins said something that worries me. He thinks the attack on the White House might have been arranged just to create a crisis. So extra security measures would be called for."

"Do you believe George Rushton would do that?"

"No."

She shook her head. "This is getting a little too much for me. I think we should go out and get something to eat."

They went to the restaurant next door to the hotel. As they were leaving, he picked up a newspaper at the corner kiosk. The lead story reported that the reaction to the President's speech had been overwhelmingly favorable. Telegrams and letters and telephone calls were inundating the White House.

He turned to *Elkins's Corner*. Jack Elkins said some of the President's advisers had pressed him to make an even stronger statement. General Ziffren, for example, wanted the President to declare a state of national emergency. . . .

Back in the hotel room, Carter was subdued.

"Of course, Elkins could be making it up," he said. "But it doesn't read that way."

"Why don't you check with him?" Joyce suggested.

He dialed Jack Elkins's number and got a busy signal. On the next dozen tries the lines remained busy. Finally, when a call went through, a recording told him no one was available just then but he could leave a message and his phone number.

Carter slammed down the receiver with annoyance.

Jack Elkins sat in the private office of his home with a broad-shouldered black man who had a strong hooked nose and eyes that shone in the lamplight—Harry Wade, leader of the John Brown Society.

Locating Harry Wade had not been difficult. People talked who would never have talked to the police. They remembered Jack Elkins as the man to whom the top Mafia boss in the United States had chosen to surrender when he was afraid either his enemies or the law would gun him down on sight, as the man who had uncovered the evidence that cleared the John Brown Society of complicity in the ambush slaying of two policemen.

That morning Elkins had finally reached Harry Wade's mistress, a woman who had served two prison terms for assault on an officer and for the knife mutilation of a white man who had called her a "nigger." She and Harry Wade made a pair.

Elkins asked her to get word to Wade that he had vitally important information. She told him how Wade would identify himself when he called, and what his responses would have to be. For extra security, Jack arranged for the call to be made to him at his brother's home.

When Harry Wade agreed to meet him, Jack Elkins gave the address of his home and told him where to find a parked TV repair truck; there would be a change of clothes inside it and he could drive right up to the door and enter, carrying a portable bag of tools, without creating suspicion.

— 137 —

"You know someone named Duncan?" Elkins asked now. "Thomas Duncan?"

Hard bright eyes stared into Elkins's face as if to decipher the meaning of the question.

"What you pushing at, man?"

"Duncan is a police agent. Planted in your organization by the Security Bureau."

Wade's face lacked expression. "*You* say so."

"He got picked up for armed robbery when he was nineteen. A cop was killed. With the capital punishment laws for cop murder he could have burned. But he didn't. Okay he was young, okay he didn't pull the trigger. But that wouldn't have got him off. Somebody decided to let him work off his debt a different way."

"You got proof?"

"A photostat of a document from the federal files. I brought it along."

He watched Wade examine it. Thomas Duncan, alias Tommy the Toff, was the son of a black man and a Siamese woman. After the armed robbery incident, he had started work in the SDS among campus agitators and graduated to more radical movements, showing the militants how to make bombs and use an M-1 rifle. When fire bombs were thrown into an ROTC office, the culprits, including Duncan, were arrested quickly—but Duncan was quietly released shortly afterward. There was another arrest for arson, followed by a curious dismissal of charges. Another case in which Duncan was indicted never came to trial because he had left town. And no one pursued the matter. At the bottom of his record was the damning notation: *Local police authorities who pick up Duncan's record through the usual channels should check with the Major Crimes Division of the New York Police or with the federal offices of the Security Bureau before arresting him.*

Wade flicked an edge of the photostat with a finger. "Why you showing me this?"

"Just to prove we can trust each other. Duncan put your people up to the attack on the White House."

"What's the difference to you?"

"I want to find out who put *him* up to it."

Wade was silent. "That's all you're after?"

"That's it. Duncan won't talk unless you convince him he ought to."

"If you're right, you know what'll happen to him."

"Not until after I get my story."

"How do I know you're not shilling for the pigs? The pigs are itching for a chance to get something started. That White House gig anted things up, and it's our lives against theirs."

"All I'm asking is that you talk to Duncan."

Wade cracked the knuckles of a strong dark hand. "You're pretty sure of yourself. But you still might be bulling me."

"I'm not."

"You'll come along?"

"Sure."

As they were leaving the house, a car pulled up in the driveway and parked beside the TV repair truck. Wade stiffened as the car turned off its headlights.

"Take it easy," Elkins said. "I'll handle this."

Carter Fitzsimmons got out of the car and ambled toward them with a lanky stride.

"I'd like a word with you. I couldn't reach you on the telephone." Carter glanced at Harry Wade, noting his repairman's uniform. "It has to do with what you wrote in today's column."

"Later," Elkins said.

He heard a steely whisper at his ear.

"Who is he?"

"Don't worry about it," he told Wade. "It's all right."

"That's how I am," Wade said. "I worry." He took his hand out of his pocket, and it was holding a gun. Wade said clearly, "Both of you get into the front seat of the truck. I'll be right behind you."

Carter stared at the gun. "What's this about?"

"You picked the wrong time to come calling," Elkins said. "Do what the man tells you and you won't get hurt."

Elkins got behind the wheel and backed the TV repair truck out of the driveway. It took twenty minutes to drive where they were going. They doubled back twice, so Harry Wade could make sure they were not followed.

On the way, Carter tried once to start a conversation, but Wade quickly silenced him. He moved the gun. "Hang loose," he said. "Anything you got to say can wait."

Elkins parked the truck on a side street a half block from an apartment house. The street had no lights and was quite dark.

Wade said, "Watch the window on the sixth floor. When the shade drops, you come in."

"I need Duncan in one piece," Elkins said.

"You'll get him that way. I want to see you and your friend from that window. *Outside* the truck."

Harry Wade opened the door, got out, and after a quick look up and down the street crossed to the other sidewalk.

"Would you explain what this is all about?" Carter asked Elkins.

"He's taking me to a guy who can prove that the attack on the White House was a setup." Elkins watched Harry Wade's dim figure reach the alleyway behind the building, then duck out of sight. "Okay, do as he says. Out. He wants to see us. To make sure we haven't gone for the cops."

"Listen, Jack . . ."

"Don't argue. Just move. That man's Harry Wade."

They had been standing by the truck less than a minute when on the sixth floor a window shade was lowered, then raised again. As they were starting across the street, a police squad car moved past them. Its headlights were on, but the turret lights were dark.

"What in Christ's name is he doing here?" Elkins asked.

The police car pulled up a short distance away, directly opposite the apartment house. The rear lights blinked out.

"There's another," Carter said.

A second squad car turned into the street, cruised slowly past, and stopped at the curb nearest the building, parallel with the police car across the street. Then its lights went out. A third squad car moved across the intersection beyond, going to the front entrance of the apartment building.

"Goddamn!" Elkins said.

He debated whether to try to get back to the repair truck and leave as fast as possible. But the minute he made that move, they would start blasting from that window.

"What's the matter?" Carter asked him.

"We're in a situation. The best thing is to follow Wade's instructions as long as we can."

He began walking slowly. After an instant's delay, Carter followed him and his long legs caught him up in a stride.

"Are we going up there anyhow?" he asked.

"I don't think they'll let us," Elkins said.

A cop was on the sidewalk near the squad car directly ahead, partially shielded by the overhanging branches of a tree. He peered toward them, then raised his hand to wave them back.

Elkins put his hand on Carter's elbow to keep him moving. There was no choice. The cop wouldn't shoot them, but the people watching at the window might.

Suddenly the street exploded in gray puffs of smoke, and stuttering gunfire followed. The cop ran out, gun at the ready. He appeared to trip over something and went down. The gray puffs moved beyond him toward the squad car.

Elkins hit the sidewalk, and Carter was a split second behind him.

Around the corner, racing, came one of the big trucks of the Special Operations Division. Elkins knew the kind of firepower the truck was packing, everything from machine guns to tear gas, rifles and grenades. It stopped. From the rear of the truck a rattling fusillade of fire erupted. At the sixth-floor window, glass shattered and the wall was stitched with bullet holes.

Then the law arrived in force. There must have been fifty uniformed and nonuniformed men on the scene. The attack had been carefully prepared. With police fire raking the building, Elkins decided it was safe to get up. He ran fast to the TV repair truck, jumped in, and slammed the door behind him. The sound of the door slamming was like an explosion. Then he realized it *had* been an explosion. A mushroom of orange flame sprouted on the dark street. The people barricaded in the apartment had an arsenal that included hand grenades.

He reached beneath the dashboard of the truck for the tape recorder mike. While gunfire made authoritative punctuation sounds, he began dictating impressions. Thinking ahead to the dramatic moment on his television show when he would run this tape, Elkins gave his voice added urgency. He was not in the direct line of fire, but there was no reason for anyone to know that. He heard the rattle of a submachine gun, the whining of high-powered rifles, the intermittent bark of pistols.

Someone rapped on the window of the truck. Elkins pulled up the lock button and Carter Fitzsimmons scrambled in.

"Let's get the hell out of here!" Carter said.

"Not yet."

Four men ran across the street from the Special Operations Division truck. They were not in uniform but their clothes bulked. Bulletproof vests. *Security Bureau*, thought Elkins. He sat frozen in the front seat, watching them until they disappeared into the alleyway that Harry Wade had entered.

The police, using cars as protection, kept up a steady fire. From the Special Operations truck, a tear gas launcher sent a canister whooshing upward. Elkins saw it go directly through the window of the sixth-floor apartment.

A haze drifted out.

The gunfire from the window diminished. Then suddenly the sound of shooting broke out within the apartment. The Security Bureau men must have forced their way in.

A few seconds later Carter said, "Look!"

A man was crawling out onto the window ledge. He was as naked as the day he came into the world.

"Why'd he take off his clothes?" Carter asked.

"To show he isn't carrying concealed weapons."

The man on the ledge began to scream something.

"What's he yelling?" Elkins asked.

"I think it's *Don't shoot!*"

A searchlight pinned him on the ledge in a glaring bright circle. A police bullhorn roared.

The man on the ledge was Harry Wade. He held up both hands to indicate surrender.

There was dead silence. The police stopped firing. They were standing, looking up. Suddenly, dust spurted on the wall near Harry Wade. In the window, a man was pointing a gun. Harry screamed just as the man fired.

Harry Wade's arms and elbows seemed to draw in and then his body started to fold. He put one arm out into space, feeling for support, but there was none.

He fell outward, slowly turning like a pinwheel in the air.

13

Except for the light from a flickering television screen, the living room in Joyce's apartment was dark. An excited newscaster was saying, "Among the known dead are Harry Wade, Joshua Johnson, George Field, Thomas Duncan. . . ."

"Come in," she said.

Carter followed her into a room where the television was now showing the apartment house where the shootout had occurred. That image was all too vivid in Carter's memory.

"Do you want to listen to this?" he asked.

"I've heard it."

He pushed a button and the images on the screen stopped. The room became darker still.

"It was a brutal business," he said.

"Did they have to do it?"

"What?"

"Go in there and butcher them all."

Only a misty haze from streetlights penetrated the drawn curtains.

"It didn't happen quite that way."

"Explain it to me. You're so good at explaining things." Her tone was angry. "I'll bet I know what you're going to say. You're so damn *predictable*."

"Am I?" He turned on the light, and whiteness leaped from the ceiling light fixture to the bare wall opposite. The painting of the satyr and nymphs had been removed and lay tipped against the sofa. On the wall, in its place, was a large wavering untidy scrawl: *Black Is Beautiful.*

"I see you've been making some changes," he said.

"They aren't the last I'm going to make around here."

He shrugged. "It's your apartment."

Her face was puffy and a little swollen, and her hair looked touseled. He smelled the pungent odor of liquor. A bottle of Scotch was on a table with a partially empty glass.

Half smiling, he said, "Solitary drinking is dangerous. I know from experience."

"Very funny." She stood watching him, swaying slightly.

"Are you going to tell me why you're being hostile, or are we going to keep on like this?"

"If you don't like it, get out."

Carter nodded, accepting this as if it were an ordinary remark. "I can go back out the door, count ten, and come in again. Then we can start all over." When she didn't reply, he looked around the room. "What have you been doing outside of listening to TV?"

"I'd love to hear you explain," she said. "The police didn't have any choice. Those men were armed and dangerous."

"You don't believe it?"

"Not a word."

"What do you believe?"

Her hand lifted accusingly, and the fingers curled. "You won't be satisfied until you've killed us all. One by one. Two by two.

Whenever you get enough of us together to make it worth your while."

"If you're talking about the shootout. . . ."

"Massacre! They even used that word on the news report. *Some* of the truth gets through."

"I was there."

She drew in her breath sharply.

He continued, "Jack Elkins and I were taken there by a man with a gun. One of the men who was killed later. We were outside the apartment building when the shooting started."

Her voice rasped, "I don't believe you!"

"It's true."

With a strange intensity she asked, "Who was it? Who took you there?"

"If it makes any difference, Harry Wade."

She stared as if she were still trying to understand or had not quite heard. Then she muttered, "Oh, Jesus!" and slumped into a chair.

"What is it?" He moved toward her quickly.

"Leave me alone!"

When he touched her shoulder, she pulled away.

"Whatever it is," he said, "you can tell me."

She put a hand over her eyes. "It doesn't make sense! It's crazy."

"What is?"

"He always said they'd kill him if they got the chance."

"Harry Wade? You knew him?"

She answered in an exhausted whisper, "Yes." She leaned back and shut her eyes. "He's the man I told you about."

There was a small initial jolt of surprise, then nothing. Harry Wade had been her lover. Carter had known everything but his name, and the name didn't matter. It merely rescued his rival from faceless anonymity.

A clear picture opened in his mind: Harry Wade, gun in hand, standing in the driveway of Jack Elkins's home. The strong, dark, sharply etched face became more graphic with every moment.

"I'm sorry," he said.

Wetness stained her tight-closed lashes. "I've been listening to them tell me he's dead for an hour."

"We don't have to talk about it."

When her eyes opened, there was sullen anger in them. "Some people get away with anything. Lie, steal, hurt people. As long as they work inside the system, it's all right. They let you commit any sort of crime. But if you try to wake people up to how it really is, they shoot you down like an animal that broke out of the zoo!"

He watched her, thinking: *Harry Wade was not the man you believe he was, nor what you'd like to make him into.*

"He really knew where it was at," she said. "He grew up in a section called Nigger Town. White men came over the dividing line to pick out the women they wanted. When police raided the whorehouse where his mother worked, the white boss went to jail but the girls made the street. Because whitey had to keep his black women available."

A terrible legacy of bitterness. He didn't excuse it. There wasn't any excuse. But somehow, sometime, people had to face away from the past.

He said gently, "We have to deal with things as they are today. There's still a long way to go, but a lot of people are trying . . ."

She was biting her lip. Then she asked, "You were there. You saw him. Tell me about it."

He shook his head. He had no desire to be a lightning rod through which she could discharge her unexpressed hatred.

"I want to know," she insisted.

"You've seen it on television."

"Only when it was over."

For God's sake, he thought, *this isn't fair. I know what you'd like to hear and I can't tell you that.*

"Why did they kill him?" she persevered.

Because Harry Wade was a violent man carrying on a bloody vendetta against everyone he considered an enemy of his race.

Because he had shot a man to death during a gunfight in a bar. Because he had taken part in a bank robbery in which a guard had been killed.

"Please," she repeated.

He looked at her as if to ask, Don't you see how impossible this is for me? But if he did not tell her, she would go on re-creating Harry Wade out of her memory. So he began to describe exactly what happened from the moment he arrived in Jack Elkins's driveway, not changing anything or altering an emphasis. He could not risk a false note, or she would reject everything. He led her up to the moment a naked man began falling from a window ledge, and heard her choked breath. For a moment he had the eerie sensation of falling through space himself, grabbing at nothing.

When he finished, he did not know what to expect. "I know he was important to you," he said.

There was no anger in her eyes now, only hurt and bewilderment. "He was fighting for something he believed in."

Impulsively, he took her hand. "You couldn't live in his world." He held her hand against a slight resistance, an almost-desire to pull away.

"Carter, help me," she whispered, and suddenly turned into his arms.

Her grief and confusion and fear released in a storm of tears while he held her close, trying to convey without words, *everything's going to be all right. The world is not a zoo. The only cages are those we build to imprison ourselves.*

He sat with her a long time until her sobbing gradually weakened. Her head was resting quietly on his shoulder, and her breath came unevenly. A tiny white froth had appeared on her lip. He brushed it away with his handkerchief.

Across the roof the defiant scrawl stretched out on the bare wall. *Black Is Beautiful.*

He felt the salt sting at his eyes. He was so deeply sorry for everyone, including Harry Wade.

In the heated pink tent over the west terrace, discreet waiters were in place at the tables. The occasion was a White House luncheon for the deputy prime minister of the Ivory Coast, and the guest of honor was arriving at that moment in a marine helicopter on the south lawn.

Marie Rushton came toward Carter, smiling.

"There's going to be a delay," the girl announced. "Mother asked me to keep you amused."

He was relieved to have a little more time. He hadn't slept much, and the events of last night were graven in his memory.

"What's the problem?"

"Protocol. Our guest has to review an honor guard before the lunch. Actually, I volunteered to take care of you. I thought we might get to know each other."

"I'm flattered."

"Why don't we sit here?" She indicated a bench under the shade of a magnolia tree. "The delay means Dad can't be at the luncheon. He has an important meeting with General Ziffren." She sighed. "Dad always seems to be locked up with that man. . . ."

"What's it about this time?"

"Those people shot in that apartment. Some news reports called it a massacre. General Ziffren's furious. He wants Dad to issue a statement that the people who got killed were responsible for the attack on the White House and that it was a fine job of hunting them down."

"We may never know the truth."

"Well, I don't trust Mark Ziffren."

"Why not?"

"He's always talking about revolutionaries, and I'm not sure who he means. And he's so against young people. I know a lot of kids my age put up a big show about being radical, but I'll bet when they grow up and get families and settle down, they'll end up as conservative as their parents."

She had a direct naïveté which did not bother to disguise feelings or pretend to sophistication.

"You could be right."

"It happens all the time." She smoothed her dress over her knees. "Do you think I'm attractive?"

"Very." He smiled.

"There's someone I think has a crush on me. He's standing over there."

A young man in a gray suit was standing at a corner of the tent, watching them.

"Isn't he Secret Service?"

"Even so, there's something special about the way he looks at me. His name is William Chalmers. Is there much of a future in the Secret Service?"

"There is," Carter said, "if you marry the President's daughter."

She made a face. "The White House is a terrible place for making new boyfriends, or even keeping old ones. Boys are either so impressed when they come here that they don't act naturally, or else they think they can make a good thing out of knowing me." She gave him a sidelong curious glance. "Is it true you and Mother were once engaged? Before Dad?"

"I never had a chance once your father came along."

"He is pretty terrific, isn't he?" Quickly she added, "I don't think she'd have done so bad with you either."

If he had married Claire, the very existence of this vivacious young girl would have been forbidden by the mysteries of genetics.

Abruptly she said, "I hope Dad starts feeling better soon."

He was becoming accustomed to the sudden darting turns in her conversation. "Hasn't he been well?"

"He's been so nervous. You won't believe it, but about an hour before he gave his speech the other night Mother and I didn't think he could make it."

"Really?"

"Dr. Thatcher had to come over and give him a treatment. Dad was just sitting on a chair in the bedroom, holding the back of his neck. I felt so sorry for him. He told Mother it felt as if he had an open wound back there. She gave him pills, but they didn't help. And finally she had to call the doctor."

"Is he all right now?"

"Oh, yes. He's always fine after he sees Dr. Thatcher. . . . Here's Mother."

Claire was coming toward them across the lawn. In the sunlight, in her shimmering pale green dress, she seemed to him an apparition from vanished years. As he stood up to greet her, his heart ached with the heavy weight of years gone by.

As soon as Jack Elkins entered his private office, he knew something was wrong. The color TV set was playing too loudly. He was standing near the desk when Adele Moyer entered quickly.

She said, "Hello, Jack. Well, I might as well get the bad news over with." Her voice was shaky, and her bony hand with its neatly manicured nails was not quite steady. "We've had visitors."

"When?"

"Sometime early this morning. They disconnected the alarm system, moved right in, and took over. Didn't even bother trying to cover up."

"Any idea what they were looking for?"

"Nope. They dumped out all the files. The computer was locked up and I've got the key. But they got it working. What they didn't know was our code."

"Thank God for that."

"I haven't called the police. The last time this happened you didn't want any publicity."

"Smart girl. Why the television?"

"For company. Everyone is downstairs putting things back in order. It's creepy up here all alone, and I didn't want to wake you."

"Well, before you go down and help the others, get General Ziffren on the telephone. Tell him it's urgent."

He watched the television set, which was showing a Road

Runner cartoon, until finally Adele signaled that she had his party on the telephone.

"Say, General, when are your boys going to get tired of nosing into my affairs? I don't see what you accomplished with all this breaking and entering."

"If you're trying to be funny, Elkins, you're failing miserably."

"You won't think it's funny when you see me on TV this week. I'm going to show everyone a nice closeup picture of a secret FBI report. It proves one of the men killed in that apartment was your own undercover agent."

"That's a damned lie."

"I've got the facts, General. His name was Thomas Duncan, alias Tommy the Toff. He infiltrated the John Brown organization, and he was the one who fired them up for that attack on the White House. Of course, he needed some help from the inside, too. I can't prove yet where he got it."

"Just how irresponsible can you get, Elkins?"

The tense emphasis in General Ziffren's voice was a promising sign.

"Isn't it possible your Security Bureau boys were acting under orders when they finished off Duncan?"

"Careful."

"I'm not saying whose orders, General, but you've got to admit it would have been dangerous to let Duncan live. The poor bastard knew too much. Always a chance he might spill his guts." He heard what might have been a gargle of suppressed rage. "Things are tough when you have to start shooting your own guys."

"Elkins, I look forward to the satisfaction of dealing with you someday personally."

The telephone clicked off.

Elkins leaned back in his chair and put his feet up on the desk. "Had the old boy really going there for a while," he said to Adele.

In the pink tent the guests were leaving and the tables were being cleared. The deputy prime minister of the Ivory Coast paused for a few minutes with Carter. He was a tall, well-built black man.

"If you talk to the President, I wish you would urge him to grant recognition to Monzania. When we look at what is happening to our sister nation, we are oppressed by a great helplessness and impatience." He spoke with the formal stilted eloquence that was a curious mode of speech among African leaders, a tradition that had begun with Nkrumah. "What is your great country waiting for? Black people must be free to govern themselves. They will do so, even if the future of their land has to be written in blood."

"I'll give him your message, sir."

The deputy prime minister departed soon afterward.

Claire said, "You were a lifesaver, Carter. I'd have been lost without you. When it turned out you actually *knew* him. . . ."

"We've met twice."

"He's so formidable looking. If he's only the deputy, what is the prime minister like?"

"A short, potbellied fellow with absolutely no physical presence."

Claire smiled. "George wants to find something to keep you in Washington. Now I know what it should be. Undersecretary for African Affairs."

"There is one. And he's very capable."

"Oh, well, I don't care what it is as long as you don't go away again. I thought the luncheon went well, didn't you?"

"Everyone says you're the most successful hostess since Jacqueline Kennedy."

She smiled at the compliment. "Let's take a stroll. I've been trying to find time to be with you alone."

They walked onto the south lawn, strangely empty now that the honor guard had departed.

"You know, Carter, everything seems to fall in place for me when you're around. I've always felt I understood you. There's a kind of . . . dependableness about you. You never change."

"I'm still the tallest man you know."

The steps she was taking seemed to become aimless, and then she stopped. "Oh, Carter . . ." She turned to him. "I have to talk to someone."

"Try me."

Their mingled shadows stretched out eerily. One night on a dimly lighted campus she had put her head back to look at the stars and he had kissed her. He had sensed her uncertainty then. Another man would have put her feelings to a test. He had not, and on such small decisions a future may depend.

She said quietly, "It has to do with George. . . ."

She told him about what happened the day of George's television speech. Earlier she had accompanied him to an affair at the Newspaper Photographers Association, and he had been in fine spirits. But by the time they left, she could sense trouble starting. At the White House he hovered over the AP and UPI tickers. When the clacking keys took too long, he reached under the glass to wrench the paper along. His mood turned irritable. He snapped at Chad Oliver, and at her. Later, when he was supposed to be getting ready for his speech on television, he had been in terrible pain. Every minute had seemed to induce more pain, until finally she had called Dr. Thatcher.

"Dr. Thatcher helped get him in shape to carry on. But it doesn't last. I—I think he's getting worse."

Carter said cautiously, "It sounds as though there may be a serious problem."

"What can I do?"

"We've got to find out what's really wrong. If Dr. Thatcher can't tell us, we'll get another doctor."

"George won't hear of it. He has complete faith in Dr. Thatcher."

"Well, I don't."

Carter called Jack Elkins and arranged to meet him at the Whaler's Bar. At four o'clock in the afternoon, the bar was almost deserted.

He held a wine glass between thumb and forefinger, lifting it slightly in Elkins's direction. "I think you were right about that informer."

Elkins grinned. "I'll drink to that." He tossed off his Scotch in a swallow. "That was some scene, huh?"

Carter shook his head in agreement.

Elkins said, "You were a pretty cool cat during that shootout. I may have been underestimating you."

"Is that offer of cooperation still open?"

"I can always use someone with good access to the White House. What's your angle?"

"I want to know why you think Thatcher is responsible for the President's troubles."

"Call it a hunch. Or a reporter's instinct."

"Is that all?"

"Don't knock it. I've made a good living by trusting it."

"Nothing more definite?"

"There was the Ordiveras cremation. Smelled of something being covered up."

"Why?"

"Too big a hurry. And I did some checking on the cause of death. Myocarditis—inflammation of the heart—usually results from either an infection or the ingestion of toxic chemicals."

Carter was thinking again of Dr. Vancell's theory concerning Ordiveras's symptoms, and the Institute of Psychiatry report on how certain personality types behaved under prolonged treatment with amphetamines. The report had included a frighteningly accurate description of George Rushton's symptoms.

He asked, "Anything else?"

"What more do you need? I've started with less. Thatcher is supposed to be treating the President for a simple pain in the neck. It doesn't add up."

"What can I do?"

"Help me find out what kind of treatment Thatcher is giving him."

For the present, Carter decided against confiding too much in Jack Elkins—their collaboration would have to remain limited. "I can tell Dr. Thatcher that the President's wife and daughter are very worried about him. That they don't think his condition is getting better. And they're going to bring in another doctor unless he tells them exactly what's wrong with the President, and what he's doing for him."

"Thatcher won't give you the straight story. I have a better idea. Become his patient."

"What for?"

"You go in for a problem like the President's, and maybe he'll give you the same treatment he's giving the President."

"What kind of a problem?"

"Bursitis. One of those painful things doctors can't really do much for. And it's similar enough to what the President's supposed to have."

"I don't think Thatcher is taking private patients. Not new ones, anyhow."

"But if Claire Rushton asked a favor—for an old friend—he'd find it hard to turn her down."

After a moment Carter said, "You really think of the angles, don't you?"

"That's the name of the game."

A small red light glowed on Jack Elkins's telephone. The call was from Joe Simons, his syndicate chief in New York.

Joe said, "I need a fill-in piece. By tomorrow."

"What the hell is it now?" Elkins demanded.

"That one about the shootout is too risky. You imply somebody gave orders to get an FBI informer who was in the apartment."

Some years ago, after a prolonged legal battle, the syndicate had lost an expensive lawsuit on an Elkins column. Since then, their lawyers have had the right to approve copy.

"He was there," Elkins said. "I'm going to prove it on my TV show this week."

"That doesn't mean anybody had orders to kill him."

"Joe, be reasonable. It's a hot story. If you hold it up, it'll break somewhere else."

"One story against a million-dollar libel suit. We can live without the story."

Elkins's highly sensitized radar gave him a signal. "Joe, how's the weather up there?"

"Not as hot as in Washington."

"Okay. I'll put another piece on the teletype."

Joe Simons had told him where the heat was coming from.

Elkins hung up, grimacing as if he had just tasted yesterday's coffee. He called Adele Moyer into his office. For the next half hour they checked other story possibilities. There was one about a $19,600 aide to a powerful congressman who had become a millionaire during five years of service. His outside activities included an insurance company and a radio-television station. He had used the congressman's name in setting up his deals, and the congressman had a financial interest in the businesses although his shares were owned by nominees and his name had never been listed.

Elkins decided that would make a more interesting interview for his TV show, if he could line up either the congressman or his aide and then confront him with the facts without warning. Something like that might edge him up a notch in the ratings.

He settled on a short piece about suite 436 at the Sheraton-Carlton Hotel. That happened to be the suite leased by the State Department to entertain visiting dignitaries. Through an electronics expert who had placed a telephone tap, Jack had learned the Security Bureau was illegally listening in on the private conversations emanating from the suite.

"That ought to shake up that bastard Ziffren," he told Adele. "He's screwing up our foreign relations."

His desk was piled so high with proofs, memos and correspondence, tear sheets and photostats, it would not have surprised him if there were no desk beneath it at all. He dug into the pile, and was still hard at work when an informant on the White House press corps called to tell him about Chad Oliver's news conference.

"Chad really took off on Senator Halliwell for saying the summit conference couldn't change the fact that China is a Marxist-Leninist country and no friend of ours. Chad said, in effect, Halliwell doesn't know beans about foreign policy and ought to stick to pacifying voters in his own state."

"Old stuff. The President will invite Halliwell to a private meeting and they'll kiss and make up."

It was time for him to make his afternoon rounds. As he was leaving, Francoise was in the outer office transcribing letters from a Dictaphone.

She smiled at him, and removed the earphone. "Do we still have our appointment?"

"We certainly do, honey."

He toured the Sans Souci, the Federal Club, the Metropolitan Club, exchanged lies about current stories and sources with Reston, Buchwald, Conine, Evans, Kraft, and Gold. Jack quoted Chad Oliver as having told him privately that if it were up to people like Senator Halliwell, this country would never be able to act in a crisis. We'd just have to hang like a spider in a web, waiting for a fly that's never going to appear. That last sounded so much like a quote that Chad would get angry telephone calls demanding to know why he was feeding Jack Elkins exclusive material.

This was the public side of his activity; the other side was the people he met at secret rendezvous. He had to work a sixteen-hour day to keep up with the demands of his column and TV show. At times he appeared to be feeding a great devouring machine which was never placated. The machine kept grinding away while he desperately searched for more scraps to throw in—his personal belongings, his acquaintances, his friends, probably in the end, himself.

During the afternoon rounds he had an unpleasant encounter. A woman rushed up to him on the street, screaming something about the "disgraceful stuff" he was printing. Apparently she was a disciple of General Ziffren's. "Honey," Elkins told her, "you ain't seen nothin' yet!" She spat at him.

At five-thirty he had a pleasant interlude. He went to the rooming house where he often interviewed informants. Francoise, the brunette secretary, was waiting. She came out of the bathroom, surrounded in pleasant steamy vapors and wrapping a yellow towel around her slim body. While he got on the telephone to make a few word changes in the copy that would go out by messenger from his office later in the evening, she sat combing her hair before a mirror. She stroked slowly, watching him in the mirror, listening to his impatient inflection and terse responses. "Give me a few minutes, I'll feel better," he said when he hung up. He opened his collar and tie, and sat back in a chair with his feet on a hassock. She came over and began quiet ministrations. His eyes closed, and he breathed so regularly he might almost have been asleep. At last she unbuttoned his trousers, and rolled them down to the middle of his heavy strong thighs.

She smiled. "Everything's going to be fine," she said, with just that delicious trace of French accent.

She bent to him, her face clenched like a hungry baby's expecting his bottle. She held him with both hands, as if to contain and control the source of his power. With every passing second he was growing.

"Would you like it now?" she asked.

"Sure. Go ahead."

She moved on top of him and, with both hands on his chest, held herself so his penis barely touched her moist vagina. She lowered herself very slowly while moving her hips to make his penis do small circles inside her. Then she settled down on him and began to ride.

He lay on his back, watching the ceiling resolve itself out of dimness. In the early years he had often asked women if they enjoyed it, and they always answered "Oh, yes!" in a way that convinced him. He had stopped asking.

When he finally came in great shuddering thrusts, her body quivered.

She leaned over him, caressing his cheek with her own. "Now I know why I've had a crush on you."

He admired her long symmetry atop him. "Okay, honey."

When he finished dressing, she was still lying naked on the bed. He looked at her. "By the way, you're fired."

"What?"

"Fired."

She smiled, a bit uncertainly. "You're not serious."

"Too many strange things have been happening since you came to work at the office. This morning was the clincher. They knew how to short-circuit the alarm, they even knew how to start the computer. What they didn't know was how the files are coded. Funny thing. You don't know that either."

She sat up. "I had nothing to do with it."

"I can't take chances, honey. You'll get a good severance and great references. But you probably don't need them if you're working for the government."

"It isn't fair! If you thought that, why did you . . ." Suddenly aware, she picked up the sheet and held it against her.

"I couldn't resist letting you give your all for the Security Bureau one last time."

"You son of a bitch!" she screamed at him.

He grinned. "It wouldn't have worked out anyway, honey," he said from the door. "You're a lousy lay."

He arrived at the Highbank Club shortly past seven o'clock, entering through the simulated-iron door. Inside the foyer he nodded to Douglas, the ancient black guardian of the club's checking room.

It was important to stay on friendly terms with people like Douglas. They often supplied tidbits of news for his column.

He checked the bulletin board, which announced an upcoming backgammon tournament and an exhibition of billiards by a former champion. Elkins's chief interest was in the posting of members who had not paid their bar and restaurant bills for at least sixty days. There was nothing unusual in bills going unpaid that long in a gentlemen's club, but there was a chance that the list might contain advance information about a member in real financial difficulties.

Elkins had gone to a great deal of trouble to obtain a membership in Highbank. Not many club members were willing to sponsor him, and three blackballs were enough to bar him from membership. His sponsor had to be someone with sufficient influence to ride roughshod over objectors. He found the right man in a vice-president of the World Bank, who wanted to keep an unpleasant item about his son from appearing in Jack Elkins's column. The vice-president let it be known that he would consider it a personal affront if Elkins were blackballed. Nevertheless, there were two blackballs.

At dinner, his guest was Paul Jayson, the industrialist. He had insured Paul Jayson's acceptance of the invitation by simply mentioning that he was calling at the suggestion of their mutual friend, Michele Alpen. Jayson, a short, bald, pleasant-looking man, was waiting in the roof-garden bar with its spectacular skyline view of the Capitol. They ordered cocktails, and Jayson sat back in a luxurious leather chair to regard Elkins with cool suspicion.

"You said you wanted to talk about our mutual friend."

"You've got that wrong. I only said she *was* a mutual friend."

Cool suspicion became cool appraisal. "Then what do you want to see me about?"

"You were a patient of Dr. Thatcher's."

"What of it?"

"Michele was with you when you had a seizure. I have reason

to believe the treatment you were getting from Dr. Thatcher caused it."

"Ridiculous."

"You don't deny it happened?"

"A symptom of my illness. Dr. Thatcher cured me. I haven't had a recurrence in years."

"You were lucky. A number of Dr. Thatcher's other patients haven't done so well. He's had a lot of people crack up. Physically and mentally."

"I don't know what you're after, Elkins. But Dr. Thatcher is one of the finest men I know, and I have no use for anyone who tries to discredit the work he is doing."

He recognized another dead end. Keep plugging, that was the answer; continue putting one thing with another.

In the third-floor men's room of Garfinckel's department store, shortly before closing, he found Marty Brokaw waiting.

"Hi, Mr. Elkins."

"I have a little job for you, Marty. A confidential job. Needing your special skills."

"You'd better pass me by this time. My license is under suspension. While I'm waiting for a hearing I can't take any chances."

"I want you to get something for me."

"I'd like to help you, Mr. Elkins, but you know how it is. If anything went wrong now, I'd lose my license for sure."

"Nothing will go wrong. And it's worth five hundred to me."

"Nice money, but sorry."

"Do this for me and I may be able to help with your license."

"You mean it?"

"A favor for a favor."

"Mr. Elkins, just tell me what this job is."

"I'm looking for patients of a doctor who may have reason not to like him. That kind of information is probably locked away in his private files."

"A plumbing operation?"

"It has a lot more to do with national security than the one they did on Ellsberg's psychiatrist."

"You want the actual files? Or just microfilm?"

"Microfilm will do fine."

Shortly after leaving Garfinckel's, he had a nasty near-accident. A car suddenly veered from the street and surged toward him on the sidewalk.

"Hey!"

He had time for one quick strangled shout. Then the car was upon him, tires screeching. He left his feet in an instinctive headlong dive. The army had taught him a few things that remained useful. Never stop to figure it out. Act. Think and you'll be killed with the thought half-formed.

It was so close that he felt the brush of the fender and the heated air of its passage. Then he hit the pavement and his hands skidded, breaking the fall. Rough concrete scraped skin off his palms.

Sound broke over him in a deafening gust, followed by the high-pitched whine of a racing motor, the growl of shifting gears, and the jounce of tires as the car slid back over the curbing to the street. He looked up, too late to catch the license number. The driver was only a dim blur through the rear window.

"Crazy stupid bastard!"

Several people began moving toward him as he picked himself up from the sidewalk. It had all taken only a few seconds.

"Are you all right, mister? I saw the whole thing. The driver lost control."

"He could've killed you!"

"Why didn't he stop?"

"Did he hit you? Are you hurt?"

His palms burned where the skin was scraped and a little blood was oozing. There was a small jagged tear in one trouser leg.

"I'm fine," he said. "Did anybody catch the license plate?"

"I think it was a rented car. Don't they start with Z?"

"Whaddya mean, rented? It was an out-of-town license."

"Did anyone get a good look at who was driving?" Elkins asked.

"Some kid. One of those crazy youngsters. They're a real menace behind the wheel."

"You're blind, grandpa. It was a woman driver. An old lady."

Eyewitness testimony.

Elkins thanked them, said he didn't need help and wasn't hurt. At the corner he hailed a cab.

The taxi's radio was playing a muffled blare of rock. He looked out the side window at streets that seemed strangely empty. It might not have been an accident. The car had seemed to come up over the sidewalk looking for him. And it had sped away without stopping to find out if he'd been hurt.

He settled back in his seat. *Jesus*, he thought, *I could be lying back there this minute with a broken chest. I could be dying.*

He shivered.

14

Marvin Thatcher's clinic was located seven miles from the District of Columbia, in a gray stone-and-brick Tudor mansion that had formerly been a school. Among the signs of its previous occupancy were tall green hedges surrounding an open area of lawn with a volleyball net. The mansion was set back from the street and had spreading wings which gave it a wide front on the road. The terrace and gardens commanded a fine view.

Carter parked his car at the end of a cement driveway in front of a garage that still had a basketball hoop. He was ushered into a bright small room where a woman introduced herself as Dr. Thatcher's assistant. She gave him a form to fill out, but did not glance at it when he returned it to her.

"Please remove your jacket and follow me."

He waited in a starkly furnished room with cream-colored walls, until Dr. Thatcher came in, holding a clipboard. They shook hands amiably.

"Well, now, Mr. Fitzsimmons. What seems to be the problem?"

"I've got this pain in my shoulder, Doctor. I think it's bursitis."

"Let's not jump to conclusions. If patients could diagnose their own aches and pains there wouldn't be any need for doctors."

Half an hour later, after a physical examination and X-rays, Carter was back in Dr. Thatcher's private office.

"You appear to be in excellent shape, Mr. Fitzsimmons," the doctor said, leaning back in his swivel chair. "In fact, if you were a corporation, I'd buy stock in you."

"How about the bursitis?"

"If there's calcium in there, it doesn't show up on the XRG. And there's no sign of inhibited articulation. Your condition isn't that serious. Aspirin is probably the best remedy."

"Can you prescribe anything stronger?"

"Cortisone might help. Or Butazolidin. But there can be side effects."

"Sometimes it hurts so much I can't work or concentrate."

"If the pain becomes that acute, come in and I'll have another look. We can always do something until the worst is over."

"Isn't there something you could give me meanwhile to at least make me feel better . . . give me a psychological lift?"

Dr. Thatcher's left eyebrow registered a slight surprise. "No, I'm afraid I can't recommend anything like that. The danger with any strong drug is that it can develop a dependence worse than the original malady. Do you mind if I ask a personal question?"

"Not at all."

"Anything else troubling you? Some emotional problem, perhaps?"

"I can't think of any. Why?"

"When a patient complains of a physical symptom and there is no readily apparent reason, it's time to ask what else may be bothering him. Emotional trauma can act like a magnifying glass to make physical symptoms appear larger and more intractable."

"I can't think of anything like that, Doctor. I'm in reasonably sound mental shape."

Dr. Thatcher smiled. "Then take aspirin. I'm ashamed to say that's the best advice I can give you."

The door opened and the nurse said, "Your next patient is waiting, Doctor."

Thatcher walked Carter to the door, and shook hands again. "I hope we'll run into each other soon—at the White House. Meanwhile, try not to worry too much about the pain in your shoulder. Worry never helps anything. It'll probably go away by itself."

As Carter was leaving, a man in the waiting room was talking to the receptionist. It took Carter a moment to identify him as Blue Berry, the television comic, because he was not in his familiar uniform of wide trousers, suspenders, and long flat shoes. Berry was a tall man of about forty-five, and in person unexpectedly good-looking.

He was saying in a highly excited tone, "Look, baby, tell the doctor I can't hang around here all day. A whole studio is waiting. It's costing a thousand dollars a minute for me to stand here talking. Is that fair? Is that right?"

"You don't have an appointment. I'm sorry."

His broad, freckled face made a rubbery grimace. "How could I call for an appointment? Cut right out in the middle of a belly laugh? Leave them standing there with custard on their faces? Look, I'm going to be late getting back as it is. Tell ol' Thatch he's gotta see me right away." He became aware of Carter, and his staccato speech and enforced gaiety took a new turn. "Maybe I shouldn't see Doc, after all. Look how he stretched *this* one! Mister, you could play male lead to the fifty-foot woman. Or just lie down and play the bridge of San Luis Rey. You don't mind a little kidding, do you?"

Carter smiled. "It's been happening all my life."

"You're a good sport. I like a good sport. Maybe you could pose for one of those nude centerfolds. You'd look great in a foldout. But you'd need plenty of hair on your chest." It was a ritual monologue, devoid of a real attempt to amuse. He turned back to the receptionist. "Look, baby, get me in to 'ol Thatch and I'll give you a season's free passes to my show."

The receptionist rewarded him with a frosty smile. "I've already told Dr. Thatcher you're waiting. He may be too busy to see you today."

"Hey, now, that's no way. I can't go back to work. I can't concentrate. I get depressed. He can't do this to me!"

The receptionist said coolly, "I'll call again and see if he can schedule you." She closed the glass partition to make the call.

Blue Berry turned to Carter, who was putting on his jacket.

"Did'ja ever hear of anything like this? Crazy! A man's sick, he can't even see his doctor. What've you got to be, dead?"

The receptionist opened the partition. "I'm sorry. The doctor is definitely too busy to see you today."

Berry rubbed both hands over his face, molding rubbery flesh. "Jess-zuzz C. Keerist!" His mouth began twitching. "How about that other thing? He gave me it when I hadda go on tour a year ago. You know."

"I'm afraid I don't."

"Ask the doc. He'll know."

At that point, the receptionist looked at Carter with a slight question in her eyes. He nodded, waved pleasantly, and left. He waited in the driveway until Blue Berry emerged ten minutes later, carrying a small square box and heading toward a gray Mercedes parked in the driveway.

"Mr. Berry?"

"Well, if it isn't Mr. Stilt." He nodded toward the nearby basketball hoop. "Ol' Jabbar ain't gonna stuff baskets on you, fella. What can I do for you?"

"I think a mistake has been made."

Berry blinked nervously. "No hard feelings. You know how it is. All in fun. Here, have a cigar."

He reached toward a breast pocket.

"I think you took something that belongs to me," Carter said.

"What? This?" Berry glanced down apprehensively at the small box in his hand. Then he was reassured. "Naw. You got it wrong. I just picked this up."

"I left it in the waiting room."

"Your mistake, pal. Maybe you can't see too good from way up there." Grinning, he moved toward the car.

Carter's hand on his arm delayed him. "I'm not joking. That's mine."

"Don't touch the merchandise!" Berry pulled his arm away. "I don't like people to maul me." His eyes became crafty. "You know how it is. In my business all kinds of nuts try to press the flesh. Turns my nerves into banjo wire."

"I'm still sure that's my property."

"Take my word. This isn't your box of Havanas. What you want is probably back where you left it."

"There's an easy way to prove it. Open it up and have a look."

"I've got no time to play hide and seek." He put his hand on the car door. " 'Bye now. Don't take any wooden giraffes."

"Of course, if you'd rather have me call a policeman," Carter said.

Blue Berry whirled with sudden anger. "Are you some kind of a nut? I don't mean to sound nasty, but a gag's a gag, fella."

"Open it up."

"Go to hell!" The words burst out in a voice that had veered sharply toward hysteria. "On your way, Ichabod! Or you'll be carrying your head around in your hands."

He turned the handle of the car door and opened it. Carter slammed it shut.

"Son of a bitch!" Berry swung his left hand, but Carter easily fended the awkward blow. He grabbed Berry by the lapel of his coat jacket, and was a little surprised at how soft the husky body suddenly became.

"Hold on! Hold on!" Berry's voice was a shrill falsetto. Trying to guard against an expected blow, he raised his right hand defensively and let the small box drop to the ground.

At the splintering crash, he whimpered, "Now you've done it. It broke!"

The accident seemed to completely unnerve him. He stood immobilized, staring, then stepped back as if he expected the box to explode.

Carter knelt beside the box. It had landed on one corner and the hasp had snapped. Inside, in six neat cushioned spaces were six vials, and horizontally aligned at the bottom a small hypodermic and syringe.

"Bastard," Berry mumbled. He slumped against the car as if the bones had been taken out of him.

Carter got to his feet and handed the box back. "I'm sorry. It isn't mine, after all."

Berry stared at him like an offended child who had been done injury by a grownup. Then he nodded numbly, took the box, and hastily drove his Mercedes out of the parking lot. Carter was sure he would not notice until much later, if at all, that one of his precious vials was missing.

Carter met Joyce at the medical center. It was the first time they had met since the night he learned about Harry Wade. He had found the rivalry with her dead lover hard to cope with. He could not think of himself in mythic terms. Strong. Resolute. Honest. Brave. Yet he was sure she thought of Wade that way.

While other hospital employees passed by in the corridor, he told her what had happened at Thatcher's clinic.

"You mean you actually stole something?"

"If you don't mind, I'd prefer a less blunt description."

She grinned. "I was beginning to think you were the kind who would never give a girl any surprises."

"I need your help."

"Me Jane. You John Q. Spy."

"That paper from the Institute. It mentioned a type of druguser that could have been a double for Blue Berry. Almost as if they had been watching how he behaved at Dr. Thatcher's clinic."

"You think Berry is hooked? But what's that got to do with you?"

"I'm interested in the President. Thatcher happens to be his doctor too."

She blinked. "I'd rather you didn't get mixed up in anything as heavy as that." She frowned. "And besides, Dr. Thatcher would never do anything like that to the President."

"You didn't think so when only Blue Berry was involved. Or Felix Ordiveras. What makes the President immune?"

"It's too irresponsible." She shook her head, "Not Dr. Thatcher."

"Even if conventional methods of treatment weren't working?"

"Amphetamines are a known quantity. They can cause anything from high blood pressure to paranoid delusions." She hesitated. "Of course, he might only use amphetamines as part of something he'd invented himself. A mixture. Like Miss Emma."

"Miss Who?"

"Addict's name for morphine. Great stuff for pain, but knocks you out. So they mix it with cocaine to get a speedball and think that solves the problem. Only it makes worse problems. The effects are synergistic."

"What's that?"

"Instead of adding to each other, they're multiplied. Like with alcohol and Valium. Somebody who's on Valium may get really looped on just one drink. When you start mixing chemicals, you really buy a basketful of trouble."

"Thatcher was a professor of pharmacology. He could have thought he had the answer."

"You can't make me believe it."

"We have a way to find out." He took the vial out of his pocket and showed it to her. "I'd like you to have this analyzed."

She took the vial and turned it over without really examining it.

"It might be harmless," he said.

She put the vial into the pocket of her nurse's uniform. "I've got a friend who works in the lab. He'll run a test, strictly as a favor." She shook her head stubbornly. "But I know Dr. Thatcher wouldn't do anything really wrong."

Joyce called him at the hotel at four o'clock, her quitting time, to say there was no word yet from the lab but that she would wait until there was.

She arrived at his hotel room at almost six, and took from her purse a typewritten page that seemed a dense mass of chemical symbols and indecipherable phrases.

"Are you any good at reading this?" she asked.

"Better tell me what it says."

"The long and short is that the contents, in addition to some well-known and not so well-known ingredients from the pharmacy, contain methamphetamine in a solution ready for injection. . . ."

"Good Lord!"

She added with mocking amusement, "But it's not in sufficient quantity to cause symptoms even in long-term use."

"What do you mean?"

"It's a perfectly legitimate prescription, the equivalent of about a ten-milligram tablet—which you can buy for fifteen cents at any drugstore. Approximately eight billion pills as strong as this are produced every year and sold under popular brand names."

He had been prepared for quite different news. "All right, I was a damned fool. Thatcher is in the clear."

On the telephone, Jack Elkins did not seem impressed by the news. "I'd like to see the lab report. Would you drop it in the mail?"

"It was done as a favor. Not for publication."

"If it's as innocent as you say, it isn't worth publishing."

"I'm willing to say I was wrong. Why can't you?"

"How many doctors hand out medical kits with hypodermic needles and syringes? A man who can do one thing is capable of another. That's how I look at it. Besides, what was in the kit isn't necessarily what Thatcher gives his other patients."

"What does it take to convince you?"

"Maybe I'm not as anxious to be convinced as you are."

"Or I'm not as interested as you are in working up a scandal," Carter answered. He hung up, pleased with himself. Elkins and he had quickly come to a parting of the ways, and that in itself proved he had chosen the right path.

He hesitated a moment before turning to Joyce, sensitive to anything that might waken her memory of Harry Wade. "Well, I wouldn't mind celebrating my mistake. How about dinner at La Potiniere tonight?"

Her head was tilted back and a little away. "I'd have to go home and change."

"You can wear the new white dress. And this time I promise to be bowled over."

Her face at that moment seemed to hold, as if in suspension, a number of conflicting emotions, but the most surprising to him was desire.

"I'd rather stay."

He felt as if a noose were being loosened about his throat. His whole body pulsed with life, and suddenly he was quite unreasonably happy.

Later, in bed, in the lamplight, he saw her beneath him, hair dark on the white pillow, coppery-nippled breasts rising and falling. She was so beautiful. Her body had incredibly soft contours.

She lifted her arms to him. "Darling," she whispered, and that was the last word either of them spoke for a long time.

15

Carter drove toward Abramson's office the next morning in an ebullient mood. Along Connecticut Avenue repairs were being made on the new transit system, and the street was uprooted, intersected with barricaded trenches like a World War I battlefield, blocked by bulldozers and seventy-foot cranes. Workers in bright green hats watched the black limousines of ambassadors, congressmen, and government bureaucrats slow into long, congested metal lines that stretched past elegant boutiques and office buildings. During the half-hour delay, tempers grew short, horns stuttered, drivers and pedestrians glared at each other at street crossings. Carter remained in good humor, waving pleasantly to the muddy-clothed workers who often waved back, grinning.

When Carter arrived at the office, Abramson peered at him uncertainly. "I'm glad you're in such a good mood."

It took Carter only a moment to recognize that something was wrong.

He asked, "What is it, Dolph?"

"Can I depend on you not to tell anyone what I'm going to show you?"

"Of course."

From his topmost bookshelf, Abramson took down a heavy volume from a leather-bound edition of State Department papers, and from its hollowed insides he removed a tiny microphone.

"I don't know how long it's been here. Apparently, everything said in this office has been overheard."

Carter was stunned. "Who would do a thing like that?"

"I seem to recall Dr. Kissinger making a similar remark when he discovered he was being spied on. In that case, it turned out to be the Pentagon. This time I'm more inclined to think it's Mark Ziffren."

"Have you told the President?"

Abramson shook his head. "If he didn't actually approve the wiretapping in the first place, he'd certainly support Ziffren now. In the name of national security."

"How did you find out?"

"I was alerted by the Vice-President, who had just discovered his own office was bugged." Abramson smiled faintly. "Incidentally, I've never heard such fine extemporaneous profanity. Elmer Tate was practically sulfuric. He surpassed himself."

"What are you going to do?"

Abramson took a few moments to answer. "I've considered various possibilities, but I think the only honorable course for me is to resign. I was appointed by the President, and can only serve while I have his confidence."

"You can't be sure he even knows about this."

The intercom buzzer sounded, and Abramson flicked the speaker switch.

"Mr. Secretary," said his receptionist's voice, "the President urgently requests your presence in the Oval Office. He'd like you to bring Mr. Fitzsimmons with you."

"I wasn't aware he knew I was here," Carter said.

Abramson flicked off the switch. "Do you mind accompanying me?"

"Not at all. I'd like to see George Rushton myself."

They went down in the private elevator to the basement where a car and chauffeur were waiting, as they waited all day for the secretary until needed. It was just starting to rain.

"What do you think he wants?" Carter asked on their way to the White House.

"I haven't any idea."

George Rushton was standing staring out the French windows of the Oval Office at the rain. When they entered, he swung around and surveyed them for several seconds.

He said harshly, "There was a burglary last night. Someone broke into Dr. Thatcher's office."

Carter became aware of Dr. Thatcher seated in a wing chair in a shadowed corner. The doctor sat quietly, but his nervousness was as visible as a facial tic.

"Do you know who it was, Doctor?" Carter asked.

"I—I have no idea. I can't imagine who. . . ."

George Rushton said, "We know this much. It was a professional job. There were hardly any signs of forced entry. He picked the lock to the office door. And once inside, he broke into the small safe that contained the doctor's medical records."

"What do you think he was after?" Carter asked Rushton. "Your medical history?"

"Of course. There are people who want to discredit me in any way they can. They'd like to make everyone think I'm a sick man who shouldn't remain in office."

Dr. Thatcher smoothed the hair at the back of his head. "Fortunately, the President's medical record was not in that safe. I keep it separate. They never found it."

"Did they take any of the others?" Carter asked.

"No. Everything was left intact. But the safe had been opened."

"The records were photographed," Rushton said impatiently. "They didn't know which were valuable and which were not.

And they certainly didn't have time to study them. What do you make of this, Dolph?"

Abramson sighed. "I'm afraid it doesn't come under the heading of State Department business."

"Well, I know what to make of it!"

"What, Mr. President?"

"Obviously, the people involved in this conspiracy are desperate. It isn't possible to deal with them any longer in the ordinary way."

A frown made a parenthesis between Abramson's eyebrows. "Before you assume this is a political plot, Mr. President, wouldn't it be wise to consider that it might have been an ordinary burglary? Someone might have broken into Dr. Thatcher's office, opened the safe expecting to find cash or valuables, and, finding nothing, simply closed it and gone his way. Hoping no one would be the wiser."

The silence in the Oval Office was interrupted only by an intermittent splash of raindrops against the windows.

"An ingenious idea," George Rushton said, "and I'm not surprised that you thought of it. Unfortunately, it's wrong. The man who broke into Dr. Thatcher's office was not only a professional, he was acting for someone who knew exactly what he wanted." He looked toward Thatcher. "Doctor, I don't think we need to detain you any longer."

Thatcher left, and Rushton turned to Abramson. "I want to know who and where my enemies are, and what they are up to. General Ziffren and his Security Bureau are going to investigate everyone and anyone, including those high in my administration."

"That's going to have a bad effect on morale."

"Can't be helped. This is a question of the highest national security." Unexpectedly, he added, "You can go now, Dolph. I want a few words alone with Carter."

Abramson was taken aback at the sudden dismissal, but after a moment's hesitation, he left. As soon as the door closed, Rushton came around the desk toward Carter.

"You heard Abramson. What do you think?"

"About what?"

"This little interview finally convinced me. He's the leader."

Carter stared at him incredulously.

George said, "I had reason to suspect him before this, but I was studying his reactions just now. He knew about that break-in. He gave himself away."

Carter searched for a possible response. "It doesn't make sense. Why would he do anything like that?"

"He's willing to do anything, anything, to destroy me." With the fingers of one hand George appeared to be nervously rolling small balls of bread. "But the Grand Alliance is going to go forward no matter what spies and traitors try to do to stop it."

"The Grand Alliance?"

Rushton took several strides about the room, then returned. "I can tell you, Carter, because you're loyal." The intensity in his voice made it seem queerly pitched. "We're going to be military allies with China. An alliance that will change the whole future of mankind."

A strange chill moved through Carter's body, the reflection of what was occurring in his mind.

Rushton's tone was triumphant. "Guarantees of each other's borders, agreements to come to each other's aid in event of attack, a full exchange of nuclear weaponry. The works! All that remains is the formal signing in Peking."

Carter could hardly believe George Rushton meant it. The Russians, maneuvered into isolation, feeling themselves cornered, might strike first. If they did not, the Chinese could provoke them—knowing they were backed by the most modern nuclear arsenal in the world. It was a prescription for catastrophe.

Carter said, "I don't think a military treaty between China and the United States could be approved by the Senate."

"There won't be a treaty. Just an executive agreement between the Chinese Premier and myself." He lifted his hand to forestall reply. "I know all the arguments, Carter. Every man elected to public office confronts the dilemma of whether to obey the will of the people—if anyone can discover what it is—or to do what he knows is right. As for the Constitution, you have to keep a sense of perspective. There would have been no way for a strict Constitutionalist to have approved the acquisition of the Louisiana Territory, or to fight a war to keep the Union intact, or even for an income tax to be levied. What people call evasions of the Constitution are really just practical means to make the old document work in new ways."

George Rushton was looking at him eagerly. He appeared to be trembling with excitement.

Carter said, "No one can foresee what would happen. It might have . . . terrible consequences."

"I'm aware of the risks, but in my judgment they're worthwhile. The Grand Alliance will work, Carter, and insure peace for all mankind."

Carter was too stunned to reply. There had to be a way to stop this. The thought was compelling and terrible: At any cost, George Rushton *had* to be stopped.

Driving south toward the Virginia line, Carter was almost certain he was being followed. In the rear-vision mirror he picked out a car and watched it keep a steady distance for six miles before it turned off the highway.

Carter shook his head with annoyance. He was becoming paranoid.

He had called ahead to ask John McMullen's permission to visit the farm. Now, driving the familiar route, he was thinking ahead to what it would be like when they met again. Since the divorce, relations with Janet's father had been chilly. But he desperately needed Judge McMullen to hear him out and render advice. There was no one whose advice he trusted more. Although no longer a member of the judge's family, he still thought of him in terms of friendship and admiration, and missed the times when he had been a welcome visitor at the McMullen farm.

He stopped the car near the front entrance, under the great willow tree that offered shade and respite from the hot Virginia sun, and went up the short walk, treading in the footsteps of the great and famous who had come to knock at this same door.

A stout, aging, red-cheeked woman answered the summons of the antique iron clapper.

Her expression wrinkled with pleasure. "Why, Mr. Fitzsimmons. How nice. The judge told me you were coming. I'll tell him you're here."

"Thank you, Marian."

In a few moments she returned to lead him through the comfortable, high-ceilinged living room and down the narrow wood-paneled hall to the library.

Surrounded by floor-to-ceiling bookshelves, John McMullen, wearing a gray eyeshade, was hunched forward in his chair watching a baseball game on television. A batter swung, the excited voice of the announcer leaped an octave, and the camera whirled to show the outfielder going back in great loping strides with his eyes riveted somewhere in the air. At the fence he made a leap, and came down with the ball in his glove.

"How do you like *that!*" McMullen yelled.

"Not bad," Carter said.

McMullen turned, saw him standing on the threshold, and stood up. "Carter! It's been a long time." He had bowed a bit further to the years; his slight body now appeared frail, his thin face gaunt.

"Much too long for me," Carter said.

"Lucky thing he was playing deep. Or he'd never have got that ball. As it is, he'll have to take a bus back to the dugout." The handshake was as firm as Carter remembered it.

"I've come on rather urgent business."

"Ah, well, in that case," McMullen said, with a glance at the television set.

"It can wait until after the game."

"This isn't one I have to worry much about. We're ahead eleven to two in the top of the ninth." He waved Carter toward one of the two battered leather armchairs. "I'll just turn off the sound, and keep an eye on it from time to time. To make sure they don't hand it away."

"Is their pitching as bad as last year?"

"Worse. I was at the ball park last week and they blew a five-run lead. When the fourth Baltimore pitcher started coming in from the bullpen and we saw who it was, a poor distracted fellow jumped up and started beating his chest and crying, 'Oh, no! *Take me!*'"

Many pleasant afternoons and evenings they had shared at the Orioles' stadium.

McMullen sat down and Carter took the other chair. They made desultory conversation until the last batter grounded out in the top of the ninth inning. Then the judge relaxed and began patiently stuffing tobacco into his pipe. It was a customary preliminary to any discussion, and served the purpose of bridging over the transition from social pleasantry.

"Well, Carter, what's on your mind?"

"Something that concerns the safety of our country."

The judge struck a match and lit his pipe. "Sounds rather ominous."

"I don't know any better way to put it." He leaned forward. "Suppose the President were suffering from a disorder that rendered him incapable of making rational judgments?"

McMullen appeared to be studying the bowl of his pipe. "Hypothesis?"

"Fact."

"What has led you to such a startling conclusion?"

Carter arranged in his thoughts the sequence of events that had taken him to this moment. As he began his recital, he was confident that the description would be enough to convince Judge McMullen. Midway, he was no longer sure. Without the invisible data that supported it—the behavior and other indications of stress—his mere testimony was not enough.

He finished lamely, "I've observed George closely ever since I came home. He's a changed man—obviously disturbed. There's no other way he could do the things he's doing."

McMullen appeared to consider this before he replied gently, "I wouldn't have difficulty rounding up a good many people who would say directly the opposite."

"What about the things I mentioned? Including this so-called Grand Alliance? Don't you agree it would be a catastrophe?"

"Suppose a majority thought he was acting reasonably? What then? Should we declare all those people to be mentally disturbed also?"

"If people had any idea of what he was doing, they would never support him."

McMullen said patiently, "All right, suppose he would not have a majority. That would still make no difference. A President is elected for four years."

"That doesn't give him carte blanche to do anything he wants to. We proved that with other Presidents."

"You've heard of our system of checks and balances."

"It isn't working. Congress and the courts don't even know what he's planning to do."

"They usually don't. A smart President is like a smart pitcher. He doesn't let the batter know what his next pitch is going to be."

"This executive agreement is a clear evasion of the Constitution."

"He wouldn't be the first President to slip a fast one past that sacred document. Want some examples? Abraham Lincoln called up the state militias, spent money not appropriated by Congress, censored the mails, and suspended the writ of habeas corpus. FDR closed down all the banks and ruled the country for a while virtually by executive fiat. Lyndon Johnson and Nixon committed the nation to acts of war for which there was no precedent or excuse in our Constitution. In none of those actions was there a real challenge to the President's power, although there were people who considered those actions fully as irresponsible as you consider George Rushton's."

"Something has to be done."

"What would you suggest? Impeachment?"

"I agree that's out of the question, but isn't there any other way?"

"I'd be neglecting my duty as a lawyer if I didn't point out an alternative—although it exists more in theory than as an actual practical possibility."

"What is it?"

"I believe it is set forth in section four of the Twenty-fifth Amendment. Would you care to read it?"

"Very much."

McMullen brought a volume to his chair and soon found the relevant passage.

Carter read: *Section Four: Whenever the Vice-President and a majority of either the principal officers of the executive department, or of such other body as Congress may by law provide, transmit to the president pro tempore of the Senate and the speaker of the House of Representatives their written declaration that the President is unable to discharge the powers and duties of his office, the Vice-President shall immediately assume the powers and duties of acting President.*

"That seems clear enough," Carter said. "Why isn't it a practical possibility?"

Another expression—almost a new color—had come into McMullen's gaunt features, a calculated glint of pleasure into his eyes. Since his retirement, the judge had lacked for an audience.

"Remember, the President's cabinet is appointed by him. They serve entirely at his pleasure. Do you reasonably expect men in that position to swear in writing that their leader is incompetent?"

"They might, if they became convinced it was true."

"Think of what it would mean—cabinet ministers, not elected to office, would take it upon themselves to reverse the results of a national election. In effect, they'd nullify the votes of everyone who voted for George Rushton as President."

"That's what the amendment provides for, isn't it?"

"There's a further provision to the amendment. If the President claims that he *is* able to discharge his duties, Congress has to assemble within forty-eight hours to decide the question. In all honesty, Carter, how do you think Congress would decide?"

"The President would win hands down."

"Good man. At least you're in touch with the political realities. You put congressmen on that kind of a griddle and they all turn into poached eggs." McMullen clapped his thin hands onto the chair arm. "That reminds me, it must be dinnertime. Why not stay?"

The invitation was not simply a reflex of courtesy; it signaled a closing of the breach. Carter had to clear his throat before he answered, "Thank you, Judge. I'd like that very much."

Over dishes that resembled a Chinese-style dinner, they discussed the Baltimore Orioles' pennant chances. The dining room was cheerful, with cherrywood paneling and a large yellow tapestry that showed a picture of King John being forced to sign the Magna Carta at Runnymede in the presence of his nobles.

"We've come a long way since then," McMullen said smiling as he noticed Carter looking at the tapestry. "But basic problems don't change too much. We're always trying to set some limits on the power of our leaders."

"I still can't accept that once the people put a President into office, they surrender their right to self-preservation."

"That's putting it a bit strong. I agree that some limit ought to be put on the power of the Presidency. But you're taking it too seriously. After all, we've muddled through for over two hundred years with all kinds of Presidents. Strong ones and weak ones, villains and clowns. Bismarck once said that fortune apparently favors drunks, fools, and the United States of America."

"Nobody's luck lasts forever," Carter said.

He left half an hour later, with a promise that he would come soon again. Driving home, his feeling of helplessness increased. It seemed clear to him that his old friend, George Rushton, the man in the Oval Office, was behaving irrationally. But how could anyone set a norm for irrational behavior and apply it to the nation's leader? An attempt to replace the President by the Vice-President and a majority of the cabinet would tear the country apart.

Judge McMullen had put his finger precisely on the difficult point. A patina of logic can be laid over any course of action— and history is proof of it.

The car was speeding past the maple and oak trees on Canal Street when Carter turned on the radio, hoping music would cheer his reflections. Instead, he caught the middle of a news bulletin:

". . . the President's declaration of a national emergency. Acting under the extraordinary powers given him by the new declaration, General Ziffren has ordered a roundup of all subversive elements. Among the first arrested was Jack Elkins, well-known columnist and television personality. . . ."

Carter's hands were clammy on the wheel.

16

Twenty-four hours before it was publicly announced that he was an enemy of the nation, Jack Elkins took the midnight plane to Las Vegas to interview Peggy Delaney.

Peggy Delaney was an overly voluptuous blond pop singer whose popularity had lasted a phenomenal twenty years. Now, with her weight increasing and her looks fading, her popularity had dwindled, although she was still a name in the smaller supper clubs. What interested Jack Elkins about her was the microfilmed record of her medical history with Dr. Thatcher. Of all the records Marty Brokaw had brought back from the Thatcher clinic, hers was the most promising.

At two-thirty in the afternoon, Jack was in Peggy's suite at a hotel. With the aid of two bottles of Veuve Clicquot they got along famously. He noted her appreciation for his massive physique, and he pretended to be fascinated by her life story, which included a brief marriage to a former lieutenant governor of a western state. That being her only connection, however tenuous, to politics, Peggy thought he was mainly interested in hearing about her marriage. He finally got her talking about her career, and she began telling him about the time she had a painful laryngitis.

"It really had me uptight. My throat was killing me, and I had no money because I wasn't working. Then I heard about this doctor who could fix me up."

Elkins poured another glass for her. "What's his name?"

"He's a big shot now. Dr. Marvin Thatcher." She pronounced the name slowly, drawing out the syllables. "The President's very own private doctor."

"No kidding?"

"That's a story I don't want to talk about."

"Did something go wrong?"

She raised an unnaturally arched, pencil-thin eyebrow. "Why are you interested?"

"I'm interested in everything about you."

She touched her shoulder-length, blond pageboy hair. "I don't feel too much like talking."

He admired the ample curves of her body and the white softness of her arms and shoulders. Her full mouth had a rosy gloss.

He smiled. "All of a sudden, neither do I."

When he kissed her, she parted his lips with her tongue and aggressively searched his mouth.

"Now, that's better," she said. "You got anything else to do this afternoon?"

"Not a thing."

"I hate to turn a man out on an afternoon like this."

They went into the bedroom, and he undressed her with provocative deliberate care. She pressed to him in a squirming embrace while his hands kneaded lush full breasts, and her hand moved down to his crotch.

When it was time, he moved onto her slick and flaccid whiteness in bed and she literally pulled him into her. The veins in her neck corded, and her tongue lolled. As the first spasms began, he was startled by the fierceness of her response. When she opened her mouth to kiss him, he was afraid he was going to be devoured.

She tore her mouth away to cry, "Give it to me, ah, give it to me."

Her climax came quickly. He shuddered in uncontrollable depths as the long, lovely feeling began. He pummeled into her. They were bathed in sweat, clutching and straining at each other; he was bruising her with the rough weight of his body.

Long minutes later, she cuddled against him while he sucked at a brown nipple, drawing it in between his teeth.

"Why don't you stay tonight?" she asked.

"You really want me to?"

"You'd be surprised the kind of creeps that try to get me into bed. They don't really care if I'm having fun. All they're trying to do is prove to themselves if they're really AC or DC."

"There can't be that many."

"Most men are latent when you come down to it. They don't dig women."

"Really?"

"I could tell you some stories." And with his subtle encouragement, she did. Anxious to please and amaze him, she told him about some of the lovers she had known while the tape recorder in the inside breast pocket of his jacket on the nearby chair was taking down every word.

She began to giggle and finally just lay back on the bed laughing.

He sat up on one elbow to smile at her. "Tell me more about you and Dr. Thatcher."

"Nothing like *that*. He's an old man."

"You said it was something you didn't want to talk about. What did he do to you?"

"Oh, well, if you really want to know." She waved a hand indifferently. "I'd gone to him with this throat condition like I told you. And for a while he really had me feeling better. I thought he was some kind of miracle man."

"He wasn't?"

Her chuckle was bitter. "I was all right as long as I kept getting regular treatments. But I had to go off on a tour. London, Paris, the works, and all of a sudden queer things started happening."

"What queer things?"

"I got spells. Saw double. Busted out into tears for almost no reason. I really felt beat up emotionally. It got so bad I called him from Paris for help. He sent me something he called a self-medication kit. By the time it arrived things had gotten so bad with me I'd checked into a funny farm. That's where a French doc said he thought my condition was caused by an overdose."

"Of what?"

"Amphetamines. I don't say I'd never touched the stuff—everybody does in this racket—but I'd been clean for months. So it didn't make sense when he ran tests on me and . . . sure enough. When Thatcher's kit arrived I gave it to the doctor to analyze but he said there was only a small amount of amphetamines. Not enough to cause my kind of symptoms. Just the same, he thought I shouldn't use it. And I didn't. I found a French doctor who cured my throat problem without the use of drugs. It was all emotional. Right then I was busting up my second marriage and it got me right here." She put her thumb and forefinger at her throat. "Naturally, 'cause that's where I make my living."

"Did you ever ask Thatcher about the amphetamines?"

"Say, why are you so fixed on Dr. Thatcher?" The razor-edge of purple eye liner intensified the directness of her gaze. "All of a sudden, I don't trust you."

Elkins sat up, propping a pillow behind him. "I'd like a written statement of everything you've told me. And the name of that French doctor so I can get a deposition from him."

"So that's it."

"That's the story I'm after. The President's doctor."

Her full lower lip protruded angrily. "Pack your ass out of here, buster. You think I'd let any of that get in print?"

"I've got it all down on tape anyway."

"You *what?*"

Elkins got out of bed, and from his coat jacket on the chair removed a tiny microphone bugging device.

"A lovely verbal record. Including the boozy memoirs about your love life. I'm not interested in your past, honey. But I am interested in Dr. Thatcher. If he's giving the President the same kind of treatment he gave you, that's news."

"Slimy bastard! Get out of here before I start hollering rape."

"That would sound pretty funny when the cops heard this tape."

"You couldn't be that big a skunk."

He was dressing as he spoke to her. "You don't have to make up your mind right away. How about tonight?"

"I'm working the early show."

He pulled on his trousers and zipped up. "I'll be back to catch your act."

"That's only a couple of hours."

He stooped to adjust his tie in front of a dresser mirror. "When I get your written statement, signed before a witness, and the name of that French doctor, you won't have to worry about anyone hearing that tape."

"Screw you, you lousy blackmailer!"

"Love you too," he said, and went out.

From a pay phone in the hotel lobby, Elkins made a long-distance call to a number that connected with the transcribing machine in his Washington office. He dictated a memorandum: "I'm pretty sure now the President is off his rocker, and Thatcher is at least partly responsible. Peggy Delaney today told me what Thatcher had done to her. I've got it all on tape." He then gave a thorough rundown, including the verdict of the French doctor, and the lab report that showed amphetamines were present although not in dangerous quantities. "My guess is that Thatcher's self-medication kit doesn't have as much amphetamines as he gives in a regular treatment. Naturally, he doesn't want the full dosage used when he isn't around to supervise. Also, it's insurance. If a kit fell into the wrong hands it wouldn't show an illegal amount of drugs. Take this off the reel, honey, and put it you know where." This last instruction was for Adele Moyer, the only one in his office with access to the transcribing machine.

Upstairs in his hotel room, he drew a warm bath and lounged in it. He had no doubt that Peggy Delaney would have mixed emotions thinking back on what had happened in her bedroom. He was also sure she would do exactly as he told her. She would be too scared to do anything else, because she really thought he would go through with his threat to publish those tapes.

He gave himself a quick shave before the bathroom mirror, just to keep the blue shadow from showing. Twice a day for all these years. All that precious time gone to waste. He could have been learning Spanish or something.

When he went into the living room he saw a tiny flashing red light on the telephone. He called the hotel desk and got the message. Please telephone Schuyler 7-7997 as soon as possible. That was Joe Simons's home number. It was after office hours in New York.

He dressed and went down to the lobby, and put through the call from another pay phone.

When Joe answered he said simply, "Jack Elkins. Okay to talk. What's up?"

"The President's going to back Ziffren all the way. But Ziffren isn't waiting. He's starting to clamp down already. Arresting people. One guy is dead. Poor bastard name of Tony Gramalia. The Security Bureau raided his home. No warrant. No identification. Gramalia tried to run and was shot in the back."

"What did they want him for?"

"Supposedly for printing subversive pamphlets. But it turned out he was in the porno business. Something got fouled up. Gramalia's dead, just the same. They're playing rough, Jack. If you're after the wrong story, you can get in real trouble."

"There isn't any wrong story," Elkins said, "if it's news."

When he returned to his hotel room, he thought about it. He'd been expecting something like this. And it wouldn't be the first time it had happened in the good old U.S.A. The Palmer raids had left a permanent scar on the Twenties, and as late as the summer of 1970 a secret police plan had actually been put into operation by Nixon and his Intelligence Evaluation Committee. It had lasted only a short time because J. Edgar Hoover had been unwilling to go along. But Nixon's blueprint for a supersecret police to deal with domestic dissidence might become a fearsome reality under a man like Mark Ziffren.

Suppose Jack Elkins got a bullet in the back.

The thought of his own death moved him, invoked a vision of his youth—Latrobe Street on a soft spring morning, the smooth paths of used brick beneath tall graceful elms, the neat white fences with manicured green lawns and the haughty immaculate houses rising behind them, the well-dressed men and women going to church on a Sunday morning. The vision caused a familiar tight envy—comparing Latrobe Street with the harbor area, with its decaying shacks and broken cement sidewalks and the air of poverty that rose from its shabbily dressed inhabitants. His parents had been honest working poor, not the drinking or the loafing kind, not shiftless whiners—but the kind of faceless people never recognized by the arrogant rich. He could recall his childhood with unsentimental exactness, for it was then that the complex of instinctive resentments had been formed that led him to break out. He still had the old rankling hatreds. When the high and mighty were scalpeled daily in *Elkins's Corner*, he was paying back some of what he owed the cool, cutting snobs of Latrobe Street.

He got ahead in the world by boldness, by not showing fear of anything or anybody, and he had no intention of backing down now. Even Ziffren would not dare to attack a prominent newspaperman, or challenge the power of the press. There were too many ways of hitting back.

Meanwhile, there was a story to work on. For the next half hour he roughed out on a sheet of paper the column he would write about the President's doctor, based on what Peggy Delaney had told him. What he tried to get over in the rough penciled draft was an implication that if Doc Thatcher were treating some patients with amphetamines, then he might be giving drugs to the President too. . . .

At six o'clock that evening he was at a ringside table watching Peggy on the small stage in the lounge of the Hotel Les Diamantes. A few hours had worked a magical transformation. Her shimmering, sequined gown made her figure appear lush, and her new wig was an interwoven embroidered blond tapestry that seemed specially made to show off her glittering jewels.

When she left the stage twenty minutes later, there was enough applause from the early-show crowd for an encore. Before she returned, Elkins left his table to make his way backstage to her dressing room. He was stopped at the stage door by a watchman who said he would have to check with Miss Delaney.

A short time later the watchman came back. "She'll see you now. Third door down."

The door had a silver nameplate: MISS PEGGY DELANEY.

"Who is it?"

"Jack."

The door opened. Peggy was wearing a maroon robe that did nothing to conceal the lines of her ripe figure. A towel was wrapped around the fabulous hairdo, and she had removed most of her makeup. Her looks were definitely frazzling around the edges.

"Come in." She stepped aside, and he went into a small room with two chairs, a dressing table with a mirror lined with small lights, and a screen in the corner.

"You're alone?"

"Who'd you think would be here? You don't trust anybody, do you?" She sat down before the mirror. "I suppose you came for that statement."

"You have it?" He was checking the room. Behind the mirror would be the most likely spot for a concealed microphone. But there was no need to worry. Just be sure not to sound as if he was using coercion.

"You'll have to tell me what to say."

"I couldn't do that, Peggy. It's your story."

She began working in cold cream on her cheeks. "What have you got against Dr. Thatcher, anyway?"

"Me? Nothing at all." Something about her attitude made him uneasy. "Look, if you'd like me to come back later, I will."

A peculiar fixity of smile. "I may not want to say anything."

Looming behind her image in the mirror was the screen at the other end of the room. His attention centered on it.

"That isn't the impression you gave me a few hours ago." He began backing slowly toward the screen. "Think it over, Peggy."

Her eyes flickered at him. "I've been thinking. A lot of people might get the idea that because he's the White House doctor he's doing something to the President. That wouldn't be fair. . . . *Say!*" She got up so hastily that she knocked over a perfume bottle. A cloying fragrance instantly filled the tiny room. "What are you doing?" She reached him before he reached the screen. "Cut it out! You're making me nervous."

"Why?"

"I don't like people barging around in my room."

"Okay. When you've made up your mind to talk, we'll talk."

"What are you trying to . . ."

Her voice escalated into a near scream as Elkins suddenly kicked the screen aside to reveal two men behind it.

"I thought so," Elkins said.

The two men moved into the room. "You're under arrest, Elkins." A coat lapel was turned to show a badge.

"Anybody can buy a badge."

The other man took out a pair of handcuffs.

"Take it easy," Elkins said. "You're going off the deep end."

From the corner of his eye, he saw Peggy half standing, half leaning against the edge of her dressing table. She looked scared.

Her fingers were squeezing one arm until flab bulged under the robe.

"You're coming with us, Elkins." The man with the handcuffs moved forward.

"I'm not going anywhere until I call my lawyer." He shoved the handcuffs away. "Do you guys know what you're doing?" He spotted a telephone on a small table. "My lawyer will straighten you out."

As he started toward the telephone, a rough pull on his shoulder stayed him.

"Keep your goddamn hands off!" Elkins warned.

Something spun him around. He lifted his fist, and something hit him on the nape of the neck. Despite the jarring impact he managed to stay erect.

"I've got a right. . . ."

His breath exploded as a fist drove into his stomach.

"What the hell!" He lunged. He was clipped again from behind and went down to his knees. Then the edge of a hand slammed into his throat and sent him sprawling. He was semi-conscious when his arms were pulled roughly behind him, and a punishing knee dug into the small of his back.

Handcuffs clicked.

"Okay. He won't make trouble now."

17

Jack Elkins's home, a few miles below Frederick, also contained his office. Set apart from the living quarters, the office had rich, dark-grained furniture, caricatures and photographs of the famous on the walls, and a petite young blond seated at a wide, curving desk with an electric typewriter, three telephones, and boxes marked IN and OUT.

She smiled graciously. "Mr. Fitzsimmons?"

Carter nodded. She picked up one of the telephones, dialed a number and spoke into the muted mouthpiece, then hung up.

"Ms. Moyer is busy at the moment, but you can go downstairs if you like."

"Downstairs?"

She indicated a door. "Go right through there and down the flight of steps."

The upstairs office was the visible tip of the iceberg—only the smallest part of the whole. Below, he emerged into a mammoth basement room divided by four long corridors. Lining each corridor were rows of filing cabinets, interrupted at intervals by tables on which were reference books, journals, and magazines. Two girls clattered away on electric typewriters, and in the background a news ticker clacked.

Adele Moyer was at work beside a small computer, feeding pages into its data bank. When she saw him she pulled a switch, and the computer's humming stopped.

She indicated the papers piled on a table beside the computer. "As you see, work goes on. Even when the boss isn't around."

"Have you heard anything more about Jack?"

She took off rimless eyeglasses to stuff them into a pocket of her suit. "Not a word. We can't even find out for sure what charge he's being held on. All we've been told is that it involves some violation of the Espionage Act. That's ridiculous, Mr. Fitzsimmons. Jack doesn't keep secrets from me. If he was doing anything like that I'd be the first to know."

"Have you called a lawyer?"

She nodded. "As soon as I heard about it. He promised he'd take care of everything. Since then I haven't been able to get him on the telephone."

"Busy?"

"He keeps not being in. I got hold of the syndicate lawyer today, but he says there's nothing he can do. The lawyer for the TV network told me this isn't in his field and suggested I get a good constitutional lawyer. I don't know what's happening, but everybody sounds scared."

"I'll get someone to handle it. But first I'd like to know a few things. What was Jack doing when he was arrested?"

"He was in Vegas."

"I mean, was he working on a story?"

"That's confidential."

"I'm trying to help, Miss Moyer. I don't think Jack has much to lose right now."

She nervously fingered the glasses in the pocket of her gray suit. "He was checking out a woman who'd been a patient of Dr. Thatcher's. Peggy Delaney, the singer."

"Why?"

"He thinks there may be a connection between how the President is behaving and the kind of medical treatment he's getting."

On the console of the computer someone had pasted a quotation: *The father of evil is not malice but ignorance.*

"We can dismiss that, Miss Moyer. I checked it and there's nothing to it."

"Don't be too sure. Jack is very thorough. And he knows what he's doing."

The lab test on the vial Carter had acquired at Dr. Thatcher's clinic had convinced him the amphetamine dosage was not harmful. If George Rushton was emotionally disturbed, there had to be another reason.

"Well, there's no use arguing about it," he said. "Our first job is to get Jack out of jail. And I think I know the man who can do it."

Her smile caused innumerable wrinkles in her tanned skin. "It's good to know Jack has a couple of friends. Keep in touch."

He had tentatively arranged to meet Joyce at the medical center during her lunch hour. He called her to say he couldn't make it.

"I feel rotten canceling like this."

"I won't starve. Hospitals specialize in jiffy food machines."

"I'll miss you. That's why I feel rotten."

He arrived at the State Department building and had to wait in the anteroom of Abramson's office. After a while he began to wish he'd had something to eat. He picked up a *Foreign Affairs* magazine and leafed through it.

"Who's with him?" he finally asked the receptionist.

"General Ziffren. He arrived just a few minutes before you did."

"Will they be at it much longer?"

"I don't know. It wasn't a scheduled appointment."

Carter heard raised voices from behind the door of the private office, loud enough to penetrate the soundproofing. The receptionist sat with self-conscious erectness. Carter returned to the pages of *Foreign Affairs.*

After a while the door to the private office opened and Abramson emerged with Ziffren. There were no clues in their expressions to what might have transpired in the office. They exchanged a few quiet words before Ziffren limped away. He did not appear to notice Carter in the anteroom.

Abramson said, "Come in. I apologize for the delay."

"That's all right."

Carter entered and the door closed them into the privacy of the slightly antique-looking office.

"Would you like a drink?" Abramson asked, starting to the portable bar.

"No thanks."

"I'm going to have a Scotch and soda. An hour of Mark Ziffren is about all I can take."

"I gather it was a rough session."

Abramson poured Scotch into a glass and siphoned in soda. "Ziffren informed me that several people in my department would be, as he put it, detained for questioning."

"You can't let him get away with that!"

"He told me he is acting with full authority from the President. At that point I asked him whether he had also been acting with the President's authority when he wiretapped my office and the office of the Vice-President."

"What did he say?"

"That the President has put him in full charge of national security and he doesn't always check out his methods of operation with him."

"In other words, he admitted it."

"He also told me that the new declaration of national emergency gives him power to lock up everyone he pleases—and hold them incommunicado—without interference from the courts."

"Does it?"

"Legally, I don't know. My guess is it allows the President to do almost anything he wants. And if Ziffren is acting in the President's name. . . ." Abramson shook his head wearily.

A few minutes later Carter was in his car speeding toward Judge McMullen's farm in Vanceville. He thought of the judge as something like the great willow tree in front of his house—they both offered integrity and steadfastness and wide-branching comfort.

He found the judge in his backyard, pruning a rosebush.

"Glad you came," McMullen said. "The game is going on soon."

"I won't be able to watch. I suppose you've heard what's been happening?"

"I listened to the news this morning."

"Mark Ziffren's arresting anyone he thinks may be a threat to national security. He claims he has the power to do it under the new declaration of national emergency."

Judge McMullen snapped off another twig. "He doesn't. But the President has. In fact, there's some question in my mind if the President even needed a declaration of national emergency. He could have relied on his inherent emergency power as commander-in-chief."

"I never expected to hear you say that American citizens could be thrown into jail and held without a formal charge or arraignment."

McMullen replied mildly, "During World War Two, FDR rounded up all the Japanese-Americans and put them into detention camps for the duration. And the United States Supreme Court said he was within his rights."

"That happened in wartime."

"From what you told me on your last visit, we may be facing the threat of another war."

"That still doesn't put the President above the law."

McMullen put down the pruning knife. He stood up, holding his back. "Might be an interesting subject for a debate. It seems a number of citizens of this republic hold a contrary view."

"Are you telling me there isn't anything that can be done to protect the rights of innocent people?"

"No, I'm saying there isn't any question in this case of the President being above the law. The declaration of emergency triggered more than two hundred laws allowing the President to take action in many areas without approval of Congress or of the courts."

"That's unconstitutional!"

"In order to challenge it, you'd have to come up with somebody who's been treated unfairly because of it. The courts don't decide questions in the abstract."

"Jack Elkins is being held for gross violation of the Espionage Act. And he's certainly not a spy!"

"Elkins?" McMullen took off his glasses to wipe them carefully. "That kind of man can be bought—and a man who can be bought might do anything. It's only a question of price."

"You know him?"

McMullen nodded. "Indirectly. Some years ago I presided at the trial of an investment company accused of having defrauded thousands of small investors. I saw a pretrial motion supported by an affidavit that Jack Elkins knew about the swindle long before it became public knowledge. He didn't tell what he knew because he was paid a considerable sum of money."

"Why wasn't he called as a witness at the trial?"

"The case was settled out of court. I'll grant you that an accusation isn't proof, but the evidence against him was substantial. At least it confirmed my impression that he is a contemptible man."

Carter realized that his only chance was the bone-bred reverence the judge had for the basic law.

"He may be contemptible, but he isn't a traitor—and that's what he's been arrested for. It doesn't matter what you think of him. It's enough that he's being held on a ridiculous charge, without being allowed to talk to a lawyer."

"What do you expect me to do about it?"

"There are scores, maybe hundreds of people in his predicament.

Defend him. You have to start somewhere, so start with Elkins. If you can establish that he's being held illegally, it will apply to everyone else."

"I don't practice law any more. If I did, I would not welcome a client like Mr. Elkins."

"You told me once that justice doesn't deal in personalities."

"A lawyer deals in clients. He isn't required to defend anyone he doesn't want to. I grant you that when I was in active practice I didn't defend only those clients I approved of. But I never took a case where I didn't believe my client was in the right." He mopped perspiration with a handkerchief and smiled. "I was not always correct in that belief."

"Elkins needs a lawyer who really knows constitutional law. Someone who can make this a test case."

"There are hundreds as qualified as I am."

"There isn't anyone with your reputation and authority."

"It's pretty hot out here," McMullen said. "Let's go inside and have a lemonade. And I'll make a few phone calls. There's time before the game."

He made the telephone calls from the library. When he hung up on the last, his mood had changed. "You weren't exaggerating. Right now there seems to be quite a number of Americans sitting in jail, God knows where, charged with God knows what. We'll have to do something about that."

Before they left the house, the judge consulted his address book. In it he found the unlisted telephone number of Charles Deckter, an old friend and former confederate on the district bench. He put through a call and, speaking quickly in a voice bright as a young man's, explained the situation. Apparently Deckter at the other end expressed surprise because McMullen said, "I'm calling you beforehand, Charlie, so you can verify what I've just told you. I'm coming right over."

Carter drove, and Judge McMullen asked him to turn on the radio so they could listen to the ball game.

"It helps me to concentrate," he said.

Carter kept his attention on the rear-vision mirror. Soon a gray sedan appeared about a mile behind him. When he sped up, so did the sedan. When he slowed down, the gray sedan kept a discreet distance.

McMullen said, "You're driving erratically. It's distracting. Is that three and two on the batter?"

Charles Deckter lived in a two-story stone farmhouse a few miles from the outskirts of the Capitol. As the car passed through high walls onto the grounds, Carter was relieved. For some minutes he had seen no sign of the gray sedan.

Charles Deckter heaved himself ponderously out of an easy chair. He was wearing a faded blue bathrobe with a tear visible beneath one shoulder. He had a long, sagging, mournful face.

McMullen shook hands, then Carter did. The justice's handshake was large and fleshy.

"You didn't waste any time getting here," he said to McMullen. "I just hung up on my last call. Seems like you had it right, John. The man's being held. Been there since yesterday. No charges, no arraignment, not even a lawyer. This is the first time I've heard of anything like this in peacetime."

"What are we going to do about it, Charlie?" Judge McMullen demanded. He was like a small aged terrier snapping at a Basset hound.

Deckter sat down again with the slow paunchy movements of a man not accustomed to being rushed. "Apparently, the orders came from pretty high up, John. Maybe we ought to find out what's at stake before we mess in."

"The thing at stake is the Constitution of the United States. Charlie, if you don't sit right down and dictate a habeas writ, you're not fit to sit on a federal bench."

"You always were able to see the right and wrong of things faster than anybody, John."

"We can't have police going around and willy-nilly throwing citizens into jail."

Deckter looked dubious. "How about a simple visitation order? That'll let you see your client—if he is your client."

"No use beating around the bush—not when the fundamental law of the land is circumvented."

"The President has declared a national emergency. He can suspend the rights of habeas corpus if he wants to."

"If he does, we'll fight that through the courts, too."

"All right, John." Deckter sighed gustily. "If you're going to jump into a vat of boiling oil, I guess I have to go along."

McMullen rubbed his hands together. "Now you're talking. This ball game is just beginning!"

In a cell-like furnished room Jack Elkins sat fuming, rubbing chafed wrists where the handcuffs had been put on too tightly. His head ached and his shoulders were sore from having been wrenched behind him.

Nothing was in the room but the cot on which he was sitting, a basin, and a toilet. He was in shirt-sleeves and trousers. When they brought him in they had taken away his jacket, shoes, watch, wallet, keys, and money.

How long ago? It must have been hours.

A young man entered the room. He had an outthrust jaw and his shoulders were squared like those of a military man. He sat near Jack on a folding stool he brought with him.

The young man did not identify himself, but began at once with questions. Name? Occupation? Names and addresses of living relatives?"

Finally Elkins looked at him sourly. "Look, I'm not applying for a job."

The young man was not amused. "Among your belongings, Mr. Elkins, we found a recording device. Can you tell me what it was used for?"

"I'm a reporter. R-e-p-o-r-t-e-r. I like to know exactly what was said to me. That way, no one can claim later they were misquoted."

"Were you recording anyone at the time you were apprehended?"

"I don't like that word. *Apprehended.*"

The young man had a patient, businesslike air. "You were in
the dressing room of a Miss Peggy Delaney. Isn't that so?"

"If you know, why ask me?"

"Why did you feel it necessary to record Miss Delaney's conversation?"

"I'm not going to answer any questions until I see a lawyer."

"Let's try again. Isn't it true that you expected to get a written
deposition from Miss Delaney concerning her experiences with a
certain Dr. Marvin Thatcher?"

"You heard that on my tape."

"You also wanted a deposition from a certain French doctor
who treated her for a throat ailment."

"You're the one with the answers."

"We also found this in your coat pocket."

Elkins recognized the rough, handwritten draft of his column
based on a statement he never got from Peggy Delaney.

"I was just trying to work up a story."

"In other words, you wrote this without knowing what she'd
swear to."

"I was getting a jump on it. In my business you have to meet
deadlines."

The young man returned the clipping to his pocket. "Why were
you trying to discredit Dr. Thatcher?"

"I wasn't."

"We have proof you were assigned to this job in order to create
rumors about the President's health."

"Don't be a damned fool."

The young man got up and walked a few steps away. Then
he suddenly turned. "You are part of a conspiracy against the
President!"

"Me? I'm a newspaperman. I don't know anything about conspiracies."

"You don't understand the serious trouble you're in. The charges against you involve the highest national security."

"Somebody's got to be kidding. If I could only talk to the right person, I could clear up everything."

"By pretending you're a journalist? It won't work, Mr. Elkins. We know who gives you orders."

"Transcontinental News Service? The ABC television network? When you've got an audience of thirty million people, nobody bosses you around much."

"You have the ability to subvert public opinion. That makes you a valuable tool."

Elkins rolled the word tentatively around in his head. "Tool?" He brushed his face as if a snowflake had settled on it. "What the hell are you talking about? Listen, you officious little ninny. You can't treat me like a second-class citizen. I've got friends in some pretty influential positions. When they hear about this. . . ."

"Your friends will be surprised to discover that you're a paid agent of the Soviet Union."

"A what?"

"You made a trip to Moscow some years ago."

"What of it?"

"During your visit you had a personal interview with Brezhnev. That courtesy isn't usually extended to visiting American journalists."

"I'm not your usual journalist."

"You also had a private meeting with Vladimir Rokkosky."

"That's no secret. I wrote half a dozen newspaper columns about it."

"It lasted almost five hours. Was it during that meeting you were recruited?"

For an instance Elkins contemplated swinging at him. "Recruited to do what?"

"Political propaganda for the Soviet Union."

Elkins made a sound through gritted teeth. "If you repeat that to me on the street I'll bash your goddamn teeth in. Look in my wallet. You'll find that I'm a reserve officer in the army, a member of the Boston Patriots, a registered voter, an Elk, a Mason, and last but not least an officer of the Newspaper Guild. If that doesn't add up to you, let me spell it out. I'm a damn sight better American than you are!"

The young man was neither impressed nor perturbed. He said evenly, "It's my duty to inform you that you will be detained indefinitely for questioning."

"I want to see a lawyer."

"You will not be allowed to communicate with anyone."

"What the hell is this? I've got a right. . . ."

"That's what you don't understand, Mr. Elkins. People like you don't have any rights. Not any more."

On the drive toward Washington, D.C., with Judge McMullen, Carter again glimpsed a gray sedan following him. It was only a glimpse, and when he looked again the road behind was clear.

There was a delay at the Federal Building, where no one would admit being authorized to accept a writ.

McMullen's eyes narrowed as he confronted the tall, spare, bald man in an office of the Security Bureau. He said with crisp impatience, "You hold a writ of habeas corpus signed by a federal district judge. You have to honor it. There is no higher authority than our Constitution, and the right of habeas corpus is embodied in that document."

"I really can't do anything until I consult with my superiors. . . ."

"Use your common sense, man. Habeas corpus. Produce the body. You don't have any choice."

"I'll get back to you with an answer as soon as I can."

"Do you realize that what you're doing, keeping a man in custody without preferring charges, is against the law? Against the *basic* law?"

The man shook his head wearily. "I'm sorry. I don't make the rules around here. As soon as I can talk with someone. . . ."

"I'm not going to stand around waiting until you do. While you go through your channels, or whatever you call it, I want to see my client."

Confronted with the assertive certainty of Judge McMullen, the man visibly weakened. "Well, I don't see any harm in your just visiting with him."

"You can't prevent me from visiting him. I'm his lawyer."

Tapping the writ against the back of his hand, the man glanced at the telephone. Then apparently deciding there was no hope of getting through channels quickly enough to resolve the dilemma, he reluctantly made up his mind.

He rose, went to the door, and called a guard. "Take these two to Elkins."

When the door opened to the bare room, Jack Elkins was reclining on the cot with a pillow propped behind him for support. He jumped up when he saw Carter enter, then gave a puzzled glance of semirecognition at the man with him.

"You've heard of Judge John McMullen," Carter said.

"I sure have." Elkins offered his hand.

McMullen did not appear to notice. He took a chair, brought it up to the cot, and indicated with a gesture that Elkins should sit down again.

"Apparently you're in serious trouble," he began without preamble. "Violating the Espionage Act is nothing to sneeze at. It could put you away for life. What did you do to get yourself in such a fix?"

"Not a damn thing!" Elkins exploded.

"Do you have a lawyer?"

"You're the first person I've even been able to talk to."

"Would you like me to represent you?"

"I'd have to be nuts not to. And I'll pay any price you name."

McMullen said, "Before I agree to anything, I'd like one question answered. What was your involvement with Southwestern Investment Company?"

Elkins looked startled. "That's way out of left field."

"Do I have to jog your memory?"

Elkins fingered his lower jaw. "The statute of limitations must have run out on that one. I have your word that nothing I say will be repeated to anybody?"

Judge McMullen gave a quick small nod.

"Okay, I don't mind admitting I knew about it before anybody else did. They came to me with an offer I couldn't refuse. All I had to do was forget to publish."

"And so you took a bribe?"

"Yes and no. I grabbed the money, sure, and kept my end of the bargain." Elkins's wide mouth creased. "But somehow or other, the facts found their way to the office of the federal commission. I'm not saying how."

Huddled in his chair, McMullen stared at him. "That's just what I would have expected, considering your character. However, what's important is that you told the truth when you might have lied. I can defend a scoundrel when it involves a principle as important as this. But I couldn't defend a man who lied to me."

"Thanks a lot." Elkins looked both amused and irritated. "What happens next?" he asked.

"There are more questions I'll have to ask, but those can wait. First I have to arrange a hearing on the charges. I'd better get started on that right away." He stood up, a shrunken, frail little man who somehow seemed formidable. "Coming, Carter?"

"Not yet, Judge, if you don't mind. I'd like to talk a few minutes to Elkins."

McMullen left the room. The guard who had opened the door looked at Carter questioningly, but Carter waved him away.

"Spunky little guy," Elkins said. "Got a tongue sharp as a razor but says what he means."

"I'm glad you told him about the investment case. I want you to level with me, too."

"Sure."

"What do you know about Dr. Thatcher that I don't know?"

"I don't get it."

"You were in Vegas running down a story on him. Obviously, you still think there's some connection between Dr. Thatcher and the way the President's been. . . ."

"What gives you an idea like that?" Elkins's eyes made the smallest possible shift. "I was just checking up to find out if Thatcher is as good a doctor as he's cracked up to be."

This was such an obvious evasion that Carter was about to reply indignantly. Then he saw Jack Elkins tug gently at the lobe of his ear. It suddenly occurred to him that the room might be tapped. Others might even be watching.

"Well, I'm glad that's all there is to it, Jack," he said. "I was a little worried. Personally, I've got a lot of faith in Dr. Thatcher."

"You're probably right. I've got to admit the leads I was following never came to anything. Even that bitch in Vegas. She was just leading me on so she could hop into bed with me."

"It'll all straighten out, Jack. As soon as they find out you weren't really up to anything."

"Yeah, I hope so. Meanwhile, if you see Adele Moyer, tell her I'm fine, they're treating me okay, and to keep things going until I get back."

"I'm sure she will."

"I'm not really worried. She knows as much as I know," he said with a slight additional emphasis.

The door opened again; the tall bald man was standing there with the guard.

"Time is up," he said harshly.

The guard moved into the room to emphasize that this was a command.

Carter stood up. "Don't worry," he told Elkins. "Judge Mc-Mullen is handling your case from now on."

He stepped outside. The tall man was annoyed and did not mind showing it.

"It was a mistake letting you in here. I really got scrubbed for it. Your friend isn't going to get very far with his writ either."

They walked along the gray corridor.

"Judge McMullen was telling you the truth," Carter said. "You have to honor a writ of habeas corpus."

The man said bitterly, "All I know is nobody gets in to see Elkins. And he stays put. Those are my orders."

At the end of the corridor near the elevator, two men were standing, neatly dressed clean-shaven men with unlined faces.

"Mr. Fitzsimmons?"

"Yes?"

"Would you mind coming with us, sir?"

"Where to?"

"General Ziffren would like to see you."

"Oh? Suppose I don't care to see him?"

"He's waiting for you in his office. I hope you will be cooperative, Mr. Fitzsimmons."

"And if I'm not cooperative?"

He was rather enjoying this. It was like watching computers that were not programmed to receive certain kinds of information. Their distress signals were blinking. Finally, one man pushed a button for the elevator, and the other stepped forward and took Carter by the arm.

"General Ziffren has an office right here in the building," he said as matter-of-factly as a tour guide.

When they opened the door to Mark Ziffren's private office it was late afternoon and the descending sun had turned a bank of clouds crimson. Ziffren was not at his desk. He was standing in a corner beside a bird cage on a five-foot pedestal, feeding bits of cracker to a green parakeet.

"Mr. Fitzsimmons to see you, sir."

"Very well. You can go."

The two men departed, closing the door.

Ziffren fed the last of the cracker to the parakeet before he turned to Carter with an apologetic smile.

"It was a favorite of my wife's. I keep it around to remind me of happier days." He brushed the crumbs off his fingers. "You don't mind if I come directly to the point, do you?"

"I imagine you must be pressed for time, with all the people you have to arrest."

Ziffren replied without anger, "You don't approve of me, but that isn't important. People on the same side don't have to like each other. What is important is to find out exactly whose side you're on. That's particularly true in view of your close relationship with the President."

"You're free to ask questions."

"Thank you."

"I'm also free not to answer—if I find them out of order."

"Let me begin by saying I know you were visiting Jack Elkins. You even brought Judge McMullen into his case."

"Your information is correct."

"Are you aware that he is charged with a very serious crime?"

"As I understand it, General, he hasn't been formally charged with anything. He hasn't even been allowed to see a lawyer."

"The case against him is being developed."

"You can't put a man in jail and then set about finding out if there's any reason to put him there. Innocent until proved guilty, remember?"

"We have every reason to expect results. These are extraordinary times. We can't treat everyone with kid gloves."

"The kid gloves you refer to are a basic part of our Constitution."

"And this is a question of national security. Which is more important?"

"It isn't an either/or question, General. The Constitution is a large part of our national security. But *you* don't really believe in the way a democracy operates."

They were interrupted by a squawk from the parakeet's cage where the beady-eyed bird was rocking sidewise, lifting one claw and then another.

After a moment, Ziffren said coolly, "I want to know why you've chosen to ally yourself with those who are the enemies of your country."

"I don't think I have. You seem to think patriotism is some kind of personal possession something you're privileged to share with others."

"You don't acknowledge that there is a conspiracy in this country?"

"I do."

"Well, then?"

"The conspiracy exists on a much higher level than the fanatics of the John Brown Society. It's people like you."

Ziffren's lips looked as if fastened with a zipper. "If you're helping people like Jack Elkins, then you're a fool or a traitor. There's no other explanation. He's the spokesman for a group of revolutionaries. He's working side by side with those who are trying to create anarchy in this country."

"Well, you'll have the devil's own time proving it. In court you dot *is* and cross *ts*. You can't bring charges supported by no evidence."

"We'll have his confession by then."

"I doubt that very much."

"It will be a confession that, in your words, dots all the *is* and crosses all the *ts*. We're going to keep him in custody until he tells everything he knows. Including who he's working for, how much he's being paid, and the names of other people involved in the conspiracy. And we're not going to allow any legal tricks to stop us. The writ of habeas corpus Judge McMullen got isn't worth its weight in scrap paper. There is no way that the judge who issued it, or any other court in this land, can enforce it."

"I don't think President Rushton is prepared to go quite that far."

"I know what you're thinking. You'll go to Rushton and persuade him I'm a dangerous man. Well, I wouldn't count on that succeeding, Mr. Fitzsimmons. The President no longer believes you're his friend."

"Why wouldn't he? I am."

"Certain facts have been brought to his attention."

Carter's eyes narrowed. "What have you been telling him?"

Ziffren appeared to bite off every word. "What you've been doing in Nigeria the past few years. And the contacts you've had with the Russians there."

It was quite unbearable to be civil to this man, but Carter managed to ask, "Are you trying to say I'm a spy, too?"

"Anyone who gives aid and comfort to the enemy is the enemy. A hard rule, but a necessary one."

Something seemed to tear loose in Carter. "General, if you believe that, you ought to be taking sanity pills."

He had the satisfaction of seeing Ziffren's effort to control his own anger.

"Let me warn you. If you make any further attempts to aid Elkins, I'll see to it that you end up in jail with him."

"Why don't you arrest me now?"

"Time enough for that."

Carter went down in the elevator with stabbing sensations going through him. Fascist zealot! *Son of a bitch!* Everything around him seemed to be in an orange haze. He had never been so furious.

In lighted cabinets lining the lobby walls, awards and citations and exhibits were on display. One cabinet was devoted to an exhibit on Communism. A placard warned that "THE COMMUNIST PARTY IN AMERICA IS A TOOL OF MOSCOW," offering a free brochure on request: "How *You* Can Help Fight Communism." In a Communist country, the exhibit noted, "secret police can arrest you at any time."

As Carter left the Federal Building he saw the gray sedan parked a half block away. He moved angrily toward it, but the sedan swung out and was soon lost in traffic.

18

"On your call to the President," Chad Oliver said, "is there anything special you'd like to talk to him about? If you could give me a clue, I'd be glad to pass it on to the President."

Carter, holding the receiver at his ear while lying full length on the bed in his hotel, said, "Listen, if he can't talk now, could you ask him to call me back when it's convenient?"

"I'll ask, but it doesn't look too promising. You're about twenty-seventh in line."

"Tell him it's something very definitely in his interest."

Carter placed another call, this time to Claire. Again he was forced to go through the ritual of the press office and clearances, only to be informed that the call could not be put through at present.

"Is Mrs. Rushton in the White House?"

"I really can't say, Mr. Fitzsimmons."

"Will you leave a message and ask her to call me as soon as possible?"

By then it was time to pick up Joyce at the medical center. She had been working late because of a mild flu epidemic. He drove into the parking lot, a wide area of striped asphalt bordered on the south by trees. The day's heat hung like an invisible blanket in the night air even though the temperature had fallen to reasonable levels. The hospital's broad facade was alive with lighted windows. At a wide glass corridor window, an old man was sweeping up in ultramarine light—his slow motions were like someone moving under water.

At eight o'clock Joyce came down the gray, stone steps at the side entrance. She looked tired.

"Do you mind if we don't go anywhere special for dinner?" she asked.

"What would you like?"

"Maybe a hamburger."

In the red plastic chain restaurant, he discovered that more than weariness was afflicting her mood. A young flu patient who was an epileptic had had a seizure, swallowed his tongue, and suffocated.

"There isn't enough trained help to look after all the patients. If we'd made a regular room check, it wouldn't have happened."

"I know how you must feel. But it wasn't your fault."

"Doctor error. Nurse error. Plain and simple neglect. It happens all the time. This was different. The boy had been kicked around all his life."

"You knew him?"

"I didn't have to. He was black."

Her mood was like a sullen undercurrent that ran against his own concerns.

"Look, we've both had some awful days, and this isn't the right time to say it. But if I don't I may never get up my courage again." He was suddenly rendered speechless, like an actor who has forgotten his next line.

She looked at him curiously. "Yes?" she said.

The distant sound of taxis, trucks, and passenger cars from the avenue was muted, but his voice barely carried over it. "Will you marry me?"

She had picked up her coffee cup, but she put it down. "It wouldn't work," she said, and gave a quick shake of her head for emphasis.

"Why not?"

"We're better off to leave things the way they are. I've seen too many people who were happy together get married and become enemies."

"That wouldn't happen to us."

"You remind me of my father. He wasn't very practical either. He loved my mother, but when the pressure got too much she cracked. She left him—and broke his heart."

His reply was tenderly mocking. "Which of us is going to do that to the other?"

"Neither. Because I won't let it happen." She gave a small hurt sound. "Oh, why couldn't you let it alone? I'm not going to marry you. I can't. I'd be trying to prove something, like my mother. Offering herself on the altar of racial equality."

"Cut that out."

"Please take me home."

Seated in the car outside her apartment house, he took her face in his hands and said urgently, "Listen to me, darling. This isn't a perfect world. But it happens to be the only one we've got, so it has to be good enough. We can handle any problems. Believe me."

She stared with wide-open eyes, and for a moment he actually felt suspended in their motionless translucence.

"I'd like to believe you," she said, "but I just don't know how." Then she opened the car door and ran into the lobby.

At the hotel, Carter spoke to the girl at the switchboard who told him there had been no calls. He had left his number for George or Claire Rushton to call back. In his room, he placed a long-distance call to Vanceville. When Judge McMullen heard that the writ was not being honored, his voice shook. "By God, this is still a country of laws! And we'll prove it to 'em!"

Just before midnight, the telephone rang.

"Hello."

"Carter Fitzsimmons, please."

"Speaking."

"This is Marie Rushton." Her voice had a faint betraying tremor. "Something's happened and I must talk to you. Can you meet me?"

"Now?"

"I couldn't leave now. Tomorrow morning, when Dad's busy in his office."

"Where?"

"Would it be all right if I came to your hotel?"

"Of course. I'll be waiting for you."

"About ten?"

"About ten."

After breakfast at a Hot Shoppe, Carter returned to the hotel. At exactly ten, there was a hesitant rap on the door. He opened it to a girl with a strange hairdo, dark glasses, and a shapeless linen dress.

"This is my walking-around-Washington outfit," Marie Rushton explained, entering, and glancing at him with what appeared to be a nervous apology. "No one ever recognizes me in it."

"I imagine there must be a Secret Service man tailing not far behind."

His remark unsettled her in an extraordinary way. Her jaw muscles tightened, her fingers plucked at the dark tinted glasses, and she burst into tears.

He stood for a moment bewildered, then recovered enough to help her to a chair.

"I'm so sorry," she said in a shaky voice. "I didn't mean to do that. In fact, I'd made up my mind I wouldn't. I came to you because I don't know anyone else to turn to. It's about my father."

"What about him?"

"We had a quarrel last night. He flew into a terrible temper."

"What were you quarreling about?"

"Because I was talking with someone. The White House security guard I told you about, William Chalmers. We weren't doing anything. Just having a conversation. It's the first time we've ever *talked*."

"And then?"

"We were right outside father's study on the second floor. Father came out and saw us together. He didn't say anything right then, but afterward he was awful."

"What exactly did he say?"

She looked at him helplessly, as if to convey the inadequacy of words. "He accused me of carrying on with a man behind his back. He kept saying, 'How could you do a thing like this to me? How could you?' I hardly knew what to tell him."

"Then?"

"He asked how long it had been going on." Her mouth remained open to speak, but for seconds no words came. "And when I asked him, 'What?' he said, 'This cheap affair.'" She bit her lip. "Then he said he was going to p-punish me. I couldn't even answer him. I just ran back to my room."

She might be concealing part of the story. There might be more reason for George Rushton's anger than she was admitting. But if she had contributed in any way to his outburst, would she have come to him now seeking help, acting as if her whole world was collapsing?

"Have you told your mother?"

"I don't want to upset her. And there isn't anything she could do about it."

"You'd better talk to her, Marie."

She shook her head. "It wouldn't do any good. She knows. She just doesn't want anyone else to find out."

"To find out what?"

"How bad the situation is. We've both seen it happening. At

first it was just that he couldn't sleep. He was getting up at any hour of the night and making notes or reading. He never slept through. And he was always so tired in the morning. We couldn't talk to him about anything. . . . He wasn't listening. . . . And there were other things."

"Like?"

"I was with him on *Air Force One* when he began talking, and it was as if he couldn't stop. Chad Oliver interrupted with papers to sign, but then he started in again. The same thing happened when he started dictating. He went on and on. I remember the girl who was typing it up on one of those special typewriters— you know, seventy words to a page—and she finally began to look at him. Another time, Mother and I were with him in a motorcade and he stopped the car and got out to talk to people lined up at a fence. He asked them questions and never let them answer. When one of his aides tried to get him to move on, Dad shoved him away roughly."

The Institute of Psychiatry paper had called it the "pressure of speech," a compulsive need to talk coupled with an inability to listen.

"Does Dr. Thatcher see him often?"

"Every day. Usually only for a few minutes."

"I think your father needs other medical help. Your mother might convince him to see another doctor. Would it be all right if I discussed this with her?"

"She's been keeping it to herself. She needs someone."

"Can you arrange for me to meet her—alone? Without your father knowing?"

"I don't know. I'll try."

Carter waited in a sitting room on the second floor of the White House. The closet doors were covered with bright *trompe l'oeils*, the rug was a vivid geometric design, and he caught a gleam of china, a shimmer of crystal, on the shelves of a burnished wood cabinet. It was an exquisite room.

"Mother decorated it herself," Marie said. "She has lovely taste."

"Where's your father?"

"Resting. He had another bad night, and Dr. Thatcher had to come over. I'd better go now. Mother's due in a few minutes."

Claire came into the room soon afterward. She sat stiffly in a chair before a low table with a silver tea service. She seemed composed, but did not radiate her usual warmth and charm.

"Would you like tea?"

"No, thanks."

"Marie told me you wanted to see me about something important."

"It has to do with George."

She gave him a simple, questioning look.

He said, "He isn't well. I think he should have a complete physical examination."

"Dr. Thatcher . . ."

"I mean by someone other than Dr. Thatcher."

She seemed to withdraw a little. "I don't really think that's necessary."

"Have you heard what happened last night?" He told her of the episode with Marie and the White House guard while she listened intently, her face white. "You don't believe Marie was doing anything wrong, do you?" he asked. "Anything that would call for that kind of emotional outburst?"

"Of course not. But you have to understand the circumstances. If he's upset, a thing like that can happen. I'm surprised Marie would have come to you with such a story." Carter looked at her steadily, and her assurance faltered. "Perhaps it's because she knows you're such a good friend. . . ."

"George's condition is serious."

"We mustn't make too much of it. No one understands the enormous terrible burden. . . ."

He brushed past the flimsy defense. "You can't explain it away like that, Claire."

"He's exhausted. I've tried to make him rest, but he doesn't seem able to." She blinked, looking at him as if she were not quite sure whether to go on. "One night he got up at four in the morning. Told me that he'd thought of something he had to write down. When I went out to get him, he showed me what he'd written. He thought it was very important—page after page filled with illegible scrawls. Not a single word. I told him I would keep the notes for him until morning. He never asked for them, and I destroyed them." Her eyelids fluttered down, weighted with the load of memory. "I don't know what to do any more. He's at the end of his strength, and there's always some new crisis. It isn't fair!"

"He's asking too much of himself. The job may be more than he can handle." He paused. "Maybe more than any one man can handle."

"But he's trying so hard. Trying to find solutions to problems beyond my understanding." He face seemed to become smaller and more pointed. "When I think of what he went through to get where he is. . . ."

Carter was reminded of a bright morning in Lagos, high white clouds sailing lazily past while he sat on a veranda reading the copy of *The Making of the President* that had just arrived in the mail. George Rushton had campaigned with the incredible drive and vitality that had always been his hallmark as a politician. Seven days a week he had toured the nation—one day in Massachusetts, another in Georgia, a third in Tennessee, a fourth in Texas—shaking hands at factory gates, walking through tobacco and cotton fields to greet the farmworkers, visiting wealthy ranchers in their fine houses. He campaigned for weeks, months. Television and radio speeches, party rallies, parades. Like Harry Truman in 1948, he went out to meet the people where they lived and worked. He was up before six o'clock in the morning to greet men on their way to work, making a street tour before lunch, attending a business luncheon to make a speech, and then on his way again to visit lofts and offices, supermarkets and taverns,

fire stations and police stations. At closing time he would be back
to greet workers leaving their factories. After a shower and a
change of clothes, he would begin his nightly routine of house
parties and political rallies, interviews and speeches, visits to local
campaign headquarters to speak with the volunteers addressing
envelopes or calling people on the telephone.

Yes, George Rushton earned his job. But how much nervous
vitality, emotional strength, had been drained out of him in the
process?

"I don't mean to frighten you, Claire, but he can't go on like
this."

Her eyes were suddenly wide and bright, as if she had removed
dark glasses.

He continued in a strong but gentle voice. "You must persuade
him to see another doctor. I know how he feels about Dr. Thatcher. But another opinion can't hurt."

"Dr. Thatcher says it's his neck injury. And it's getting better."

"Do you think it is?"

The query was hardly needed; he merely had to stay in touch
while fear worked its way to the surface.

"Suppose it turned out to be . . . as you say . . . something
serious? Would he be able to keep . . . going?"

"We'd have to wait and see exactly what the trouble was."

"If he had to . . . resign . . . that would kill him."

"Claire, he isn't only your husband. He's President of the United
States."

She stood up. "He's still my husband. I won't do anything to
hurt him." She led the way into the wide second-floor corridor
lined with grim Catlin portraits of Indian chiefs. "As it is, he
thinks everyone is against him."

"Is there anything I can do to help?"

"No, not you."

There was a surprising, slight stress on the last word.

"Doesn't he trust me?" he asked.

"George thinks—oh, I know it's silly—that you and I. . . ."

"Yes?"

She answered with a terrible weariness, a swimmer whose strength is gone and can struggle no further. "He's sure it's happening again."

He knew what she meant, but he wanted to compel her to say it.

"What is happening again, Claire?"

"That we've . . . fallen in love with each other."

"Did he really suggest that?"

"I told him how foolish it is."

"When did this happen?"

"Last night. He heard you'd called, and he wouldn't call back. He wouldn't let me call you either. We had an argument. He kept on and on, and finally began insisting that I still . . . cared for you." She turned to him with quick apology. "Of course I *do* care . . . but not in that way."

"Has he ever been jealous before?"

"Never."

"Claire, you must get him to see someone other than Thatcher. This isn't normal. Can't you see it?"

"That isn't for me to decide. He's fought his own way to where he is, and I can't help anyone throw him down. Even if everyone turned against him, I wouldn't. I'd never do *anything* that might cost him the Presidency."

Her face was as stern as the Catlin Indian portrait on the wall above her head.

Carter met Joyce at the opening of an African art exhibition at the National Gallery. The paintings were on loan from various governments, and there had been a private showing for important government figures before the public display.

But Carter's thoughts were occupied elsewhere. He clung to the idea that George Rushton was simply reacting badly to tension. All he would need was a safety valve—a rest, some means of recreation. George liked sailing, but hadn't done much recently.

Carter knew he was deceiving himself.

Joyce had stopped in front of a painting that showed bare-chested black workers digging irrigation channels in a field.

"What did she think of the native art?" Joyce asked.

"Who?"

"The sister of that plantation owner. The one you knew in Lagos."

"Oh. Her."

"You said she was an artist."

"Yes—and she taught black artists, but she didn't think much of them. She told me once that if I were making a survey of Nigeria's economic resources, not to bother including their art."

"Was she good?"

"She painted enormous still lifes. Very enameled." He had one in storage, a green vase of flowers on a table with yellow and brown fruit. Disciplined and lifeless. "To tell you the truth, the native artists she was teaching were more talented than she was."

"I'm glad. I don't like her."

They moved on. His thoughts wandered to George Rushton sitting up at 4 A.M. writing page after page of gibberish.

He said to Joyce, "You never did mention what was in that vial. Outside of amphetamines."

"Niacin and calcium glutonate, as I remember."

"What effect would they have?"

"Probably make anyone who took them feel better, at least temporarily. Niacin is a vitamin, and calcium glutonate produces a nice warm flush but very little else." She gave him a slightly quizzical look, but did not force the issue.

Later, when he dropped her off at her apartment, his thoughts returned to the problem. If drugs were not causing George's condition, what was? One man certainly knew the answer—Dr. Marvin Thatcher.

In his hotel room, he placed a call to Jack Elkins's home. Adele

Moyer's gruff, near-masculine voice turned mellow when Carter identified himself.

"We all appreciate what you're doing for Jack. What's the latest word?"

"Judge McMullen is trying to get an arraignment. As far as I can make out, they don't have any reason to keep him in custody. That business about violating the Espionage Act is too ridiculous to hold up in court."

"I hope we'll get him back soon."

"Judge McMullen is doing his best."

"In the meanwhile, if there's anything I can do to help. . . ."

"There is. Thatcher was the story Jack was investigating when he was arrested. I'd like to see what you have in your files on him."

She sounded doubtful. "You'd have to limit your inquiry strictly to Dr. Thatcher. And I'd be there to make sure."

"That's fine with me."

When Carter arrived at the office in Jack Elkins's home, Adele was working at the desk. She had a manuscript before her on which she was making penciled inserts. As she snipped off part of a page to paste onto another, she looked up and saw Carter in the doorway.

"Jack never lets anyone see his files," she said. "I'm making an exception in your case."

He followed her down to the subterranean room with its long rows of filing cabinets. It took only seconds for the computer to search its data banks and to begin typing a list of coded references to Dr. Thatcher, with the filing cabinets and indexes where the original documents could be found. At the end of ten minutes the computer was still typing.

Carter asked impatiently, "Suppose I want to see a particular item now. How do you turn this thing off?"

"No need. It will continue listing while I order any item you want."

"Let's start with Thatcher's professional credentials."

She pushed a key for facsimile transmission, and tiny lights on the console blinked irregularly. Electrical impulses traveled to the commanded conduit, and within seconds, on a small transmission screen on the side of the console, appeared a list of the universities where Dr. Marvin Thatcher had studied, his service in the Korean war, and a record of a subsequent year of study in Germany.

Carter asked, "Who is this Dr. Heinrich Bruening he studied with? Any information on him?"

The computer printed out a brief paragraph. Dr. Bruening had established himself in general practice in 1953 in a fashionable area of Berlin and died there in 1964. Dr. Thatcher had made a last trip to Germany to visit him. An obituary notice from a weekly news magazine noted that Dr. Bruening had been criticized by some of his colleagues because he prescribed medicines not to attack underlying causes of illness but merely to make his patients feel better. It also mentioned that Dr. Bruening had once worked with the doctor "whose treatment of Hitler by glucose and drugs was responsible for the decline in the Führer's nervous stability during the war years."

"Remember," Adele said, "this is raw data. You can't believe it all."

"Let's go back to Thatcher," Carter said. "Try another. The one called 'personal data.'"

The computer blinked and began typing out a report on Henry and Miriam Thatcher, married in Kwangsi province. Henry Thatcher, a doctor, had been executed in Nanking in 1936 for having failed to save the life of a Japanese officer. Shortly afterward, his wife emigrated to the United States, bringing her young son. She died some years later. There followed a record of Dr. Marvin Thatcher's own marriage to a woman of South Korean parentage whom he had met in a hospital during his term of military service in Korea in 1951. The computer showed a facsimile of a report on Dr. Thatcher's application for an army discharge based on a "service-connected" injury. Elkins added a note that the discharge did not mention that it had been for nervous ex-

haustion brought on by overwork and by the horrors he had wit-
nessed. On Thatcher's return to the United States, his wife gave
birth to a daughter. They were divorced five years later, and his
wife returned to South Korea with their child. Here was appended
another personal memo from Elkins concerning "temperamental
differences" remarked upon by those who knew the couple, apparently growing out of Dr. Marvin Thatcher's compulsive work
habits and neglect of his family. "A man obsessed, literally obsessed
with the fear of failure," said one doctor who had served with
Thatcher in a Baltimore hospital.

Understandable, Carter thought, in a man whose father was
executed for having failed.

The final item was a transcript of notes Elkins had dictated
following his interview with Greg Hazen, the male attendant
who had worked in Thatcher's clinic. Elkins appended a comment: *Deal carefully with this material.*

Adele Moyer said, "It's like the unclassified files of the FBI.
That's one reason we don't like anyone else to see it."

"How about this one? Dr. Thatcher's patients."

The computer responded with notes that Jack Elkins had filed
following interviews with several patients, including Paul Jayson.

"They all think well of Dr. Thatcher. Isn't there anyone who
doesn't?"

"That's all we've coded into the computer."

"How about his trip to Las Vegas? Peggy Delaney was Thatcher's patient, too."

She hesitated. If there was more, she was reluctant to admit it.

"The last thing Jack told me, Miss Moyer, was that I was to
come to you for any information I needed."

She weighed this for several moments. "Jack did make a call
from Las Vegas," she said finally. "He called directly into the
transcriber. I haven't coded anything or put it into the computer."

"May I hear it?"

She shrugged. "I hope I don't get into trouble for this."

Upstairs, in Elkins's living quarters, she opened a closet and chose brown saddle shoes from a rack that held at least thirty pairs. She removed the shoe tree from a left-foot shoe and flexed up the rear of the tree, revealing a small wooden cubbyhole from which she extracted a tightly wound roll of recording tape. She took it to a recording machine, and Carter heard the sad story of Peggy Delaney—and why the medical kit did not contain as much amphetamines as one of Thatcher's regular treatments. A final link snapped into place.

The tape ran out.

"Thank you, Miss Moyer," Carter said on his way out. "And don't worry. Jack won't mind your breaking the rules this time."

19

Adolph Abramson lived on the outskirts of Falls Church, not far from the junction of Routes 50 and 7, in a white colonial house with an immaculate green lawn and stately trees.

Sara Abramson, a tall spare woman with a solemn engaging manner, met Carter at the door. He knew only a little about her. She was a few years older than Adolph, had managed a tea shop, and once published a volume of poetry. Her first husband had been killed in the Second World War, and she had not married Abramson until she was almost forty.

"Dolph is in the music room," she said. "You can hear him." He heard a piano. "He has so little time for music nowadays."

"He's very accomplished."

"You must tell him so."

They waited in a high-ceilinged corridor until the playing stopped with a bravura flourish.

Sara Abramson gestured toward the door and turned quietly away.

Abramson was seated before a well-burnished baby grand, his hands loosely in his lap, his head bent forward slightly toward the keys, as if listening to the sounds he had been making.

Carter cleared his throat.

Abramson looked at him vaguely; then his glance sharpened.

"Carter!" He pulled the lid down over the piano keys and stood up to shake hands. "Can I offer you a drink?"

"No, thanks. This isn't a social visit. There's something I need to talk over with you."

"You sound as if it's bad news."

"It is. And you're the only man I can think of who's in a position to do anything about it."

"I don't know what position I'm in these days. Most of the time I feel as though I have both feet planted firmly in midair. But tell me what's on your mind."

"George Rushton has to step down from the Presidency."

"What?"

"If he won't resign, he has to be forced out."

"On what grounds?"

"That we can't afford a man in the job who's no longer in control of his reasoning faculties."

"That's a pretty extreme statement, Carter. Do you have the facts to back it up?"

Carter began by telling Abramson about the tape he had just heard in Elkins's office. To this he added other evidence: the episode with Marie Rushton, George Rushton's unmotivated jealousy of Claire, and the curious effects of Dr. Thatcher's treatment on some other patients. He included Dr. Vancell's unwitting diagnosis of Felix Ordiveras's symptoms and what he had learned from the Institute of Psychiatry report. There was no need to buttress his argument with examples of Rushton's actions on the governmental level, for Abramson was all too aware of them.

Abramson listened carefully until Carter finished his recital. Then he said, "But even if you're right—and George Rushton's mind and personality have been affected—it would take a great deal of proof before the President could be forced to resign."

Sara Abramson appeared in the doorway. "This is your day for visitors, dear. The Vice-President just arrived, and wants to talk to you right away."

"Just the person I'd like to see."

"I came from the White House," Elmer Tate said as he entered the room. Then he stopped, looking at Carter Fitzsimmons. "I didn't know you had company."

"Would you rather I left?" Carter asked.

"No, that's all right. What the hell. I've got enough worries to go around."

Abramson said, "What's on your mind, Elmer?"

"I was in conference with the President—getting last-minute instructions about what to do while he's in Peking—when we got word that the Russian ambassador, that fellow what's-his-name. . . ."

"Stolypin," Abramson said.

"All those Russian names are jawbreakers. This Stolypin wanted to see him right away. Said his government wanted him to deliver a message."

"Unusual," Abramson murmured. "He would ordinarily have come to me first."

Carter had never seen Elmer Tate look so serious or determined. "He told the President his government has come into possession of some very secret information. A memorandum of agreement between President Rushton and the Chinese Premier."

"How could he have gotten hold of that?"

"It didn't come from our side. Stolypin practically admitted that. So it's the Chinese."

"What did the President tell him?"

"What the hell else could he tell him? He said the damn thing was a forgery."

"Did Stolypin believe him?"

"I couldn't tell. He answered nice and polite. Said he was glad to hear it, and then asked assurances that what the memo said wasn't true."

"What did it say?"

"I'd better not reveal that."

Carter said, "The memo indicated that agreement had been reached on a full military alliance between the People's Republic of China and the United States. And the details are going to be worked out during the summit meeting in Peking."

"How do *you* know about that?" Elmer Tate demanded.

"George Rushton told me."

Abramson sat unmoving, but there was shock in his voice. "What did the President say when Stolypin asked for assurances?"

"He exploded. *Boom.* Straight up. Said he wouldn't let himself be browbeaten. I kind of enjoyed listening to him tell that Russian off."

"We may not enjoy what happens next," Abramson replied.

"What do you think will?" Carter asked.

Abramson took a minute to answer. "Well, assuming they believe the alliance is really going ahead, they might strike first and try to eliminate China's nuclear power. All they need to do it are seventy to a hundred missiles carrying two-thousand-pound nuclear warheads."

"If we're allies with China, we'd never let 'em get away with that," Elmer Tate said.

"They'd have to anticipate that. And guard against retaliation from us."

"How?"

"A simultaneous attack on us. They'd have plenty left in their nuclear arsenal for that."

Elmer Tate said harshly, "They'd be committing suicide."

"They may believe that an alliance between the Chinese and the United States means a slower and more agonizing death for them."

"You really think it could happen?" Elmer Tate had stopped, facing away from the fireplace, his hands clasped behind his back.

"Are those Commies stupid enough to blow up the world?"

In a whisper that seemed somehow undimensional, Abramson replied, "You know, Count Tolstoy used to believe there was a green stick, buried at the edge of a ravine in the forest at Yasnaya Polyana, on which the magic words were inscribed that would destroy evil in the hearts of men. Sooner or later, each of us learns there is no such green stick."

Elmer Tate answered impatiently, "What kind of jackass talk is that, Dolph? Green sticks! What we've got to do is get it through the Russians' thick heads that we're not looking for a war with them or with anybody else!"

Carter was struck by the contrast between these two men. Abramson had the qualities of mind and spirit needed to be a chief executive, which Elmer Tate did not. But Elmer had the will to act.

"Only George Rushton can persuade the Russians of that," Abramson said. "And he isn't going to."

A screw of tension tightened in Carter's head. "That leaves us with one alternative," he said. "Rushton has to be replaced as President."

Elmer Tate stared at him. "What the hell country do you think you're living in? This isn't some goddamned banana republic. We've had our belly full of replacing Presidents!"

"Carter has other reasons for what he said, Elmer," Abramson said. "I think you'd better hear him out."

Slowly, carefully, Carter repeated what he had told Abramson. He spoke, uninterrupted, for twenty minutes. As he finished, Elmer took out a handkerchief and mopped his face.

"That's the damndest thing I ever heard. You believe it, Dolph?"

"I'm afraid it's true."

"Then we better get off our keesters. We can't just sit around talking about it. If George Rushton isn't in charge of things, that son of a bitch Mark Ziffren will be. And time's running out. The President goes to Peking the day after tomorrow. If he's—damn it, I can't even *say* it!—if he's hooked on something, he sure as shot-puttin' shouldn't be trying to match wits with the Chinese!"

"What do you suggest, Elmer?"

Elmer Tate looked from Abramson to Carter, and sat down abruptly. "It's a damn stinking situation," he said.

"I have a suggestion," Carter said.

"Let's hear it!"

"Others in the cabinet must have noticed the way George Rush-ton has been behaving. Talk to them. Tell them what's going on."

"Where will that get us?" Elmer Tate asked skeptically.

"It might confirm their suspicions. If you get enough people worried, you might get together and make him postpone his trip to Peking."

Elmer Tate shook his head. "It'd be like throwing confetti at a tank."

"It isn't much of a chance," Abramson agreed, "but I can't think of anything else."

Carter said, "I'm also going to pay a personal call on Dr. That-cher. He's got to tell the President to consult some other doctor."

"Why would he do that?" Elmer Tate asked. "Especially if you're right about what's going on."

"I'll persuade him," Carter answered grimly.

The starchy young receptionist said, "I'm terribly sorry. Dr. Thatcher isn't accepting unscheduled appointments."

Carter said, "Tell him it's about the President."

She plugged into her switchboard and spoke guardedly.

Then she said, "Go straight down the corridor, turn, and there are steps leading up. The door at the top leads to the doctor's private living quarters."

As he was climbing the steps the door opened, and Dr. That-cher asked, "Is anything wrong?"

"I'm afraid so, Doctor."

He entered a large living room with a handmade tile floor that gave a fine coppery glow. There were tall bookcases, and paintings on the walls that varied from baroque miniatures to retablos to primitives.

"The President? Why didn't he call me? Why send you?"

"He didn't send me."

Thatcher looked puzzled. "The girl told me. . . ."

"I know what she told you."

Dr. Thatcher closed the door. "You'd better make yourself clear."

"The President is a very sick man. You know that already, so don't make me go into the symptoms. If people close to him have noticed, you must have."

"Noticed what?"

"I'm talking about impaired judgment and emotional instability. If you deny that, then I can only assume it's because you're responsible for it."

"I?"

"And you're trying to cover up, as you did with Felix Ordiveras."

"What *are* you talking about?"

"Dr. Vancell gave me the clue. When I described Ordiveras's symptoms, he thought they might be those of a man suffering from prolonged dosage with amphetamines."

"Ordiveras was *my* patient."

"Dr. Vancell didn't know that. He didn't even know Ordiveras's name."

"A diagnosis without having met the patient. I see."

"Ordiveras died before I could take him to another doctor for an examination. His body was cremated before there was a chance for an autopsy. But other little things began to add up. Jack Elkins has quite a dossier on your former and present patients. Surprising how many of them suffered some sort of emotional derangement."

"Mr. Fitzsimmons, this is really the most extraordinary conversation." He had developed a slight stammer. "If you have nothing further to say, I must ask you to leave."

"You're going to tell the President he's too ill to make the trip to Peking. And bring in a specialist to consult about his condition. Or Jack Elkins is going to publish what your treatment has done to many of your patients."

"If the President wishes to consult another doctor, that's his business." The voice firmed with decision. "As for his going to Peking, I will not say anything to him about that."

"Doctor, you force me to mention something I hoped I wouldn't have to. Does the name Greg Hazen mean anything to you?"

"He was an attendant at my clinic."

"And he has quite a story to tell about what went on here."

Thatcher regarded him narrowly. "What did go on?"

Carter hesitated, feeling himself start to flush, but he repeated the story Greg Hazen had told of the orgies in Thatcher's private clinic. As he finished, blood was tingling in his ears.

Dr. Thatcher's tone was tolerant. "I'm surprised that a man of your reputation would stoop to this. That story is completely false. But even if it were true, you would never be a party to its publication. I am a better judge of character than you give me credit for."

"I'm prepared to do whatever I have to, Doctor. This isn't just a matter of your reputation, or even the President's health. It's a question of world survival."

For just an instant something surfaced in Thatcher's eyes, a look that Carter thought he could identify. Uncertainty. The first crack in what had appeared to be a wall of granite. With renewed hope, Carter explained some of the dangers that the President's trip to Peking might entail. At the end, Thatcher seemed to be watching him as an accused man might watch a prosecutor presenting evidence.

"I am a doctor, Mr. Fitzsimmons. I don't know anything about politics. I have no way of knowing if you are right when you tell me these things."

"You know the President's condition. Do you think he should

be trusted now to make judgments on which the peace of the world may depend?"

"I am a doctor," Thatcher repeated. "I only try to help people."

"The way you helped Felix Ordiveras?"

"Ordiveras was a very ill man. There was nothing I could have done for him." He raised his hand, reaching out as if he had something important to say and his hand was preparing the way. "As for the President . . ." he began.

The telephone rang.

Dr. Thatcher let it ring a second time, then picked it up. "Thatcher speaking." In an instant his voice became tense. "Keep him quiet and as comfortable as you can." He hung up. "It's the White House. They need me at once."

"My car's outside," Carter said. "I'll drive you."

Thatcher hesitated, frowning slightly. "Mr. Fitzsimmons, did you believe that story of Greg Hazen's?"

"No, I did not."

Thatcher studied Carter's face before he gave a quick nod. "All right. We will trust each other from now on."

20

A guard pressed the elevator button and turned to Carter. "My instructions are to take the doctor in alone."

As the elevator doors slid open to reveal the cubicle of walnut paneling and brown carpeting, Carter asked, "Will you let me know how he is?"

"Of course," Dr. Thatcher said.

After a few minutes the guard came back. "Mrs. Rushton and her daughter are in the living quarters. They'd like to see you."

The elevator took them to the second floor, and Carter followed the guard down the cavernous hall to double doors marked with the Presidential seal. He entered alone. Inside, Claire was seated on a sofa and Marie was with her.

Claire's hand was bandaged to the wrist.

"What happened?" he asked.

"I'm all right." She was quite pale. "I cut my hand."

"How?"

Marie said, "He was going to kill himself. She tried to stop him, and that's how she got hurt."

She told the story, with occasional interpolations from Claire. ("It wasn't as bad as that, dear." "It was really more of an accident.") It seemed that George had been brooding over the episode in which he found Marie with the Secret Service agent, William Chalmers. He accused Chalmers flatly of being paid by Rushton's enemies to infiltrate the White House. Chalmers felt it his duty to report the incident to Claire, who asked him not to inform his superiors.

Claire went to see George, and was subjected to a violent harangue in which he rebuked her for allowing "intrigues" to go on right under his eyes while he was busy struggling on all fronts with secret enemies. "You should have known what they were up to!" he shouted.

"And then?" Carter asked.

Claire bit her lower lip and gave Marie a pleading glance, but her daughter answered with a tiny shake of her head and continued the story: George had demanded that she be brought to him to confess her role in the affair. "How long has it been going on? Don't deny you're involved with him!" Marie, close to tears, nevertheless did deny it. That only infuriated him. He shouted that "because he's gotten you into bed, he needn't think he can force you to marry him!" Claire tried to intervene, pointing out that he seemed determined to think the worst, but all she accomplished was to direct his fury against her. He accused her of having known about Marie's affair for some time and not telling him because she was afraid Marie might turn the tables and reveal Claire's own "liaisons"! "It's bad enough that my daughter is sleeping around without my wife betraying me."

Marie concluded the narrative. "Father accused her of carrying on with you, Carter. He said you were simply using her to land yourself an important government job."

Claire looked down, unable to meet Carter's eyes. He sensed the reverberations of shock that must be going through her.

She spoke listlessly. "I don't think he really meant. . . ." Then she fell silent, her attention focused inward.

Carter said gently to Marie, "You were going to tell me how he tried to kill himself."

She began in a hushed whisper. "He'd been rocking back and forth, clutching both hands to his neck. I couldn't quite make out what he was saying. But it was something to do with enemies trying to get at him through his family. . . ."

"What happened then?"

"He was up on his feet, ranting, and Mother told me to call Dr. Thatcher." She stopped, staring with blank inert bewilderment. Her slouched shoulders refused to straighten and her fingers slowly tightened on the chair arm. She had reached her breaking point.

Claire recognized what had happened and took over. "When I told Marie to call the doctor, George was saying incoherent, meaningless things, a jumble."

"Can you remember anything?"

"He said I was trying to punish him for something that had happened a long time ago. 'What more do you want?' he kept asking." Her gaze met and held Carter's. "Suddenly he jumped up and strode to the writing desk over there. He said, 'If it's my blood you want, you can have that too!' He grabbed the letter opener from the desk and I realized what he might do. I ran toward him. . . ."

In a detached, almost clinical way Carter observed the scene through Claire's eyes.

"I don't think he'd have actually tried to. . . . It was my fault. I caught his arm and held on, and shouted for Marie to get help. He tried to push me away. . . ."

The despairing, grotesque struggle.

". . . And it was then I cut myself . . . and fell. . . .

The soft tumbling down into nothingness, the slow touch and slide on the carpet.

"It was an accident," she said.

"Claire," he said, after an interval, "he's going to need care, a long period of recuperation. . . ."

She gave him an odd look, and murmured, "I don't blame George."

For too many years his emotional life had been bound up with those candid transparent-looking blue eyes and that softly sibilant little-girl voice. In some indissoluble way she was linked to his very soul.

He asked brusquely, "Do I have your permission to call another doctor?"

She sat rigidly, unseeing. "I'd have to talk to George."

"He can't make that kind of decision, Claire."

"He'll be all right if we stand behind him. He needs our support." She looked vaguely at her bandaged hand. "No one really understands."

"Trust me," he said. "I know a very good doctor. And I only want what's best for George. Let me handle this now."

She turned slowly toward her daughter. "What do you think?"

Without looking up, Marie said, "Carter should do whatever he thinks best."

Carter placed the call from a telephone in the study. Dr. Vancell was not in his office and not at home.

He told the White House operator, "Locate him as soon as you can."

In less than two minutes the phone rang.

"The doctor is on the telephone now."

He waited for the switchboard to click off. "Doctor, this is Carter Fitzsimmons calling from the White House. Are you where you can't be heard?"

"I can hardly hear myself. I'm at the opera. They called me out during the overture. I'm in the lobby and they've got the door open and this is Wagner."

Through the telephone he now heard soaring, swelling melody.

"A very important person has been taken quite ill. A violent episode, with an attempt at suicide. His wife would like you to join Dr. Thatcher for a consultation."

"Is this Dr. Thatcher's patient you're talking about?"

"Yes."

"I'll come right away."

As soon as the call was completed, Carter phoned Abramson to explain the situation briefly. "You can find an explanation for the press that won't sound too alarming."

"Indisposition," Abramson said, "is a word that covers a multitude of complaints. Well, I suppose this means the summit meeting will be postponed."

In his own mind, Carter was forecasting beyond this to a special meeting of the cabinet at which the whole question of the President's competence could be brought up. A majority of the cabinet could at least compel him to take an indeterminate leave under proper medical supervision.

He hurried down to the northwest gate, where he had to wait a few minutes for Dr. Vancell to arrive in a taxicab.

Carter paid the driver. "I apologize for taking you away from the opera," he said to Vancell.

Dr. Vancell said, "To tell you the truth, I can't stand Wagner. Everybody sings too loud and the women wear breastplates."

They returned to the White House and took the elevator to the second floor. They were directed to the room where Claire and Marie Rushton were sitting with Dr. Thatcher.

Thatcher said, smiling benignly, "Good to see you again, Dr. Vancell. I was just telling Mrs. Rushton how much better her husband is."

Carter felt a strange numbness. "He's better?"

"Oh, yes, much better. A slight case of exhaustion," Thatcher said, addressing himself to Dr. Vancell. "I gave him a sedative to assure a good night's rest."

Vancell turned to Carter. "Obviously, my services aren't required here."

"Don't go yet, Doctor." Carter looked imploringly toward Claire and Marie for support.

Claire asked Dr. Thatcher, "Can I see my husband now?"

Thatcher nodded. "He'll be getting sleepy in a few minutes, so don't stay too long."

"Would you like to come too, Carter?" Marie asked suddenly.

"I'd like to very much," he said.

George Rushton was sitting up in a chair in the bedroom with a pillow propped behind him. He smiled at Claire and Marie as they entered, but when Carter appeared behind them his smile faded a little.

"I guess I gave everybody a pretty good scare," he said. "Thatcher says I've just been working too hard." He held out his hand, and Claire went over and put her hand in his. "I'll take a real vacation after I get back from Peking," he said.

Carter said, "George, you shouldn't dismiss what's happened too lightly. You've had a bad experience. You need time to get over it."

Tight lines formed about George's eyes. "Dr. Thatcher's handling my case," he answered shortly.

"I realize that, but. . . ."

"Right now, if you don't mind, Carter, I'd prefer to be alone with my wife and daughter."

Carter shrugged resignedly. He said good night, and when he emerged Dr. Thatcher and Dr. Vancell were chatting together.

The whole situation was impossible. There was nothing left to try but audacity.

Carter went over to them. "You say it's nervous exhaustion, Doctor?"

"Yes."

"How does that diagnosis account for the fact he tried to kill himself a little while before you got here?"

Dr. Thatcher paled slightly. "I believe that's exaggerating things somewhat. Both the President and Mrs. Rushton told me it was an accident."

"That isn't what his daughter says."

"She may have misinterpreted what she saw."

"Or she's the only one telling the truth."

Dr. Vancell was regarding Carter now with clear irritation. "In any event, this has nothing to do with the reason I was brought here."

"It does, in a way, Doctor."

"May I ask how?"

"I read that paper by the Institute of Psychiatry. And I think the President's illness fits into one of the four basic categories of people who've been suffering from an overdose of drugs."

Dr. Vancell was startled. "That's very hard to believe. I'm sure Dr. Thatcher would know if—"

"He knows all right."

Vancell glanced at Thatcher, who shook his head slightly.

"I'm afraid you may have read too much into it." Dr. Vancell's face was set in disapproving lines.

"Doctor, won't you at least see the President? Won't you give him an examination?"

"Certainly not. I am quite willing to accept Dr. Thatcher's diagnosis of the case. And I hope he understands I only came tonight because you assured me that I'd been asked for as a consultant."

"You were, by Mrs. Rushton and her daughter. But they apparently changed their minds."

Thatcher said quietly, "I should tell you, Doctor, that Mr. Fitzsimmons is a very good friend of the President's. I'm sure he had only the best motives for asking you here."

Dr. Vancell glanced at his watch. "I'll catch a cab. I can probably get back in time for the fourth act." He did not appear too pleased at the prospect.

The elevator took Dr. Vancell down.

"Believe me, everything is under control," Dr. Thatcher told Carter reassuringly. "He'll sleep through the night. And feel much better. Oh, perhaps a bit nervous—a secondary relapse is only to be expected."

"But there's nothing to worry about," Carter said acidly. "Because you'll be here first thing in the morning if he needs further attention."

Thatcher answered softly, "Yes. That's true."

"And Peking? Are you going to let him make the trip in this condition?"

"Mr. Fitzsimmons, I know how upset you are, but you must leave the President's care to me. I am his physician. If it's any comfort to you, I am going to urge him to postpone the trip for a few days."

"And if he won't?"

Dr. Thatcher shrugged. "There is only so much I can do. After all, he is the President."

Carter made another phone call to Abramson to tell him of the drastic change in the situation. Then he left the White House. He did not ask for his car downstairs. Instead, he strolled slowly around, past the southwest gate. He was trying to clear his mind, to order his thoughts in a way that could accept final defeat.

A siren's wail cut through the soft hot August evening. A fire engine appeared, turning at headlong speed, with a fireman swaying on the back like a drunken man. Carter watched the engine caterwaul down the avenue, flashing its panic-red signal.

Then the nerves in his skull seemed to light up like a darkened theater suddenly illuminated. He felt as if he were sitting in the last row of the balcony, and a faraway voice was speaking to him from the stage. He passed the east gate again, and the White House policeman on duty looked at him curiously. Carter's knees felt weak. He walked on slowly, lost in reflection. He was confronting a previously unthinkable possibility, a solution that ran counter to all past and present loyalties and even to previous concepts of what was honorable and right.

A quote leaped from his memory: *The hottest places in hell are reserved for those who, in a period of moral crisis, maintain their neutrality.* He would have only himself to blame if he stood by and did nothing. That was intolerable; everything else was merely unwise or reckless.

He went to the nearest telephone booth. Joyce was at home. She was pleased to hear from him until he told her why he was calling.

He had to be very forceful to persuade her he really meant what he was saying. Then: "How long will it take you to get to the medical center?"

"Twenty minutes. But, darling, this is crazy. As soon as you think about it, you'll change your mind."

"There isn't any other way. Leave now, and I'll be there as quickly as I can."

He had to wait a moment for her reply.

"I'll want a chance to talk to you first."

He walked along the north fence on Pennsylvania Avenue, returning through the northwest gate to the White House. The plan, still dimly formulating, was seeping through his mind like water finding its way through underground channels. It depended on Dr. Thatcher's still being there.

Half-hoping he would be too late, he met Thatcher coming out.

"Doctor . . ."

"Yes?"

He extended his hand. "I owe you an apology. I sincerely hope you'll forget everything I said."

Thatcher's hand met Carter's warmly. "All is forgiven. George Rushton is your friend. I understand perfectly."

"May I drive you back to your clinic?" Carter gave a slight rueful shrug. "Call it a form of penance."

"Of course." Thatcher's cherubic face brightened further. "No penance is necessary. And I'd be delighted to have your company, Mr. Fitzsimmons."

The White House attendant brought the car around to the driveway, and Carter squeezed down into the front seat. Dr. Thatcher got in beside him, putting his black medical bag into the rear. He leaned back. "It's been a long, exhausting day," he said.

Carter drove past the gate and the policeman in his cubicle, and turned left on Pennsylvania Avenue. He turned left again on New Hampshire, heading toward the medical center. "I have to pick up my date for the evening first. I hope you don't mind. She's a nurse at the medical center. And an old admirer of yours. Joyce Hatton."

"Oh, yes." Dr. Thatcher was smiling. "I remember her well."

Carter pulled into the driveway of the hospital's emergency entrance. Joyce was waiting. She had slipped on a light coat. She came quietly to the car, and said, "Can I speak to you a minute?"

"Can't it wait?"

"It really can't. Hello, Dr. Thatcher."

"How are you, Joyce?"

Carter got out, and they moved a short distance out of hearing. An ambulance pulled into the dark driveway, and white-coated interns and attendants busily unloaded a stretcher and hurried inside.

"Did you bring it with you?" he asked.

"Yes," she said. "But I've never heard of anything so insane."

"Trust me."

"How can I?"

"We can't let the President go to Peking," he said. "And this is the only way I can think of to stop him."

In her light coat with a kerchief holding her hair, she looked like a young girl except for the anxious lines around her eyes.

"I'll do anything else you want," she said. "Anything. But please don't make me do this."

He had a sudden impulse to yield. *We don't need this. What does any of it have to do with us? With two people who ought to be thinking about getting married and making a life together?*

As if he had been speaking his thought and she had been listening, she said, "There's so much we should talk about. . . . Darling, I've had a chance to think. I was wrong. We belong together. I don't want to lose you."

"We're going to be okay," he told her, and gave her hand a

hypocritical squeeze. He knew he was not telling her the truth.

They went back to the car. "Sorry we took so long," Carter said to Dr. Thatcher. He buckled his seat belt while Joyce got quietly into the rear. When he risked a glance at her in the rear-vision mirror, she met his gaze calmly. Good girl.

He drove on for a few minutes before he said loudly, "Dr. Thatcher, there is one thing I'd like to ask you."

As Thatcher shifted his attention toward him, he gave a puzzled grimace. He turned. Joyce had the hypodermic needle in his arm.

He quickly yanked his arm away. "What was that?"

"He didn't get all of it," Joyce said.

"What are you doing?" Thatcher put his hand over his arm. "Let me out!"

He made a confused movement toward the car door. Carter tried to hold him, but using only one hand, it was hard to keep control of the wheel. Carter guided the car to a wavering stop near a curb.

By then Dr. Thatcher had the door partly open, and his struggle to free himself had become frenzied. But Carter was much stronger and managed to hold him while Joyce coolly administered the rest of the injection.

"It's nothing that will hurt you, Doctor," she said as she returned the hypodermic to its case. "Don't be frightened."

"What . . . what was it?"

"Sodium Amytal." She put the hypodermic case into the pocket of her coat.

Thatcher's mouth made a small "oh" of alarm. He lunged for the open door of the car, but the seat harness held him, and so did Carter.

"*Why?*" Dr. Thatcher asked. He was breathing heavily.

Carter reached across to pull the door closed. "I don't want you to keep that appointment with the President tomorrow morning." The car pulled away from the curb. "That's the only reason we're doing this."

Dr. Thatcher fumbled with his seat harness.

"Please don't, Doctor." Joyce leaned over the seat to pull his hands away from the buckle.

Thatcher's lips trembled. "Oh, my God." His stiff resisting movements became sodden. The angry lines in his face began to iron out. "Let me go," he said faintly. "I won't tell . . . police." His head appeared to wobble, and he made a vague bewildered gesture. Then his eyes rolled up into their sockets until the sclera was exposed, and his breath congealed into a sigh.

Dr. Thatcher snored gently.

On the way to the mountain cabin Carter tried to explain. He told Joyce briefly what had happened since he visited Dr. Thatcher at his clinic and the emergency call came from the White House. She sat quietly, listening, and when he finished she gave him a long, dubious glance.

"I suppose it still sounds a little crazy," he said.

"More than a little."

"The important thing is, as long as I have Thatcher, President Rushton will be in no condition to leave for Peking. There'll be a relapse tomorrow morning. It will be worse if Rushton doesn't get another of Thatcher's timely treatments."

"Suppose you're right? What then?"

"They'll be forced to call another doctor. And we'll find out the truth about his condition."

Her eyes narrowed in speculation. She looked at Dr. Thatcher, his face pink with sweat, his chest rising and falling with each slow breath. "He'll come around in a few hours. How long do you expect to keep him?"

"As long as I can manage."

"By force?"

"I don't think it will be necessary. There's no phone in the cabin. And no way he can escape."

"You realize it's kidnapping."

"You take the car and go back. If anything goes wrong, I'll swear you didn't know what I intended to do."

Thatcher's head was lolling, and she turned it gently to rest against the seat back. "*He* will tell quite a different story."

"It will be his word against ours."

"They'll know about us and our meeting at the medical center. I had to sign a slip to get sodium Amytal from the drug closet. That will support Dr. Thatcher's story.

Cars approached steadily along the other side, and their headlights seemed to peer inquiringly at him.

"What would you do in my place?"

"I'd consider turning around and taking Dr. Thatcher back. He did make some mention of not telling the police."

He shook his head. "What happens to me—even you—isn't important. "I don't have time to explain everything. But if the President goes to Peking, the consequences could be too terrible to think about."

"The consequences of what we're doing aren't going to be too pleasant either." Thatcher stirred with a tiny restlessness and, watching him, Joyce asked, "How long do you think it will be before they connect you with his disappearance?"

"I don't know."

"It'll come a lot quicker if you're among the missing. They'll be looking for you *and* him. People will know you went to the White House with him. You'll be the first person they'll want to question."

He turned off the highway and onto the road that led up the side of the mountain. The car's headlights illumined the darkness for only a short distance ahead.

"I can't help that," he said.

"It would make more sense if you take the car and go back."

"What about you?"

"I've got more sodium Amytal. I can keep him resting nicely. When he wakes up, he won't even have a hangover."

He stopped the car near the woodshed. The cabin was on his left.

"I can't leave you here. It isn't fair."

She asked, "Do you have provisions in the cabin?"

"A lot of canned goods."

"And water?"

"A well."

"Then there doesn't seem to be much of a problem."

"What about the hospital? Won't they expect you at work in the morning?"

"Call in. Say I'm sick."

He felt adrift, confused, drained even of self-anger.

"I'm tired of making decisions," he said.

"Let me make this one. They won't connect me with his disappearance. And if they question you, you can invent a story that will throw them off the trail."

She was more clear-eyed about the danger than he—yet willing to stand by and try to salvage what could be salvaged.

"This was all my idea," he said. "It should be my responsibility."

"Let's move Dr. Thatcher inside. Then show me where to find the canned food. I'm hungry."

21

Adolph Abramson had never quite accustomed himself to life in Washington, D.C. By contrast, his term as governor of Pennsylvania had been quiet and uneventful.

After their move to Washington, Sara did her best to maintain a quiet home atmosphere, but the odds were hopeless. The job was too demanding. As secretary of state, he had to transact business with more than 170 countries, keep a watch on the affairs of the United Nations, travel to foreign lands, and with what time and energy remained had to maintain close working relationships with other government agencies that had responsibilities in foreign affairs—agencies ranging from the Pentagon and the USIA, to the Agency for International Development and a score of other independent and semi-independent agencies like the Export-Import Bank. That did not include ceremonial duties, handling protocol and social affairs, attending formal dinners, receiving ambassadors.

There was no way to preserve a semblance of private life. The phone rang at any hour. Even when he went out for a walk with Sara, someone would come running after them with a message. He had given up his very occasional golf game. Hardest of all had been giving up the daily half hour at the piano. Some evenings he did not get home at all but slept on a couch in a cubbyhole adjacent to his office.

This morning at home, before breakfast, he had already been interrupted by a telephone call from the Libyan ambassador, who began in an irritatingly pseudohumble manner. "You, of course, Mr. Secretary, are an official of a very great government, and I am merely the representative of a very small one. . . ." How to deal with such sly provocation? The ambassador had been leading up to an impertinent request: another huge loan to build oil refineries after his country had seized American-built refineries without adequate compensation.

He was summoned from the shower to accept a telephone call from Carter Fitzsimmons.

"Isn't the cabinet meeting scheduled for ten o'clock this morning?" Carter asked.

"Yes." He wrapped the bath towel tightly about him.

"I have a feeling the President is going to be very upset. If he is, suggest a postponement of his trip to Peking."

Carter hung up, leaving Abramson to puzzle about the significance of the remark.

At ten o'clock the members of the cabinet were gathering in the conference room in the west wing of the White House. Abramson chatted with Elmer Tate while he clocked late arrivals. Ed Fahey, the blunt, tough secretary of labor came in, and a moment later was joined by the immaculately dressed slender Elias Crankshaw, the secretary for health, education and welfare. That left only two absentees: the President, and Mark Ziffren, whose post as head of the Security Bureau had recently been elevated to cabinet rank.

Elmer Tate was looking at the paintings on the wall, one called

The Relief Ship and the other *Distributing Supplies,* that depicted American efforts to assist the Russian people during the devastating famine of 1891 to 1892.

"Those Commies never appreciated what we did for them," Elmer said.

"It was the Czar then," Abramson reminded him.

"Well, they're no better off now."

Nearby, Abramson overheard a conversation between Peter Mackleby, the brash young secretary for urban affairs, and Fred Wilson, the attorney general.

Mackleby said, "I understand General Ziffren called a news conference for nine-thirty this morning. I wonder what the old boy is up to."

"Probably trying to soothe ruffled feathers," Fred Wilson said. "We've been catching forty kinds of hell from the press and TV about this national emergency. They think it means a wholesale invasion of civil rights."

"If you ask me, they've got reason to worry. Ziffren's the last man I like to see with dictatorial powers."

No doubt, Abramson thought, Mark Ziffren was the least popular member of the cabinet. The general's insistence on exposing what he called "conspirators in government" never had exempted members of the cabinet.

"Well, gentlemen," Abramson said, "shall we continue to wait? Or shall we call the meeting to order?"

Elmer Tate said, "You're presiding officer in the President's absence. Let's get started. We can clear off some matters on the agenda before he gets here."

At a few minutes after ten, Abramson called the meeting to order around the twenty-six-foot mahogany table. Each chair had the nameplate of the cabinet member who occupied it. Abramson's own place, as secretary of state, was adjacent to the President's high-backed chair at center right.

There were still two unoccupied chairs, the one reserved for the President, and the one on the opposite side that Mark Ziffren usually filled.

During the next half hour, as various topics were brought up for discussion, Abramson sensed a distinct air of tension. Everyone knew this was the meeting at which the President would disclose the agenda for the summit in Peking.

Shortly before eleven o'clock, one of the three doors to the conference room opened and General Ziffren limped in, stood behind his empty chair, and waited until there was silence.

"The President will be delayed. He has an appointment with his doctor, and for some reason Dr. Thatcher hasn't shown up."

"Of course, if it's a question of illness . . ." Abramson said.

"The President is not ill."

Mackleby said, "Then why can't he see his doctor after the meeting? Makes more sense to keep his doctor waiting than his whole cabinet."

Abramson decided to exploit the collective mood of restiveness. "After all, Dr. Thatcher saw him only last night."

"Who told you that?" Ziffren asked sharply.

"Someone who was there. Dr. Thatcher answered an emergency call to the White House." He was aware of the impact this news had on the others present.

"There was no emergency," Ziffren said coldly. "Whoever said that was misinformed."

"I'm sure the members of the cabinet would appreciate some further reassurance on the subject."

"The President will give that to you, in person, when he arrives."

The faint accent on the words "in person" carried with it an implicit warning.

From the other end of the room, Elmer Tate said, "Well, let's get on with it then. His health isn't on the agenda as far as I can make out."

At eleven-thirty, after a detailed tedious review of the fuel situation from Tim Loughran, secretary of the interior, General Ziffren was clearly restive.

"I see no reason to prolong this. I suggest we simply adjourn this meeting until a time more convenient for the President."

Abramson remembered his early-morning call from Carter Fitz-simmons. Ever so slightly he shook his head at the Vice-President.

"We don't have to adjourn just yet," Elmer Tate said. "I'd like to hear the secretary of defense report on his tour of military bases and the conditions he found there."

Secretary Hawkins was still in the middle of his report when Ed Fahey signaled for recognition.

Fahey said, "I have an important lunch with the UAW chief. If I can be excused. . . ."

Abramson replied, "I think it's time to find out if the President intends to join us this morning."

Before the President's empty chair was a green blotter and a telephone. Abramson used the telephone to call Chad Oliver and ask him to find out if and when the President would be free.

Chad called back a minute later. "The President is still waiting for his doctor. Sorry." From his tone it was clear the inquiry had met with an unpleasant reception from the President.

Abramson hung up to report what Chad had told him.

"Under the circumstances," Ziffren said, "I move that we adjourn this meeting indefinitely. We all have a great deal of other work to do."

Loughran, the secretary of the interior, and three others joined Ziffren in voting for indefinite adjournment. The others voted with Abramson and Elmer Tate to resume the meeting at three o'clock that afternoon.

When Abramson returned with the Vice-President to his private office, he found Carter Fitzsimmons waiting.

"Cancel my other appointments," Abramson told his receptionist. He turned to Carter. "Will you join us at lunch?"

It was a warm day, so they were served luncheon on the eighth-floor terrace that looked down on E Street and on the green canopy covering the walk to the private elevator. In the distance loomed the Lincoln Memorial and the great octagonal bulk of the Pentagon building.

Carter reviewed for Abramson and Elmer Tate the events of last night, ending with the emergency call to the White House and what had transpired there.

"You mean to tell me the President actually tried to kill himself?" Elmer Tate asked harshly.

"That's what his wife and daughter told me. Claire Rushton hurt herself trying to stop him."

Elmer Tate sat back, pushing his plate of grilled sole away from him. "Goddamn," he said. "His condition must be even worse than we thought. And that's sure the understatement of the year. Even this crazy goddamn year."

"I'm afraid I agree with you," Abramson said.

Carter said, "I'm almost sure some drug is causing it, probably an amphetamine. Nothing else would account for the President's sudden dramatic improvement last night. But, of course, the improvement won't last long."

"How long?" Elmer Tate asked.

"The maximum is twelve hours."

Abramson said, "That means, if he got a treatment last night, the withdrawal started sometime this morning."

Carter nodded. "Until now, withdrawal symptoms have been comparatively mild. But judging from what I've seen, they're getting serious."

"You sound like a doctor," Elmer Tate said, a bit sourly.

"I've read up on it."

"Is it dangerous?" Abramson asked.

Carter said, "He might become aggressive, violent, even attack those he comes to distrust. The final stage is collapse. And blackout. A semicoma that can last for a day or more."

"It isn't going to happen," Elmer Tate observed. "He'll be okay as soon as Doc Thatcher shows up to give him another treatment."

"He may not get another treatment."

Elmer Tate looked at Carter suspiciously. "Are you keeping something from us?"

Carter was tempted to say, Nothing good for you to know. But he answered, "What would I have to gain?"

At three o'clock, Abramson reconvened the cabinet. The President's chair was the only one unoccupied.

Mark Ziffren asked for the floor and was recognized. "Gentlemen, the President's personal physician still cannot be located. He seems to have disappeared."

"Are you implying he's met with foul play?" asked Secretary of Defense Hawkins.

"All I can tell you is that Dr. Thatcher is not in his office, did not sleep in his living quarters last night, and no one in his employ seems to know what's happened to him. The President has asked me to begin an investigation at once, and to report to him." His commanding gaze swept the room. "I'm sure that under the circumstances you will excuse me."

He picked up his briefcase and left.

"Does this mean the President isn't going to show up at all?" Hawkins asked.

"Apparently," Abramson said.

"I don't understand. This was the most important cabinet meeting in months. A helluva lot more important than worrying about his doctor."

Abramson was struggling with a private sense of shock. He had not thought of Carter Fitzsimmons as a reckless man, but if Carter had had a part in the disappearance of the President's doctor, that certainly qualified him as reckless.

He avoided looking at Elmer Tate, who was probably having the same thoughts. "I think it's obvious, gentlemen, we're not being given the entire truth."

"The truth about what?" asked John Lohnes, the secretary for housing.

Abramson squinted thoughtfully down the table at him. "In

my opinion, the President is ill. We know Dr. Thatcher was called to the White House during an emergency last night. Obviously, his presence is so vital again today that the President is going to pass up the final cabinet meeting before Peking."

A solitary cough and some nervous shuffling of papers were the only audible responses.

Elmer Tate appeared to be almost crouching, his head drawn in against his shoulders. "We've heard rumors about his health before," he said. "It's my guess people are getting scared. And maybe they have a right to be."

"What do you expect us to do about it?" asked Fred Wilson, the attorney general.

"I have a suggestion," Abramson said.

Everyone turned toward him.

"We might prepare a resolution, stating our concern for the President. Accompany it with a request that he undergo a complete physical examination to reassure the country."

A tense silence followed.

"That wouldn't accomplish a damn thing," Wilson said.

"I agree," said Loughran. "What d'you think would happen? Rushton isn't going to read that and go running off to have a physical."

"I don't think it goes far enough," Mackleby said unexpectedly. "It isn't just the President's health at issue. It's whether he's in shape to bargain with the Chinese leaders. I'd like to see the Peking summit postponed until it's clear that President Rushton is in satisfactory physical condition."

Paul Bridges, secretary of transportation said, "I can just picture what George Rushton would say to that."

"If the summit isn't postponed," Mackleby replied, "then the results will be subject to all sorts of damaging questions. It'll be FDR at Yalta all over again."

Loughran said levelly, "If we even start to debate such a resolution, I'm not going to stay in this room. I want the President to know exactly where I stand."

"Hear, hear," Hawkins said.

"I have made a motion," Abramson observed mildly. "Does any-one second it?"

Elmer Tate's hand shot up at once. So, he noted, did four others.

"The motion is approved. We should now appoint someone to compose a resolution that will meet with the approval of the majority."

Loughran said, "I said I'd walk if we started to talk about it. That includes starting to write it."

Abramson had a foretaste of defeat. No doubt the secretary of the interior's exit would precipitate a mass exodus, for others would be anxious to demonstrate their loyalty to the President.

However, he had committed himself.

He said, "Let's proceed along parliamentary lines. The meeting is open for suggestions. Whom do you nominate to write a draft of the proposed resolution?"

"What resolution are you talking about?" a familiar voice de-manded.

Abramson turned. Striding through the door was a tight-lipped and obviously angry George Rushton.

The opening of the door wakened Jack Elkins.

The young man came in, walked directly to where Jack was lying on the stiff cushioned cot, and stood over him with his feet planted close together.

"There've been some new developments," he said.

In Elkins's sleep-blurred vision, the young man's face was hardly more than a suggestion of eyes, ears, nose, and mouth.

"What the hell do you want?" he said.

Then he saw another man in the room. He was slight of build and had delicate white hands that looked plastic and unreal.

"We're not going to waste any more time," the young man said. "When I ask questions this time, you will answer."

Elkins sat up, his creaking bones adding their separate outrage to his own. Sleeping on the cot was like being twisted on the rack. Bastards.

"What's happened to Dr. Thatcher?" the young man asked.

Elkins moistened the dryness inside his mouth with his tongue. "Thatcher? What about him?"

"He's been kidnapped. You know who's responsible."

Elkins shook heavy shoulders like a horse twitching off a bothersome fly. "I don't know a damn thing about it."

"Very well. Mr. McNeil is taking over." The young man inclined his head toward the other person in the room. "Mr. McNeil was formerly with the CIA special unit in Vietnam. In charge of interrogating Vietcong prisoners."

Elkins stared without moving. "That kind of stuff doesn't scare me. Nobody's going to do anything like that."

McNeil spoke for the first time, in a voice half an octave too high.

"Bring in the equipment," he said.

Minutes later, spread-eagled on the cot, with padded straps holding his hands and feet and a sponge filling his mouth and taped in place, Elkins was still unwilling to believe they would actually go through with it. When the first pain flamed, he roared so hard the muffled sound penetrated the occluding sponge. His nerve centers seemed to flare up in one bright interminable excruciating agony.

He managed to convey that he wanted to speak. The young man removed the tape and took the sponge from his mouth. McNeil's delicate white hands ceased moving knobs on the control panel.

Elkins found it hard to catch his breath. Tiny muscles still jumped galvanically in his body. "Listen, I'm willing to tell you anything. You don't have to convince me any more."

"Who has Dr. Thatcher?" the young man asked. "And where are they keeping him?"

"Jesus, I didn't know they were going to kidnap him. That's the truth. They don't let me in on things like that. But I'm not too surprised. They know how much the President relies on him."

"Who are 'they'?"

"The ones in charge."

"Their names."

He drew a deep breath. "Naturally, I don't know everybody. At the level I operate they don't want me to. My job is to handle publicity and public relations. Kind of a front man. Like Lord Haw-Haw."

"Lord who?"

"Never mind. Anyway, they're very careful about keeping their identities secret. I only know the people I work with."

"Stop stalling."

"They've got spies planted in all branches of government. Out-side it too. I'm just trying to explain how it works."

"Go on."

"You just want the names, right?"

"Right."

"Carter Fitzsimmons."

"Who's that again?" The young man touched something inside his shirt. He was wired for sound.

"Fitzsimmons. Carter."

"What's he do?"

"Inside man at the White House. A good friend of the President and his whole family. Reports back on everything that goes on there."

The young man's face moved closer, and his eyes looked almost directly into Elkins's eyes.

"I hope for your sake you're telling the truth."

"You don't think I'd pull any tricks, do you?" He kept his ex-pression meek and compliant, his eyes pleading.

The young man went on, "In less than a minute, McNeil can fix it so that you'll never be able to do anything with a woman. A simple little thing, but no surgery would make you whole again. You understand?"

Elkins shuddered. "I get it. Ask me anything you want to know."

"Who are the leaders of the conspiracy?"

"Well, there's the Vice-President and the secretary of state. . . ."

Carter Fitzsimmons emerged into the hot August afternoon, leaving behind the air-conditioned interior of a movie theater. He had been killing time. Now he would return to his hotel to await a telephone call from Abramson. The secretary had promised to call him as soon as the cabinet meeting ended.

A news truck was delivering tightly wrapped bundles of papers to a sidewalk stand. He strolled over to glance at the headline. MASS ARRESTS! ZIFFREN VOWS CRACKDOWN ON THOSE WHO "PLOT AGAINST AMERICA."

He reached into his pocket for a coin, intending to buy a newspaper to take back to the hotel with him.

"Mr. Fitzsimmons?" General Ziffren opened the rear door of a limousine parked at the curb. "I've been looking for you." He moved over so Carter could get into the backseat of the limousine. "When was the last time you saw Dr. Thatcher?" he asked.

After the initial surprise, Carter felt remarkably self-possessed. "Last night. At the White House."

"You drove him there in your car?"

"Yes, I did."

"And waited for him to leave?"

"We happened to meet again as we were leaving."

"Accidentally?"

"He was coming out as I returned for my car. I asked if he'd like a drive back to the clinic."

"And is that where you took him?"

Carter nodded. "Why all the questions?"

"We haven't been able to trace Dr. Thatcher since he got into your car at a little after eight o'clock last evening. What time did you arrive at his clinic?"

"I really can't recall. Is it important?"

"The caretaker lives in an apartment over the garage. He says no car came in after eight o'clock."

"I think I can explain that. Dr. Thatcher didn't want to disturb anyone. I let him off outside the grounds."

"Were the lights on?"

"I really don't remember."

"The lights are triggered by an automatic system. They went on at eight-eleven last evening."

"What are you driving at, General?"

"I'd like to go back over the preceding events. How did you happen to take Dr. Thatcher to the White House?"

"I was with him in his apartment when a call came, saying it was an emergency. When I heard it was the President, naturally I volunteered to drive him."

"What were you doing at Dr. Thatcher's at that hour?"

Carter said carefully, "I'd been to see him before about a bursitis condition."

"Was that why you were in his office last night?"

Weighing the chances of evasion, Carter decided Ziffren had probably been too thorough. "Not entirely."

"You told the receptionist that it was about the President. What was it?"

"The President's wife and daughter were concerned about his condition. I volunteered to find out what I could from Dr. Thatcher."

"And what did he tell you?"

"That he saw no reason for their concern. A few moments later the call came from Marie Rushton, and we left."

"When you arrived there, what happened?"

"Dr. Thatcher went in to the President. I visited with Mrs. Rushton and her daughter."

"During that time, did you make a telephone call?"

"To a doctor." Carter added irritably, "His name is Vancell. I called him at the request of the President's wife and daughter. I thought he might be needed. It turned out I was wrong."

"You also called Secretary Abramson. Why?"

"To report that the President was ill."

"Why Abramson?"

"He's the man in government I know best, with the exception of the President. Now look here, General . . ."

"What was the result of your conversation?"

"Secretary Abramson agreed to give out a story to the press that wouldn't be too alarming."

"Did you call him again?"

"Yes. By then it was obvious that President Rushton was not in need of further medical help. I told him it wouldn't be necessary to give any statement to the press."

"When you drove Dr. Thatcher back to the clinic, did he mention he was going to see the President this morning?"

"I'm beginning to resent this. Just what authority do you have to interrogate me?"

"The President asked me to conduct an investigation into Thatcher's disappearance. We already know it was the result of a conspiracy. One of the people involved has talked, and the others are soon going to be in custody."

"Are you accusing me?"

"I could arrest you here and now if I wanted to. You would be well advised to put no obstacles in my way."

"I'm trying not to."

"Fine. Then I repeat, Did Dr. Thatcher mention he intended to see the President this morning?"

"He might have." Carter made a determined effort to appear relaxed.

"Did he give any indication that he had anything else in mind?"

"For example?"

"Going away."

"No."

Across the park Carter saw the Capitol, with its pillars and arches scrubbed and sandblasted to a gleaming whiteness. It seemed to float on that hill against the sky.

Ziffren asked, "Are you acquainted with a nurse at the medical center named Joyce Hatton?"

"I am."

"Would you say you're on intimate terms?"

"I won't answer that, General."

"In any event, you spend a great deal of your time with her. Have you seen her recently?"

"How recently?"

"Since last night?"

His heart was beating fast. "No."

"Miss Hatton didn't go to work at the medical center today. Early this morning a man called to report that she was sick. Was that you?"

"No."

"Do you have any idea who that man was?"

"You might ask Miss Hatton."

"We haven't been able to locate her. She isn't at her apartment. Do you know where she is?"

"I'm afraid I can't help you. And I can't see what she has to do with it."

"Last night she returned to the medical center shortly after eight o'clock. She went to the medical supply room, then downstairs to wait for a car that came to the emergency entrance. A blue sedan, make unknown. That fits the description of your rental car, doesn't it?"

"There are a lot of blue sedans around, General."

"We know she got into that car, and that's the last anyone has seen of her." Steel entered the general's voice. "Does it strike you as a remarkable coincidence that Miss Hatton and Dr. Thatcher should have disappeared at almost exactly the same time?"

Within a few moments of George Rushton's entrance into the cabinet room, it was obvious to Abramson that something was terribly wrong. After a brief reference to the pending resolution as being out of order, even if well meant (the remark might have been engaging if not said with such a grim countenance), the President looked around the room.

"Gentlemen, only a few minutes ago I received word from our intelligence people that Soviet Russia has put its armed forces on full alert."

He might as well have exploded a bomb on the center of the table. In the aftermath, there was dazed stunned bewilderment.

"Incredible," Wilson said. "A full alert?"

"Including nuclear weapons?" Hawkins asked.

"That's the information I have received," Rushton replied.

"Holy God," breathed Elmer Tate. "They'll be in position to launch nuclear war within a matter of minutes."

Mackleby shook his head. "What possible reason would they have for going to the brink?"

"What's more important," Tim Loughran said, "is what are we doing about it?"

"I have given orders to prepare for instant retaliation," Rushton said. "In a few minutes our missile bases in Europe, our nuclear submarines, all our forces will also be on full alert. Then we'll find out if the Russians are bluffing."

Mackleby glanced at the secretary of defense. "Hawkins, what's your estimate of what would happen to us in a nuclear war?"

"The best estimate I've been able to get from our military is that our defenses would knock ninety percent of all enemy missiles out of the air."

"And what about the ten percent that got through?"

"They would kill one hundred and eighty million Americans in the first fifteen minutes."

Fred Wilson said, "My God." He took a pill and swallowed it without water. "Have the Russians lost their minds? The same thing—or worse—would happen to them."

When George Rushton did not reply, Abramson said in a low voice, "Nothing that Russia, or any other nation, does takes place in a vacuum. If they've taken such a drastic step, we must try to find out why. Their actions don't exist entirely apart from our own behavior."

Beside him, Rushton stirred. Abramson looked into the President's cold blue eyes.

"Are you trying to fix the blame on us, Adolph?"

"All I'm saying, Mr. President, is that the Russians are not devils, and not madmen. Nor are they inscrutable. What they do is in large part a reaction to what we do. We should ask what result they're trying to achieve with what otherwise seems to be a wholly unmotivated action."

"I can tell you what they want," Rushton answered. "They want me to back away from the Peking summit. They're afraid they've been outsmarted, outmaneuvered. That's what they're afraid of."

Elmer Tate said, "If you've got something up your sleeve, Mr. President, something connected with the Peking summit, we ought to know about it."

Mackleby said, "More important, the American people should know about it."

Rushton appeared taken aback by opposition from the youngest member of his cabinet; Mackleby was a personal favorite. He glanced at the other cabinet members, apparently gauging their reaction.

"Very well. I intended to brief you anyway on why I am going to Peking. Let me put it simply. Our nation and China have reached a point in history when it is necessary for us to forget our past differences in Korea and in Vietnam, and move on to a new level of cooperation. I don't mean a simple nonaggression pact, but an agreement that will provide for our mutual defense and a full military alliance with the People's Republic of China."

There were shocked murmurs before Elmer Tate's voice rumbled, "Mr. President, anybody can tell you that's why the Russians are so goddamned upset!"

In a moment rife with electricity, Abramson became aware that the Vice-President had scored an inadvertent direct hit on George Rushton's precarious self-control.

The President asked, "Are you in league with them?"

"In league with who?"

"Are you speaking for yourself—or for the people behind you?"

The air in the cabinet room actually seemed to become a little heavier to breathe. Elmer Tate looked puzzled, searching for some significance other than personal attack. Throughout the room other members were engaged in the same process of checking through the words for some hidden pertinence. About then, Elmer reached the conclusion that nothing but a vicious slander was intended.

He flushed the color of used brick. "If that's a slur on my patriotism, Mr. President . . ."

"I'm sure the President didn't mean that," Abramson said placatingly. Then, with persevering quietness, "However, the Russian action may be connected to your impending visit to Peking, Mr. President. It might go a long way toward helping us understand if you explained the purpose of the alliance you mentioned."

Elmer Tate said belligerently, "We've got no business meddling between the Russians and Chinese. That's how I feel about it, and that's what Congress will tell you if you try to put us into one camp or the other."

Rushton gave a meaningless reflex grimace. "I don't propose to ask for the approval of Congress."

"And how do you expect to get away with that? The Senate has to approve any treaty. That's in plain English right in the Constitution."

Rushton's face turned dark and mottled. "Good God, what kind of an idiot are you?" Perspiration broke out on his forehead. "Russia is aiming her missiles at us this minute, and you're fiddling around with whether we have a right to sign a treaty with the only country that can help us!" He finally managed to contain himself, but his tone remained contemptuous. "You've heard of an executive agreement. This won't be the first time an executive agreement took the place of a treaty. And it won't be the last."

Fred Wilson said, "Perhaps if you'd go into more detail about what we'd be committing ourselves to, Mr. President. . . ."

A muscle twitched in Rushton's cheek. "I don't care to do that at this time. There are traitors opposed to my policy. Some of them are in this very room."

The collective exhalation of breath was like a single gasp.

Elmer Tate said, "I'd like to get this straight, Mr. President. Are you suggesting someone here is a traitor to his country? In that case, you'd damn well better start naming names!"

Rushton touched fingertips to his head as if to focus a thought. "Ziffren warned me about . . . a conspiracy. I couldn't believe. . . ." He moistened dry lips while confusion deepened in his eyes, then continued in a barely audible voice. "The guilty ones know who they are. . . . They *know!*"

"What guilty ones, Mr. President?" Mackleby asked.

Rushton's answer seemed to lurch forward. "They will be dealt with. We must all stand by our battle stations, ready to defend the nation . . . to back up the Grand Alliance. . . ."

Abramson looked into the President's face and caught his breath. He felt as if he were looking at someone he had not seen before.

Secretary of the Treasury Charles Lancourt, a man known to reserve his opinion until the facts were in, said quietly, "Mr. President, it might be useful if we polled the members of the cabinet now to see how they feel about this proposed alliance."

Rushton appeared to sway and then, with an effort, straightened. His eyes swept the room with baffled fury. "That's not necessary." Then he paused, muttering, "Lincoln said seven nays, one aye, the ayes have it. . . ." He appeared to summon strength for a last effort at reasonableness: "In a showdown . . . a billion Chinese on our side. Anyone who can't see that . . ." a tide of anger swept him ". . . is a traitor unfit to serve this government!"

Elmer Tate was up out of his chair, and Wilson was trying to restrain him, and Mackleby was saying something that couldn't be heard in the tumult.

In a voice that cut across the room, Abramson said, "Mr. President, it's clear to everyone you're not well. I move to adjourn this meeting."

At the height of the uproar, the door opened. Chad Oliver entered and hurried to the President. As Chad whispered to him, Rushton pursed his lips and severe lines appeared at the mouth corners. He shook his head slightly.

Chad left, closing the door, and with painfully visible effort George Rushton prepared to speak. His erect posture seemed to have broken at the shoulders; he was struggling against some force that threatened to pull him down.

"It has just been confirmed that my personal physician, Dr. Thatcher, was kidnapped," he said distinctly.

"Who would do a crazy thing like that?" Fahey asked in a loud voice.

Deep in the well of what had once been an inexhaustible vitality, some reserves remained. Rushton brought his fist down with such abrupt force that a heavy ashtray jumped. "Typical . . . of the criminal mentality . . . that rules in Moscow."

"Mr. President, are you seriously suggesting. . . ."

The questioner was John Lohnes, the secretary for housing, but he broke off midway as he saw that George Rushton was not listening.

Rushton's lips were moving, but no words came out. "You fools . . . you blind fools . . ."

He brushed his cheek lightly and turned toward Abramson with a slight surprise, as if something had just been said to him. His eyes were staring and fixed.

Too late Abramson saw what was about to happen.

The President of the United States fell forward unconscious across the conference table.

22

Carter Fitzsimmons did not go back to his hotel after leaving General Ziffren. It was clear the net was closing rapidly. The Security Bureau knew of the connection between him and Joyce, and Joyce and Dr. Thatcher. Ziffren had hinted that he knew who was involved in the "conspiracy" and that one member had already been persuaded to talk. That was a lie, of course, because no one else was involved, but the overtones of accusation were clear.

He entered the hotel lobby, took the elevator down to the garage, and made a call to the car rental agency.

"I rented a car from you that isn't running well. Now it won't start."

"Where are you, sir?"

"In my hotel garage."

"If you'll give me your name and the address, we'll send someone over right away with a replacement."

"Hurry, please. I have an urgent appointment."

Ten minutes later the new car arrived. It was copper-colored. Carter exchanged keys with the driver, and pointed out his dark blue car in the garage.

"I don't know what's the matter. But I hope I never see it again."

As he drove the new car out of the garage, he looked in the rear-vision mirror. The man got into the dark blue sedan and started the engine up quickly. Sorry about that, fella.

Not until he reached the highway heading south was he sure no one was following him.

He pushed the speedometer up ten miles over the posted speed limit and drove steadily, keeping a wary eye on the highway behind him. Anyone following would have to exceed the speed limit too, and therefore could be spotted. He was taking a chance on being stopped by a highway patrol, but that couldn't be helped. He had to get to Joyce as quickly as possible.

At five-thirty he arrived at the narrow dirt road that led up to the cabin. For some time, he had heard something at the very edge of awareness. A distant thrumming. He heard it fitfully again now, but there was nothing in his rear-vision mirror.

As he turned up the dirt road, the car's chassis tilted, and through the windshield and veiny interlacing tree branches he saw a great dark whirling blade against the sky.

A helicopter!

Ungainly circling black bird. In a moment it would go away. He *willed* it to go away. He held to a desperate forlorn hope. It might be a traffic helicopter, a mere coincidence.

The helicopter began to descend.

He grasped the wheel, jamming his foot down on the gas pedal. The car leaped up the hill, leaving a wake of dust. Joyce! She mustn't be found in the cabin with Dr. Thatcher.

At the top of the hill he drove up to the shed, cut the ignition, and jumped out while the car was moving. It nosed into the shed wall and stopped with a heavy thump. He ran toward the cabin.

The helicopter resembled a great bird of prey getting ready to pounce. They had been following him all the way from the city. And he had thought he was being careful by watching the highway!

He reached the cabin door, pounded on it. Joyce opened it.

"Get out," he said. *"Now!"*

Not quite comprehending, she followed with her eyes the directionless sweep of his arm. The helicopter's great whirling blade was just barely visible over the treetops. It was settling down, and Carter knew where. A cleared patch of ground two hundred yards away.

They would be here in minutes.

He thrust the car keys at her. "Drive as fast as you can! I'll try to delay them."

"What about him?" She indicated the open door of the bedroom inside

"I'll take care of everything."

She said suddenly, "I can't leave you!"

Nervous anger exploded. *"Damn it!* Do what I tell you!"

She stopped only to get her handbag and grab her coat. As they went out the front door onto the small porch, he was listening.

The faint thrumming sound ceased.

"That way!" he told her peremptorarily, indicating the trail that led around the far side of the cabin into the woods. The men from the helicopter would take a different route.

He watched her hurry along the trail. That man, Tony Gramalia, had been running like that when Security Bureau operatives shot him down. Suddenly fearful, he almost called to her, but by then she was out of sight amid the trees.

He traced ahead in his mind the route that led past the small garbage dump and emerged at the woodshed. There was no point at which she became visible to anyone following the trail through the woods from that clearing. She would be safe.

He returned to the cabin, closed and locked the door and put the crossbar into place. He went into the bedroom. Dr. Thatcher was lying in bed, his arms crossed peacefully on his chest, his white hair splayed out on the pillow.

Pleasant dreams, Dr. Thatcher.

In the living room he drew two window shades completely, allowed an open inch at the bottom of another so he could watch that part of the woods from which they should emerge.

They came out exactly where he expected. All three in civilian clothes. Soldierly, gimpy-legged Mark Ziffren and two tall young men with guns in their hands.

They came steadily toward the house. At a command from Ziffren, the two young men angled a few yards away. Deploying. Still coming.

They stopped.

Ziffren turned quickly, tilting his head. Listening.

Carter heard it too—the starting roar of a car engine. Joyce had reached the shed.

He yelled, "General! What do you want here?"

Without a glance at the cabin Ziffren lifted his arm, and one young man started back at a run. Carter reckoned the distances. Joyce would be down the dirt road before he reached the shed. Even running downhill he wouldn't reach the asphalt until she had gone a quarter of a mile and the winding road had taken her out of sight.

He breathed again.

Ziffren and the man with him had stopped about twenty feet away.

"Is that you, Fitzsimmons?"

"It's me."

"Are you armed?"

"I'd like to know why you followed me."

"We think Dr. Thatcher is in the cabin. We'd like to come in for a look."

"This is private property. You're trespassing."

"We're coming in."

In a moment Carter heard footsteps on the porch, then a rat- tling at the door.

"You'd better have a search warrant with you," he warned.

The door shuddered. Carter picked up a chair to jam under the door handle.

Glass suddenly shattered behind him. Something heavy thud- ded inside. He turned, holding the chair, and saw someone run- ning toward him from the kitchen. It was the young man who had been with General Ziffren a moment before. He was running as hard as a football linebacker.

The young man barreled past the chair and plunged into Car- ter, smashing him down with a force that knocked the air out of his lungs.

He was lying there gagging when the front door was unlocked and Ziffren came in.

"Thatcher's here," the young man said. "In the bedroom."

"I just heard from the roadblock. We've got the girl too."

Sick despair gripped Carter.

Abramson broke the stunned silence in the cabinet room by going to the door and telling the guard on duty to send for a doctor.

That call went to the man in charge of the White House infirm- ary, a former pharmacist's mate in the navy. He arrived within minutes and examined the unconscious President.

"I can't tell what's wrong. We'd better get him to the hospital."

Elmer Tate said, "Bring a stretcher up here and we'll move him quietly before the press room gets wind of what's happening."

"What hospital are we taking him to?" Abramson asked.

The man replied, "There isn't a better equipped hospital in the United States than the medical center. They can handle any emergency."

Elmer Tate said, "When their ambulance gets here, make sure the siren is turned off. Have them come in the back way."

"We'd better speak to the agent-in-charge," Abramson said. "I think his name is Chalmers."

While they were waiting for a stretcher to be sent up from the first-aid room, William Chalmers came in and saw George Rushton lying supine on the single slab table. "Is he dead?"

"Passed out," Elmer Tate said brusquely. "We're having him taken to the hospital for a checkup. I want maximum security. No panic."

Chalmers nodded, then went directly to the President's chair at the desk. From the blotter he removed the tray with the silver thermos jug and water glass.

"He didn't drink anything," Abramson said.

"Just routine, sir," Chalmers assured him. "The thermos and the glass will be sent for a chemical analysis."

The men who guarded the President did not miss a trick. Every morning they inspected the President's office, lifting blotters, seat cushions, rug corners, even disassembling the desk phone to see that a transistor set hadn't been put in overnight. They used Geiger counters on radiators and other metal objects to make certain that nuclear active products had not been introduced into furnace boilers or drilled into tiny holes in letter openers. They even examined the mechanism of clocks.

In the job of maintaining security, Abramson thought, there were no details too small to be checked.

By the time the ambulance arrived at the medical center, two residents were waiting outside the emergency entrance.

Chalmers jumped out of the lead car to supervise unloading the stretcher. He took off his suit jacket and shaded the President's head to conceal his identity. Then, with the ambulance attendants and the two doctors, the stretcher was hurried to trauma room one, where specialists had been summoned from their stations in the huge hospital-school complex.

Abramson and the Vice-President waited in a private room a

short distance down the hall. In a few minutes a doctor in a white smock entered.

"I'm Dr. Vancell. Our preliminary examination indicates that the President is in no immediate danger. His life signs are stable. Can you tell me what happened?"

Abramson described the scene in the conference room, ending with George Rushton's sudden collapse.

"Had he complained of anything prior to his collapse? A headache, for example? Gastric upset? We'll check everything. But it might save time if you could give me a clue as to what you think may have caused it."

Abramson said, "Try to find out if it's a toxic condition—from an overdose of drugs."

Dr. Vancell stared at him, saying nothing. His glance shifted uneasily toward Elmer Tate. "I'll be back as soon as I have word," he said finally.

After the doctor left, there was an uncomfortable silence.

Elmer Tate said, "For all we know, it could have been anything. A heart attack or a stroke."

"We both know what it is," Abramson said. "More important now, Elmer, is to figure out what the next step should be. The President may need a long convalescence."

"I don't know what you're driving at," Elmer said doubtfully.

"There must be a private disability agreement between you and George Rushton, just as there has been between most recent Presidents and their Vice-Presidents. What does it provide for?"

"I have to take over. But I'm not going to. For one thing, the agreement says on 'clear evidence of disability.' We don't have that. George Rushton's disability isn't permanent. This isn't the first time a President was unable to function for a while."

Abramson had to acknowledge that. James Garfield had been out of action for months before he died from an assassin's bullet. And Grover Cleveland had had his whole upper jaw removed in a secret cancer operation that the public never even heard about for twenty-five years. Woodrow Wilson's stroke incapacitated him for the last eighteen months of his term. And no one but Ike's doctors ever knew how serious his heart attack was. Yet they all stayed in office.

"There's a crucial difference, Elmer. With a problem of mental or emotional disability, no one can be sure of full recovery. If it happens to an ordinary person doing an ordinary job, it isn't serious. But with the President?"

"George is going to be okay. I know what you're trying to make me do, Dolph, but I don't want the job—not even temporarily. I know my limitations. I'm not big enough to handle it."

Abramson was touched by the genuine humility of this honest man. "You knew there was a possibility of this when you became Vice-President," he reminded Elmer.

"Nobody gave me a choice. The party picked me because they wanted to head you off. There was a lot of sentiment among the delegates for you."

Abramson smiled. A Jew next in line for the Presidency was an idea whose time hadn't come, whereas he had been perfect for secretary of state. After Dr. Kissinger, nobody would have risked giving the job to anybody who *wasn't* Jewish."

"I wish to hell they'd picked you, Dolph. Then I wouldn't be in this fix. Trying to make a President out of me is like trying to build a house around a keyhole."

"You'll do better than I would have. You can make decisions. We need to know what to do about the Peking summit, Mark Ziffren—and most urgently, about the Russian nuclear alert. And there's no time to waste."

The door opened and Dr. Vancell reentered. "I thought you'd like to know. Your guess was right on the button. The President is in a withdrawal coma."

"Will he be all right?" Elmer Tate asked anxiously.

"We've started treatment. He's beginning to come out of it already."

"What kind of drug was he being given?" Abramson asked.

"We can't be sure yet. My guess is equal parts of amphetamine and a drug that's supposed to cancel out the bad effects of amphetamines. But it doesn't always act that way. In some cases, it actually intensifies the effects."

"I want you to stay in charge of the case from now on, Doctor," Abramson said.

"I'll have to speak to Dr. Thatcher first."

"You're in charge, Doctor," Elmer Tate said in a voice that brooked no argument. "That's an order."

Through the Plexiglas bubble Carter saw one of General Ziffren's men at the controls and Dr. Thatcher in the seat beside him. Thatcher appeared to be still unconscious. The helicopter rose two feet and hovered, an incredibly heavy machine poised near the ground but not a part of it. It made a great deal of noise, and the downdraft from its great revolving blade stirred up the clearing and sent leaves flying in all directions.

Carter stood between Ziffren and the other young man. They watched the helicopter surge a few unsteady feet forward, then rise vertically. In a moment it was above the trees and whizzing off through a cloudless darkening sky.

The young man beside him asked, "Shall I handcuff him, sir?"

"Wait until we get into the car. Easier walking."

Not much chance, Carter was thinking, that he would try to escape. That might give someone an excuse to put a bullet in his back.

He kept himself carefully in control, trying not to look afraid. But he began to experience a sense of panic. Not so much for himself as for Joyce.

What would happen to her?

They began to walk down the trail, twigs crackling beneath their feet. General Ziffren was slightly ahead, hobbling along, and the young man was close behind Carter.

"General," Carter said suddenly, "there is something I'd like you to know."

"Yes?"

"Miss Hatton only came to visit me a few minutes before you arrived. She has nothing to do with this." As he pushed a branch out of his way, he seemed to feel inside his hand the agitated pulsing of his blood. "Believe me, it was simply coincidence that she was in the cabin. She can't be punished for that."

Ziffren answered in a flat tone slightly tinged with irony. "The penalty for kidnapping is set by the Lindbergh law."

"She isn't guilty!"

"As far as I'm concerned, the case is open and shut."

"If you'll let her go, I'll cooperate fully. I'll admit my own part in it."

They moved down the slope of a hill.

"Are you willing to name the leaders of the conspiracy?" Ziffren asked.

"There is no conspiracy."

"Don't take me for a fool."

They arrived on the road and Ziffren started off. Carter caught up to him. All that mattered to him was to protect Joyce.

"I was acting alone. This was my idea. I'm the only one responsible."

"We know you were obeying orders. We've got the names of the leaders. All I want from you is confirmation. Jack Elkins has already told us his part in the conspiracy."

"Elkins?" Carter felt as if he were helplessly drifting into a dream state.

From behind, the young man said suddenly, "There's the road-block."

Beyond the next turn of the dirt road, a Cadillac limousine horizontally blocked both lanes of traffic. Nearby, on the shoulder of the road, Carter's copper-colored rental car was parked. Joyce was inside it. Beside the cars, two Security Bureau men were on guard.

"Put the handcuffs on now," Ziffren said.

23

Joyce rode in the rented car with two Security Bureau agents and General Ziffren. Carter rode in the Cadillac. One agent drove, and another sat in the rear seat with him. Carter's hands were handcuffed behind his back.

They entered the city and drove up before the Security Bureau building in the Federal triangle. An olive-green truck with army insignia and half a dozen soldiers was parked in front. General Ziffren got out of the car at the curb and an officer came forward to meet him from the truck. The officer wore a major's insignia.

There was a short, heated colloquy.

General Ziffren's high voice rose angrily. "Ridiculous, Major. I'm in charge now. You're relieved of further responsibility."

The major stood his ground, apparently ignoring Ziffren's order. Carter became interested. He leaned forward slightly to hear more.

The major, speaking in low calm tones, could not be heard.

But Ziffren's impatient voice was clear. "What's your name? Who gave you your orders?"

A moment later Ziffren clumped over to the limousine. "Get me General Grissom," he told the driver. "There's some confusion here."

The driver put through the call on the limousine's telephone. All he said was, "Volunteer calling. Get General Grissom," and after a few seconds, he turned the telephone over to Mark Ziffren.

"Dwight?" Ziffren said. "Would you mind telling me what's going on? Your Major Sherwood tells me he has orders to take my prisoners into his custody. . . . From who? I don't believe it! You've been taken in by an impostor. . . . I'll go over there now and prove it. . . . Until you hear from me, you keep one of the prisoners. I'm taking the other with me. I want the President to see him, and hear for himself the story he's got to tell."

Ziffren got into the front seat beside the driver. "White House," he said shortly.

At the sentry gate, they were waved through. A moment later Carter, still handcuffed, followed Ziffren down a short corridor in the west wing. Both Security Bureau agents trailed behind. Before they reached the door connecting to the office of the President's secretary, a man in a colonel's uniform intercepted them.

He said to Ziffren embarrassedly, "I'm sorry, sir. I'll have to ask for your weapons."

Ziffren nodded to the agents, who handed over their guns. The colonel then looked inquiringly at Ziffren.

"Are you armed, General?"

"Does this order apply to me?"

"As I understand it, sir."

"A damned outrage!" Ziffren said. Nevertheless, he removed a gun from his shoulder holster and handed it over.

"The President will be with you shortly in the cabinet room," the colonel told him.

"He's going to hear about this," Ziffren promised.

When Carter and Ziffren entered the cabinet room, they found Abramson standing by the window.

"Is it really necessary to keep him in handcuffs?" Abramson asked.

Ziffren replied, "He happens to be under arrest."

"On what charge?"

"I'll tell that to the President when I see him." Ziffren permitted himself a tight little smile. "Actually, I'm glad you're here, Mr. Secretary. Whether or not you realize it, you've played right into my hands."

A door to the cabinet room, the one that led directly from the President's office via the office of his personal secretary, swung open. Elmer Tate came in.

"Here's the President," Abramson said.

Ziffren's gaze moved from Elmer Tate to the high-backed chair at the conference table as if he expected George Rushton to be sitting there ready to contradict Abramson's statement. "If this is meant to be a joke, it's in very poor taste."

Abramson said, "I'm afraid this will come as a shock to you, General. A lot has happened since we last met. George Rushton is in the hospital. Elmer Tate has taken over as the acting President."

Carter felt a sudden emptiness in the pit of his stomach. "George is in the hospital?" he asked.

Elmer Tate said, "He collapsed during the cabinet meeting. He'll be all right, though. Meanwhile, I'm in charge. And my first official act, General, is to relieve you of your responsibilities as head of the Security Bureau."

Ziffren's chill survey traveled from Carter to Abramson to Elmer Tate. "I warn you, gentlemen, it won't work. You're trying to save yourselves, but you can't do it by seizing power."

Elmer Tate said impatiently, "General, the only one who's been trying to seize power around here is you. But that's over now."

Ziffren's cheeks flushed shiny red. "You're all part of a conspiracy, and you've been scheming from the first to get rid of the President. You won't get away with it."

Tate gave him a frowning look. "I was going to let you off easy, General," he answered. "I intended to accept your resignation. But I've just changed my mind. You're fired. You're through, discharged, out on your ear. Finished."

Ziffren replied stiffly, "Do what you like. I'll take my case to the Congress and the people."

"General, if you go around shooting off your mouth now, you could probably cause some trouble. In a day or two it won't matter because everyone will know the truth. So until then we'll just keep you under wraps."

"How are you going to do that?"

Carter saw that Abramson was also puzzled by Elmer Tate's remark.

Elmer said, "I'm placing you under arrest. We'll think up a nice fancy charge. Maybe the one you're so fond of—violating the Espionage Act."

"You wouldn't dare!"

"Wouldn't I?" Elmer walked over to the President's chair and picked up the telephone on the conference table. "Send a couple of guards in here. On the double."

Ziffren regarded the President with baleful anger. "That's the worst mistake you ever made. I'll be free again as soon as I get to a lawyer. And if you repeat that absurd charge at the arraignment. . . ."

Elmer Tate's eyes widened slightly. "Lawyer? Arraignment? Hell, General, ain't you heard the news? We don't mess around with that any more. Something called a declaration of emergency is in force around here."

Carter was relieved when the handcuffs came off. He managed a weak smile. "Those things hurt after a while." He rubbed his wrists to restore circulation. "I was beginning to think gangrene would set in."

Abramson waited until the Security Bureau agent left the room. "Carter, you're not off the legal hook. A serious crime was committed. If Dr. Thatcher wants to prosecute you for kidnapping, you could be in a very sticky situation."

Elmer Tate turned from staring out the window. "When you took the law in your own hands, you knew what the consequences might be."

Carter said, "I'm prepared to face the consequences. But I don't think Joyce Hatton, who helped me, should have to face them."

"From everything you've told us, she's in this up to the neck," Elmer Tate said. "Anything may happen in a courtroom. The hell of it is, if you're convicted, I can't even grant you a presidential pardon. That would only back up Ziffren's claim that this is some kind of conspiracy. And a lot of people would believe him."

"I guess everybody still remembers the uproar after President Ford handed out his pardon," Carter said.

Elmer Tate turned to Abramson abruptly. "Where's Thatcher now?"

"In a private room at the medical center."

"Get him the hell over here. We'll try to talk sense to him."

A short time later, agent-in-charge Chalmers entered the room ahead of Dr. Marvin Thatcher. Thatcher was still in the suit he had worn when taken to Carter's cabin. He looked disheveled and did not appear to have shaken off all the effects of the sedation.

Abramson pulled out a chair from the conference table. "Won't you sit down?"

At that moment Thatcher became aware of Carter's presence. He gave a slight but perceptible start.

"How are you feeling?" Abramson asked.

"Much better, thank you." With his fingers he pushed back an untidy lock of gray hair. "Not quite as clear in my head as I'd like to be."

"Do you think you can answer a few questions?"

Thatcher nodded, and his glance strayed toward Carter. It was obvious what he expected the questions to be about.

Elmer Tate said abruptly, "What kind of goddamned drugs were you feeding to the President?"

Thatcher's uncertainty edged toward confusion. "I—I don't know what you mean."

"You were giving him something. What was it?"

"Is this why you asked me here?" Thatcher directed the question toward Abramson. "I—I've been through quite an ordeal. I would like to help, but an interrogation at this time. . . ." He gave a tiny head shake of refusal.

Abramson said, "George Rushton is now in the hospital. A council of doctors has examined him and confirmed that he's suffering from toxicity caused by drugs."

"I really must ask to be excused. I—I don't feel up to this."

Elmer Tate said grimly, "Yes or no, Doctor. Were you giving President Rushton drugs as part of a regular treatment?"

"If there are charges against me . . ."

"When that council of doctors publishes its report, there are going to be plenty of charges. In fact, you'll be lucky if they don't get up a lynching party. What the blazes gave you the right to turn the President of the United States into an addict?"

Dr. Thatcher replied without anger. "All doctors prescribe drugs to treat undesirable mental or physical conditions. You can purchase them at any drugstore. Aspirin, reducing pills, cough drops . . ." His voice trailed off.

"Cough drops!" Elmer Tate roared. "Goddammit, Doctor . . ."

Abramson interrupted, "We're not talking about drugs in approved use, Doctor. We mean volatile, harmful ones like the stimulants, depressants, hallucinogens, narcotics. Did you treat President Rushton with any of those?"

"In all fairness, Mr. Abramson, there is a problem of confidentiality between doctor and patient."

"Are you trying to imply that George Rushton *knew* what he was getting?" Elmer Tate demanded. "If you are, I'm calling you a brass-plated liar."

Dr. Thatcher appeared bewildered. "As far as I know, I am the injured party in this case. Why aren't you interested in this man," he indicated Carter, "and what he has done to me?"

Elmer Tate exploded. "He was trying to save the President from more of your damn mind-destroying treatments! He took one bitch of a gamble in order to expose what kind of a quack you are."

Thatcher's large moist eyes expressed a mild surprise. "I am a physician, and I've spent all my working life as a physician. I resent that characterization."

Abramson reminded him gently, "The council of doctors will submit a report on its medical findings. That report will be forwarded to other authorities, including the state department of education, which has the power to revoke your license to practice medicine."

Dr. Thatcher winced. His lips moved, repeating the words. Then he said aloud, "Hundreds of people will tell you what I have done for them. Does that count for nothing?" Receiving no answer, he paused, and his head slowly dropped until all Carter could see was his thin gray hair and the pink scalp beneath. "I thought I could help. . . ." He sat shaking his head slowly.

And then he began to talk. He began with the first time he had been asked to see the President. It was shortly after he published a paper on how malfunctioning of the temporal-mandibular joint, a commonly undiagnosed condition, can be a factor in ailments ranging from migraine and vertigo to persistent neck and shoulder aches. There had been a paragraph on it in *Newsweek*, and George Rushton read it, checked Thatcher's qualifications, and sent for him.

It was noon when he had arrived at the White House, flattered but wondering what the President wanted. He found Rushton sitting up in a chair, wearing a surgical collar. Rushton said impatiently, "Well, do you think this ailment you wrote about is causing my neck trouble?" After a brief examination, Thatcher had determined the cause of the neck pain and told him frankly that the only cure for the problem was time.

"Isn't there *anything* you can do?" Rushton demanded. Thatcher prescribed certain exercises, and pills to help ease the pain. Then Rushton dismissed him abruptly. He was sure he would not hear from the President again. But he did. On his next visit, Rushton said, "Someone has to keep an eye on my health. Will you take on the job?" The painful neck injury was Rushton's sole complaint, and Thatcher tried to deal with it by massage, diathermy, and pills. One day, several months later, he called at the White House and was told the First Lady wanted to see him. She asked for the truth about her husband's condition, and he told her there was no cause for alarm.

"You must try to do more for him, Doctor. The pain makes it impossible for him to concentrate. His nerves are being affected. There must be something you can suggest that would make it easier for him to carry on."

For two years Thatcher had been experimenting in his clinic with injections that combined amphetamines with a chemical substance developed by his friend and teacher, Dr. Bruening, in Germany. The chemical counteracted the undesirable side effects of amphetamines. The results in blocking pain and improving morale of a few selected patients had been striking—more than he had hoped for. He decided to try it on the President, who was so delighted with the results that when he was suffering a spasm he would not accept anything less.

Abramson asked, "When did you begin to suspect anything might be wrong?"

Thatcher's hand trembled as if with a slight palsy. "Some of my other patients, a few, began to exhibit classic symptoms of chronic amphetamine users. I tried to change the mixture, using less amphetamines, but that made the symptoms worse. And then . . . then I read that the German company that manufactured the chemical had withdrawn it from the market. They had learned it actually intensified reactions in some patients."

"You could have warned him!" Elmer Tate said angrily.

"As long as he got regular treatment he was able to function.

Without it, he came very close to a breakdown. I had no choice but to keep on . . . to keep experimenting to find an answer." He joined his hands tightly together in his lap. "How could I admit I had failed? *How could I?*"

Abramson said, "You realize that you will probably face criminal charges."

Carter could not see the expression on Dr. Thatcher's face, but he did not need to. The doctor sat with forearms resting loosely on his thighs, hands still tightly clasped between his knees, his head bowed.

He said, "I didn't realize the consequences. Not at first. When it was too late, I saw what could happen. I was frightened by what the President might do if he were not in control, if his judgment was affected. God knows, I didn't want the responsibility!" His head drooped further, as if it were on a broken stalk. "But I kept hoping, praying. . . ."

The facade was dissolving, coming down piece by piece to reveal the pitiable, frightened man trapped within. Carter could not watch.

He asked, "Why didn't you admit you needed help when Dr. Vancell came to the White House?"

"I wanted to, but President Rushton had snapped back . . . like he always did. He has incredible vitality. I thought perhaps if I stayed with him, he could get through the trip to Peking. And after that . . ." A wrenching noise came from deep inside his body, a groan of despair. "Oh, my God!" He covered his face with his hands.

Elmer Tate said, "There is one way out, Doctor. You haven't been charged with anything. Nobody can stop you from leaving the country."

Dr. Thatcher's head came up slowly.

"I'm making this offer conditional on your promise never to practice medicine again. Your license would be revoked anyway if you stay here. And you'd probably end up in jail."

For an instant Dr. Thatcher seemed to be staring beyond the

room, focused on some other vision. It occurred to Carter that the doctor was staring at the ruins of his life.

"My clinic," he murmured. "My patients." He looked from Abramson to Elmer Tate, searching for some sign of relenting. "Medicine is my life."

Finally his eyes met Carter's with a baffled pleading. Carter was the first to look away. He felt somehow that he owed Dr. Thatcher an apology, although for what he did not know.

After Dr. Thatcher left, Carter stayed to join Abramson and Elmer Tate in a discussion of what to do about the Russian and American nuclear confrontation.

Elmer said, "The way it stands, any spark will set off an explosion. We could blow up the goddamn world. But I don't know what in sam dunghill to do about it."

"How about the hot line?" Carter suggested.

In the Situation Room in the basement of the west wing stood a teleprinter in an unbreakable glass shield—the direct communication line to Moscow.

Elmer Tate said, "That bastard Rokkosky wouldn't pay any attention to me. As far as he's concerned, George Rushton is still President of the United States."

"That brings us up against our real problem," Abramson said. "The country can't remain in limbo, hoping to muddle through crises while the President is convalescing. On the other hand, we certainly can't let him decide. We don't know when, if ever, he can be fully trusted again."

"What's the alternative?" Carter asked.

"The cabinet is meeting in an emergency session tonight. That's where you come in, Carter. If the vote goes the way I think, then I have a favor to ask of you. You're so close to the President and his family that you're the best man for the job. . . ."

Claire Rushton led the way into a magazine-littered room that served as the hospital visitor's lounge. It was off limits now to anyone not on an accredited visit to the President.

"How is George?" Carter asked.

"Better. I'm thankful the worst is over. I haven't had the courage to look at the newspapers."

"So far they've only mentioned that he collapsed and is undergoing tests to discover the reason."

"It's bound to come out. I can imagine the scare headlines: 'PRESIDENT EXPOSED AS DRUG ADDICT.' " She turned her head away quickly.

"I don't think that will happen," he said with as much assurance as he could muster. "Everyone knows that the best thing for the country is to play it down as much as possible."

"What I can't get through my head is why Dr. Thatcher would do it. How could he be so irresponsible?"

"Apparently he'd gotten good results with other patients. The bad effects don't show up for a time, and then only in some cases."

"He was experimenting!"

"In a sense."

At the window, Claire held the draperies aside to look out. "It's all incredible. I can't believe it really happened."

The thought was painful to Carter that he might have to do something to cause a permanent breach between them. He had gone over and over the arguments that could prove persuasive, but in the end there was every likelihood they would not be persuasive enough. George Rushton had a stubborn will; it had carried him to the heights, and was likely to carry him past any arguments Carter could devise. In that event, Carter had one other weapon, a weapon unknown even to Abramson and Elmer Tate who had sent him on this mission.

Claire said, "Everything in the last twenty-four hours has been a nightmare. I'll never get over it."

"Yes, you will. You'll put it all behind you and start over again."

She turned to him. "You don't know what it means to have you standing by, Carter. This is when he needs us most, isn't it?"

He felt the muscles of his face tighten. "Can I speak to George now? I have an important message from the cabinet."

She sensed something in his attitude. "Is it anything that will ... disturb him?"

"They've decided George should resign."

She turned pale. "You're not serious!"

"Claire, they admire and respect him. It was a difficult decision. They're trying to put the interests of the country first."

The edge of her voice made him flinch. "George will think it a betrayal."

He might have explained that for them to do otherwise would have been to betray a higher allegiance. But all he said was, "They thought it might be better coming from me."

"Tell them it's impossible! How can they even consider it at a time like this? It's out of the question!"

In her sharpness of tone, her assumption he would comply, there was a fresh affirmation of his role as Old Friend. He could never step out of his role.

"Frankly," she said, "I'm a little disappointed that you would even agree to do their dirty work."

He felt the sting of the rebuke. "We'd all like to avoid a compulsory transfer of power."

Her first reaction was shock. "Compulsory!" Then she looked at him narrowly but with increasing certainty. "You can't agree with their decision!"

"Under the circumstances, I don't believe what they're asking is wrong."

She was incredulous. After a moment she answered, "I'll see if George is willing to talk to you."

When Carter entered the living room of the hospital suite, he found George sitting in a chair with a quilt robe over his knees. The window blinds were drawn, and Claire was standing in a far corner near the window.

George's strong friendly handshake revealed Claire had not told him the reason for this visit.

"How are you feeling?" Carter asked.

"Much better. I've made up my mind to lick this thing in jig time. I'm going to do it cold turkey. Just to prove something to myself."

The irresistible force in motion. Toward a new goal.

"You're looking well," Carter said.

"I hope you'll forgive the way I acted the last time we met. We know the reason for it now."

"No problem."

"I keep going back over things I said and did, trying to figure out when I was myself and when I wasn't. It's an eerie feeling." He shook his head, smiling. "I'm afraid to even take aspirin now."

"You'll be fine. All you need is rest."

"Yes, I know. But I can't help worrying about leaving Elmer Tate in charge."

"Elmer's a good man."

"He made a big mistake when he fired Ziffren."

"I don't agree with you about that."

"I won't deny Mark is monomaniacal. But that's probably true of anyone who rises to a position of leadership. Only a neurotic compulsion makes anyone want to be a leader in the first place." His small, deprecating laugh indicated he was aware he might be accusing himself.

"You don't believe that, George," Claire said.

"Not entirely. But it could be argued. Anyway, you can't deny Mark Ziffren is sincere," he told Carter.

"I've always thought sincerity was a highly overrated virtue. Hitler was sincere. So are most racists and bigots."

George made a gesture of disagreement. "I don't think we'd better discuss Mark Ziffren any more."

"All right, George. Let's discuss you."

"One thing I've promised myself. I won't go back until I'm satisfied there won't be a recurrence. Of course, I suppose there will always be some who will wonder about me. They'll ask, Is it my best judgment or the decision of a man not entirely his own master?"

You've analyzed it well, Carter thought. *But you haven't suggested the answer.*

He said, "Your recuperation may take a long time, George. Too long for the country to be without a President."

George Rushton's intuitions had always been quick. "Is that what you came to tell me?"

"That's what the cabinet decided."

"I can imagine who is pushing that idea."

"The vote in the cabinet was unanimous. They want you to resign."

From a distance Carter felt Claire's reproachful stare.

"Unanimous?" George said. "Not one was for me?"

"You know a President can't really function without the confidence of the people," Carter said. "It's unlikely you can regain it to a point where you could govern the country again. The trouble is, with your kind of problem no one can be sure when you are well again."

He could sense resistance even before George spoke.

"Suppose I promise to stay in office just to the end of my term and not seek renomination?"

"What about the big decisions? What would you do, sit in the Oval Office for a year and do nothing? If a crisis developed, would you just ignore it?"

George searched Carter's face, then turned to where Claire stood in dimness. "What do you think?"

"You haven't done anything wrong. None of this was your fault. Why should you be punished?"

"The country hasn't done anything wrong either," Carter said.

George Rushton answered, "If they want me out, let them force me out. Let them try to impeach me. There aren't any grounds and they know it."

"They won't do it that way. The Twenty-fifth Amendment takes care of the procedure."

An angry expression crossed George Rushton's face. "I've never backed away from a fight."

"And what would be the result? Your own party split. A divided nation. If it's vindication you want, you'll get it more easily by resigning. Say you're doing it in the interests of national unity and the whole country will be in your debt."

"I won't resign. That's final."

Carter saw there was only one way; the secret drawer would have to be opened.

"It isn't a question of how you feel about it, George." He saw Claire near the window, and his imagination painted in little accusing lines around her mouth and with a fine brush etched hurt into her eyes. "You have to resign. I won't allow you to do anything else."

"You won't allow?" George asked with irony.

Carter said quietly, "I will do anything I can. Absolutely anything."

He heard Claire's sharp indrawn breath. Then George's puzzled stare gave way to an understanding that this was an ultimatum.

His hand began slowly rubbing the back of his neck. "I don't think you realize what you're asking, Carter. You want me to give up the most important job on earth. And then what? I can't even join all those former senators and congressmen who refuse to go back home—to leave Washington and the power they once had. Once you've held center stage, no one knows how to treat you afterward. There's no place in Washington for former Presidents."

George was as adroit as ever in weighting the scales in his favor. But what he said didn't really change anything. It simply drew a starker picture of the personal consequences.

Carter hesitated. To spell out the alternative in Claire's hearing would be a despicable thing. There seemed to be no choice, but that did not change the fact that it was despicable.

While he was gathering courage to speak, he received support from an unexpected source.

Claire said, "It might all be for the best, George."

George looked at her as if he did not quite accept that she had spoken. "Do you believe I should resign?"

"I'm thinking of your health. I'm sure Carter is too, although he won't say so. You need a rest."

"I'm a little young to spend my time just relaxing and enjoying myself."

"It isn't as if you won't have anything else to do. When you're ready for it, you'll have all kinds of offers. You'll be able to pick any job you want."

George said with mocking emphasis, "From the Presidency of the United States to the presidency of the General Typewriter Corporation. Swallowed up like Jonah in the whale, but unlike Jonah, never heard from again."

"That couldn't happen to you, dear. Why, Elmer Tate would call every day to get your ideas. After all, he's worked for you, and knows you're better qualified to make those judgments. He can't fill your shoes."

George's hand now moved to shield his eyes, as if against a glare.

"I have to give them your answer," Carter said.

There was a long, painful hesitation. Then George Rushton said slowly, "I wonder if there's ever been a President who, after he left the White House, didn't live much of his life in the past."

Looking at George Rushton's drawn face, Carter understood that whatever had sustained him until now had reached the end of its motivating power.

"I haven't been such a bad President, have I?" George asked.

Carter was grateful for a chance to make small amends. "You've been a damn good one."

George looked down at the quilt on his lap. "I'd have a chance to do some sailing. It's never been much fun with those Secret Service men tailing me." Then he seemed to find it hard to go on.

Claire began to cry quietly.

Carter suddenly remembered a sunny afternoon many years ago when he and Claire and George had been crossing a college campus together. He could almost hear their vanished laughter, in that precious scene preserved in amber memory. Everything had been ahead of them then. They were so sure of the future, seeing themselves not as they were but as very wise, already a little disenchanted with life, skeptical and clear-eyed. They had been children, really, with a marvelous sense of time standing still and waiting for them to make up their minds what they wished to do.

"All right," George Rushton said.

Carter waited. He knew what was coming next.

"Tell the cabinet they can have my resignation."

24

On a grim, showery day, Carter met Joyce at Duke Zeibert's restaurant. News kiosks still blazoned the startling announcement of Rushton's resignation; the front pages of the newspapers featured a stiffly posed photograph of Elmer Tate being sworn in.

"I can't see Elmer Tate visiting world capitals and meeting famous leaders," Joyce said across the table. "He's just not the type."

"Neither was Harry Truman."

"Gloria Tate isn't going to give any of those marvelous receptions, and for sure no one is going to talk about *her* wardrobe."

"The republic will survive."

"I know it's a superficial standard. I'm just saying that a lot of style will leave with the Rushtons."

They were at a corner table and the nearest diners were several feet away. The piped-in music was loud enough to discourage eavesdroppers. That was probably why, Carter thought, it was featured in most Washington restaurants.

Carter looked up as someone came to their table.

Jack Elkins leaned over. "Try the marinated herring in sour cream. And chicken in the pot with matzoh balls."

"How are you, Jack?"

"First rate."

"I'm glad you're at liberty again."

"You'll never know. Ziffren's boys play rough. Did you hear that bastard wants to run for President next year?"

"I can't see him getting nominated."

"Not while I'm around. I've got my knives sharpened. And I'll go right for the jugular." Elkins drew up a chair and sat down. "If I could prove he was behind that attack on the White House, I could send him to jail for life."

"You can't. There aren't any living witnesses."

"But I think I can get hold of that paper he wrote. You know, *The Suppression of Civil Disorder*. When I'm through showing up that bastard, he couldn't get elected a sewer rat." Elkins grinned. "Even though he has every qualification for the office."

"I'd just as soon forget about him."

"By the way, I'm going to make you a hero."

"What?"

"I'm going to tell what I know about you and the President's doctor. I put it together. You had him stashed away in your cabin."

Carter noted Joyce's slight involuntary quiver.

"You always did have a vivid imagination, Jack."

"That's why they let him hightail it to England without having to face criminal charges. So he wouldn't be around to testify against you."

"Another fishing expedition?"

Elkins laughed. "You know, I like you. I really like you. Are you telling me it didn't happen?"

"It's as wild a story as the one about you and the Southwestern Investment Company."

Elkins's laughter diminished and stopped. "You wouldn't be trying to scare me?"

"Why would I do that, Jack?"

"Better men than you have tried. I'm looking to do you a favor. You're responsible for Rushton's resignation and that bastard Ziffren getting dehorsed. The way I see it, that makes you a hero."

"Everyone might not see it that way."

"You want me to forget it?"

"It's up to you. I never interfere with freedom of the press."

"Okay. I figure I owe you one. Back it goes into the computer." Elkins smiled again. "And we're still friends. Don't eat the seafood here, they prepare it in advance. Seafood and news more than a day old stink a little."

"Thanks for the tip."

"You can level with me about one thing. The way I hear it, you may be our new ambassador to Monzania."

"We haven't recognized Monzania."

"We're going to."

"Are we?"

"Come on. Not even *off* the record? Will you accept the job when they offer it to you?"

"All right. I'll tell you I've had meetings with President Tate and Secretary Abramson and that we discussed the situation. Including my becoming the new ambassador. But if you repeat what I've just said, I'll deny it."

"You can't." Chuckling, Elkins lifted his sleeve to show a small mike taped to his wrist. "I've got it all right here. Nice talking to you, Carter."

Carter took the oblique turn in the road, keeping the tires parallel with the yellow center line.

Joyce said, "I've never been so nervous about meeting anyone." She touched a lighter from the dashboard to her cigarette. "I still don't know why they included me in the invitation. Did you tell them?"

"That's our secret. I'd rather keep it that way."

He suspected the invitation might be a pretext for George and

Claire to vent feelings that had simmered since their encounter several weeks ago in the hospital: *I never thought it of you, Carter. I never thought you could do it.* It was common knowledge that George Rushton had seen almost no one since his resignation. There was no telling what conclusions he might have reached in his isolation.

Joyce blew out a reflective smoke spiral. If it came to the point of recriminations, Carter promised himself that Joyce would not bear any of the brunt. What they said to him didn't matter. Not at all.

He parked the car in the driveway and led Joyce along a stone pathway that circled between rows of dark hedges to the rear of the mansion. Here was a wide expanse of green lawn and a free-form pool set into a concrete plateau.

Beneath an orange beach umbrella, George and Claire were seated at a table sipping drinks in tall, ice-filled glasses.

George leaped up, a lean, muscled, deeply tanned man in brief swimming trunks. As he came toward them, Carter had a silly thought: He wondered how President Elmer Tate would look in bathing trunks.

They shook hands. "I'm so glad you could bring Joyce, Carter. We've been looking forward to meeting her."

"It was nice of you to ask me," she murmured.

They followed George toward the beach umbrella. Claire was standing; she wore a light halter dress and sandals.

Joyce whispered, "She's just as pretty as she looks in her photographs."

"You don't have a thing to worry about."

Then they reached Claire, and George made the introduction. It pleased Carter that Joyce was more than a match in attractiveness, although there was also a touch of pathos, of something lost. For years he had believed no woman to be Claire's equal.

They sat making inconsequential talk, until Carter began to feel as if they were walking on a sparkling snow crust that was not really strong enough to hold their weight.

"Would anyone like a swim?" George asked.

"I'm afraid I didn't bring a bathing suit," Joyce replied.

"We can supply those," Claire said. "Size fourteen?"

"Twelve," Joyce corrected her.

Carter sat back in his chair looking at sunlight glinting in his tonic water. Opening skirmish—even.

"I'd really prefer not to swim," Joyce said, smiling graciously. "I spent an hour just getting my hair ready."

Good sacrificial move, Carter thought.

"Have another drink then," George suggested.

With the second drink, talk seemed to become easier. Perhaps there were not going to be any ambushes and this was exactly what it appeared to be, an opportunity for old friends to repair misunderstandings.

George swirled his glass and downed the remaining contents in a swallow. "How do you think Elmer Tate is doing so far?"

"Well, I like the fact he's giving up all his emergency powers. And he's selected a Vice-President who's extremely well qualified, perhaps the best qualified since L.B.J."

"I understand he's planning to share some of the Presidential duties. Letting the Vice-President help him formulate domestic policy. And take care of the routine contacts with the cabinet and the White House staff and Congressional leaders. I wish I'd been smart enough to do that." George was talking rapidly, as though hurrying to his main point. "But what do you think of his deal with Marshal Rokkosky?"

"It makes sense to me, George."

In a series of communications via the hot line, President Tate and the Soviet leader had agreed to cancel their mutual military alerts, and for the United States to abandon plans for a military alliance with China in return for immediate cessation of Soviet provocation in Malaysia and the Middle East. Details still to be worked out, of course.

"If we can trust the Soviets to keep their side of the bargain,"

George Rushton said, with an air of misgiving.

"That's probably how they feel about us."

Claire was saying to Joyce, "This has been exactly what we need. No worries or tensions. George goes sailing every day. Salt air and sun do wonders for him."

Carter felt like telling her: At the moment, what George needs is some assurance of a future that will matter. George will only have meaning to himself if he shares in meaningful events. It was hard to believe that Claire did not understand that.

Late afternoon sun penetrated to do its healing work.

He asked George, "Isn't Marie here with you?"

"No. Marie has a romantic interest."

"Name of William Chalmers?"

Smiling, George shook his head. "A young man she met at a wedding. He's a law clerk for a Supreme Court justice."

"Serious?"

"Serious enough so she won't leave Washington. He's a nice young man. We'll just have to wait and see. That's all parents are good for these days, anyhow."

As they moved to the buffet table, Carter tried to evaluate how everyone was behaving. Joyce was a bit nervous but did not show it. George, now balancing a plate of food, was performing as gracious host. Claire moved and spoke with increasing animation, her lean face creasing at the cheeks into very fine invisible lines. Of the four, she seemed the most self-conscious.

She was talking now about the long holiday they were going to take—halfway around the world, stopping at most of the world capitals, and at places like Tangiers and Casablanca and Majorca.

"We're going to take the better part of a year," she said. "We've already had invitations from heads of government in every country."

"Sounds like great fun," Joyce said.

George, slumped in his beach chair with his plate of cold cuts, remarked, "I'll have time to think about what to do with the rest of my life." There was an awkward silence in which George realized he had revealed too much. He looked around smiling, as if to banish the implication of self-pity.

"I still think of you as the First Lady," Joyce said to Claire. "Gloria Tate just doesn't seem to fit that role."

"Gloria's a very sweet person," Claire responded. "Very down to earth."

George made a small *tsking* sound.

"I don't mean to sound condescending," Claire added quickly. "I admit I was sad at first. After we packed up to move out of the White House, I was showing Gloria around and I felt as if she were an intruder, as if she were forcing me out of my home."

"The arrogance of power," George said lightly. Then he got up to get another round of drinks.

"I was feeling bitter toward everyone," Claire went on. "Even you," she said to Carter.

"I hope I'm forgiven," Carter said, and tensed for what might come.

"Oh, more than that. The announcement today made this an especially happy occasion for us."

Carter asked, "What announcement?"

"In this morning's newspaper. Jack Elkins reported that you and Joyce are getting married next week."

Joyce flushed—a rose tint beneath bronze.

"He did?" Carter said weakly.

Claire looked at Carter inquiringly. "He said you were going to spend your honeymoon traveling about the U.S. until your appointment as ambassador is confirmed."

"It's true, isn't it?" George asked, returning with the drinks.

"Well, yes," Carter admitted. "But I'll be damned if I can figure out how Jack Elkins knew."

George chuckled. "That's how it happens when you're in the public eye."

As the late afternoon sun lost its warmth, they started back to the house. George and Joyce were ahead, with Carter and Claire following.

Claire's hand on his arm delayed him until the others were out of earshot. She said quickly, "I'm grateful for all you've done, Carter. I've waited a long time to tell you. But I've always known you weren't involved with Anne Demas."

He had an unpleasant, dislocated sense of irritation, the reaction he might have felt on reading the first few lines of a letter containing bad news—a feeling he would like to put it aside and not read the rest.

She went on, "It was George in the cabin that night. With her."

He became rooted where he stood. "George wasn't near the cabin. That was the night of his accident. Don't you remember?"

"When he came out of the anesthetic he was muttering, 'Oh, my God, dead.' It didn't make much sense to me at the time. I thought he was . . . hallucinating . . . about himself. But it was really guilt."

"Claire, you're wrong George was a hundred miles away."

"I'd guessed there was someone. There are so many little ways a woman can tell. When he told me he had to go away for a few days, it was the first thought that jumped into my mind." She looked composed, in control. "Afterward, when he was hurt, I blocked it out. Not until he was well again did I begin to realize what you'd done, the kind of sacrifice you'd made for him."

It had nothing to do with George. The thought rolled itself up in words but his lips and tongue would not speak them.

"It was magnificent of you, Carter. I've always wanted to be able to tell you that."

"I hope you haven't said anything like this to George."

"How could I? I've never given him any reason to suspect I know the truth. I never will."

The metallic taste of the lie was on his lips when he said, "Frankly, Claire, he wouldn't know what you were talking about."

They went into the house together.

As they were driving back along a two-lane highway, a billboard promoting a soft drink inquired: GETTING ENOUGH OUT OF LIFE? The world was full of such unasked-for challenges.

Joyce said, "He's much nicer than I thought he would be. I couldn't help feeling a little sorry for him."

"Sorry?"

"It was all his. And at an age when most men are just starting, it's all anticlimax."

"I guess it is something like that."

"Is that what you and Claire were talking about? I noticed you lingering behind. And you were both pretty quiet when you got inside the house."

Carter debated briefly whether to tell her, finally deciding not to keep any secrets. She sat smoking a cigarette until he had finished.

"Quite a story," she said, rubbing the glowing cigarette end into the ashtray. "Exactly what were you trying to accomplish?"

"I'm not sure I know what you mean."

"Playing hero. The white Christian knight riding off to rescue the fair maiden. Don Quijote."

He bristled slightly. "It seemed the best thing to do at the time. I wasn't especially trying to be heroic."

"Were you in love with her?"

Certain risks had to be taken. "I was," he said.

"Well, that explains a little. You don't come off quite as foolish."

"Thank you."

"And I can see why you felt that way."

"It's been over for some time." He glanced at her. "Do you have anything in particular against white Christian knights?"

"Sure. The last ones rode out of our world with the Confederacy. And good riddance."

He replied with tender amusement, "I promise never to buckle on my armor, if you'll put down your lance."

"I have no choice." She leaned over to kiss him on the cheek. "I'm in love with a white Christian knight."

"Hold that thought."

"I will. It makes all the difference."

After a while, she leaned back against the head rest. She began to hum softly,

> Let us cheer the weary traveler,
> Cheer the weary traveler.
> Let us cheer the weary traveler
> Along the heavenly way.

Carter reached over and took her hand. He kept his eyes firmly on the road widening ahead, leading toward a world in which all things were possible.